NOW COMES THEODORA

Books by Daniel Ford

Cowboy: The Interpreter Who Became a Soldier, a Warlord, and One More Casualty of Our War in Vietnam

Flying Tigers: Claire Chennault and His American Volunteers, 1941-1942

Tales of the Flying Tigers

Poland's Daughter: How I Met Basia, Hitchhiked to Italy, and Learned About Love, War, and Exile

A Vision So Noble: John Boyd, the OODA Loop, and America's War on Terror

The Lady and the Tigers (with Olga Greenlaw)

Glen Edwards: The Diary of a Bomber Pilot

The Only War We've Got: Early Days in South Vietnam

The Country Northward: A Hiker's Journal

Fiction

Michael's War: A Story of the Irish Republican Army

Remains: A Story of the Flying Tigers

The High Country Illuminator: A Tale of Light and Darkness and the Ski Bums of Avalon

Incident at Muc Wa: A Story of the Vietnam War

Now Comes Theodora: A Story of the 1960s

Thank you for your interest. For more about the author and his work, or to sign up for his monthly electronic newsletter, visit his website at danfordbooks.com

Now Comes Theodora
A Story of the 1960s

Daniel Ford

Warbird Books

Durham, New Hampshire, USA

2018

NOW COMES THEODORA published 1965 by Doubleday & Co.
Library of Congress Catalog Card Number 65-14007.
Avon paperback edition published 1966, 1972.
Author Guild Back-in-Print edition published 2000.
Warbird Books revised edition published 2018.

No character in this book is a portrait of any actual person.

Lines from "What Have They Done to the Rain?" by Malvina Reynolds reprinted by permission of Schroder Music Company.

Cover design by Janet Halverson

ISBN 978-1-7322300-1-9

1 - Don't Cut the Cord

When Boris was a young man, he had a dream to this effect: he was a warder in a madhouse. He had a great many keys on a silver chain. Somehow, at some undefined moment in his dream, the keys were taken from him. His life did not change; he toured the madhouse as before; but he was no longer in charge of it. He was one of the insane.

The discovery frightened him awake. He searched his waist for the silver chain, from fright to fright, and it was a very long time before he convinced himself that he had been dreaming, that he had no use for keys.

BORIS YEARNED to photograph Marvin Peabody's wife. She was pregnant—superbly so. By February she was pushing the unborn child ahead of her like a shopping cart, showing off her belly much as the college girls displayed their breasts. Boris trembled when she was near. He longed to get her into his bedroom, in something flimsy with her dark hair combed straight back, with a kitten or a ball of yarn or something else small and soft, to set off the swollen belly, and Prudence herself lost in a dream of motherhood. What a picture she would make! The hope of that photograph was the only reason Boris kept inviting Marvin Peabody to the Hut. Taken by himself, Marvin was a bore.

"What we need," Marvin was saying to a circle of his admirers, "—ah, thank you, Boris—what we need in Narwich is a small *direct action*. The propaganda of the deed! We'll picket the air base or send a boarding party to the navy yard next time they launch a nuclear submarine."

Having refreshed Marvin's drink, Boris crouched down to collect some empty glasses from the floor. While there he pinched the firm bronze curve of Prudence Peabody's calf. She began a shriek but swallowed it. "*Bastard,*" she whispered as he rose again on his long legs.

"Tomorrow?" he said into her ear.

"No! *No more pictures.*"

She'd posed for him once, when she was between babies.

Marvin frowned at Prudy, who smiled like the Madonna. Content, Boris ambled across the room to the couch, where a different sort of party was in progress. Three or four couples were furiously drinking and necking, while a leftover youth watched them from the armchair. "Gee, thanks," the young man said, taking a glass from the tray Boris was carrying. "Nice party," he added, but not as if he meant it.

This was Georgie Morris. He belonged with the intellectuals, but Marvin regarded him as a rival and snubbed him cruelly. Boris perched on the arm of Georgie's chair (well, *his* chair, actually) and together they watched the necking couples. Boris was especially fascinated by a blonde in a bulky knit sweater and tight jeans. She was with Hal Pappajohn, a husky lad with a black eye. He was tempting her to kiss. The blonde's lips were swollen with desire, but Hal would not come down to them; finally she heaved herself up and fused her mouth with his. Boris dug Georgie's ribs with his elbow. "Who's that?" he asked. "Hal's blonde?"

Georgie squinted at the kissing pair. "Her?" he said. "Oh, that's Carol Phipps."

Boris sighed, seeing the dream go glimmering as dreams so often did. Mr. Phipps was the University Development Officer, and therefore the immediate supervisor of the University Photographer, who was Boris. He couldn't ask his boss's daughter to pose in the nude.

~ ~ ~ ~

As the evening wore on and the peaceniks grew tipsy, they began to talk about the Bomb. Marvin Peabody was obsessed by the Bomb. He worried it so frequently and at such great length that Boris had come to think of it as Marvin's opposite in every way—hard and gray where he was soft and pale; angular, cold, and gleaming with the one great purpose of its existence, which was to snuff out Marvin Peabody's life.

Since the last party, the United States or the Soviet Union had exploded a nuclear weapon. Boris was not sure of the details. He didn't read a daily newspaper, but bought the Sunday edition of the *New York Times* and read the Week in Review at his leisure. That way he could be sure that any crisis he was studying had already been resolved. Once, when the New York printers went on strike, Boris had spent an entire month without knowing that the world was on the brink of war. He was almost sorry when the *Times* began to publish its weekly review again.

"It's unfortunate we were on vacation," Marvin said. "Otherwise we might have organized a protest march against Washington." So the explosion must have been an American one.

"What good would that have done?" asked Georgie, venturing into the intellectual circle. "The embassy doesn't pay any attention to pickets." Boris changed his mind: the bomb had been set off by the Russians.

"The *embassy*?" Marvin echoed. His face, like an egg balanced upon its heavy end, registered scorn. "Did I mention the *embassy*? You don't understand the uses of publicity, George. I was thinking of—the Overseas Press Club."

The pacifists gasped at his wisdom.

"Gosh," said Boris. "Has the Press Club got the Bomb?"

Hal Pappajohn whooped with laughter, and after a hesitation some of the pacifists joined in. Georgie, who for some reason was unable to laugh or even to smile, pounded his knee to show the glee that otherwise was beyond his powers of expression. Marvin glared at him, but Georgie was wise enough not to meet the leader's eye.

"Well," said Marvin, nailing a lid upon the laughter. "We'll go to Washington anyway! It's not too late for a protest, and even if the publicity value is diminished, that's not the most important thing, is it?" He glanced around the faces that once more were his to command. "What should be uppermost in

9

our minds," he said, shooting a glance at Georgie, "is the effect our protest has upon *us*. We are the ones who are involved." He pointed to his wife's swollen belly, and the others dutifully looked at this proof of Marvin's manhood. "Ambassadors are not important," Marvin continued, with all the assurance of a man who has gotten his wife with child. "Presidents are not important. Even the *press corps* is not important. But *we* are. The world is comprised of individuals, and if the individual doesn't protest, he deserves to be destroyed." Marvin punched the arm of his chair with a pudgy index finger. "If we do not protest, then we have chosen war."

As a combat photographer in the South Pacific, Boris had devoted four years of his life to recording the real War. Now Marvin Peabody, the professional student, was suggesting that those four years shouldn't have happened. Snotty bastard. He talked about war and had never seen combat; he talked about misery and never missed a meal in his life. Boris had earned the right to be cynical, while Marvin Peabody had not. "Hey, Marvie," he said. "What would you do if war broke out tomorrow?"

"A nuclear war?" Marvin said.

"Yeah. The big one."

"I would take my wife and my children," Marvin said, looking firm-lipped at Prudence, "and I would go to the loneliest stretch of seashore I could find. We would have a picnic."

"A picnic?" Hal Pappajohn bounded from the couch, letting Carol Phipps slide to the floor. "Why, you silly son of a bitch," he said. "Do you know how your mother-loving *picnic* would end, for Christ's sake?"

"In death," Marvin said grandly.

"Death by puking," Hal said. "You'd vomit your guts out for a day or two or three, and finally you'd die. They'll put a tombstone on the beach: *Here lies Marvin Peabody, who puked himself to death*. Radiation sickness," Hal said proudly. "I read it in a magazine."

"Propaganda," Marvin said. "The trouble with you, Harold,

is that you believe what you read in the popular press."

"Horseshit," Hal said. But he was baffled. What was the point in winning a fight, if the other guy wouldn't admit there had been one? Hal clenched and unclenched his fists. "I also read about firestorms," he went on. "A nuclear explosion would set the woods on fire, see? A firestorm is when the trees burn so hot that they make their own wind, and nothing can stop the fire, not rivers or highways or anything."

"In the winter?" said Marvin, flicking his white fingers.

Hal raised his fists. "Stand up, you son of a bitch!" he yelled. "I'll winterize your ass!"

A couple of his friends wrestled him to the floor, and Carol Phipps led him off to another part of the room, cooing and mussing his crouched, angry head.

"What would *you* do, Boris?" said one of the intellectuals, a long-haired girl named Judy who just before vacation had agreed to pose for him, if he promised to photograph her only from the rear.

Boris leered at her. "Honey," he said, "I'd grab you by the hair and run for the hills."

They laughed, all except Georgie, who leaned toward Boris. "Seriously," he said, "what would you do?"

"Yes, what?" chimed another of the girls.

Boris thought back to his years in the South Pacific, where the climate was so foul that he'd rolled his film in condoms, to keep it from rotting. He remembered the fear, and sores and rashes and insect bites, and how he'd hated the civilians safe at home. Ah, the civilians! There was some comfort in the knowledge that a nuclear war would involve everyone, not just the soldiers. And it would be quick! That had been the trouble with the South Pacific—death had come one bullet at a time, so slowly that four years were required to kill a hundred thousand Americans, and few of them civilians.

He went to the bureau that stood against one curving wall of the Hut, and took his father's pistol from the top drawer. Its weight restored his good humor. Turning, he swung the gray

11

muzzle upon Marvin Peabody, who went pale. "I'd look out for Number One," Boris said. "In spite of what old Marvie says, I think that when the balloon goes up, he'll run like hell. And I don't want him to run over me. He's too heavy."

Marvin looked away. Except for the moment when he was frightened by the pistol, he hadn't conceded a single point to any of them. No matter if all the magazines in the world declared to the contrary, Marvin would still believe that he could expire against the sunset on a lonely beach, nobly and without pain.

When Boris returned the pistol to the bureau, Marvin stood up. "This is all very interesting," he said, "but beside the point. How many of you are coming to Washington with me? For myself, it doesn't matter, but our gesture will receive more attention if we can get together two or three carloads." Like a cat with its mouse, he pounced on Georgie: "You'll go, of course?"

"Ah," said Georgie. "I can't, Marvin. I have a personal matter to take care of."

"He has a pregnant girl at his place," one of the younger students whispered to Boris. "Do you remember Colin Merchant? *His* wife."

"I don't know," Boris said. The name was familiar, but he couldn't find a face to go with it. So many faces had passed through the Hut in the past ten years. "Is she a good-looker?"

"I haven't seen her since she got back," his informant whispered. "She used to be cute enough, I guess, but Colin walked out on her." He laughed as if this were a good joke on the girl. "They were living in Boston. She didn't want to go home, so she came back here and Georgie took her in."

Boris stirred with interest. "When's she expecting the baby?" he asked.

"Any day now. That's why Georgie can't go to D.C."

Marvin looked at his watch. With his rival crushed, he announced that he was leaving; it was nearly mid-night—curfew for the girls who lived in dormitories—and his

12

announcement ended the party. The Hut swiftly drained of its guests. "Jeepers," said the first out the door. "A blizzard."

Yes, snow was whipping across the yard, and had already risen above the threshold. The guests floundered to their automobiles, suddenly in a hurry. Boris grabbed Georgie and held him until the others were gone. "Why didn't you bring Colin's wife with you?" he asked. "I'd like to meet her."

"Teddy?"

"Yeah, Teddy Merchant. When are you gonna bring her over?"

"Well, gee. . . ."

"Tomorrow," Boris said. "Bring her for supper tomorrow. Steaks and beer, okay?"

"Well, sure, if she wants to come."

"Of course she'll come," Boris said. "We're neighbors!" Georgie rented a house trailer not far from the Hut and on the same back road. "Tomorrow," Boris said, and pushed him into the blizzard before he could change his mind. "Seven o'clock!" he shouted.

He stood in the doorway, his shadow stretching across the snow like a buzzard's, until the last of his chicks had left the yard.

~ ~ ~ ~

When nobody was there to laugh at him, Boris prided himself on two things: he was gentle and he was neat. He could talk to chipmunks, and he could persuade chickadees to take sunflower seeds from his thin, pursed lips. These creatures came to him out of College Woods. Boris had a feeding station behind the Hut to keep them coming; it was a replica of the Hut that Boris had fashioned from a large tin can. He went out there now and tipped a pound of sunflower seeds into the miniature Quonset. Returning, he lost his way. Yesterday's path had vanished; he stumbled up to his knees in the drifts that had appeared from nowhere, unable to see the Hut because its edgeless steel shape was so nearly the color of the storm. He stopped and oriented himself by the rattle of wind-driven snow against the metal. "All for a couple of nit-ridden *birds*," he grumbled when he was inside, kicking the snow from his overshoes. He was glad that none of the students had witnessed his trek through the night. "You skinny boob," he said to his reflection in the bureau mirror.

Stooped by all the defeats of its thirty-nine years—or perhaps by the reality of living in a Quonset hut—the reflection stared back at him. Boris was too tough for wrinkles. Instead, the years had cut grooves around his mouth and eyes, so that his mirror image resembled a wooden statue cracked by the weather, its features smooth but beginning to drift apart.

He took off his jacket and indulged his second secret virtue. He swept the main room, emptied the ashtrays, and washed the glasses. The Hut had a sink and a gas range and a tiny German refrigerator, fitted like jigsaw pieces into cabinets the Narwich handyman had built in exchange for a portrait of his wife and four children. There once was an actual kitchen, but Boris had turned it into a darkroom. Otherwise, the Hut contained a bedroom and a bath, jammed with the darkroom into the westerly third of the Quonset's length. After tidying the main room, Boris went to work on this section of the Hut. Somebody had been sick in the bathroom, of course. He cleaned up the mess, then wiped the porcelain with a sponge and flushed it off with cold water. Then he went into the bedroom.

A couple was in his bed, gently sleeping, with arms and legs entwined like some curious monster. Boris switched on the overhead lights and a few of the fixtures along the walls, until the bedroom was as brightly lighted as a photographer's studio, which indeed it was. The couple remained locked in its narcissistic embrace, as if each half had attempted to crawl into the other and disappear. It was resting now in the exhaustion of failure.

Boris got his twin-lens Rolleiflex from the other room and

tried to capture this notion on film, stepping lightly around the bed, seeking the angle where reality became truth. After twelve exposures he returned the camera to the living room and switched off most of the lights. Then he grabbed a naked ankle and pulled the monster apart, whereupon the masculine half woke up. "Hey?" it said, morphing into Hal Pappajohn. "What's that?" Hal peered at Boris with eyes that refused to focus.

"Party's over," Boris said. "Take her home, for Christ's sake—that's my boss's daughter."

"Grrr," said Hal, shaking his head. "Had a funny dream. Dreamed that somebody had a spotlight on me, and people were walking all around, inspecting me."

"Imagine that," Boris said. He got Hal on his feet and dressed, but Carol Phipps refused to open her eyes. Together they wrapped her in a coat and carried her out to the car. Boris drove them into the village and abandoned them in front of the Laundromat. "I'll take her up to my place," Hal said, to show he held no grudge. "Her folks'll think she's at the dorm, and her house mother will think she's at home."

"Okay," Boris said.

"Thanks for the lift," Hal said, yawning. He held the girl casually by one elbow, her clothing a bundle tucked under his other arm; she stood wide-legged on the sidewalk, gently swaying in his grip. "Nice party."

"Any time," said Boris.

He drove back to the Hut, almost not getting into the driveway because of the drifting snow, and went to bed. It was after one o'clock.

~ ~ ~ ~

Boris dreamed that he was with his wife and child at the beach, at night, in a storm. The woman and the infant were faceless, but he knew that they were Teddy and her child, Colin Merchant's child, though it had become his by some process he did not fully understand. There was an orange glow in the west, and all around them the pulsating drone of the

15

bombers. It was the evening of the last day of the world. Boris ran circles on the beach, trying to protect Teddy and the child from radiation, but they vomited themselves onto the sand and vanished, leaving only two dark stains upon the beach. Boris cleaned them up with wads of toilet paper. Then he looked about for a means of killing himself, since he had lost the pistol in his hurry. There was nothing suitable on the beach, no rocks or broken bottles, and the drone of the jet bombers grew louder, and the orange glow that was civilization burned brighter on the horizon. Accordingly, he decided to swim out to sea and kill himself that way.

But as soon as he was in the water, Boris found himself back in the Hut, drowning beneath twisted blankets and sheets. The roaring and the pounding, however, continued to fill his ears. He crawled out of bed and groped for the light switch. In the sudden white glare, he decided that there was indeed a bomber flying overhead, although how the bastard could fly through a blizzard was more than he could understand. The pounding came from the door. Boris dressed and went to open it. "Oooof!" said Georgie, plunging into the Hut. "I thought you'd never wake up."

"Me too," Boris said. He waited until Georgie's feet were out of the way, then he closed the door against the blizzard. "What the hell do you want, this time of night?"

"It's Teddy," Georgie said. He picked himself up, dusted his knees, then waved his hands at Boris, like an old woman seized with despair. "Don't just stand there," he cried. "Boris! Teddy is having a *baby* out there in my car."

Boris saw himself cheated of his finest photograph to date. "Are you sure?" he said. "How do you know?"

"Her baby," Georgie insisted. "Boris, for God's sake! *Do* something!"

Georgie's car was stuck in a snowbank just beyond the Hut, its headlights glowing through the storm. Boris pulled on his overshoes and loped down the path Georgie had made. Together they managed to half-carry, half-drag the girl into

16

the Hut. She collapsed in the armchair and stared trustfully at Boris out of a white, strained face. She was not pretty, not even female; she was a shapeless, frightened child in a green duffel coat dusted with snow.

"Can't we take your car?" Georgie said.

"A Volkswagen?" Boris said, jumping up and down to get his blood moving again. "You want to deliver a baby in a Volkswagen?"

"I forgot." Georgie was wringing his hands, staring first at the girl and then at Boris, like a spectator at a ping-pong match. "What then?" he pleaded. "Will you go for a doctor?"

Boris quivered with indecision. Let Georgie stay here? Trust him with the Volkswagen? Which? "No, you go," he said. He didn't want to leave the girl, not after she had looked at him so trustfully. "You take my car and go for the Doc. . . . You okay, honey?" he said to the girl. "Can you hold on for a few more minutes?"

"The pains aren't so bad now," she said. The words came in bunches from pale lips. "I'm all right, really I am."

Boris ran into the bedroom and pulled on a jacket. "Come on," he said to Georgie, and led the way outside, buttoning the jacket. There was a shovel under the Volkswagen's hood. While Georgie worked the clutch, Boris hacked at the snow-drifts and then ran back to heave at the rear fender, running from front to rear, shovel and heave, with a frenzy he had not known since Bougainville, when his Jeep had bogged down in a sector still infested with Japanese. Soon he was sweating as if he were back in the jungle, instead of blizzard-bound in New Hampshire. While he sweated, his fingers numbed on the shovel and his ears filled with snow.

"Almost," he panted. "Let me try." He pulled Georgie out of the driver's seat, tossed the shovel into the rear, and backed the car toward the Hut. Then he put the gearshift into low, eased out the clutch, and rammed the little car into the road that the town plows had cleared not long ago. "How the hell did you get stuck?" he asked, getting out again.

"Teddy grabbed my arm. I'll have a bruise there tomorrow."

"Well, go!" Boris said. "You where Doc Perkins lives? I'll call him, so he'll be expecting you."

"All right," Georgie said.

Boris watched him out of sight, then went up the road and extinguished the lights on Georgie's old Chevrolet. More shoveling tomorrow. The plows would bury the car on their next trip along the woods road. When he returned to the Hut, the girl was not in sight. "Hey!" he yelled.

"I'm in here," said her voice from the bedroom. "I hope you don't mind, but I had to lie down for a minute." She had a throaty voice, very pleasant.

"Well, keep a tight grip on the situation," Boris said. "We'll have the Doc here in a jiffy." He jackknifed himself into the armchair she had vacated, his favorite chair, and dialed the number with a finger that felt like an ice cube. "Sawbones!" Boris shouted when the old man answered, on the third ring. "Get your ass over here or I'll sue for malpractice. What are you doing asleep on a night like this?"

The doctor cussed him out, slowly, his voice still hoarse with sleep and probably whiskey. Then, the ritual done, Boris explained what had happened. "Well, you can tell her this for me," Doc said. "The little critter is gonna come out a hell of a lot harder than he went in." He burst into laughter, which ended in a fit of coughing. "*Ack*," he said, clearing his throat. "I'll try to get my own car out. Otherwise I'll wait for your friend. If we don't get there in time, just wrap the kid up, good and warm. And don't cut the cord. Leave that to me."

"Don't cut the cord," Boris repeated, and cradled the receiver. He dragged off his overshoes and went into the bedroom. "Doc's on his way," he told the girl.

"You're awfully kind," she said. "Please don't hate me."

"For Christ's sake," Boris protested. He switched on the bedside lamp and turned off the overhead lights. The girl was lying on the covers, still twisted from his nightmare. She had a

18

small, heart-shaped face, so white he could hardly distinguish it from the pillow. She was wearing a ruffled nightgown beneath her coat, and moccasins that were dripping snowmelt on his blankets. "Let's lighten the load, honey," Boris said. He removed the wet moccasins. Then, with the girl helping, he freed her arms from the duffel coat and pulled it from beneath her. The belly was huge under the nightgown; there seemed to be more belly than girl. Boris realized that he'd been wrong about the photograph. She was too pregnant for the picture he had in mind, something gentle and soft.

"Oh!" she said when he was folding the coat. She grabbed his arm, hard, her fingers threatening to pinch right through the bones and tendons. No wonder Georgie had lost control of the car! "I'm sorry," she said, letting go. "Oh!" She twisted away, rolling onto her side, biting into the knuckles of her hand. She had nice teeth. Her face glistened with sweat. "Please don't hate me," she said again.

Boris went out to the other room. He drew a saucepan of warm water, collected some towels and a pint of vodka from the bureau, and returned to her. "Swallow this," he said.

"I don't drink, as a rule," she gasped.

"Well, you don't have babies as a rule, do you? Go ahead—drink up. It'll make me feel better." He got maybe an ounce of the clear liquor between her lips, spilling another ounce on the pillow. Then he dipped a towel in water and washed her face. She immediately began to sweat again. "Christ," he muttered, looking at his watch.

"Please don't hate me," she begged. She managed a pale smile. "I won't do it again, I promise—*oh!*"

"I've got a medical dictionary somewhere," Boris said.

"I have one too, at home. Oh! Will you hold my hand? If you don't mind? Oh, God! It's no good—the dictionary, I mean. I looked up Pregnancy—oh!—and it gave all the symptoms, but not a word about the cure."

"Horseback riding is supposed to be good," Boris said.

"Yes, and taking hot baths, and jumping downstairs, and

eating slippery elm—oh, I know. Colin made me try them all." Her hand was clamped on his. "I'm sorry," she said, "I'm terribly sorry, but I'm afraid I just can't wait."

Boris grabbed the bottle and applied it to her lips. "Drink up," he said. "Please." The girl obeyed, sucking at the vodka like a child with a bottle of soda pop. She stared at him with huge eyes—hazel, Boris guessed, with flecks of brown floating in them, although the pupils were so huge he could not tell for sure.

She took her time, after all. Between contractions she swallowed quite a bit of the vodka, until finally her eyes were blurred enough that Boris could ignore them. He worked the blankets out from under her, until she was lying on the bottom sheet. He placed his supply of towels on the bedside table. Then he sat back to wait. After one particularly long contraction, in which the girl seemed to be trying to tie herself into a pretzel, she suddenly straightened and looked at him, cold sober. "Please don't hate me," she said.

"Can't you hold on a minute longer? The Doc will be right here."

"No," she said. "Just don't hate me, that's all."

"Well, okay," Boris said. "If that's the way you want it. But maybe we'd better get that nightgown off. Do you mind?"

"No, not at all," she said with a curious dignity.

Boris began to sweat, and soon he was as damp as the girl. What if he did the wrong thing? What if she died?

He tried without success to ease the nightgown past her hips, so he got up and brought a paring knife from the kitchen. "Cut up the seam, " she said. "That's my best nightie."

Boris tried, but the cloth ripped away in a zigzag pattern. Finally she was free up to the ribs. Her belly was impossibly big and white, like a mushroom ready to burst; the triangle of pubic hair seemed almost black against that gleaming white mountain of a belly.

"I'd turn out the light," Boris said, wiping the sweat from his eyes, "except maybe I ought to see what I'm doing."

"Don't mind me," the girl said. "It doesn't feel like my body, anyhow."

Then, in the circle of light from the bedside lamp, she delivered her child into his hands. Boris held the creature for a long blank instant, trying to remember what the Doc had said. There was a swampy stench in his nostrils and a dying moan in his ears. The baby was an angry red, wrinkled like a prune, and slippery in his hands. It was a boy, although the proof seemed stuck on at the last minute, as an afterthought.

The rag of humanity balled its fists and shrieked. Boris nodded. Oh yeah: he should have picked it up by the heels and slapped its bottom—a fitting introduction to the world, by God. But that didn't seem necessary in this case. Furious at the insult of his birth, the baby balled his fists, screwed up his eyes, and screamed. He wanted to get back to the womb, and Boris couldn't find it in his heart to blame him. "If I could manage it, buddy, I'd send you right back," Boris told him. "We haven't burned your bridges yet." The umbilical cord, remarkably stout and thick, ran like a vacuum cleaner hose back into the mother's body. Boris studied it. What the hell did the hospital do with all these extras?

Eventually, as a thunder in the other room announced the Doc's arrival, Boris came to his senses enough to wrap the child in towels, leaving it sufficient space to breath and yell in its thin, indignant voice.

"Well, well," roared Doc Perkins from the doorway. "Wouldn't wait, eh? That's the new generation for you, Boris; that's the new generation all over. She'll know better next time." Huge, bearlike in his topcoat the color and smell of a dead cigar, Doc dropped his medical bag and surveyed the bedroom. "Everything seems in order," he said. "Mother, child, midwife. . . . Of the lot, Boris, you look the worst, I'd say. What's this?" He picked up the vodka bottle and emptied it into his grizzled face. "That's better," he said, wiping his lips. "You'd be surprised how many folks never spare a thought for what the Doc has to go through." He gave Boris a bone-shaking slap on the back. "Well, well! What have you got there, m'boy?"

Boris surrendered the child, still linked to its mother by the slippery spiral cord, and staggered out to the main room, where Georgie sat wringing his hands. Boris booted him out of the armchair and sat down. "I'll be a son of a bitch," he said. "I didn't think to take a single picture."

"Gee, that's too bad," Georgie said. "How is Teddy? Is she all right?"

Boris focused on him. There was nothing wrong with Georgie, nothing in the world, but if there were two people in sight Georgie would be overlooked. Now, with nobody to distract his attention, Boris was surprised that such a sturdy young man could be so insignificant.

"She didn't say," Boris told him. The baby was still wailing in the other room. "Why don't you fix yourself a drink? You make me nervous, jiggling up and down like that."

"I'm sorry, Boris." Georgie sat down on the couch and began to bite his knuckles. "I hope Teddy is okay," he said after a while. "She's a sweet kid, you know?"

Boris stared at him. "What?" he asked.

"Well, now she isn't pregnant any more. . . . I mean, she can't very well stay with me at the trailer otherwise, can she?"

"Huh," Boris said. "You mentioned this to her yet?"

"I thought I'd better wait."

"I'll be a son of a bitch," Boris said.

2 - *Peace Is Our Profession*

BY WEDNESDAY AFTERNOON, Boris had caught up with most of his assignments, so he locked the photo lab at two o'clock and drove over to the University greenhouse. "I need some roses," he said.

Stanley, the ancient gardener, was surprised to see him. "Hey, Boris," he said, peering out from the turtle shell of his shoulders. "I just transplanted some nice geraniums. *There's* a plant you can live with. Dollar-fifty."

"Roses," Boris said. "A dozen of them. *Yellow* roses." Muttering, Stanley filled the order. Once a month for ten years—a ritual that paralleled his career as University Photographer—Boris had purchased a potted plant for his mother, who was an inmate at the New Hampshire State Hospital. Stanley thought she was in a nursing home. Actually, she was nutty as a fruitcake.

The roses made a great shout against the snow, and Boris hid them beneath a newspaper in the Volkswagen's back seat. Then he drove into the village, where he heard a shout: "Hey, Boris!" He double-parked the car and got out. There were a dozen people on campus who had the right to hail him and send him out to photograph a prize watermelon or hockey player. But it was all right this time: just some students, his guests of Sunday night, standing on the sidewalk in front of the Greek barbershop. He walked over to them with his hands in his pockets, staring at Prudence Peabody, gestating proudly beneath her winter coat. Didn't she ever think about the pain, the smell, the sopping bedclothes'?

"Honey," he said to her, "why don't you let that kid out on a leash? I can give you a hand if you need it." Prudence stared at a point just south of his elbow. The others made a circle around Boris, congratulating him upon the delivery, all except Georgie. He was probably upset that somebody else took care of Teddy while he was driving into snowbanks. "You going to

Washington too?" Boris asked him.

"I guess so." Georgie looked at Marvin Peabody. "I hate to cut so many classes, but I can do it if everybody else can. And Teddy's in the hospital, so that's okay. Maybe you'll drop in and say hello for me, Boris?"

"You bet!" Boris slapped him on that surprisingly sturdy shoulder. "Any girlfriend of yours is a girlfriend of mine." The others laughed. "That goes for the rest of you, too," Boris told them. He winked at Carol Phipps. "Where's your admirer?" he asked.

"Hal? He's drunk. He's been drinking since . . . Sunday night."

Marvin Peabody cleared his throat. "Just leaving!" Boris said, pretending to shield his face with his arm.

At that moment, a low-pitched droning that had been bothering his ears morphed into a swept-wing bomber. It flashed low over Narwich, then vanished beyond the Victorian bell tower of the University administration building. Boris remembered the planes of World War II, at least two of them and sometimes hundreds, like bats, darkening the sky. Then they had traveled in swarms; now there was only one, and one was enough. "Son of a bitch," somebody said. It was hard not to be awed by the swept-wing Boeing B-52.

"That's why we're here, people," Marvin Peabody said, like a good preacher, adapting his sermon to the weather. "That's why we're going to Washington!" He was delighted that the Strategic Air Command had arranged a send-off for him.

They had three cars, two decrepit Chevrolets and a Dodge, their doors and fenders whitewashed by salt from the highway. Marvin supervised the loading, four students in each car. "I don't suppose you'd like to come?" he said to Boris.

"Maybe next time," Boris said. "I gotta look after Georgie's girlfriend."

But he envied them. They were going somewhere and doing something, however foolish. He watched them out of sight, then jackknifed into his Volkswagen and drove to

24

Oldfield between the high banks of snow. As was often the case when he encountered Marvin Peabody, the edge was gone from his good humor. He cursed the orange truck that crept along with its plow raised two or three feet off the pavement. It was lowering the snowbank to make room for the next blizzard, while a hopper fed blue crystals of rock salt onto the pavement. These were portents that winter would never end.

At the hospital, on the far side of Oldfield, he held his bouquet behind his knee and told the receptionist he wanted to see Teddy Merchant. "Do you know his ward?" she asked.

"Maternity," said Boris.

"I beg your pardon?"

"Maternity," Boris said. "Teddy's a she."

"Oh," the receptionist said, flipping through her card file. "Theodora Merchant. Yes. She was scheduled to go home today."

Boris felt a twinge of disappointment. "Has her husband been here?" he asked. He moved closer to the desk to keep the flowers out of sight.

"She's had no visitors," the receptionist said. "I take it *you're* not Mr. Merchant?" Her expression added: Or *is* there a Mr. Merchant?

He didn't want to be expelled from Oldfield Hospital with a dozen yellow roses, so he turned and went down a corridor that seemed to lead into the center of the building. He passed several nurses until he found a pretty one. She led him down a cross corridor, her buttocks twitching nicely beneath the starched uniform skirt. "Mrs. Merchant is in Children's, not Maternity," she told him. "It's a little rule we have for babies born outside the hospital." Boris wanted to flee. Babies, flowers, hospitals—what the hell was he doing here? But the nurse opened a door with a flourish, and he was sucked inside.

Teddy greeted him shyly. She was in a private room, with a bassinette on wheels and a bedside table that contained nothing except a pack of cigarettes. "I even forgot my purse," she said.

"How come Georgie didn't bring your stuff over?"

"I don't know," she said. "Maybe he was afraid they'd take him for the father. Nobody here believes I'm married."

The nurse returned with a vase. She took the roses and fussed with them until they were glowing like a Japanese lantern on the table. Boris meanwhile studied the girl. She was small and passably pretty, even lovely, except for a wrongness about the mouth: she kept nibbling at the lower lip and forcing it against her teeth. Boris felt an odd little tug. He wanted to tell her that it was all right; she didn't have to bite her lip. "The receptionist says you're supposed to go home today," he said when the nurse was gone.

"Oh—maybe tomorrow." Poor kid! She was waiting for Colin to come, and he probably didn't know where she was.

"For Christ's sake," Boris said. "He can find you in Narwich as easy as here. Easier! You got that kind of money, to stay all week in a hospital, in a private room?"

"Well," she said, and her eyes blanked out on him, not permitting him to see what she felt about Colin's absence. "It's not that, really. But I can't just move in on Georgie again."

"No, I guess you can't. He's gone to Washington, anyhow, with Marvin and the peaceniks. . . . Well," he said, scratching his head and wishing he'd taken time for a haircut, "you can sleep on my couch for a day or two, until you find a better place." She stared at him, her big eyes functioning again. They seemed brown in the daylight. "After all, we're old friends," he urged. "Didn't I deliver that kid of yours?"

"Ohhh!" she said. "Have you *seen* him?"

She twisted around to uncover the bassinette. She was wearing a hospital smock, open at the throat, and with her movement Boris caught a glimpse of shoulder, collarbone, and breast, all lightly dusted with freckles. Then the brown eyes glowed upon him again, so he bent his attention to her son. The baby was pink now, instead of the angry red he'd worn the other night, and his miniature hands were relaxed and drawn up as if to protect his ears. He was asleep. "Well," said Boris, "I

26

have to admit he improves with age."

"Yes, isn't he marvelous? All last week, you know, I prayed and prayed that I would have a girl. Because Colin wasn't here? A boy needs a father, that's what I kept thinking; he needs somebody to play baseball with him. . . . Oh, I *know*," she said, as if Boris had protested. "I can play baseball ten times better than Colin, but that's what I was thinking, until Dr. Perkins told me it was a boy. Oh! You can't imagine how I felt—I was in paradise, simply in heaven. You'd think he was the first boy to be born on earth in a hundred years." Her eyes brimmed with tears. "What a wonderful thing it is," she said, "to create a man."

"Yeah. What are you gonna call him?"

"I don't know," she said, looking away. "That's Colin's job, isn't it? I mean, what if I named him Robert or Johnny or something and Colin didn't like it?"

"For Christ's sake," Boris said. "If—"

Teddy rushed on: "Can you imagine? They wouldn't let us into the maternity ward because he might *give something* to the other babies. Because he was born outside the hospital? So they put us in here. But it's marvelous, really; I have him all to myself. In the maternity ward, I'd see him only at meal-times. . . . Boris?" He quivered as if she had touched him. "Did you really mean it, what you said?" she asked, biting her lower lip. "That I could stay with you for a day or two?"

"Yeah, sure. As long as you like."

"Oh, it would only be a few days, until Colin comes for us."

"That's what I meant." Boris decided to beat it before she changed her mind, or he changed his. "I'll wait outside," he told her. "Have them send the bill to you at this address." He gave her one of the business cards that the University provided for its senior staff, and that were a great help in recruiting models, they were so dignified.

"Thank you," she said, impressed. "Really—thank you."

Boris left the room and searched his way through fluorescent corridors to the exit. He waited in the Volkswagen for half

27

an hour, chain-lighting cigarettes. Finally they appeared at the hospital door, Teddy in a wheelchair pushed by the pretty nurse. She was a diminutive figure in the green duffel coat, with the frilly hem of her nightgown appearing beneath it, and worn black moccasins upon her feet. They had given her a blanket for the baby. She cradled her son in both arms, looking like a wayward teenager. An elderly couple, just going up the hospital steps, looked at her with something between outrage and pity. Teddy stared them down. A tough little girl! Boris felt better about the whole thing.

He got out of the car and went to meet them. Teddy seemed relieved to have someone walking at her side, and indeed the next couple they encountered gave them a warm smile. Boris wondered if they had mistaken him for the baby's father, or for Teddy's.

~ ~ ~ ~

When they reached the Hut, they found Georgie sitting on the doorstep with his hands in his pockets, looking chilly and sad. "My car broke down," he told them. "At the Portsmouth traffic circle?" This was about ten miles from Narwich at the entrance to the New Hampshire Turnpike. "Marvin put my riders in the other cars, but it was really crowded and anyhow I couldn't leave my buggy by the side of the road, you know, in case it snowed again, so I hitched back here. . . . How are you, Teddy?"

"Fine, Georgie," the girl said fondly. "See what I've got." She shifted her pink-blanketed son, so that the tiny face was peering out at them with a puzzled expression. "Isn't he marvelous?" she demanded.

"Oh, a boy," Georgie said, looking at Boris for inspiration. Boris gave him none. "Gee, congratulations, Teddy. That's swell."

They went inside, where Georgie made a move to help Teddy off with her coat. "Oh, no," she said. "This is my bathrobe. . . . Remember? I left your place without a stitch on except for my nightie."

28

"Speaking of stitches," Boris said, "did you get that night-gown fixed?"

"Yes, that nice nurse mended it and washed it out, but it's pretty much of a ruin all the same."

"I'll get you a new one, honey," Boris said. At home in the Hut, with Georgie for an audience, he felt more confident about this venture. "Well." He scratched his head. "You'd better take the bedroom. Why don't you get settled while Georgie and I have a look at his car? Then we'll move your stuff down here from the trailer." He spread his hands in an inclusive gesture. "Make yourself at home."

Georgie was listening openmouthed. When they were in the Volkswagen, driving into Narwich, he blurted: "You mean Teddy is going to stay at the Hut with you?"

"Sure. I told you I'd look after her for you, kid."

On their way through Narwich, he saw Hal Pappajohn and stopped. Hal was that useful sort of American who could fix anything that moved on wheels. During his Army days, Boris had learned how to spot such men wherever he went. Hal, who was only slightly drunk, roared at Georgie's story. "The Portsmouth traffic circle!" he shouted. "You might at least have made it as far as Boston."

"Thank God he didn't," Boris said.

Hal chuckled happily in the back seat. "I wish it was Marvin," he said. "Would I like to see that bastard hung up by the side of the road? Son of a bitch! You know, he came over to La Cantina last night and drank a beer with me, trying to talk me into joining his goddamn Children's Crusade." Hal leaned between the bucket seats to demonstrate how Marvin Peabody held a glass of beer, between his thumb and forefinger. Hal's knuckles had been recently skinned. "It took him an hour to get it down," he said. "Say, Boris, you didn't happen to notice any rubbers around your bed the other night?"

"No, but I got a pair of high-buckle overshoes you can borrow."

"No joke," Hal said. "That was Carol's pregnant-getting

time. She almost clawed my eyes out when we woke up next morning."

"Then you'd better buy a ring," Boris said. "Or a ticket to Mexico City. I didn't find a thing."

"Well, Mexico City would be nice in February," Hal said, settling back. They were just passing the main gate of Powell Air Force Base, where a billboard told them: PEACE IS OUR PROFESSION. Powell was the home field of the bomber that had swept over Narwich a few hours earlier.

"I guess Marvin hasn't reached Washington yet," Boris said. "The Strategic Air Command is still open for business. Maybe we should picket them."

"Just the three of us?" Georgie said.

"Naw," Hal said. "There's no press club here. What's the use of picketing if you don't get your picture in the papers?"

"There's my car," Georgie said. He had abandoned the old Chevrolet a mile or so beyond the air base, just before the traffic circle that fed this highway into the Turnpike. The wind across the snowfields was chilly. Boris and Georgie sat in the Volkswagen while Hal, in his shirt sleeves, disappeared beneath the hood of the stranded car. "Boris?" said Georgie then. "Why . . . I mean, look at Hal."

"I can't," Boris said. He hated to wait by the side of the road while someone tinkered with machinery. "He's out of sight."

"I mean, look at him *for example*. He's always a big deal with the women, you know? How does he do it?"

"Why don't you ask him?"

Georgie was silent for a while, then burst out: "Boris, why don't the girls like me?"

Boris softened when he saw how serious Georgie was. "Well, for one thing, you never laugh," he said.

"Laugh?"

"Yeah. Hah-hah. You know. All you do is waggle your chin a bit and pound your knee. Girls like to hear a big sexy hah-hah."

"You never laugh, either, Boris."

"Fuck you," Boris said. "You *asked* me, didn't you? Why did you ask if you weren't going to believe what I told you?"

"I'm sorry, Boris." He was silent again, and Boris looked at him side-glance. The corners of Georgie's mouth were twisted, as if he were about to cry; his eyes were screwed up like an infant's. This expression rapidly grew worse. His lips peeled away from the teeth, and between them at last issued a series of short, breathless explosions, like the cries of an animal caught in a trap. "Like that?" he asked.

"What?"

"The laugh. Was that better?"

"Well, I think you need a little more practice before you try that on the girls. *Alone*," he added when Georgie's face began to twist again. "These things go better when you're alone. . . . What's all this about women, anyway?"

"Well. . . ."

"That Teddy," Boris said. "How come I never saw her at the Hut?"

"Gee, Boris, she didn't want to see *any*body. I guess she felt pretty bad about Colin. They were living in Boston, you know, but Colin went off somewhere, and when Teddy ran out of money she called me up, but she didn't want to see anybody else. . . . That's what she said," he finished proudly.

Hal Pappajohn emerged from beneath the Chevy's hood. "Fuel pump," he said triumphantly, blowing on his hands. "No sweat. I can install a new one in ten minutes." He climbed in, and Boris drove down to the traffic circle, around it, and back toward Narwich in the westbound lane. There was a garage almost directly across from the stranded car. Boris loaned Georgie ten dollars for the new fuel pump, then allowed that he ought to get back to the photo lab before closing time.

"Call the Hut if you have any trouble," he said. "And, Georgie? Give me the key to your trailer so I can pick up Teddy's things."

Georgie dug into his pocket and produced the key. "All her

31

stuff is in a blue suitcase on the couch, I think. We had it packed for the hospital, but we forgot it at the last minute."

Boris left them at the garage and drove back to Narwich. There were no messages at the photo lab, so he went out the woods road, collected the suitcase, and returned to the Hut. It was nice to know that somebody was there waiting for him.

Teddy was wearing one of his shirts, with the sleeves rolled up to show the warm brown flesh of her arms. The legs beneath the flapping shirttail were the same rich hue, and more rounded than curved. She was a small girl, and did indeed look like a teenager with her short hair and the baggy man's shirt.

"Goodness," she said, "but it's nice to be *flat* again." She smoothed the shirt across her belly, betraying the fact that her hips were quite wide. Boris decided that she was more female than feminine—a baby machine. She looked at the suitcase, which he had placed on the floor, and giggled. "I can't bend over," she said. "I'm not wearing pants."

With any other girl, Boris would have flipped up the shirt-tail to admire her bottom, but with Teddy his hand would not move from his side. So he picked up the suitcase and carried it into the bedroom, where Baby Merchant was sleeping in a bureau drawer, with a folded blanket for a mattress. "Isn't he cute?" Teddy demanded, glowing with motherhood. "I saw it in a movie one time, and ever since I've wanted to sleep my baby in a drawer."

"Yeah," said Boris, a little disturbed at how completely she had settled in. "Well, I'd better let you unpack."

He returned to the other room and sat down in his armchair. What the hell had he let himself in for? Perhaps Colin Merchant would collect his wife, but Boris had be-friended enough college men to know that they did not take fatherhood very seriously. No, the chances were that Teddy and her child would be his guests for quite a while. They would ruin his solitude—but then! Wasn't that what he needed? If a lousy greenhouse attendant knew his schedule for

32

buying flowers, and what kind, wasn't it time to break the pattern of his life?

Besides: think of the picture possibilities!

Boris trembled to a delicious melting in his groin. It was like the sensation—half fear and half joy—he had felt when volunteering for combat patrols in the South Pacific, from which he had returned with some of the finest photographs of his life.

3 - *Seven Months and a Bit*

THE DAYS WERE TOO SHORT. And the nights! What Colin needed was a Daylight Saving Time that added an hour to the morning without subtracting one from the evening, though even then he'd come up short. He needed more hours than any clock could provide. He needed time to create, to cry protest against a world that was trying to destroy itself, and him with it; he needed time to learn. He needed time to live, to enjoy himself; and time for a job to feed himself. That was the pinching shoe of his existence. He had to cram his eager feet into the same twenty-four hours that were allotted to every man, regardless of the distance he planned to travel. Colin snatched at the hours but they were never sufficient to his needs.

His apartment—not the place he'd shared with Teddy, but a one-room walk-up on Sherman Street—testified to the flying hours. There were books on the icebox, books on the windowsill, and books on the floor, turned face down with their spines endangered. Most of them he hadn't finished, but had gutted of their substance. There was an unmade bed and a pile of empties. Lastly, most significantly, there was a piece of sculpture sitting on newspapers in the middle of the room. This was Mankind Cowering. It was white, squat, and amorphous, and when Colin was elated it seemed to embody all the vague fears of his generation, and when he was depressed it looked like — an unfinished statue.

Oh, and there was a photograph of his wife. Incredibly, he was married. Sometimes he halted, when working on Mankind Cowering or reading fiercely through Jean-Paul Sartre, struck with the lunatic awareness that he possessed a *wife*. He gazed long minutes at Teddy's photograph. It was a wedding gift from her parents, head and shoulders only, since a full-length view would have showed her pregnancy. The face was in soft focus, but still it burned with the love she had awarded him,

34

and the greater love she wanted in return: more love, more attention, and more time than he could spare for her. His *wife*. And the mother of his child, for all he knew.

Since returning to Boston and finding Teddy gone, Colin had worked at an electrical repair shop on Charles Street, at the foot of Beacon Hill. He liked the job. He bent over his soldering iron for hours at a stretch, and these hours were not something lost, because he had rented them out to Mr. Fasinelli, whose shop it was. He'd exchanged them for two dollars each, and having done so he could forget them. The rush began only when he left the shop, which he did at six o'clock each evening. He bought an Italian sandwich and a copy of the *Christian Science Monitor*, then hurried up the steep sidewalk of Sherman Street. None of his friends were still living in Boston, at least not in their former haunts on the Hill, and he'd made no new friends since his return; of the people in Narwich, only Hal Pappajohn knew his address and sometimes came down to visit. Colin had no time for friendship. Or for sex: he hadn't slept with a woman for months. He studied those who passed him on the sidewalk. In the February night, their heels clicking on the uneven bricks, they were all beautiful. Sometimes, on a payday evening, he thought of taking five dollars from the envelope and trolling the bars for a woman, but he never did.

This was such a night, but there were few women on the sidewalk. The wind whistled down Sherman Street, as through a tunnel, and Colin was cold and sexless by the time he reached its crest. He turned into Number 42, a wooden doorway in an otherwise blank stucco wall, and walked up the narrow stairs to the top floor. His apartment was under the eaves, overlooking the brick backsides of the houses on Joy Street, and above them the gilded and floodlit dome of the Massachusetts State Capitol.

Colin settled in his armchair and squirmed until the broken spring was out of the way. Then he ate his sandwich and turned the pages of the *Monitor*.

35

On page four he saw a photograph of Marvin Peabody, of all the people in the world. He was carrying a sign demanding: DESTROY THE WEAPONS OF WAR! He had shifted the placard enough that his face was visible, but not so much that the sign could be cropped out of the picture. Colin shook his head. Marvin was a bit of a turd, but he knew what he wanted and could persuade people to help him get it. Even Colin had signed up as a member of the Committee for Militant Pacifism. He had paid his dues more or less faithfully until he quit school last September, though he'd never taken part in the committee's crusades —what Marvin called his "actions." They were too time-consuming. Pacifists had a habit of walking to their goals, and distances in America were vast.

They hadn't walked this time, it seemed. The wire-service dispatch told how the young graduate student and his companions drove down from New Hampshire to picket the White House in the teeth of a blizzard, and how students from Georgetown and American University had turned out to help them appeal for an end to the arms race.

Colin threw down the newspaper, but his lust for work was gone. Marvin's face kept coming between him and Mankind Cowering. So he read *Fear and Trembling* instead. He'd been on a philosophy kick for the past month or so, tracing the convoluted stream of Existentialism back to its beginnings. He'd read Sartre, Jaspers, Marcel, Heidegger, and now Kierkegaard, as much as he could understand of them. How they tortured their minds! Like snakes eating their tails, or incandescent hammers forging each other. (And what did the Old Testament have to do with it, anyhow?)

~ ~ ~ ~

Fear and Trembling gave way to the sound of an army, tramping up the stairs and halting outside his door. What the hell? The knob turned before he could get up. Marvin Peabody burst into the room, close-followed by Prudence and three young men from Narwich. "Hal said we'd find you here," yelled one.

"My God," Colin said. "I thought you were in D.C. I saw your picture just now, in the paper."

"Where?" said Marvin. Colin pointed to the newspaper on the floor. Marvin stooped to pick it up, then sprawled in the armchair while Colin marveled at his other visitors. They punched one another on the shoulder, grinning and exchanging insults. Prudence Peabody stood apart while the men mauled each other. Finally Colin turned to her, to the one upon whom half of his mind had all the time been fixed.

"*Prue*," he said in his sexy voice, "how *are* you?"

"As you see," she said.

Even through the winter coat, Colin could see. If anything, she was more pregnant than Teddy last time he'd seen her, three months ago. "Congratulations," he said. "Is that what I'm supposed to say?"

"It'll do." Prudence watched him while she removed the coat, but Colin refused to look at her belly. Instead he studied her face, trying to find a handle for this mystery: the small dark face with the waxy skin, sexual and secretive. "It's been a while, hasn't it, Colin?" she said at last.

"Yes," Marvin said. He was carefully tearing the photograph from page four. "At Provincetown, wasn't it?"

"In July," Colin said, and he could resist the temptation no longer. He glanced down at the ripeness of Prudence's pregnancy. He counted them off: August, September, October, November, December, January, *February*, pressing a finger against his thigh for each month. Seven months and a bit more.

At Cape Cod last Fourth of July, when they had visited him in the fisherman's shack he rented, Colin had seduced Prudence Peabody. Or so he had remembered it. Now, looking at the dark and enigmatic beauty of her face, he wondered if it might not have been the other way around. A burning afternoon. While Marvin remained in the shack to work on his thesis, Prudence and Colin took a picnic lunch and went out among the dunes, where he or she, he couldn't remember

37

which, suggested that they strip and go for a swim. Prudy was heavy-breasted and dark as an Indian. Returning, they did not reach the picnic basket, but fell naked upon the beach, still wet from the outgoing tide. She had cried out in the sun like a gull.

"What?" he said, realizing that his name had been spoken.

"Theodora," Marvin said. "Your wife. She's in Narwich, did you know?"

"Yes. Hal Pappajohn was here a couple weekends ago." Colin was torn between his memories. They blurred in his mind: hot afternoons with Teddy in College Woods, with Prudence on the beach. The sun burning his back.

"Did you know you're a father?" asked one of the other men.

"You have a son," Marvin added. They told him how Georgie had started for the hospital and driven into a snowdrift, and how Boris had delivered the baby.

"The guy who lives in that Quonset hut?" He'd seldom gone to the parties at the Hut. They were too political, and there was so much else to do—making love to Teddy, for one thing. And now he was a father! "I guess you think I'm pretty much of a shit," he said.

"Why, Colin," Prudence said sweetly, "how could we ever think such a thing?"

"A man must do . . .what he must," Marvin said. He was poking through the books on the floor. "Ah," he said. "Existentialism. Good for you, Colin. Tell me—do you really believe that the Self can be actualized?"

"I—"

"Colin can," Prudence said. "Can't you, sweetie—*actualize* yourself?"

He snatched at a diversion. "You're not going back to Narwich tonight, are you?" he cried. "I've just been paid. Let's get a bottle and celebrate." They were enthusiastic, all but Prudence, who looked at him with smiling eyes and a non-committal mouth. "Why don't you rinse out some glasses?" he suggested. She couldn't refuse, with Marvin standing there, and obeying Colin would rankle. "I'll run down to Charles Street and buy a bottle."

He did so, not running exactly but walking fast to burn off the energy that Prudence had inspired in him. The liquor store clerk gave him a handful of change from the dollar bills, as if encouraging him: go ahead, man, telephone your wife! There was a pay phone in the corner. Colin thrust the bottle into his pocket, picked up the receiver, and asked the operator to get him the number of George Morris in Narwich, New Hampshire. His hand sweated upon the cold black plastic of the telephone.

Georgie was delighted to hear his voice, but Colin cut him short. "Is Teddy there?" he asked.

"Gee, Colin, she isn't. Have you tried the Hut? She's been staying with Boris, you know, since she got out of the hospital."

"No, I didn't know." He felt as though somebody had betrayed him.

"Well, that's where she is, all right. Boris has been swell, Colin. Did you know that he delivered the baby? Boy, what a night —"

Colin hung up. The telephone digested his forty-five cents with a satisfied noise, like a cash register. "You need more change?" the clerk asked.

"What? No." He left the store and walked slowly up the hill to Number 42, remembering the stories he'd heard about the photographer who got girls to pose for him in the nude. And now Teddy was living with this man? Well, to hell with her! To hell with Teddy and Boris, and Prudence and Marvin, babies, complications—to hell with all of them. He was well out of it, by God.

Back in the apartment, he found that Prudy had washed his dishes, swept the floor, and tidied his books. She was still glowing with her secret.

The pacifists got drunk very quickly on Colin's gin, as if their Washington adventure had been a prelude to this party,

39

the hard work that justified it. Only Colin and Prudence drank cautiously. At midnight, when Marvin was half asleep and his comrades were singing to the banjo one of them had brought along, Prudence stood up. "Goodness," she said, "but I feel *woozy!*"

"Maybe you'd better take a walk," Colin said.

"Marvin?" Prudence shook her husband. "I'm just the slightest bit dizzy, darling. Would you walk me around the block?"

"Oh, God," Marvin groaned. "Can't it wait? We'll be leaving . . . soon." His chin dropped to his chest again, spreading out like a fat man's buttocks.

"I'll go with her," Colin said. "Okay, Marv?"

"Fine, fine. Splendid."

"We'll be back in fifteen minutes," Colin said to the folk singers. They nodded without losing the beat, and he grabbed Prudence's coat and his own and guided her to the door. He tried to kiss her when they were alone on the landing, but she turned away. Behind the closed door his friends were singing nasally:

This is how the world ends,
This is how the world ends,
Not with a bang or a whimper
But a fine . . . atomic . . . BELCH!"

They went down to the street without speaking. With her jutting belly and heavy winter coat, Prudence was like the compacted warmth at the earth's core, a promise out of reach. "My car's in the alley," Colin said. "We can sit there and talk, out of the wind." She didn't answer, but followed him to where the old Ford was parked and let him unlock the door for her. He slid in beside her. "*Prudence,*" he said softly. He kissed her beneath the ear, since that was all that was available to him. He put his hand into her coat and held it against her breast. "Beautiful girl," he whispered. He unbuttoned the coat and bent forward, rubbing his cheek against her breasts.

40

She pushed him away. "Men!" she said.

"What's wrong with men?"

"There's only one thing *right* about them," Prudence said, "and that's what causes women all our grief."

"Oh, Prue, for God's sake!" They wrestled on the seat for a while. She was astonishingly strong, and he didn't want to be too rough for fear of her pregnancy. Finally he gave up and slouched against the steering wheel, his breath frosting the windshield.

"Aren't you even interested whether this is your child I'm carrying?" Prudence asked, rearranging her hair with quick, deft pats.

"Haven't you told me it is?"

"No."

"All right: is it?"

"I don't know," Prudence said. "I have a husband, too."

Colin didn't believe her. "Cut it out," he said. "A woman knows these things."

"Does she?" Prudence laughed deep in her throat, a husky, sexy laugh, until his palms were itching. "Maybe, but she'd be a fool to know too much. I couldn't stay with Marvie if I was absolutely sure this was your baby, Colin. And then where would I be? Would you look after me the way you looked after Teddy?"

"I couldn't help that," he said.

"Oh, of course not!"

"Well, I couldn't. You don't know what Teddy is like—she gobbles a man right up. I almost went out of my mind, Prue. Perching on my knee when I was trying to read, wanting to come along whenever I took a walk, crying her head off if I stayed out overnight, never leaving me alone. . . ."

"I don't blame her. You're not safe, Colin; you don't give a girl anything to hold on to. You don't even notice she's around unless you're feeling horny."

"Oh, well," he said, grinning at her. "Keep 'em barefoot and pregnant, that's my motto."

41

"I'll stick with Marvin, thank you," Prudence said. "At least he can afford to buy shoes. . . . I'm *freezing*," she added.

~ ~ ~ ~

They went back to the apartment, where the folk singers had passed out on the floor and Marvin in the armchair. The place was stale with cigarette smoke. Colin opened a window, while Prudence covered Marvin with her coat and took the bed for herself. Colin debated for a while but decided not to crawl in beside her: Marvin might wake up in the night. He stretched out on the floor instead. Soon his back began to ache, so he got up and stole Prudence's coat from Marvin, for a mattress.

They had a hangover breakfast of toast and black coffee, not talking much. Only Marvin seemed unaffected by the night before. He shaved with Colin's razor, brushed his teeth with Colin's toothpaste, and herded his wife and followers down the stairs. While they were getting into the car, he drew Colin to one side. "I didn't ask you to come to Washington with us," he said, the words lingering as white steam, "because I know how very busy you are." He seemed to be conferring a great favor upon Colin. "And I need your help in another little matter. Can you come up to Narwich for a day?"

"Right now?" It all seemed so possible: he would get into the car with Marvin, and in two hours he would see Teddy again.

"Next month," Marvin said, lowering his voice although the others were already in the car. "I don't have the details worked out, but I can promise you that this will be the most important *direct action* I've ever organized. I'll need dedicated people, men and women ready to risk imprisonment for what they believe is right." He looked solemnly into Colin's eyes, until Colin had to look away. "That's why we went to Washington," Marvin continued. "I wanted to test their mettle. And that's why we stopped here on the way back to Narwich, because I know you're just such a man, Colin."

In spite of himself, Colin was pleased. "Just let me know when," he said. "I'll be there."

They shook hands on it.

He stood shivering on the sidewalk until Marvin's car had turned the corner into Charles Street, far down at the foot of the Hill, and suddenly he felt lonesome. He hadn't realized how much he had missed his friends. He yearned for them— for Narwich, for Teddy!

4 - How Could We Wait?

IN THE PAST TEN YEARS, only one other guest had spent more than one night at the Hut. That was O'Rourke, the first of the unhappy intellectuals Boris had befriended. As the first, he was granted special privileges whenever he made a pilgrimage to Narwich. But he was a man, and a transient, and childless. Teddy Merchant had none of these virtues. Within a week the Hut belonged as much to her as to Boris. The bathroom was packed with powders and oils and female gadgets, and his safety razor kept coming up dull. And because the partitions were composition board, he couldn't use the toilet unless the shower was running.

He was barred altogether from the bedroom, which was now Teddy's. It smelled of perfume, talcum powder, face cream, and dirty diapers, and there was not a single masculine odor remaining, to testify that Boris had slept ten years in that double bed. The living room had changed comparatively little: there were burlap curtains on the windows and groceries in the refrigerator and landscapes instead of the nudes that had once decorated the vertical walls. The photos were his idea. Teddy said she didn't mind the nudes—rather liked them, in fact, as long as *she* wasn't pictured—but Boris took them down anyhow. They were now in the darkroom. This was the only part of the Hut where Teddy had not left her mark, and it was here that Boris retreated whenever he wanted to do any serious thinking.

Mostly, he thought about Teddy, who had so drastically altered his life. She was marvelously complex. The longer he knew her the more complicated she seemed, until by the end of a fortnight he didn't understand her at all. "I'm terrible in bed," she would confess. "You can't imagine how clumsy I am —no sense of rhythm at all." Then she'd deny she had used his razor that day. "I shave my legs just once a week," she insisted. Yet the blade was dull again, and there was a razor nick on the

44

warm brown curve of her calf. Finally he decided that Teddy lied about trivialities and told the truth about important matters, such as her marriage to Colin Merchant.

"It was my own fault I got preggers," she said. "I was always a very *young* girl, you know? I wore pigtails and played skip-rope until I came to college, and even then I cut my pigtails only because my roommate laughed at me; and I never had a boyfriend before Colin. I didn't know the first thing about sex. I used to tell myself: you'll only be young once, so enjoy it while you can, you'll have all the rest of your life to act like a grownup. Then I met Colin and fell in love." Her voice changed when she pronounced this word, dropping an octave and taking on a vibrant quality, much as it did when talking about Baby Merchant. "Oh, nobody could tell me *anything* after I met Colin," she boasted. "Nothing could ever be like that again. I was in love, and I gave him everything I had, and I only wish it could have been more."

Colin was the hitching post of Teddy's conversation, from which she never strayed very far. "Don't bother," she would say when Boris asked if he should turn the oil heater higher for the night. "I'm pretty tough. I'm a peasant from 'way back —and a good thing, too. Colin was never very gentle with me." It was the same whether the subject was politics or money or babies: every excursion led back to Colin Merchant.

The man she described was slender and graceful, blue-eyed, artistic, a fair-haired young god whose ways were incomprehensible to the rest of the world. Boris filtered her words until only the larger facts remained: Colin Merchant was a little shit, and Teddy loved him with a deep, unquestioning, stubborn, and altogether profitless devotion.

"Do you know where he's living?" Boris asked.

"Ye-es. I asked Georgie, and he found out from Hal Pappajohn."

"Then write to him!"

"Oh, that would only put him off. You don't understand him."

45

"I understand the bastard well enough," Boris said. "You should have him arrested for nonsupport."

Teddy began to chew at her lower lip. "You needn't worry," she said. "I'll find a job as soon as I'm able, and I'll pay you back, every cent."

"For Christ's sake," Boris said. "You don't owe me anything. Hell, I'm saving money with you in the house."

"Honest?"

"Sure," he said, although it was not quite true. He had invested perhaps fifty dollars in Baby Merchant—a second-hand crib, blankets, diapers, and the like—not to mention the medicines and cigarettes and female odds and ends that went onto his grocery bill. There'd also been $500 for Oldfield Hospital and $50 for Doc Perkins. "You don't owe me a thing," he told her.

But for the first time in ten years Boris found himself without money in his pocket. Luckily February was the shortest month. While they waited—she for her husband, he for payday—Narwich alternately thawed and froze, rained and snowed.

"It's like last year, when Colin was courting me," Teddy said, hazel-eyed. "What an awful month! We couldn't find anywhere to lie down."

"You might have waited."

"Wait! How could we wait? We were in love, and the world might have blown itself up tomorrow!"

After the blizzard that began the month, there was a thaw and another storm, so that snow was piled on top of ice. Then a cold spell settled in. The town plow scraped along the woods road at night, frost snapped at the windowpanes, and Boris and Teddy spent whole evenings beside the oil stove and its radiant warmth. People blew their noses and coughed a lot. Teddy caught the bug, despite her boasted toughness, and the baby caught it from her. Then there was panic! Boris had to bring Doc Perkins over to assure her that the baby did not have pneumonia. "When I was a kid we called it croup," Doc said. "People are too damned sophisticated today. If their fingers chap they think they've got leprosy. That's what comes of reading *Time* magazine."

"He'll be all right?" Teddy pleaded.

"Right as rain," Doc said, draping a bearlike arm across her small shoulders. Boris twitched with envy. Why couldn't he comfort her like that? "As for you, young lady," Doc added, giving her a hug in which she almost disappeared, "you're hell-bent for an ulcer." He released her, tore a sheet from his prescription pad, and scribbled across it. "Sleeping pills," he said. "Take 'em. Stop trying to stay awake all night."

Teddy glowed as if she'd been praised. "You're so nice to us," she said, "and I haven't even paid you for the time Baby was born. Don't worry—I'm going to catch up with all my debts just as soon as my husband comes back." Doc looked at Boris, who looked at the floor. Teddy chattered on, oblivious.

By the time Baby Merchant had recovered from his bout with pneumonia (Teddy insisted that it was nothing less) he seemed almost human to Boris. His mild blue eyes were beginning to focus on the world. And he was discovering his body, drooling happily while he tried to locate his foot and stuff it into his mouth. Boris could watch this process for hours. Teddy, on the other hand, was becoming very deft and casual with her son, spearing giant safety pins into his diapers with a gusto that made Boris shift his weight uncomfortably. Nor was she awed any longer by the baby's gadget, stuck to his groin like a pink toy cannon.

"When the nurse was bundling him up, that day you brought us home," she said with a giggle, "his diaper slipped down and oh!—I was so shocked. I couldn't help it; I covered my eyes. The nurses must have thought I was an awful nut. . . . Life is so funny," she said, her eyes autumnal. "Who would have thought, last year when Colin was courting me, that it would have turned out like this? That I would have a *son?*"

There was no telling where Baby Merchant had been conceived. They had trysted in the University chapel, under the stone-arch steps of the administration building, in the press box at the football field . . .anywhere they could hide from the weather and the night watchman.

"My mother never guessed," Teddy said. "She was happy I was behaving like a female at last, with lipstick and a boyfriend, but my father! He came down to Narwich one weekend. We drove to the beach—I remember that afternoon so clearly, with the tide gone out and the sand all wet and gleaming. Daddy gave me a lecture about men. He told me how a man would wait for the woman he loved. He said: 'They're salesmen, Teddy. They're all salesmen! Don't I know? It's not so long since I was selling a line to your mother. But don't believe 'em. They'll wait for you if they're any good, and do you want to marry the other kind?' Then he looked at me and said: 'Teddy, is there anything you want to tell me?' He knew, you see.

"I wanted to ask him if a man would still wait, after the woman gave what he wanted, or would he just find someone else? But I couldn't get the words out. So Daddy hugged me and went home, and we never talked about it again," Teddy ended with a sniff.

She was pregnant when the University closed in June. Colin didn't know, and Teddy only suspected; so he went off to Provincetown to be in the company of other artists, and she waited on table at a restaurant near her home, like a good peasant. She didn't have her periods—she decided it was from missing Colin. Then her breasts began to swell. When finally she was convinced, she decided that before jeopardizing her young god's career she would run away from home and have his baby in San Francisco. But it seemed easier, in September, to return to Narwich for her sophomore year. Colin was bronzed and restless after his summer on Cape Cod; he talked of quitting the University and finding a job in Boston, where his talents wouldn't be cramped by lectures and homework. Only then did she admit that she was four months pregnant. Colin decided to take her with him, and they moved into an apartment on the back side of Beacon Hill. They were happy.

"I'll always respect him for that," Teddy declared. "He didn't have to take me with him."

"For Christ's sake," Boris said. "What did he have to lose?"

"It was such a wonderful autumn, Boris, you can't imagine, with the parties and the walks on Boston Common and the crazy people we knew. Nobody could guess that I was preggers —I was flat as a board. I would send my letters to Narwich, and my roommate would forward them. But then my folks decided to pay a surprise visit, and they discovered that I hadn't been at school for two months. Daddy was *frantic*. He called the state police, and he scared the life out of my roommate, and he found out where we were. Oh! What a scene that was, with my father threatening to shoot Colin on the spot. . . . So we were married."

"And that was the end of the party."

"Well, Colin was furious, of course, and we started to fight and couldn't stop. Then one day he disappeared. I stuck it out as long as I could, and then I came up here."

"Why didn't you go home?"

"Oh, I didn't want to admit that this great big wonderful romance had flopped. Anyhow, Colin wouldn't have dared visit me at home. Not after that scene in Boston. You've never met my father, Boris; you can't understand. He's the last of the great tyrants. Colin is going to come back to me some day, and I want to be where he can find me and we can talk without my father standing over us, ready to shoot him if he says the wrong thing."

"I'll shoot the bastard, too," Boris promised, "if he hands you another raw deal."

"What raw deal?" Teddy demanded. "My son? Do you think that I *regret* him? Go look at him, sleeping in his crib, and tell me I should be sorry he was born."

Boris groaned. She was delighted with her son, and therefore forgave everything his father had done. Colin Merchant had begotten him without a thought, had married her

49

under duress, and had left her to have the baby as best she could—it didn't matter! She forgave him everything, and she only wanted a chance to make the same mistake again.

5 - *Just a Little Breeze*

BORIS STRUCK OUT with Judy, the long-haired girl. "Oh no," she said. "I'm not stripping in front of Teddy Merchant. I don't mind *men* looking at me, but women —that's creepy. Can't we take the picture here?" No, the photo lab was impossible. Mr. Phipps, the janitor, a professor from the art department—half a dozen people had keys. There was no telling who might walk in.

But there was Georgie's trailer! It was nearby, it was secluded, and Georgie could wait at the Hut while Boris was taking pictures, giving Teddy some protection from the young tomcats of Narwich. An abandoned wife seemed to give off a scent that brought them in from miles around: Hal Pappa-john, his buddy Breck who lived on a houseboat in Ports-mouth harbor, and others for miles around. Teddy didn't have the experience to handle men like them.

Georgie agreed to leave his key at the photo lab each noon, retrieving it at the Hut in the evening. Meanwhile Boris cooled his heels. Judy had forbidden him to phone her at the dorm—a nice tribute to his reputation, Boris thought.

She showed up on Wednesday afternoon, treading silently on rubber-soled shoes. Boris had just finished mopping the office floor. Judy's footprints stood out on the wet linoleum like the diagrams in a textbook on ballroom dancing. "Hello, honey," he said. "What d'ye say? Let's go into the darkroom and see what develops."

Judy's lip curled scornfully. "Hello, Boris," she said, brush-ing the hair out of her eyes with the heel of her hand. "Is there a gig at your place Sunday night?"

"First Sunday of every month," Boris agreed. He leaned his mop in the corner and surveyed her, wearing black tights and a duffel coat like Teddy's. He put his arm around her, barely able to locate her waist beneath the heavy coat. Damn the winter, anyhow; you couldn't tell the women from the men.

51

"About those photos," he said; "Georgie says we can use his place. I can lock up right now and run you out there. We'll be finished before supper."

"Where?"

"Georgie Morris. His trailer.."

She swiveled away, leaving fresh prints on the linoleum, like a fox-trot turn. "Oh no!" she said. "I don't want the whole campus to know about this." And before he could protest, she'd fox-trotted out the door.

~ ~ ~ ~

Indeed, it was the last day of February. Payday! He walked over to the respectable part of campus, through a dusting of snow that fell in fat, wet flakes that kissed his cheeks and turned to slush beneath his shoes. He passed a few coeds on his way to the administration building, but of course they wore plastic rain caps, long coats, and overshoes or boots with only an inch or two of calf showing. Winter would never end, the girls would never shuck those heavy coats, Judy would never pose for him. And on Sunday—first Sunday of every month— he would visit his mother at the New Hampshire State Hospital.

He collected his money from the University cashier, an overripe blonde of about his age, who would have posed for him in a minute, probably. He went out into the wet snowfall again, walked back to the parking lot, and plucked the ticket from under the Volkswagen's windshield wiper. He blotted it with his sleeve and returned it to the glove compartment. He had been using this particular ticket for two or three months now: the campus police wouldn't bother a car that was already ticketed.

The liquor store was in Oldfield, five miles away, and Boris drove there now. The snow melted as fast as it fell; water slapped against the bottom of the car. In Oldfield the gutters were full. Boris parked in front of the liquor store, painted a bureaucratic green, the same color as Army furniture. He stepped over the gutter, went inside, and bought three bottles of vodka from the somber Greek manager. Some of the students would bring their own booze, but not enough of them.

Outside again, he spotted Carol Phipps down the block, emerging from a drugstore. Boris studied her while she in turn studied a furniture-store window, full-breasted, oblivious to the weather in skirt, sweater, and loafers. Boris took a deep breath. Well, what about Carol? She was the boss's daughter, true, but he had those photographs of her and Hal Pappajohn, as gentle blackmail if the need arose. Why not? He put the vodka bottles into the Volkswagen and walked down to where she was standing. "Hello, honey," he said. "I'll buy it for you."

"What? Oh, Boris," she said, turning her mild blue eyes upon him. "What will you buy?"

"That." He pointed to the double bed in the window. "As a matter of fact," he said, nudging her with his elbow, "I've got one at home just like it. You ought to try it out some time."

"Mmm," Carol said, pushing her lips into a pout. They seemed so ripe that if she bit them, they would burst. "Are you driving back to Narwich?" she asked. "Can I have a ride? The bus doesn't go back till five."

Boris waved at his Volkswagen, parked in front of the liquor store. Carol walked over to it without any further invitation, and when she slipped inside Boris saw a long flash of thigh. He was trembling like a fawn when he squeezed into the driver's seat. He knew better than to praise her figure, which was too obvious to call for flattery, so he needed to praise something else. "Hey now," he said, running a dark finger along her cheek, "that's a fine head of hair you've got. I'd sure like to photograph you, those big eyes and that golden hair all around."

"You would?" Carol said. "Then how come you never asked me before? Have you run out of smart girls?"

"I didn't want to get fired," Boris said, inserting the ignition key with shaking fingers: she was going to bite.

"Oh, *daddy*," Carol said. "You needn't worry. I don't tell my folks *everything*." Boris stole glimpses of her profile on the road to Narwich. It was astonishing how indefinite her features were, as if she were already a portrait, printed through a diffusion screen.

Just before they reached the village, he struck: "I've got a couple hours free this evening. Why don't we shoot off a roll or two of film, see what they look like?"

Carol touched her hair. "Well, I should study," she said. "I've got an hour exam tomorrow in Ornithology, a real stinker." She paused, but Boris said nothing, for fear of saying the wrong thing. "But I guess it'd be all right."

Boris exhaled deliciously through his mouth. Carol Phipps —the boss's daughter! She'd be the darling of his collection, with those thrusting breasts and that childish face, his finest model in years. Perhaps he would pose her in front of a mirror, a soft-faced girl suddenly discovering her womanhood. Yes, great, and she'd cup one hand under her breast, as if dreaming of a lover or a nursing child. . . .

"Is there a modeling fee?" Carol asked. "You should buy me dinner, at least."

They were just passing the Coffee Corner. Boris swung into the curb, took out his wallet, and gave her a dollar. "Be my guest," he said. "Sorry I can't watch you eat, but I got a few things to do. Meet you here at seven, okay?"

"Okay," Carol said, dropping the greenback between the jaws of her purse. She twisted his rear-view mirror so she could inspect her face. Satisfied, she got out. "Give my love to your girlfriend," she said in parting. "Colin's *wife*," she added before slamming the door.

Boris straightened the mirror, then went to the Superette and bought some groceries, a pound of steak, and a six-pack of beer. The beer would pacify Georgie while Boris was using his trailer.

~ ~ ~ ~

Teddy welcomed him joyfully. Boris had been puzzled by these greetings at first, but he concluded that she lived in a constant state of excitement, breaking dishes, redecorating the Hut, planning careers for herself, and discovering fresh beauties in her son. By nightfall she was usually bursting with the need to tell somebody about the day's adventures. "Prudy was here this afternoon," she told him, taking the bag of groceries. "Prudence Peabody? We've worked out the most marvelous scheme, Boris. You'll be ever so proud of me." She put the steak in the oven to broil and dropped frozen vegetables into a saucepan. "Groceries are cheaper in Oldfield than here, Prudy says. So, once a week, we'll organize a shopping expedition. We'll buy a week's worth of groceries at a time and save lots and lots of money. . . . And that's not all."

"What else?" Boris said, admiring the warm curve of her elbow while she salted the vegetables, which she did with a violent, left-handed shake.

"Well!" She banged the lid onto the saucepan with her right hand. "When Prudy has her baby, we'll find jobs. She'll work days and I'll work evenings, or the other way around, and whoever isn't working takes care of the children. So we won't have to hire a baby sitter. Isn't that a fine idea?"

Before Teddy had come to live with him, returning to the Hut every evening had been the dreariest part of his day. He'd hate to start that routine again. "It's a great idea," he said, since that was what she wanted to hear. "But shouldn't you take it easy for a while?"

"Oh, this won't be for a month or so, until Prudy recovers from her big moment. . . . She had a rough time with the first one," Teddy said. "Not like me." Then the fat caught fire under the broiler, and they had a panic while they rescued the meat and aired out the Hut. Baby Merchant was frightened by the noise. He began to cry, and Boris finished cooking the meal while Teddy comforted her son.

Georgie came in while they were eating. He was bundled against the weather in overshoes, topcoat, and a cap pulled down over his ears. Teddy jumped up to pour him a cup of coffee. "Goodness, Georgie," she said, "is it storming again?"

"No, but it looked pretty nasty when I went to class this

morning." He peeled off his outer garments, draped them on the couch, and pulled a chair up to the dinette table. "I didn't expect to see you here," he said to Boris. "I met Carol Phipps downtown a while ago and she said she was going to pose for you tonight." Boris didn't mind that the word was out, but he hoped it had stopped short of the University Development Office. "So I brought some stuff over to show Teddy," Georgie said. "Something I've been working on." He showed them a notebook bulging with clippings from newspapers and magazines. "Do you remember that argument at the party last month? About what would happen if a war broke out? Well, I started thinking about it, and I realized that none of us really knew what we were talking about."

"No kidding?" Boris said.

"So I decided to find out *exactly* what would happen." He spread his clippings upon the table, until Boris had to move his plate. "Do you realize that it's possible to destroy the world? Really destroy it?"

Teddy shuddered. "Oh, Georgie," she said, "why do you have to talk about such things?"

"Because they're real! It's actually possible, with present-day tools, to build a bomb that can destroy the world. It's called a Doomsday Machine. Here's an article about it." With fastidious fingers, Teddy picked up the clipping and looked at it. "Here's something else," Georgie continued, pushing a clipping toward Boris. "It's about the probability of accidental war. If there's one chance in fifty, each year, that a war might start by accident, then the chances are better than even that an accidental war will happen before the end of the twentieth century."

"I don't expect to live until the end of this century," Boris said.

"Well, *I* do," Teddy said. "And if I don't, my son will."

"That's right," Georgie said, pleased that his research had captured her interest. "I have some other clippings here about the probability of war in the next few years. Here, let me read

56

this one. . . ."

Boris stood up. "Make yourself at home," he said. "There's beer in the refrigerator. I'm gonna examine some statistics of my own—gorgeous, twenty-three, gorgeous, I think they are."

~ ~ ~ ~

Alas, there was no sign of Carol Phipps at the Coffee Corner. Probably she'd met Hal Pappajohn or one of those bullet-domed athletes from Fraternity Row, and had changed her plans. Boris skulked along Main Street, reluctant to go back to the Hut and admit defeat, hating the couples who brushed past him on the sidewalk. He walked head down through the cobwebs of their laughter. Then he saw her, trying on a kerchief inside Miss Deborah's Shoppe. "Oh, is it seven already?" she said when he appeared at her elbow. "I guess not," she said to the salesgirl, returning the kerchief with a vague smile. She tucked her purse under her elbow and followed him out to the car.

Boris drove back the way he had come. The trailer was located about a mile beyond the Hut, and Carol snickered when the Volkswagen bounced into the driveway. "This is *Georgie's* place," she said.

"Yeah. You know him, huh?"

"Oh, everybody knows Georgie. He's cute." Boris gathered his camera bag from the back seat and followed her along the unevenly shoveled walk. She fished the key from his jacket pocket and opened the door. "*Brrr*," she said, hugging her breasts. "It's cold, cold, cold." Boris turned the oil furnace to its highest heat and lighted the gas oven as well. That done, he borrowed a sheet from the tiny bedroom. He draped it across the front windows, with enough snaking along the floor to provide a seamless background in which there were no ups or downs. Into this empty world he placed a chair fashioned from steel tubing and black canvas. "I sit down, huh?" Carol said.

"Place isn't big enough for a standing view." Boris rubbed his hands. The trailer was warming up. "Perfect, perfect," he said. "No distractions." He cleared a pile of philosophy texts from the kitchen counter, then laid out his equipment. All he needed was the Rolleiflex, a light meter, and a roll of film, but women liked to have a professional setting, with mysterious accessories, black hoods, a flashgun and a sleeve of bulbs. The ritual also gave him time to consider how to get Carol's clothes off. One step at a time! "Okay," he said, patting her rump, which proved to be rather soft. "Slide down a bit and hook your leg over the edge."

Carol pouted voluptuously across a bare knee. It was cheesecake, but if that's what she expected, Boris would waste a few frames of film on it. Then he moved in closer. The Rollei was perfect for modeling, since it obliged him to crouch over the frosted-glass viewfinder, looking down, giving the model the illusion that nobody was looking. Carol's face swam up to him in the viewing mirror, the colors muted, the features vague, like Miss Rheingold of any year you wanted to name. "The sweater should go," Boris said without looking up. "Take it off."

"Huh?"

"The sweater. The pattern distracts from your face.."

"I thought you were interested in my *hair*," Carol said.

"Sure, but we need the atmosphere, you know—the surroundings."

"Oh." Carol peeled the sweater over her head. The skin of her midriff was soft and white, with a dimple where her belly button should have been. Boris was tempted to poke the dimple, but there was no sense testing his model so early in the evening. So he watched while the pink brassiere came into view, enclosing breasts as large as the cantaloupes Boris had photographed last summer at the University farm. The melons had won a prize of some sort for the horticulture department. By rights, the prize should have gone to Carol Phipps, whose breasts were rounder and riper than any cantaloupe that ever grew.

"That's a handsome pair of knockers," he told her.

Carol yanked the sweater past her head. "Now my hair's a

mess," she said. "Give me my comb."

Boris emptied her pocketbook. Among the lipsticks, keys, and pencils he found a tin of contraceptive foam. He held it up. "Better late than never, huh?"

"What's *that* supposed to mean?" Carol tried to stare him down, but didn't make a good job of it. "Put it back," she said, almost pleading.

Boris continued his search. There was a little parcel among the junk he had spilled out, a box wrapped in blue paper, and he remembered that Carol was coming out of a drugstore when he spotted her this afternoon. More contraceptives? It didn't seem likely. Maybe she was pregnant, and this was some quack remedy such as Colin Merchant had forced his wife to swallow. Hal Pappajohn would do the same; he was a bastard, too. All the Narwich men were bastards.

Boris found the long-handled plastic comb and gave it to her. He snapped one good picture while she was combing out her hair, with her breasts standing out and her face soft and pensive, but it wasn't quite what he wanted. "It's like an underwear advertisement," he complained. "You better take off the bra."

"No," she said.

"Do me a favor today, maybe I do you a favor tomorrow."

"What favor?" she asked.

"Well, you can get into all sorts of trouble in a college town. You never know when you might be needing help from good old Boris."

"*Dirty* old Boris," she said. Then she giggled and reached behind her back. She unclasped the bra and pushed the shoulder straps aside. "That's as far as I'm going." Boris was able to photograph a fine sweep of flesh in a way that would suggest the rest. Later he'd crop out the bra and nobody would know he hadn't seen it all.

He finished the roll, twelve exposures, and stored it in his gadget bag. Carol watched him with a little pucker-frown between her eyebrows. "Maybe we should quit now," she said

59

while he was loading a fresh roll into the Rolleiflex. "I have that hour exam tomorrow."

"One more roll, in case I spoiled that one."

"Some other time," she said, reaching behind her back to fasten the bra.

Boris saw his hopes go glimmering. "Aw, come on," he said. "Please."

Carol laughed in his face. "Silly old Boris," she said. "Never say please to a woman. Even if she meant to agree, *please* would change her mind. . . . Toss me that sweater, will you?"

"Go to hell."

"*Please?*" Carol said. Boris handed her the sweater. "See?" she said. "It's a woman's word. . . . That's two favors I've done you today, so don't scowl at me like that." She raised her arms and vanished under the sweater. Now! Boris reached over and prodded her navel. His index finger sank in to the first knuckle. "Eeee!" Carol shrieked, leaping up, fighting to get the sweater past her head. "You *creep*," she said, her head emerging from the folds of wool. But her good humor returned when the sweater was safely down around her hips. "There!" she said. "What do you do with these pictures, anyhow?"

"I could get fifty bucks from a girlie magazine."

"Oh, no! I'd get *killed*."

"The backs of playing cards, then. But we'll need fifty-two different poses."

Carol considered this prospect. "I'm not sure I know that many," she said, her tongue flicking out at him like a snake's. "But listen to me, Boris: if you ever let anybody see those pictures, I'll swear up and down that you raped me."

Boris patted her hip. "You're my kind of people," he told her. "So I'll tell you a secret: I like beautiful things. You got some beautiful things there, baby, and I want to make them permanent, that's all. Those knockers could be on the homeliest girl in Narwich and I'd still want to photograph them, because they're beautiful. I don't sell my pictures, for Christ's sake. Would you sell a sunset?"

Carol was puzzled for a moment, then decided she'd received a compliment. "Hey," she said, by way of reward. "Can you do the Twist?"

"In bed?" Boris said with his best leer.

Carol tuned Georgie's radio to the campus station. She began to dance to herself, as if drying her hips with an invisible towel. "C'mon," she urged. "Dance with me." But she didn't insist. She danced for her own pleasure, hypnotized by the music. "Crazy," she said when the record was finished. Her soft, sweetheart face—it really did belong on the cover of a girlie magazine—had a faint sheen of sweat. She stared at a point near his left shoulder. "I wonder what Hal is doing tonight?" she said.

Yes, what was Hal doing? Probably at the Hut right now, pestering Teddy; and if not him, some other young Narwich tomcat probably was. "Come on," he said to Carol. "Let's go."

His driveway was empty, after all, except for Georgie's car, so Boris took take his time driving Carol to her dorm. He parked on the street, away from the lights; the cars in front and behind him were tremulous with the whispers of petting couples. "Well, g'night," Carol said, fumbling for the door handle. Boris grabbed at her, but she was already in motion and he only brushed her cheek. "Oh," she said. "Do you want to kiss me?" She cupped his face and planted her lips on his: soft, wet, smelling like orange blossoms. "And that's *three* favors I've done you tonight," she said, pulling away. "So you'd better be nice to me." Then she opened the door and was gone, trailing a laugh over her shoulder.

~ ~ ~ ~

Georgie and Teddy were still at the dinette table, and the dinner dishes hadn't been cleared. "My God, Georgie," Boris said. "Are you still talking?"

"He's explaining about radioactive fallout," Teddy said, looking up. "It's dreadful. Do you know that we're living on the edge of the very worst zone of all, with the air base and the navy yard just fifteen miles away?"

"Yeah," said Boris. "I'd like to forget about it, personally, but Marvin Peabody won't let me." He went across the room to turn off the radio: a plane was passing overhead, causing the loudspeaker to go *flup-flup* like the wings of some ancient bird. "There's one of the bastards now," he said. With the radio off, they could hear the low, sullen droning of a propeller-driven plane, a tanker probably, slowing for its approach to Powell Air Force Base. Marvin Peabody had explained the phenomenon: the propeller blades were about the length of an FM antenna, and so disrupted the signal.

"The rain brings the fallout down," Georgie explained. "And the prevailing winds. I even came across a ballad about it."

"It's beautiful," Teddy confirmed. "Sing it for Boris, Georgie."

"Oh. . . ."

"Please," she urged. Georgie squared his shoulders, tilted his head back, and sang "What Have They Done to the Rain?" in a clear and melodious voice. Boris was astonished. He had never imagined that Georgie could do anything so well. The ballad was about a little boy standing in the rain, about rain that fell like teardrops, about the soft deadly rain and the prevailing winds:

Just a little breeze, out of the sky;
The leaves nod their heads as the breeze blows by;
Just a little breeze with some smoke in its eye —
And what have they done to the rain?

They were silent when Georgie finished. Finally Boris cleared his throat and said, "Yeah, well, I've got work to do," and went into the darkroom. If he left the door ajar, he could learn where this lecture-concert was leading, but he needed darkness while he handled the negatives. He worked with an open tray, sloshing the film back and forth by hand. There was no sound except the ticking of his alarm clock. He thought about Georgie's ballad, and the vision of the little boy in the rain appeared to him: he had seen something like that in Thailand, which he had visited on furlough during the war, a deal he had swung by photographing his colonel. Siam, they had called it then. The boy had carried a wooden begging bowl. Yes, and remember her, the girl in Bangkok, with the delicate bones and skin like honey, twenty years ago? He had wanted to marry her, briefly, but she couldn't speak English. Yes. Half a lifetime ago.

The alarm shrilled. Boris transferred his film to the fixing bath, reset the alarm, and tried to remember how the girl had felt. One time they'd made love next to an open window, standing up with her arms entwined around his neck and her legs around his waist, laughing. Yes. There were little golden hairs in her nostrils. Her vagina had clung to him. . . . He saw the beggar afterward, as he left the hotel in the rain.

The alarm again! Boris turned on the red safelight long enough to see twelve perfectly exposed images of Carol Phipps, though reversed black-for-white. He left them to wash in running water.

Georgie was still talking! He must have been developing this lecture ever since missing the march on Washington. Boris cleared the table and washed the dishes. By this time Georgie was explaining the mutations that would result when plants and animals tried to reproduce in the postwar era. Teddy was looking glassy-eyed, which was good. Carol thought Georgie was cute; maybe Teddy did, too.

"I'll print one picture before I quit," Boris told them. He returned to the darkroom, leaving the door open a crack, and toasted his negatives with the electric hair dryer. In a quavering voice, Georgie was describing how the leaves would wither and die in College Woods, and how weeds would spring up everywhere, choking out the plants that had managed to survive. And babies would be born with flippers instead of arms. . . . Boris pushed the door shut with his foot. He selected the last frame on the roll and inserted it into the enlarger. He chose a soft printing paper: the picture would be good enough to kiss when he was done with it. Shading parts of the image with his moving fingers, he made the exposure and slipped the print into the developing tray. The paper seemed yellow under the safelight. Breathlessly, he sloshed it back and forth, urging the developer into every invisible pore of Carol's face and breast. Ah! There was a suggestion of a mouth, as if condensed upon the paper from his own breath. This was the moment that made him feel like a magician, conjuring beauty out of nothingness by his secret arts. With his thumb, he rubbed the paper lightly where her breasts should be, so the developer would be more active there, and soon the hollow of her bosom was coming up as dark as the shadows on her face. Beautiful, beautiful. Now the woman was quite distinct, the hair gleaming with highlights, the breasts lifting proudly, the face caught in a moment of eternal invitation. She was beautiful, and she was his; he had stolen her image. Swiftly the photograph darkened, until the shadows were black and the blood was choked in his veins, while he held back for the last, best moment. There, darling—now! He flipped the print to the short-stop bath with fingers that almost refused to close.

Sweating, Boris opened the door slightly and waited for the print to be fixed. Georgie's voice came clearly to him: "Now take a look at this, Teddy, and tell me what you think."

"A contract?"

"I've got a teaching job in Nova Scotia," Georgie said. "In Canada? It's the perfect solution, Teddy, don't you see? The Russians won't drop any bombs up there, all the experts agree to that, and there won't be much fallout either. If you planned carefully you could survive the war in Nova Scotia. You'd have to build a self-contained farm, of course, and store seeds for future crops, and a rifle and plenty of ammunition. . . ."

"But you've never killed anything in your life, Georgie."

"I can learn. I'll have to learn all sorts of things! How to farm, how to preserve food, how to grind flour, lots of things, but there'd be at least a year before they became necessary. I'll have time to learn."

"Yes, but why are you telling me all this?" Oh God. Here it was!

"Teddy, you have good genes, and you're not the type of girl who needs doctors and hospitals in order to have a baby. You've proved that. It's women like you who'll have to repopulate the world after the war."

"Georgie ..."

"I want you to marry me, and next summer we'll start building a farm in Nova Scotia. It's beautiful country up there; I have some travel folders I can show you. . . . And I'll have a good job to support us until we get the farm operating. Teddy? You must, Teddy. *Somebody* has to do it."

"I can't marry you, Georgie. I already have a husband."

"You can get a divorce."

"But I don't *want* a divorce!" There was a scraping of chair legs. Boris brushed off his trousers and opened the door. Blinking in the glare, he saw them at the dinette table, both standing, Teddy wrapping herself in her arms as if she were cold.

"Jesus," Boris said, "is that Bookmobile still here?"

"I was just leaving," Georgie said. He shuffled his clippings together into a single pile. "Well, Teddy, please think it over. I'll leave this stuff here for you to look over. . . ."

"Oh, you needn't do that," Teddy said.

"It's no bother. I won't be needing it right away."

"Sure," said Boris. "Maybe I could learn something, too."

Georgie nodded uncertainly, looking first at Teddy, then at Boris. "Well, good night," he said.

"Don't forget your key," Boris said. He held the little object on his palm. Georgie took it and he went out.

"Boris," Teddy said when he was gone, "you'll never *believe*. . . ."

"I heard. The door was open a bit, you know, so I could breathe."

"You heard him propose?"

"Yeah."

65

"Poor Georgie," Teddy said softly. "Boris, love didn't enter into it *at all*. He had everything figured out, but love wasn't important, it didn't matter. Can you imagine that?"

Boris was relieved. He liked having Teddy in the Hut, even if she did spoil a photo session now and then. He had replaced Judy within an hour, but where could he find a replacement for Teddy?

"So you're not going to marry him?" he said.

"No! Oh, I'm fond of him, but there's no physical thing, you know?"

"Not like Colin, huh?"

"*Ohhh!*" she said, her eyes going misty. "You can't imagine. I simply dissolve when Colin touches me."

"Yeah. Well, don't let him make a fool out of you again."

"I probably will," she said, as if proud of it.

"It's late," he said. "Time for a midnight snack. What do you say? I'll brew some cocoa, and you take care of that son of yours, okay?"

"Okay," said Teddy, who loved to suckle her son. "Oh, Boris," she said happily, "you're so nice to me."

She danced into the bedroom, and Boris glowed. Teddy didn't think Georgie was nice, nor Colin either, probably, and that was indeed a triumph of wisdom over youth.

6 - A Splendid Piece of Direct Action

O N SUNDAY, TEDDY DECIDED to accompany Boris on his pilgrimage to Concord. "I want to meet your mother," she said. "Perhaps there's something another woman can do for her."

"She's bats," Boris said. "She's nutty like a fruitcake."

"You talk to her, don't you?"

"Yeah, but not on the same frequency. She thinks I'm my father."

"Is your father dead?" asked Teddy, sad-eyed.

"He killed himself," Boris said. "He worked in a shoe factory in Oldfield, in one of those big piles of brick near the waterfall, and ever since coming out from the Old Country he saved his money to start a business. He wanted to be a cobbler. He wanted to work on one pair of shoes at a time, I guess, instead of pushing 'em down an assembly line. Anyhow, he saved up a couple thousand dollars and my mother found it and sent it to the missions in Africa." Boris put his index finger to his temple and made a clucking sound with his tongue. "So the old man shot himself," he said. "I've still got the pistol, over there in the bureau. It's a little Colt. It's a woman's gun, really, but it did the job for him."

Teddy asked no more, but the autumnal haze was still filming her eyes when they wrapped Baby Merchant in his blanket and set out on the road to Concord. It was a dazzling, windy day, and the Volkswagen kept trying to scoot off the highway into the snowfields. Teddy wore sunglasses against the glare.

They reached the State Hospital just after two o'clock, when visiting hours began, but already the driveway in front of Baxter Building was choked with automobiles. In one of the parked cars, Boris saw a middle-aged woman and a much younger man, kissing passionately. Other patients and their visitors were walking around the grounds, arm in arm, talking too much or not talking at all; a few were skating on a pond nearby. The patients wore an odd assortment of jackets and trousers that didn't match. Boris donated his old clothes to the hospital auxiliary, so perhaps some of the mismatched garments were his.

Teddy's courage was fading when they entered the Baxter Building and stood in line at the reception desk. It vanished completely when Boris took her upstairs to the locked ward. "You can tell the warders from the patients easy enough," he said, rattling the great metal-sheathed doors. "They wear blue uniforms. Otherwise there's not much difference, except maybe the patients are a bit smarter."

Maggie, the ward supervisor, opened the door and took his visiting slip. "She's in the dormitory," Maggie said. "Poor old thing. Didn't feel very chipper this morning."

"Can't stand up to the rubber hose like she used to, huh?"

Maggie sniffed, locked the doors behind them, and went off in search of the old lady. Teddy sat down in the cane-bottomed chair Boris found for her. She kept glancing at the locked doors, their brown paint peeling away like sunburned skin, as if wondering whether they'd ever open again. Boris had brought a geranium, although in recent years the old lady had ceased to pay any attention to gifts. He placed it on the upright piano that nobody ever played.

The ward was shaped like a letter T, with visitors supposedly restricted to the vertical leg, which also the recreation area. It was furnished with a bookcase, some card tables, and a television set behind a protective cage of chicken wire. The television screen was blank, but two patients were staring at it, openmouthed, bobbing in their rocking chairs. One woman, a mild, drugged catatonic named Rose, was pacing the length of the ward on an invisible tightrope. She reached the metal-sheathed doors, shook them, and paced back to the dormitory without looking to right or left, intent on her dreadful mission. At a card table nearby, two matronly patients were sitting with a warder, covertly studying their cards. They were waiting for

Maggie to return. Elsewhere, up and down the long hall and in the dormitory beyond, patients and visitors roamed like passengers in a railroad terminal, in a turmoil that didn't amount to anything. Nobody here could remain at rest for a moment.

Teddy watched their activity with the expression of a young girl at her first funeral, clutching Baby Merchant to her breast like a doll. Boris, who had visited the ward every month for the past ten years, concentrated his attention on its newest recruit, a breasty girl in toreador pants and a tight blouse with no brassiere beneath it. She was perhaps sixteen and at the peak of her weedlike beauty—French Canadian, probably, like one of the Jutras girls in Narwich. She stood at the window nearest the door, beside the piano that nobody ever played. As Boris watched, she threw open the window and waved to somebody in the yard below. A cold sweep of March air went through the ward. "Close it, close it!" the women cried, halting their anxious bustle at the intrusion of fresh air. "You hussy!"

"Your ass," the girl said, leaning against the bars and shaking her hips. Her voice was thick.

"Is she drunk?" whispered Teddy.

"Insulin," Boris said. "It's catnip for humans."

Maggie came down the corridor then, pushing a wheelchair in which the old lady, his mother, sat fingering her rosary beads.

"Shut the window, you baggage!" insisted one of the women, a worn mountain in a pink ward dress. "Maggie, make her shut the window?"

The girl closed the window with a bang. "There," she said thickly. "Happy now, you old fart?"

"Hussy," said the pink mountain.

The girl sauntered to the piano, swinging her hips; she winked at Boris. Then she grabbed the potted plant, hefted it awkwardly, and advanced upon the woman in pink. "Put that down!" screamed Boris's mother, looking up from her rosary beads. "It's mine."

"It's hers, it's hers," the other women shouted.

69

"Oh, I'm sorry," the girl said, surrendering the plant. "I didn't know it was yours." In the same motion, she swung upon the woman in pink and fastened her fingers around the fat throat. The woman gurgled. They whirled like partners in a waltz, the girl calmly tightening her grip and the woman clawing and pounding at the young, offensive breasts. Maggie walked over, separated them, and led the girl back to the dormitory.

"Hey, Maggie," Boris said when the attendant returned, sweating slightly. "Fun with the rubber hose tonight, huh?" Not answering, Maggie parked the wheelchair beside Teddy and went back to her game of cards.

"Hello, Maw," Boris said to his mother. "How's life in the snakepit?" Teddy gasped. "She doesn't understand a word of it," he explained, looking at the withered face that had once belonged to his mother. She had returned to her prayers after claiming the potted plant. It was now slipping from her lap, and Boris rescued the pot and put it back on the piano. "See who I brought," he said then. "Look at the baby, Maw."

"Is that you, Nikolas?" the old lady asked, in a voice like the keening of a wasp. "Did you bring the money for the missions?" Boris took the folded fifties from his pocket and allowed her to hold them—one hundred and fifty dollars, her monthly maintenance at the hospital. He might have committed her as a pauper, ten years ago, but he had refused to give the state of New Hampshire the satisfaction. That was why he had sobered off and gone to work for the University. "They pray for me at the missions, you know," the old lady said wisely, fondling the money. "Think of the future, Nikolas. Think of your immortal soul."

"Sure, Maw, but take a look at who's here."

"Why, it's our baby," she said, catching sight of the child in Teddy's arms. "My Boris!" She opened her blue-veined arms, with the rosary beads dangling from her right hand, but Teddy only hugged the baby closer. The old lady halted with her arms outstretched. She stared at Teddy. If the man was her husband

70

and the child was her son, who was the young woman? She blinked several times, then shook her head. Perhaps she saw in Teddy, as in a snapshot of other days, her own young self with Boris cradled in her arms—in which case, who was she, who saw these things? "Nikolas?" she said vaguely, and her arms and eyes dropped, surrendering the puzzle to him. She picked at the rosary beads, each a sin to be washed away before her soul could ascend to paradise. The prayers won out, as always, the faded lips began to move in a ritual that Boris echoed in his own mind: *Hail, Mary, full of grace, the Lord is with thee! Blessed art thou amongst women, and blessed is the fruit of thy womb, Jesus. Holy Mary, mother of God, pray for us sinners, now and at the hour of our death. Amen.*

"Off again!" Boris said, before he was caught in another stanza. "That's as close to the world as she ever gets. If I didn't come here once in a while, she'd just melt down into one of those praying machines they have in India."

"Oh, Boris," Teddy whispered. Baby Merchant began to fuss. "It's so sad," Teddy said, rocking her son. "Hush, darling, hush. . . . She talks about the future and—and—she doesn't have any."

"Hey, Maggie!" Boris shouted. He gathered the fifties from the old lady's lap, took Teddy's duffel coat, and went to the door. Maggie pulled a key from the long chain at her waist and let them out. "See you next month, sweetheart," Boris said. "If you're not wearing pink yourself by then."

Maggie slammed the metal-sheathed doors upon his heels. The noise startled two children who were playing in the hall; they scurried like mice through an open doorway. Half in tears, Teddy moved closer to Boris and clutched his hand, cradling the baby in her free arm. She did not relax until they were in the reception room again. There Boris exchanged his hundred and fifty dollars for a mimeographed receipt—pink, like the ward dresses.

Baby Merchant was still unhappy when they emerged into the bright March afternoon. They decided he was hungry.

71

Once inside the car, Teddy opened her dress and suckled him, while Boris stared discreetly at the patients skating on the pond. Beside him the child gurgled happily at his mother's breast. Boris felt his guts dissolving at the sound. Someday he would have to photograph Teddy while she was nursing her son—that would be a picture of happiness!

~ ~ ~ ~

Boris stopped in Concord to buy the Sunday papers—the *New York Times* for himself and the *Manchester Sunday News* for Teddy, who enjoyed the comics—then headed east on Route 4. Teddy was quiet on the way back. As soon as they were home, she parked Baby Merchant in the bedroom and began to raise clouds of dust in the Hut. "I've never played hostess before," she confessed, "and I'm scared."

"Relax," Boris said, retreating to his armchair with the Week in Review. "Nobody comes but a bunch of bums." He would have preferred to spend the evening alone with Teddy. But there were no invitations to the parties at the Hut; to cancel, he'd have to telephone thirty or forty people, and even then he'd probably miss some. So he let Teddy go on with her housecleaning while he crouched in the armchair with the Review. The the first article he read concerned Civil Defense. One-way traffic, evacuation routes, fallout protection—all the things he didn't want to know about. He dropped the core of his newspaper with its outer layers, and Teddy soon scooped them up and carried them into the bedroom.

She returned with the article he had just been reading, torn from the page. "I'll save this for Georgie," she said.

"Better not. He'll get excited and start proposing."

Teddy went back to the sink. "Colin used to get all worked up about things like that," she said over her shoulder, "about Civil Defense and nuclear testing. So did I, before I met him. I used to worry about the Bomb all the time until I fell in love with Colin. But when he put his arms around me I wasn't worried any more; the Bomb didn't matter any more. . . . Oh, damn!" She'd scalded her fingers under the hot-water tap.

72

"Relax," Boris said, going over and patting her on the shoulder. "Nobody comes to these parties but a bunch of bums. They're not going to notice if the windows are dirty."

"I forgot the windows!" Teddy turned off the hot water. "Do you have any window cleaner?"

"No! They don't need washing. I washed them last fall before I put up the storm sash. Just do one thing at a time, Teddy. Finish the dishes, sweep the floor, then forget it and have a cup of coffee."

"All right," said Teddy, cheerful again. She rinsed the dishes while Boris filled the percolator. Her small face was flushed with the heat, and there was a translucent mustache of perspiration across her upper lip. "I must look horribly house-wifey," she said, catching his glance.

"Nah," Boris told her. "You look great, all warm like that." While the coffee pot perked to itself like a broody hen, Boris went back to his armchair to enjoy the peace he had created. Teddy was happy because he had told her what to do. It was a pleasant knowledge, and he sat back to savor it until she brought him his coffee.

"Someday I'm going to photograph you," he said then, "and you'll see how beautiful a housewife can be."

She blew him a kiss, glowing, and they drank their coffee in a companionable silence, as if they had indeed been husband and wife.

~ ~ ~ ~

The party started well, though Teddy's house-cleaning was far from complete. Georgie was the first to come, and Boris put him to work helping Teddy. Then came Marvin Peabody, Prudence, and four or five of his admirers, who arranged chairs in a circle and began to condemn next week's Civil Defense test, the one Boris had been reading about in the *Times*. Judy, the long-haired girl, arrived with a date she did not introduce to Boris. They sat on the couch, touching each other with nervous fingers. Hal Pappajohn was there, and Carol Phipps, although they arrived separately and elaborately avoided speaking; Carol became tipsy very early in the evening and spent the first half of it looking into men's eyes as if they were dressing-room mirrors. Hal was angry. He prowled around the Hut, unable to decide whether to pick a fight with Marvin Peabody, make up with Carol, or bird-dog a girl from the newcomers who'd wandered in.

At nine o'clock the telephone rang. Boris crossed the living room with a tray of drinks—it was empty before he finished his careful passage—and answered the phone. The caller was O'Rourke. He was stranded at the Portsmouth traffic circle and wanted to be rescued; he was hitchhiking home after losing his most recent job, teaching English at a private academy in Connecticut. O'Rourke turned up every year or two. He had spent the years since graduation chasing his sex organs up and down the Eastern Seaboard, never arriving anywhere, and visited the Hut whenever his pilgrimage brought him to New Hampshire again. Boris told Georgie to pick him up.

"In Portsmouth?"

"You're lucky," Boris told him, giving him a dollar for gas. "Last time it was raining and he didn't have enough money for the bus, so I had to drive down to Boston to fetch him. At two o'clock in the morning."

Boris had no objection to going for O'Rourke himself, but he didn't want to leave Teddy alone. She was still jittery at the idea of playing hostess; she flew into a panic whenever anybody ran out of liquor or broke a glass. And Hal Pappajohn hadn't yet settled down.

Carol Phipps asked to see the photographs Boris had taken Wednesday night, so he led her into the darkroom, where he patted one plump buttock. She didn't protest, or perhaps didn't notice. She stared at the breasts, bellies, and thighs that were represented on the walls of the little room. "Woosh!" she said. "And there's little *me*." She leaned across the counter where his photograph of Carol's head and bust was ready for mounting. She studied the image. Boris leaned against her,

74

seeing the pictured flesh across her shoulder and feeling the warmth of the real girl against his chest and groin. She was big; she probably outweighed him. What could you do with a woman who outweighed you? He ran his fingers up her dress until they were resting on her right breast. "Can I have a copy?" she asked, brushing his hand away like a fly. "Can I?"

"I thought we'd wait until we have a full-figure study. Wouldn't you like that better?"

She drew in her buttocks, and Boris backed off before she could deliver the threatened blow. "Greedy old Boris!" she cried, and danced out to join the others. Boris followed.

"What're you doing tomorrow night?" he whispered. "How about another session? I'll bring along a print for you."

"Oh, not tomorrow."

"Tuesday."

"I don't know."

"Wednesday."

"Maybe," she said, and went over to sit on Hal Pappajohn's lap. Boris had excited her; Hal got the benefit. That was the trouble with being thirty-nine years old. "Naughty boy," Carol breathed into Hal's ear.

Georgie returned with O'Rourke, who was almost as tall as Boris, almost as dark, and every bit as thin. He was one of those unhappy intellectuals who talked and drank their way through the University, two or three to a college generation, and who returned periodically for many years thereafter, never finding in real life the companionship they had known in Narwich. Like most of them, O'Rourke was writing a book. He carried the manuscript in a shabby briefcase that also contained his spare clothing. The rest of his personal effects were stuffed into the pockets of his topcoat.

"I suppose you want to stay the night," Boris said in greeting.

"My boy!" O'Rourke put his thin arm around Boris; there was a sensation of bone against bone. "A party to welcome me home? You needn't have gone to so much trouble. . . . I got

75

your letter," he added slyly.

"So why didn't you answer it?" asked Boris, who'd never sent anything to O'Rourke except the occasional money order.

O'Rourke carried his glass and a chair to the circle that had formed around Marvin Peabody, who was describing a peace march that had left San Francisco last fall and was now approaching Washington. O'Rourke blinked at Marvin, whose monologue faltered beneath the gaze and finally halted. He returned the survey with none of his usual confidence. "Ah, Boris," he said. "I don't believe I've met your brother."

"Nah, that's O'Rourke. He's writing a book."

Marvin took a deep breath. "I've often thought of writing a book," he said. "Alas, the shadow of what has been done hangs over us." He disengaged from O'Rourke and continued his speech: "I haven't *decided* to march to Moscow," he said, his voice firming as he progressed. "There may be more significant challenges here at home. But I will give all possible advice and assistance to any of you who might want to join the march. It's a splendid piece of direct action."

"Children's Crusade!" said Hal Pappajohn, glaring at them across the ramparts of Carol's breasts.

"What kind of challenges, here at home?" asked one of the pacifists.

Marvin smiled, exposing very small teeth for a man so large. "I mentioned the Civil Defense test alert scheduled for Sunday," he said. "Narwich will take part along with the rest of the nation. Think of it! One hundred and eighty million Americans are supposed to take cover at the prescribed moment—half-past one—an entire nation cowering inside drugstores and telephone booths while mythical bombs rain about their heads. *Cover!*" Marvin curled his soft upper lip. "It's the usual fraud, of course. They'll put helmets and arm bands on a few sturdy citizens, route the traffic westward on Main Street, and thus convince the good burghers of Narwich that we can survive a nuclear attack. That done, the Pentagon can continue to lead us into war."

"But what can we do, Marvin?"

"Refuse to take cover!" Marvin said. "We'll stage a non-violent protest on Main Street at the very moment this fraud is being perpetrated, and turn Civil Defense into civil disobedience."

"Won't they kick us out of the University for that?" somebody asked.

"That's a risk we must take," Marvin told him. "Don't worry about what will happen to us if we *make* this protest—worry about what will happen to the world if we *don't*." Having silenced the timid one, Marvin paused to let his epigram sink in. He paused too long.

"Why?" demanded O'Rourke, thrusting his head forward. "Why worry about what happens to the world?" Too experienced in debate to allow an answer, O'Rourke rushed on: "The world doesn't care about you, my friend, and will reward your concern with nothing but laughter. Or perhaps it will invite you to continue your education elsewhere. . . . I had occasion to watch the Freedom Riders in action while I was touring the South last year," he added. Boris knew that O'Rourke had indeed visited Georgia, for he had telegraphed urgently for twenty-five dollars to bring him North again. "They came through the quaint hamlet of Magnolia and told the darkies that the millennium had come. They danced in the streets, black and white together. It was a moving sight. The final score after the college boys had departed on their air-conditioned Greyhound: fourteen Negroes in jail, three in the hospital, and race relations set back ten years. And I!—I was advised to leave town, being rather dark-skinned myself." O'Rourke ran a finger down the hollow of his cheek, the color of rawhide. His parents were Lebanese, who'd adopted an Irish name because it sounded more American. "Why don't you leave well enough alone?" he concluded amiably.

"*Your* generation left well enough alone," Marvin said, "and that is why we are in our present situation, with nuclear war threatening to destroy civilization. Perhaps you're right!

Perhaps it's too late to make an effective protest, and we'll only succeed in alienating the common herd. But at *least we will have tried.*" He smiled at O'Rourke, reassured that this interloper had nothing very new to offer. "What did your generation do for world peace?" he asked. "Tell me; I'm very curious."

"I was awarded a Purple Heart in Korea," O'Rourke said. "Lost three teeth in a Jeep accident." The girls stared at him. He looked as though the weight of a field pack would have broken his spine, but Boris knew that a good physique was no great asset in combat. Indeed, a skinny man was a better soldier on three counts: he ate less, he was easier to transport, and he offered a smaller target. "They told us at the time that it had something to do with world peace," O'Rourke said, winking at one of the girls.

"Peace by bayonet," Marvin said. "You would have done better by refusing to fight. Peace isn't achieved by fighting wars."

"You can't argue with that bastard," said Hal Pappajohn, lifting his head from Carol's bosom. "You could bring Jesus Christ in here on a bicycle, and Marvin wouldn't blink."

~ ~ ~ ~

Teddy wasn't in sight. Boris found her in the bedroom, sitting in the dark while she nursed her son. Boris sat down beside her. The infant kneaded her skin with his tiny fingers, digging into her breast, but Teddy seemed not to mind. "Isn't he marvelous?" she asked.

"Sure."

"Son and heir!" Teddy whispered, shifting Baby Merchant to the other breast and thereby exposing less of herself to Boris. "I saw you sneaking into the darkroom with Carol," she told him. "You lech. Just because she's stacked and I'm not. You never take *me* into the darkroom."

"Just to show her the pictures I took the other day. She won't let me get near her."

"Poor Boris," Teddy crooned. She bumped him with her

78

shoulder. "Keep trying," she said. "Any girl will give in eventually—look at me!" She sighed. "Well, I suppose I should go in and play hostess some more, huh?"

They put Baby Merchant into his crib and returned to the main room. Teddy distributed the drinks as Boris mixed them, attending to Marvin Peabody last. She did not care for Marvin. "How are you, my dear?" he asked, like an honored guest talking to a poor relation.

"Fine, thanks," Teddy said, and tried to move on.

"I talked to Colin the other day," Marvin said.

"Oh! How is he? Where did you see him?"

"I phoned him at the shop where he works. He'll be coming to Narwich in a few days, I expect."

"Colin? Coming here?" She chewed her lip, trying to find the justice in having to ask Marvin Peabody about her husband. "To see me?" she asked.

"That, too, of course!" Marvin said. "And to take part in our little protest march on Sunday. We hope you'll join us, too, Theodora. We need all the wives and babies we can muster. When it comes to civil disobedience, a baby carriage is the ultimate weapon, as our friends in Britain have discovered."

"But where. . . ."

"Excuse me, my dear." Marvin touched her arm, then went over to a couple who were putting on their coats. He engaged them in low-voiced conversation.

Teddy turned to Boris. "Please," she said, "would you mix me a drink?"

She drank the glass of vodka and orange in two or three swallows, and did the same with a second drink that she mixed herself. By eleven o'clock she was as tipsy as any of the guests with the exception of Hal Pappajohn, who'd already left, taking Carol Phipps and half a bottle of vodka with him. Teddy proved to be an intractable drunk. She even kissed Georgie good night, to his astonishment and delight. "Sssssh!" she hissed loudly, closing the door upon the last departing guest. "I'm just the teeniest bit tight." She swayed, tiptoed across the floor, and collapsed into the armchair.

Boris plugged in the coffee maker, then went outside to fill the bird feeder. The moon was high; the evergreens cast black shadows on the snow. When he returned to the Hut, he found Teddy dancing dreamily to a symphony on the FM radio, which she had tuned even more badly than was her custom. She halted when she saw Boris.

"Colin is coming back," she told him, like a child delivering the news about Christmas. "He's coming back to me." Her arms were still extended in the attitude of her dance. Boris drew two cups of coffee at the kitchen alcove. What if the bastard did show up; what if he took her back to Boston? Boris would be no worse off than before, of course. But he would know it!

Teddy came up behind him and encircled his waist, hugging him tightly from shoulder blade to ankle. "*God*, how I miss him," she said. "And this is what I miss most of all. We used to sleep this way all night long, like two spoons."

"Teddy. . . ." She danced away before he could frame the question. "Drink some coffee," he said instead.

She caught his hand as she whirled around, and dragged him down to the floor with her. He could not resist for fear of spilling the coffee.

"It's the floor that gets me, every time," Teddy giggled. Close to, her face was angelic. Boris marveled at the soft shadows of her cheek, which he clumsily kissed, and inhaled her perfume with wide-open nostrils. Teddy stared sightlessly at the ceiling with her huge eyes.

"Teddy," he whispered. "Sweetheart? Can I sleep with you tonight? I'll just hold you, that's all, I promise." She did not move. "You can pretend it's somebody else," Boris offered. Her lips framed something he could not hear. "What?" he said, bending closer.

"Poor Boris," Teddy whispered.

"I thought you might like it, that's all."

"That's all?"

"What else?"

She considered the proposition for a moment, then giggled. "All right," she said.

Boris felt his heart take a running jump, but he kept the joy out of his face. She held his hand, but she seemed steady enough on her feet. Boris wondered how tipsy she actually was. How far would she allow him to go? He had a panic fear that she expected him to play at being her husband, her young god of a husband, while she feigned intoxication. And how would he compare to Colin Merchant? Not very well. Physical beauty was no asset to a soldier, but in making love. . . .

The bedroom light was on, and O'Rourke was sprawled across the bedcovers like a buzzard shot down in flight.

"Oh, Christ," Boris said. "I forgot about him." He shook O'Rourke without success. The best they could do was roll him over, take off his shoes, and cover him with a blanket. The unshod feet gave off a goatlike smell. There was no other bed in the Hut, except the couch where Boris usually slept; so Teddy took the couch and Boris stretched out beside O'Rourke.

7 - *You've Come Back to Me*

MARVIN PEABODY KNEW the uses of publicity, all right. His letter appeared in the *Manchester Union* on Tuesday, on the front page, and even the Boston papers printed stories about the young graduate student who would refuse to take cover during the Civil Defense alert. Then Tom Matthews called up and Boris found himself promising to photograph Sunday's march.

Tom was his only contemporary, or so it seemed; he had served in Europe while Boris was in the South Pacific, and they felt much the same way about the War, though they seldom talked about it. Tom edited the *New Hampshire Independent*, a weekly supplement that appeared in some of the afternoon newspapers around the state. "Your Mr. Peabody has really started something," he said. "I talked to the Governor this morning, and he's mad enough to chew nails. No damned egghead college student is going to spoil his showing in the Civil Defense test! I need a good photographer there," he said. "I want it covered from start to finish—crowd shots, faces, pictures of their signs, everything. It's your kind of story." So Boris would be part of the circus, after all. It was a nuisance. He had larger problems on his mind—how to get rid of O'Rourke, for instance.

O'Rourke was very sad. He hung around, telling Boris and Teddy how sad he was, because of a girl at Westwood Academy whom he had loved, and who since September had been ignoring his existence. "I'm afraid of him," Teddy confessed one night when O'Rourke was absent, visiting a former professor. Sometimes the professors came to the Hut, which was worse. "He stares at me as if he wanted to pull me apart and see what's inside," she said with a pretty shudder. "Why do you put up with him? I saw you giving him money the other day."

"O'Rourke's all right," Boris told her. "I give him five

dollars now and then. Otherwise he might decide to do something worthwhile with his life, and then where would I be?. . . Don't laugh! This is how I reproduce myself."

It was true. He loved the younger man like a son, and would be sad if he turned respectable. But it was also true that O'Rourke was an impossible guest. He spilled ashes, talked all night, and left his dirty socks to air upon the folding cot Boris had installed for him. On Friday, Boris decided to get rid of him. "I'll drive you home tomorrow," he told O'Rourke.

"I thought I might stay around Narwich for a few weeks," O'Rourke said, as if the duration of his visit were entirely up to him. "Until spring—comes—creeping—over the windowsill!"

"Not *my* windowsill," Boris said. "Find another place by tomorrow or I'll deposit you in the White Mountains."

O'Rourke sighed hugely. "Someday," he declared, "you'll be happy to say you knew him when he was a prophet without honor. O'Rourke? you'll say; oh, yes, I knew O'Rourke. And you'll recount the names of those who came to visit him when he stopped for a few days in Narwich, before the winds of fate drove him again into exile."

Each passing year brought an O'Rourke who was slightly more unkempt, slightly thinner, and distinctly madder than the year before. "Tomorrow morning," Boris said before he could weaken. "If you don't have another home by tomorrow, I'm driving you north if I have to strap you across the fender." O'Rourke sighed again, more quietly this time.

~ ~ ~ ~

On Saturday, Boris woke up Georgie early and gave him four dollars for a baby sitter and two movie tickets. He couldn't just dump O'Rourke in the mountains, like a cab driver with a paying passenger; he'd have to stay overnight to show there were no hard feelings, and he didn't want Hal Pappajohn hanging around the Hut in the meantime. "Gee, Boris," Georgie said, "you've been awfully good to Teddy. I really appreciate all you've done."

"Don't mention it, kid. Just look after her tonight, and

83

don't keep her out too late."

"I won't," Georgie promised. "But you'll be back in time for the Civil Defense protest, won't you? Heck, tomorrow may be our last day in Narwich." He managed a grin. "The provost sent Marvin a letter, did you know that? University students are expected to obey the law, and if we don't we can be expelled. Marvin read it to us last night."

"I'll visit you in the county jail."

"No, but do you know what I might do?" he asked, abandoning his attempt to smile. His mouth immediately went into a worried pucker. "I'm thinking of getting a real car, a roadster. I have some money saved up, but gee whiz, what am I saving it for? I might get tossed out of school next week, and that's the end of my job in Nova Scotia. So I might splurge on a sports car. The girls go for things like that, don't they?"

"I guess they do," Boris said. "But don't buy it tomorrow. You may need the money for bail."

"I never thought of that," Georgie said.

~ ~ ~ ~

O'Rourke's family lived in a picture-postcard village that was often featured on calendars, postcards, and advertisements from the state tourist bureau. It boasted a covered bridge, a white church steeple, a backdrop of snowy mountains, and no movie hall, library, or high school. It depressed Boris. It was motionless, almost dead, as if it had never recovered from the labor of producing O'Rourke.

He paid for the trip in words, as Boris knew he would. He talked without pause for the two-hour drive, and then he talked all afternoon. Mostly it was the story of O'Rourke's unsuccessful love affair with one of his students. "You're a dirty old man, and you're not even thirty," Boris told him. "Why don't you grow up and get a woman your own age?"

"Why don't you?"

"Teddy is twenty-one," Boris said, adding a year for the sake of argument.

"Looked more like nineteen, and you are—what? Forty?"

"Thirty-nine."

"Twice her age! Whereas I am twenty-nine, and little Lucia is sixteen. Relatively or absolutely, we are closer to being contemporaries than are you and your gentle lodger. . . . Have you screwed her yet, by the way?"

"Your ass," he said.

"I thought not," O'Rourke said. "Well, neither did I, and there's the pity of it! I wouldn't mind so much if I'd thrown a couple of fucks into her." He sighed deeply. "In any event, I can always plead the exigencies of my craft—I mean to celebrate Lucia in my novel. What excuse do you have?"

"For Christ's sake," Boris said. "You're nothing but a spy."

"Upon the universe!"

"That's right."

"But who sent me?" O'Rourke demanded.

"The devil, for all I know."

O'Rourke clapped his hands. "So are you a spy, my friend, so are you," he said. "I write a novel and you take photographs —don't deny it! I happened into your darkroom the other morning. We must be working for the same devil."

O'Rourke's mother had prepared roast lamb kibee in his honor, so Boris had dinner with the family, and afterward the kid brother turned up, drawing a case of beer on a sled. "Hey," Boris protested. "I should be driving back tonight." But it was hopeless.

"My boy!" O'Rourke cried in a tearful voice. "What's an hour or two between friends? Sit with me while I drink a glass of malt, and we will talk of olden times. . . . Pay the lad, will you?

Boris dug out five dollars for the kid brother and helped him drag the beer into the house. Snow was falling, a light, dry powder, as often happened in the mountains this time of night.

~ ~ ~ ~

In Boston, the evening was warm and smelled of spring. The appliance shop was supposed to be open until eight, but Mr.

Fasinelli had felt the vernal tug and gone to visit his grand-children in Lexington. Colin decided to violate the old man's trust. He locked the shop at seven o'clock and went out to Charles Street. There he encountered a bearded young man who was distributing pamphlets to those who would take them. Colin accepted one and thrust it into his jacket pocket; he had better things to think about!

The breeze coming down from Beacon Hill was soft with evening and the scent of unseen women. Colin lusted for them indiscriminately, humidly. Walking up Sherman Street, he felt as though he were steaming at the pores. He wondered if the women he passed were aware of his desire. Perhaps they were: they seemed to walk more quickly when they came abreast, as if they had seen the lust enveloping him like mist. "*Wu!*" he said to one of them, richly outlined by a street lamp. She laughed but did not linger.

Colin broke into a run, to give his blood a reason for its heat, and arrived at the crest of Sherman Street with a pain in his side. His old Ford waited there in the alley. Colin longed to slip behind the steering wheel and drive to Narwich, but he fought the weakness down. He would work on Mankind Cowering tonight, despite Marvin Peabody, despite everybody.

Marvin had phoned to the shop again that afternoon. Come up tomorrow, he said, and do your bit for world peace. Marvin had the key to world peace in his pocket. He could arrange anything—wife, kids, college, literature, music, art, Existentialism, taking a crap, anything—into neat little pigeonholes. He never had to worry about what to do next, the way Colin did. Should he stay in Boston and work? Should he go to Narwich and join the protest march and maybe go to jail? Marvin would know; Marvin always knew. But it was phony—even the baby in his wife's belly was probably Colin's.

He turned to the doorway of Number 42, then halted. Yield to the moment! Yes. He went back to the car. It started, for a wonder, and he listened to the wheezing motor—the exhaust manifold was cracked, but the engine seemed okay—

and looked at the gas gauge, a quarter full. He could make it. He closed his eyes, and the instrument panel gave way to Teddy's face, which was suffused with joy whenever he appeared. Then Teddy's in turn was replaced by the statue of Mankind Cowering.

Colin got out of the car. He recrossed the street, let himself in at Number 42, and walk up the four dark flights of stairs to his room.

The past month had altered the room somewhat. It was neater, for one thing: Colin's books were stacked in apple crates, piled sideways one atop the other, and the icebox had been washed. A single word adorned its side, chalked in huge letters:

WU!

Colin was drunk with that word, and used it where formerly he had cursed or grunted. *Wu!* It meant . . . nothing. It meant detachment, the end of strife, the beginning of wisdom. It was a Zen word, for Colin's dive into Existentialism had carried him beyond philosophy, down to the limpid beauty of Buddhism, and up again to the sunlight. The sunlight was Zen. It seemed that he had always been a Zen Buddhist and had not known it. He bought a bamboo mat, and there he squatted while reading, his legs crossed in the full lotus position, feet upon the thighs. He worked at Mankind Cowering only when the impulse struck him. Oddly, he found that he worked more when he did not attempt to keep a schedule, as he had formerly done.

Thus it was tonight. He draped his jacket across the icebox, looked at the talisman chalked upon the side, and was possessed by the need to create. *Wu!* With cold chisel and mallet, he began to coax terror from Mankind's mouth. He worked steadily until nine o'clock, sneezing occasionally from the stone dust. Then he began to itch with desire again. Where could he find a woman? There was Teddy, and there was Prudence—two women waiting for him in Narwich, just sixty miles away, but none in Boston. Dozens of friends in Narwich, but not one in this walloping great city. Just a pile of books and a blob of marble.

He took an Italian sandwich and a bottle of beer from the icebox. While he ate, he stared at the work he had done. Mankind did not seem afraid. If the mouth expressed any emotion at all, it was contempt for the universe.

Colin decided that Mankind was hopeless. He had begun it in an earlier life, at the behest of certain urgent ideas, and was finishing it when those ideas had been replaced by better ones. His jaws worked more slowly upon the day-old sandwich, finally ceasing altogether. Destroy it! Yes! Colin snatched up his mallet and hurled it at Mankind's unhappy face. The statue exploded like a stone grenade. "*Wu!*" he shouted. Free! He was free! He grabbed his jacket, ran out the door, down the stairs, across the street, into the alley where his car was waiting.

He kept the image of the girl—his wife—in front of him until he was on the freeway driving north, then his mind began to drift, so he let it drift. He became excited. Not a sexual excitement, exactly, but a tingle throughout his body, from the foot on the accelerator to the hand on the steering wheel. Enjoy it, *feel it!* He relaxed to the hum of the tires, the wheeze of the engine, the dazzle of headlights and neon signs. He relaxed so completely that a red traffic light was just another onrushing glare, and he had to slam on the brakes.

Damn it! How could a man cultivate an unstuck mind in a land full of traffic lights?

The snowdrifts reappeared as he drove north, until by the time he was on the New Hampshire Turnpike he was surrounded by winter. The moon was rising full. It gleamed on the snow, and when his lane was empty Colin switched off his headlights and drove by the light of the moon. He was a guerrilla band, taking the countryside by stealth!

He reached Narwich before midnight. Students loafed on the sidewalk, just as he had remembered them; the Coffee Corner gleamed with light, the movie theater discharged its patrons from the late show, and the girls—the girls, the girls! Colin almost cried. Not since September had he seen such a flower garden of girls. But he did not stop in the village. He drove on, past the staid brick row of dormitories, past the Victorian spire where the bell was tolling the strokes of twelve —curfew for girls, as he well remembered. Past the campus, he turned onto the road to College Woods. During his years in Narwich, the woods had been his favorite spot to love, drink, and sorrow; it was there he'd seduced Teddy (how she begged, "Let's wait, please wait; let's wait until tomorrow!" but he could not wait) last spring. He reached the Quonset hut where she now lived. In the moonlight, it resembled a length of culvert sunk in the snow.

Colin parked in the yard, murmured "*Wu*" for luck, and went to the door with his heart pounding hard enough to drive the blood out his ears. A girl with a bad complexion answered his knock. "Where's Teddy?" Colin demanded. Surely this was the right place?

"Who?" She peered at Colin. "All I know is somebody named George. I'm the baby sitter."

"Teddy is the mother's name," Colin said, smiling at the bad complexion. She warmed up to him. They were all the same, no matter how homely; they liked to see Colin smile. "It's Theodora, really, but we call her Teddy."

"A nickname."

"That's right," Colin said. "Now listen, sweetie, I want you to do me a favor. I want to surprise everybody. So don't tell them I was here, okay?"

"I guess so," she said, still dazzled by the smile. "You can come in and wait, if you want. I guess that would be all right."

He didn't want to meet Teddy in a crowd, so he winked once, for insurance, and went back to his car. He drove along the woods road until he came to Georgie's trailer, which was dark. If Georgie had hired the baby sitter, they must have gone somewhere together, Georgie and Teddy and Boris. Colin parked in the driveway and waited with his hands in his pockets and his collar turned up against the chill.

He waited twenty minutes, with the cold soaking through him, then started the car and drove back along the road. An automobile came toward him with one headlight dead. That must be Georgie, returning to his trailer. And the Hut was dark when Colin reached it. A light flashed on when he knocked, as if she had been waiting for him. "Boris?" called Teddy's voice.

"Yeah!" Colin shouted.

She opened the door, her eyes fixed at a level just above the crown of his head. She was wearing a bathrobe, holding it together at her breast with one hand; she smelled of soap, she smelled warm. "Oh, my *God!*" she said. He encircled her waist and stepped inside, carrying her with him. He could feel her tremble through the bathrobe. She locked her arms around his neck and brought up her legs and locked them around his thighs, and he didn't know whether to laugh or to yell out with love at this hilarious, vulgar, wonderful ritual of hers. He had never known another woman who fastened on to him like that. "Colin," she said, releasing him. "Oh, my *God*, and I'm such a mess!" Her hands fluttered at her hair.

Colin shut the door. Then he cupped her face in his hands and kissed her on the lips. She drank him up, trying to draw out his soul through his mouth, and her body clung to his like sea-smoke. He shivered with tenderness, with gratitude. His woman! He pulled her to the couch, and put his arms around her beneath the bathrobe; she was wearing nothing beneath it, as always. She stared at him with eyes that were glazed and shining, that eager face, shaped like a loving heart, with the delicate chin and the wide strong brow. "You've come back to me," she whispered. He kissed her at the hollow where her throat began. "Oh, God," Teddy breathed into his ear. "Oh, Colin, Colin," she whispered. "You've come back to me. Oh, how I love you; how marvelous you are."

~ ~ ~ ~

He awoke to hear the same soft babbling: "My darling,

90

darling, you've come back to me." He went into the bathroom. Seeing his reflection in the mirror—wild, blue-eyed and free!—he realized that now the claims would begin to fall on him, soft and insistent, like snowflakes. Why was everything so complicated? He flushed the toilet and went back to the living room. Teddy was still lying on the couch. Her eyes opened when he sat down beside her. "Don't worry," she said, her eyes cool and gray—her martyred look. "I'm not going to make a scene. I suppose you're going back to Boston?"

Colin laughed. She was so dignified, despite the little-girl face and the naked body. "I love you," he said, and began to massage her waist. She quivered beneath his hands. "I'm part of that Civil Defense protest Marvin is getting up," he said. "You don't have to come, probably better if you didn't, but I wish—I mean, Teddy. . . ."

"Yes," she said.

"If you would just . . .understand."

"I understand. It's something you have to do."

"Yes, and then I have to go back to Boston. I've smashed the sculpture I was working on —"

"Oh, *Colin!*"

"It wasn't any good. I don't know if refusing to take cover will do any good, either, but I have to try. I have to do something."

"Take care of me," she said. "Take care of *us*."

"That's not enough." But it almost was. He cradled his face in the hollow between her breasts, and wished that she were enough for him. He wished that he could take her back to Boston and forget about the war that crouched in a dark corner of their future. "Anyhow," he said, "I have just one room. There's not enough space, not enough money." And not enough time! "I earn eighty dollars a week."

"Eighty dollars more than I have!"

"What about your folks? Won't they help?"

"Yes, they'd love to! They want me to divorce you and come home. My father is ready to shoot you, Colin, just like last year." Colin had a vivid memory of the old man cursing him out, and Teddy not saying a word in his defense. "You should have heard the names he called you," Teddy said, giggling. "I talked to him on the telephone this afternoon. I was lonesome with Boris away."

"Yes, and what about Boris? How come you're living with that pervert?"

"He's not! He's not . . . what you said. He's been so good to me, Colin." She pushed him away from her breasts and sat up, huddled into herself. "I wish you had been as good to me."

"I suppose you're sleeping with him?" The slap caught him unaware. God, it stung. "*Bitch!*" he said. "I'll. . . ." He grabbed her shoulders and forced her against the back of the couch, not entirely certain what he meant to do. She fought him. Naked, impossible to hold without bruising, she ducked and bit his arm through the jacket and broke free. He caught her wrist. They fell to the floor, fighting breathlessly, and Colin's anger soon melted into lust. "Bitch," he whispered into her ear, "sweet old bitch."

"No," she said, "no, no, no!"

"All right, I'll rape you. It's legal. A man can take his wife any time he wants."

"I'm not your wife." But she was smiling, thrilled that he wanted her so much. Colin gave her back the smile. "You walked out on me," she insisted, "so I'm not your wife any more. . . . Oh, Colin! At least you might take your clothes off." He released her and stripped. Teddy meanwhile went to the bedroom and returned with a blanket, which she spread on the floor. "Turn out the light," she said.

The moon through the window still illumined his wife's naked body, white, smooth, and female. Colin knew that she was admiring him at the same time. They knelt at the blanket. He folded his legs in the lotus position and tried to coax Teddy on top of him, but she was shy of the position. "It's a Buddhist ritual," he said, aflame with the idea. "It's called *yabyum*."

"Looks like plain old sex to me."

"The idea is to see how long I can stand it, not going into you."

"Oh, Colin! The notions you have. . . . Can I tease you?" Then they were making love, slow and easy, sure of each other because they had loved so many times before. Afterward she made herself small in his arms. "It's like September," she said out of her dream. "Do you remember, do you remember September? When we made love three times in one night, in your car, and I was back at the dorm before curfew?"

"Let's sleep for a while." Obediently, she relaxed in his arms for a few minutes. Then she stirred again. "What?" Colin asked.

"You haven't met your son," she said. "Please come see him, Colin; he's so beautiful. He doesn't have a name. I knew you'd come back to me, and I wanted you to name him. It's your right."

His *duty*, she meant. He got up and followed her into the bedroom, where she switched on a light beside the great, inviting double bed. But she was tugging him to the crib, a little wooden cage with a colored plastic mobile hanging above it. A baby was asleep in the crib. Colin approached for a closer look. The face reminded him somewhat of Mankind Cowering, but the infant was a fairly decent replica of a human being. The hands were especially good. They were clenched into two miniature fists, and Colin fancied that the child had seized his freedom with those tiny hands and would not let him go. There was a closeness to the room, and a sweet, female smell. "What?" he said, realizing that Teddy had spoken to him.

"I said: what shall we name him?"

"I don't know. . . . I'll think about it tomorrow. Come on, Teddy, let's go to bed."

He dreamed of his son, that bald and minute creature who had a claim on him: he dreamed he threw a hammer at the infant face, and the baby cried. Colin awoke. For a long while he stared at the arc of the ceiling, still faintly visible, and wondered about the trap he had wandered into .

8 - Won't Daddy Be Wild?

THEY KEPT BUMPING in the night—it was so long since he'd shared a bed with anyone! Colin dreamed of the baby in the crib, of Mankind Cowering, and of the protest march that Sunday would bring. He awoke several times. He had the feeling that Teddy was also awake, but they did not speak. He awoke again at gray dawn to see her at the foot of the bed, naked, nursing the baby at her newly rich breasts. When he opened his eyes again, sunlight was burning at the window, set like a porthole in the wall that curved around and became a ceiling above his head. Somebody was rattling dishes in the living room—his wife. "Teddy!" he yelled.

She appeared at the doorway with a spatula in her hand, pink-faced and girlish in jeans and a white knit blouse. "You!" she cried, running to the bed and falling fully clothed on top of him.

"Ow!" he said.

"Serves you right, you brute," she said.

They loved until the square of sunlight from the window moved down the wall and touched the sheet beside Teddy's head.

"Why did you stay away so long?" she whispered. "My darling, darling man."

They slept again, until the baby woke them up. Colin went out to the other room while Teddy comforted his son. He retrieved his clothes, dressed, and sat down at the dinette table to eat the breakfast she had prepared. "Don't blame me if the eggs are cold," Teddy said in her husky, satisfied voice, following him with the baby's bottom supported by one hand and its head by the other. "You satyr," she added fondly. The baby kept reaching for her breasts.

"You make a nice picture," Colin said.

Teddy shuddered, as if she had been suddenly kissed. She deposited the baby on the couch and began to dress, alternately watching Colin and his child, which continued its groping. "Isn't he funny?" she said. "He doesn't even know how far away I am."

"Mmm," he said through a mouthful of cold egg. "Coffee?"

"I'll get it!" Still barefoot, she tilted the percolator over Colin's cup. "Poor dear," she crooned. "You look so tired."

"Once a night is enough for any man," he said.

"And once in the morning!"

Colin laughed. "It sounds like the title of a play," he said.

"Yes! You'll write it and I'll be the star. And we'll have another baby just before it opens, so I'll be all bosomy—oh!" She clapped her hand to her mouth. "I shouldn't have said that, should I?"

'You won't get pregnant again?"

"Of course not!"

"You're positive?"

"Yes! You saw me nursing Baby. I can't get preggers while I'm nursing. One thing at a time," she said. "That's nature's way."

Colin felt as though a trailer truck, having just run him down, had moved on and allowed him to rise again.

It was nine o'clock. Four hours until things began to happen downtown. After his second cup of coffee, Colin began to buzz with that wasted-Sunday feeling that had bothered him when he was living in Boston with Teddy. He got up, put on his jacket, took it off again. Then he began to explore the Quonset hut. In a little windowless room between the bedroom and the bath, he found a photo lab, wallpapered with nudes. Colin whistled. What a life this guy must lead, getting the college girls to strip for him!

"What are you doing?" Teddy called. "Boris hates to have people messing around with his darkroom."

"I don't wonder," Colin said. "Did you ever pose for this bird?"

"Of course not," she said. But he poked through the photographs, stacked in cardboard boxes on the counter. True

95

enough, there were none of Teddy, but he recognized a few of the girls he'd known in Narwich over the past three years. And there was a priceless photograph of Hal Pappajohn and Carol Phipps in bed—asleep, they looked like. Colin stuck that one inside his shirt, together with a sexy picture of Carol from the nipples up. "*Please*, Colin," Teddy called.

"Okay, okay." He emerged from the darkroom and transferred the photographs to his jacket. His hand encountered the pamphlet he'd accepted from the bearded young man on Charles Street yesterday. He sat down and began to read it, while Teddy washed the breakfast dishes.

The brochure was from the Committee for Militant Pacifism. It urged him to join a protest against the Bomb—a ten-month trek to Moscow, with recruits joining all along the route of march. Looking at the timetable, Colin judged that the pacifists (all those Marvin Peabodys!) were about to descend upon Washington like locusts, picking it barren of publicity before moving on to New York City. Then they'd go to Europe by student ship. Then across the Old World to Moscow, across the continent with the ancient names, to tell it to the Russian people: *Wars will cease when men refuse to fight!*

Colin caught a glimpse of himself, bearded and dusty, marching to the Kremlin walls, having crossed a continent to deliver his message . . . for nothing! He was a realist. Let the romantics dream of changing the world; Colin knew that nobody, least of all the Russians, would be much impressed by their march. Still. . . .

"Hey you?" a soft voice said.

He focused his eyes on the glowing face of his wife. He tucked the pamphlet into his pocket—tucked away the thought of Moscow, too, but it kept growing warmly in the dark of his mind. "I love you," he said. Teddy glowed even brighter, until it seemed that her cheeks were about to burst into flame. "I know what!" Colin said, to forestall another bout on the bed. "Let's go to the beach."

"Oh!" Teddy cried. "Oh, it's been years since you took me

to the beach. Wait until I fix Baby."

He had forgotten about his son. Watching Teddy bundle the little creature in blankets, Colin realized that his life had slipped out of his control. First there was the anxiety of last September, when Teddy came up pregnant and refused to have an abortion; then her red-faced father, threatening to jail him for abduction; then that awful civil wedding; and now this baby, bridging their bodies just as that marriage certificate had joined their lives. "We could call that girl, that baby sitter," he suggested.

"But why? He's such a good baby, Colin; you won't even notice he's along."

"All right," he said.

Fortunately the baby was asleep. It continued to doze and drool in its mother's arms during the drive to the seacoast, fifteen minutes distant, and Colin found himself growing fond of it. It was a quiet, sensible baby, unlike the ones he had seen screaming on Charles Street.

He had to stop for gas. While his wallet was out, he reached into the photograph compartment and extracted the hundred dollars hidden there, ten bills that represented his capital reserve. He gave them to Teddy. She kissed him on the ear. "I knew you were thinking about us," she said.

The morning was still bright when they reached seacoast, where the tide was high and the rocks gleamed with frozen spray. The waves lashed steadily at the shore, throwing up sparkles of water that added fresh ice to the rocks; gulls swept down to the tips of the breakers and soared up again, squawking to one another.

They left the baby sleeping in the car and ran out to the rocks, holding hands as they had often done last spring. When they had gone as far as they could go, Teddy turned and snuggled into his chest. Colin put his arms around her and stared out at the Isles of Shoals. He had always wanted to sail out to those offshore islands, which sometimes actually hung above the horizon—a mirage!—but he'd never made the trip. It was one of a great many things he had failed to do in his twenty-five years. In the Army, stationed in Hawaii, he'd dreamed of flying to Tokyo and sleeping with a geisha girl, but he didn't; afterward he planned to study ballet in New York but worked as a busboy instead; later, in college, he wanted to climb Mount Washington and learn to play chess and start a summer theater in Maine, and he hadn't done any of those things either.

All the more reason to go to Moscow! For now he knew that he would go. What matter if it accomplished nothing? At least he would have tried. He'd be out there in the world, using his feet and his shoulders to protest against the Bomb, so that the world could never say, sorry, buddy, your sculpture wasn't good enough to do the trick. Okay, maybe it wasn't; maybe he would never dent the world as an artist. But his body was as good as the next man's—better than most!—and could support a placard with as much ease.

"Hey you?" Teddy said against his chest.

"What?"

"Am I your girl?"

"Sure, Teddy. You know that."

"Yes," she said, laughing, "but I wondered if you did. . . . Colin?"

"What?"

"Why can't Baby and I come live with you? My folks would help us, I'm sure they would, once we were together again. We'd find a little apartment. . . . Wouldn't it be fun, Colin?" She looked up at him, flushed with her dream and the cold sea breeze. "I'm learning to cook, really I am. . . . Oh, let's! And we could make love every night."

"And once in the morning?"

"Yes!" Teddy clapped her hands. "I'm your girl, Colin. I'll never belong to anyone else, never, and I'll be such a good wife —you'll see!" Colin almost believed it was possible. Then he remembered the baby that had grown between them, and who must be accounted for, every day, twenty-four hours a day;

and he remembered all the things he had to do before he died. What if the world ended tomorrow or a year from tomorrow? What would he have accomplished then, with his little apartment and his wife and son; what monument would he have erected to his existence? Only let him do this one thing! "But why not?" Teddy wailed, sensing his refusal. "Do you have another girl? You do! Colin, if you have another girl I'll divorce you."

"It's not that."

"What, then?"

"I'm going to Moscow."

She stared at him. "*No!*" she cried, her voice harsh as the sound of the gulls, sailing on the wind nearby.

"Yes," he said. He told her about the march from San Francisco, why he must join it, just as he would take part in the protest today. "You said you understood that," he argued.

"You can't do it," she said, hanging her head and twisting the wedding band on her finger. "I'm your wife and that's your baby in the car, whether you like it or not, and you can't walk out on us again."

"I'm not walking out."

"What else do you call it? Is it different because you tell me in advance?"

"I've got to go," Colin said. "I've got to do this one thing before I settle down and start grubbing about my own affairs. Just this one thing! Teddy, why don't you help me, instead of making it more difficult? I'll be home before the end of the summer. That's time enough to talk about the future."

"No!" Teddy cried. "We'll talk about the future right now. Colin, if you walk out on me again I'll divorce you, I swear it.... *Please!*" She tugged at his jacket, as if she could find the thing that was troubling him and destroy it. "Colin, please say you won't go?"

"I'm going."

"Then go! But I won't be waiting when you come back, not this time." She turned, pulled the gold wedding band from her finger, and threw it into the surf. A sea gull veered to investigate the splash; finding nothing edible, he rose again on the wind and flew toward the Isles of Shoals. Colin wished he were that gull. "All right," she said. "Take us back to Narwich, please."

Colin did his best to make the ride pleasant. But she scarcely answered his questions, and about her plans said nothing at all—probably she had none. Then the baby began to howl. Teddy lifted him into the front seat and gave him a plastic nipple to keep him quiet, but he continued to fuss. "Never mind," Teddy whispered. "We'll be all right, even if your daddy doesn't care what happens to us." It was too much, and Colin abandoned his attempt to smooth things over. She was in one of those moods where she picked anything he said to pieces, no matter how reasonable. Forget it. They would only end by hating each other.

Narwich was still Sunday quiet when they reached it. A few students in long coats were walking to church, and the elm trees were spidery against the sky, all unaware that a historic protest would take place here this afternoon. Colin felt a thrill. In a few hours he would defy the United States Government— a grain of sand, thrown beneath the wheels of the mightiest war machine on earth. *Wu!* They could stop it. Enough grains of sand, and the juggernaut would be halted, impotent, useless, while wildflowers grew around it. And men would live in peace.

What did their little lives matter if he could contribute to an end like that?

~ ~ ~ ~

Boris awoke to find O'Rourke roosting at the foot of his couch like a bird of ill omen. "Your good friend Marvin Peabody," he was saying. "It's odd how certain men can contaminate even the truth. I was fired from Westwood Academy for espousing views not unlike Marvin Peabody's—"

"What are you talking about?" said Boris, who had a sore

neck. "I thought you were fired for groping little girls."

"That too." O'Rourke dismissed the contradiction with a wave of his knobby fingers. "My point is that I can say *x* in a perfectly reasonable—nay, irresistible—manner, but when Marvin Peabody says the same thing it sounds ridiculous. *Par exemple!*" O'Rourke cried in a pulpy French accent, thrusting the *Manchester Sunday News* at Boris.

The *Sunday News* was always generous with its headlines, even when nothing had happened, to make up for the fact that it contained a smaller comics section than the Boston papers. Today its thin columns of news were almost crushed beneath the great block letters that declared:

GOVERNOR TO 'THROW BOOK' AT REDS

Oh God, he was supposed to be in Narwich, photographing Marvin's little pageant for Tom Matthews and the *New Hampshire Independent*. He rolled off the couch and fumbled for his shoes. "What time is it?"

"Ten-thirty," O'Rourke said. "If you're searching for your shoes, allow me to point out that you're already wearing them. Also your trousers, shirt, and tie. You lack nothing except your jacket, which is over there on the piano bench."

Boris went out to the kitchen and rinsed his mouth with orange juice from the refrigerator. Then he washed his face, while O'Rourke hovered nearby, reading snatches from the newspaper's front page. "The editors are wondering darkly," he said in the clipped voice of a television reporter. "They are viewing with alarm. They ask: *What is the University's position in this matter? Have these self-styled pacifists been encouraged by their professors? Who is sponsoring this defiance of our laws?—laws good enough for the taxpayers of New Hampshire, but not for the eggheads in Narwich. . . .* If you're looking for a towel, you won't find one here. I suggest you use your shirttail."

Boris did so. He found a piece of dry toast on the table, crammed it into his mouth, and went through the living room

101

again to the front door. "Old friend," O'Rourke said in parting, "my severance pay might be a week or two in catching up with me. D'you have ten dollars to tide me over?"

Boris gave him the last five-dollar bill in his wallet. Then he jackknifed into the Volkswagen, shook hands through the open window, and drove out of town on the White Mountain Highway, going south. The day was brilliant. With his jacket buttoned tight and the heater turned up, he was able to drive with the windows open, so that fresh air rushed around his ears and blew away the cobwebs of his twenty-four hours with O'Rourke.

As he drove south, the mountains moved back from the highway and shrank in size, like waves subsiding. The snow-drifts also shrank. By the time he was halfway home, Boris saw brown pedestals of grass beneath the larger trees, and green splotches where the Saco River was thawing and water had seeped through to darken the snow. He was cheered by these portents of spring. Warm weather would come, the girls of Narwich would shed their winter coats, and the sap would rise in College Woods. Perhaps Carol Phipps would pose for him in the nude. Perhaps. . . . Anything might happen in the spring!

The air-cooled engine buzzed like a top behind him, and echoed from the trees and houses that he passed; and the blood ran as busily through his veins. He wanted to be home. Teddy would be there, preparing his lunch at the kitchenette—perhaps, in the excitement of return, he'd throw his arms around her, perhaps he'd kiss her. And he tell her about his trip and the signs of spring he had seen.

~ ~ ~ ~

He reached the Hut at one o'clock. She wasn't there; she must have gone into town with Georgie. Deflated, Boris grabbed his Rolleiflex and the Leica with its telephoto lens, and drove fast into Narwich. In front of the Victorian bell tower of the administration building, a campus cop waved him into the side street that led to Fraternity Row. And every time he tried to turn toward the center of the village, he encountered another policeman or a professor in a yellow Civil Defense helmet, who sent him away again. He abandoned the Volkswagen in front of the Theta Delta house. He hung the cameras from his neck, stuffed his pockets with film, and hiked through somebody's yard to Main Street, where students were gathering.

The Narwich business district was strung along the northern sidewalk of Main Street, beginning where the campus left off: the Coffee Corner, the Greek barbershop, a restaurant, Miss Deborah's Shoppe, the Laundromat, another restaurant, two or three specialty stores, and the brick post office, shaped like a fat wedge of pie on its corner lot. Each public doorway sheltered a dozen students, ready to duck inside if necessary. Others were already inside, pressing against the plate glass or leaning from second-story windows. The Main Street buildings had rental apartments on the second floor, where lived men like Hal Pappajohn who couldn't bear the regulations of a dormitory and or the antics of the fraternities.

The south side of the street was almost empty. On the west, opposite the Coffee Corner, the nearest University dorm was windowed with pink faces; at the other, across from the post office, the boys of Alpha Gamma were boozing happily on the roof of their house, dropping empties into the shrubbery and calling invitations to the girls huddled in the post-office door. Between these two outposts was the center of attraction: four black sedans. They were parked, bumpers touching, along the grassy triangle that contained the town flagstaff and the granite war memorial, a little obelisk with plaques for the Civil War, the First World War, and the Second World War. Narwich hadn't lost anyone in Korea, so the fourth side was blank, as if anticipating the future.

Boris recognized the Narwich police cruiser and a state police car, with blue gumball machines on their roofs; the other cars were unmarked. Boris photographed the lineup, then crossed over took some crowd shots along the sidewalk. He guessed that five hundred students had come out to watch the pageant. They made a noise like swarming bees. While

103

Boris photographed some girls in front of the Laundromat, the buzzing swelled into a cheer. Marvin Peabody and his troops had arrived.

Boris counted twenty-three protesters, forming up between the Coffee Corner and the Greek barbershop. Marvin and his wife, of course, with their little boy sitting in a baby carriage and carrying a sign that read SAVE ME FROM STRONTIUM 90. Boris also saw Georgie, Carol Phipps, Judy the long-haired girl, and a dozen more who were occasional visitors at the Hut. Among the strangers, he saw a tall Latin type with a scarf wound twice around his neck and dangling down his back like a pigtail, and a fair-haired young man who seemed vaguely familiar. They were carrying placards with hand-lettered messages like *No Tests East or West* and *Civil Defense Is A Fraud*. Boris photographed the signs, as Tom Matthews had requested, using the Rolleiflex to be less conspicuous. He kept Marvin Peabody out of the frame whenever possible, but that wasn't easy. Marvin was everywhere, like a big white dog keeping his charges in line.

Another cheer. Boris looked up from the viewfinder and saw a second group of pickets marching down the center of Main Street. Their signs read *Go Back to Russia* and *No Subversives In New Hampshire*. "Who's that?" asked one of the pacifists.

"The Young Americans for Liberty," another said. "I hope they don't start a fight."

"Young *fascists*," Marvin sneered, moving into range of a photographer from the *Manchester Union*. Boris walked between them in time to spoil the picture. There were three or four other photographers from Oldfield and Portsmouth, and a television cameraman from Boston. The TV man had commandeered a little Italian car in front of the barbershop and was filming through the sun roof.

"That guy is from Hollywood," Boris said to Judy, the longhaired girl. She stared at him blankly, a beautiful spook. "Why don't you take off your clothes? He might offer you a movie contract."

"The Dukhobors in Canada do that," Georgie said. 'When the government tries to make them send their children to school? They march up and down without any clothes on."

"And Lady Godiva," Boris pointed out. "She was a pacifist, wasn't she?"

"And you'll be Peeping Tom, I suppose," Judy said, masking herself behind the long black hair.

"I'd rather be the horse," Boris said, and left before she could one-up him again.

The town cop and a young Civil Defense warden hustled the Young Americans off the street. The state trooper had also emerged from his cruiser. He stood at ease in front of it, a giant in a forest-green uniform, black straps, and a tan Stetson. Boris went over to talk to him. "Hey," he said.

"Hey yourself," the trooper said. He was moon-faced, blue-eyed, full-lipped, like a Boston Irishman.

"See that spooky girl with the long hair?" Boris said, pointing at Judy across the street. "She says that if you arrest her she's gonna start taking her clothes off."

"No shit?" the state trooper said, pursing his lips. He went over to the nearest unmarked sedan and bent almost double to talk with the passenger in the rear seat, an elderly, pink-scalped man in a civilian suit.

"Who's that?" Boris asked when the state trooper returned.

"General Chase," the trooper said, spitting between the cars. He shook his head when the spittle fell short of the war memorial, landing instead on the matted dead grass. "He's in charge of Civil Defense." The trooper reached through the open window of his cruiser and extracted a microphone on a spiral cord; Boris photographed him doing it. "Hello, Concord," he said. "Fella here says the females are threatening to strip if arrested." The radio squawked at him like a flock of tame geese. "Yeah," said the state trooper. "That should do it. Ten-four." He replaced the microphone. "They're sending over blankets from the Oldfield barracks," he said, winking at

Boris. "That'll fix 'em. I'll wrap up the spooky one myself."

Boris crossed the street to tell Judy the news—but here was Teddy, standing in front of Miss Deborah's Shoppe. She was carrying a pink bundle on her shoulder, patting it while she chewed her lower lip and stared along the sidewalk at the assembled pacifists. There was a little frown between her eyebrows. "Hey!" Boris said, going over to her. He prodded the bundle in her arms, at the spot where Baby Merchant's belly should be, and was rewarded with a crow of delight. "Did Georgie drive you down?"

"No, Hal did," Teddy said in her warm voice—he had almost forgotten how warm it was. "How was your trip?"

"So-so," Boris said. The crowd shifted around them, leaving Teddy in the open. Boris saw one of the pacifists wave at her—the blond young man he'd noticed earlier. "Who's that?" he asked. "He looks familiar."

"Nobody," Teddy said, turning away.

So he *was* somebody. But how had she found an admirer overnight? Boris walked over to the Greek barbershop and photographed the stranger: small, slender, delicate face, good shoulders, wearing a red flannel shirt open at the throat, khaki trousers white from many washings, and canvas tennis shoes —a young man like a thousand who had passed through Narwich. He looked like the type who excelled at something not quite academic, editing the student newspaper perhaps, and otherwise drank a lot and made love. Probably Boris had seen him at the Hut.

The siren began to wail, hesitantly at first, as if cranked by someone reluctant to break the Sunday calm; then it gathered pitch and volume, rising like a demon over the town. Boris half expected the sky to grow dim. The students raised another cheer. Like the siren, they hesitated at first, but soon gained confidence and their full throat. Marvin Peabody had begun to march.

The pacifists walked two abreast, a strange double file behind Marvin and his wife. Prudence pushed her little boy ahead of her like a shield, though he looked unhappy in the baby carriage. She was pale. Behind her was the fair-haired young man who'd waved at Teddy, walking with Carol Phipps, and behind them were Judy and one of the beards from out of town. They went by like that, self-conscious and stiff. Three yellow-helmeted Civil Defense wardens followed them, herding the spectators off the sidewalks. Boris saw Teddy almost jostled off her feet, but before he could move he saw Hal Pappajohn elbow through the crowd and lead her into Miss Deborah's Shoppe.

"You have to go inside, Mister," one of the wardens told Boris.

"Press," he said, holding the Rolleiflex at jaw level. He recognized the warden as the janitor of a girls' dormitory, elderly and apologetic as such men always were.

"Oh," he said. "Sorry."

"That's okay," Boris assured him.

As soon as the wardens passed a doorway, the students surged onto the sidewalk again. The photographers ignored the authorities altogether. After the first sweep, an agreement was reached: newspapermen could take pictures wherever they wanted, and students could watch from the steps, but the wardens controlled the street. They blockaded it, three abreast, waiting for Marvin Peabody to return and confront them. The siren had ceased its wailing, the students had ceased to cheer, and Boris could hear the radio cackling in the state trooper's car across the street.

At the post office, the pacifists made a bad job of turning about, but after a bit of confusion they managed to reform behind the baby carriage. Back they came. Marvin looked from side to side, terrified that nothing would happen. His face ran with moisture like a pork roast fresh from the oven. Boris raised his Leica for a close-up of all that perspiration, but every time he framed Marvin in the view finder somebody got in his way, so he climbed up on the trunk of an automobile and took the picture from there.

Marvin reached the blockading yellow helmets. The Civil Defense wardens and the peaceniks stared at each other, neither quite knowing what to do. Boris photographed the encounter with his Rolleiflex, then hopped down and ran out into the street to get a long shot of the proceedings. He was almost trampled by the state trooper and the town cop. "Hey," said Boris. "How come you've got guns and they don't?" The trooper turned and lifted his riot stick at Boris, who photographed him without thinking, breath caught in his throat. What a pose!—like a bull, shaking his horns.

The wardens fell back when the uniformed police stepped in front of them. Marvin Peabody and the state trooper studied each other. They were about equal in height and weight, but Marvin was soft where the trooper was hard, and his hips seemed very wide. "Did you hear that siren?" the trooper asked.

"Yes," Marvin said, his confidence returning. He shifted his placard so it faced the photographers: NO DEFENSE FROM NUCLEAR WAR.

"That was the signal for you to take cover," the state trooper said in a formal voice, as if reading a proclamation, "according to regulations issued by the Governor under authority granted to him by the General Court. . . . Won't you take cover?"

"No," said Marvin.

"Look," the state trooper said, putting his hands on his hips. "Why don't you just step onto the sidewalk there until the all-clear sounds? Then you can march up and down all you want, carry signs, anything. Why don't you just step aside for fifteen minutes like everybody else?"

Marvin shook his head, smiling secretly.

Across the street, the boys in Alpha Theta leaned from their rooftop and chanted in unison: "Hey, Joe! Does your father work?"

And a klaxon-voiced student yelled back: *"No! He's a cop!"*

Boris saw the state trooper's neck turn red. "Okay," he

said, with a wave of his arm. "Let's take 'em in." As if they'd rehearsed this moment, the three Civil Defense wardens and the two officers cut into Marvin's column, each taking two pacifists by the arms, and hustled them across the street to the waiting cars. The photographers elbowed each other for the best angle, and again Boris had to climb on a car to get his picture. On the south side of the street, the Civil Defense director got out of his car and stood in front of it with his hands folded across his chest. Behind Boris, the students broke into their lustiest cheer of the day. The noise seemed to buoy him up, as if he could have relaxed into that swelling roar, and it would have washed him across the street and deposited him unhurt at General Chase's feet.

~ ~ ~ ~

Hearing the shouts, Colin felt as though his muscles had come unstrung. He knew the sensation from old. It followed a tough exam, or a schoolyard fight, or anything else that didn't allow you a second chance, but was suddenly and irretrievably *over*, win or lose. He was crossing the street in the grip of a perspiring Civil Defense warden, a pale young man no older than Colin. The warden held Georgie Morris with his other hand. In front of them were Carol Phipps and an olive-skinned exchange student from Peru or somewhere, whose scarf dangled almost to the ground. Colin itched to step on it.

"Won't Daddy be *wild?*" Carol said, stopping big-eyed at the state police car. Marvin Peabody disappeared through the front door, buttocks twitching like a rabbit diving into a hole. Three more pacifists were in the back seat. "They're really and truly arresting us," Carol said. "Isn't that just too much?" The South American gazed admiringly at her chest, which was heaving with excitement. She'd worn a tight sweater for the occasion.

As soon as the door slammed upon Marvin Peabody, the state police car lunged away from the curb. Five more pacifists crammed into the Narwich cruiser, which followed the first car as if tied to it by a string; their sirens howled in unison,

109

pale echoes of the alarm that had started the test alert a few minutes ago. Colin stepped over the curb and stood on the soggy grass, waiting his turn. Georgie and Carol squeezed into the next car, and a grim old man in civilian clothes was urging two more students through the rear door on the other side; he then took the front passenger seat, so there was no room for Colin and the South American. They moved back to the fourth car, but it too was full. Colin laughed. "Now what?" he asked the young Civil Defense warden. "Are we supposed to walk to jail? That doesn't seem fair." There were just the two of them now. The rest of Marvin's troops must have disappeared into the crowd of spectators.

"I think there's another car on its way," the warden said. Sure enough, a state police car appeared over the crest of the hill, narrowly missing the sedan in which Georgie and Carol were riding. It made a U-turn in front of the Laundromat and halted next to Colin, its siren fading to a growl. Across its roof, Colin saw Prudence Peabody on the opposite sidewalk. With her was another woman, also with a child; they'd been kept back by the third and oldest Civil Defense warden. Now Prudy broke free and hurried awkwardly across the street. Her little boy ran after her on his chubby legs, and after him sprang the tall, crowlike man whom Colin had decided was Boris, Teddy's landlord.

"Arrest *me*, why don't you?" Prudy cried, reaching the car just as the state policeman was emerging from it. She grabbed him by the arm. "I was marching, too," she insisted, her dark face furious and beautiful. "I won't take cover—why don't you arrest *me*?" The photographer danced around them, taking pictures, while a second camera bounced upon his narrow chest.

"Dunno what you're talking about, lady," the state policeman said, looking from Prudy to Boris and back again. "I was told that the authorities needed some blankets here, that's all I know about it."

"Well, these people were arrested, all right," the young

Civil Defense warden said. He had removed the yellow helmet and was wiping his forehead with a handkerchief. "You don't need me any longer, do you?"

Prudy snatched at the door handle. Shrugging, the trooper opened the driver's door for her. She slid across the bench seat, and Colin got in from the passenger side. The South American exchange student remained on the curbstone, impassive and handsome, waiting for somebody to tell him what to do.

"So you wanna go to jail?" the state policeman said, heaving his bulk into the front seat beside Prudy and forcing her over against Colin. "Well, I guess I can do that."

"Wait!" she said, leaning across him. "You forgot my little boy." She pointed to her son, standing in the middle of the street with tears running down his cheeks. "Arrest *him*, why don't you?" Prudy asked. "He was part of the protest, too."

But a slight figure ran out from the crowd on the other sidewalk. Teddy! She scooped up the boy and carried him back to the sidewalk, flushed and triumphant.

The state trooper put his car in gear and drove along Main Street, over the hill, and down to Gasoline Alley, the ghetto of filling stations and garages that surrounded the Narwich town hall. Colin had been jailed there one football Saturday in his sophomore year, for being drunk and disorderly; he felt a twinge of nostalgia in seeing the building again. It had a great oaken door, through which Marvin Peabody was now walking. The four black cars were parked out front.

Prudy screamed. Her eyes were screwed shut, and her lips and cheeks puffed under the strain of a second cry, which finally burst free, short and toneless like the bark of a dog. "What is it?" Colin asked. "Prudy?" Her eyelids fluttered open and she stared at him with a strange air of ownership. Colin leaned across her and said to the state policeman: "You'd better not stop. I think she's having a baby."

"What a day!" the trooper said, and plucked his hand microphone from the dashboard. At the same moment, with a

111

beautiful economy of motion for a chubby man, he kicked in the siren and veered left on the road to Oldfield. As he flashed past the town hall, Colin saw startled white faces turning to look at him, peace marchers and policemen and probably some spectators. He waved at them. Perhaps they thought he had kidnapped the state trooper, who was now exchanging number-filled sentences with somebody. "You the father?" the trooper asked, restoring the mike to its place on the dashboard.

"Yes," said Colin, then realized he should have said *no*. "I mean. . . ."

"Huh," said the trooper, slapping his thigh. "So what will you name the kid? Test Alert?"

Colin looked at Prudy, but she was hunched into herself, contemplating her secret pain. "What's your name?" he asked the state trooper.

"Me? I'm Billy."

"Okay," said Colin. "We'll name him Billy." The trooper glanced at him, uncertain whether he was being kidded. Unable to decide, he gave concentrated upon his driving, which was superb. The police cruiser flew over the hills, swooped into the valleys, and passed slower vehicles as if its siren were the rush of invisible wings. Colin remembered the times he'd been tempted to outrun a state cop, and was glad he hadn't. They reached the Oldfield Hospital ten minutes after they had left Narwich.

They surrendered Prudy to a ruddy-faced intern at the ambulance entrance, and followed them inside. A nurse intercepted them and sent them down long corridors to a waiting room, a little green cubicle without windows. It was furnished with upholstered plastic chairs that whistled when they sat down. Billy kept shifting his weight unhappily, causing the chair to whistle as if he had asthma. After a few minutes, another man joined them; he chain-smoked cigarettes and stared in turn at Colin and the state policeman. "Hey!" said Billy at last. "What's *your* name?"

The newcomer jumped.

"Colin Merchant," Colin said, and the newcomer relaxed.

"Huh. What kind of a name is that?"

"Irish, I guess."

"Yeah? Same here. I'm Billy Murphy." The state trooper hitched his chair closer to Colin's. "Just between you and me, what was you people trying to prove, back there?"

"You wouldn't be interested."

"Try me! Listen, kid, I keep up with the news. I read the *Manchester Union* every morning and the *Boston Globe* on Sunday. I'm *interested*."

"All right," Colin said. "Listen." The big man leaned so close that Colin could smell the sweat from his uniform. Colin explained how Civil Defense was making a nuclear war more likely, because it educated the people into accepting the idea of war, made them worry about how to survive it instead of how to prevent it. The state trooper said that Colin was talking like a Communist. Colin said that the state trooper sounded like an editorial in the *Manchester Union,* and the trooper said, sure, he read the *Union,* what was wrong with that? At least the *Union* was patriotic. "Horseshit," Colin said, and the state trooper was insulted.

"Well, anyways," he said, settling back in his chair with an airy whistle, "what good did it do? You got arrested."

"But that's what we wanted," Colin told him. "We'll be in all the papers tomorrow, even the *Manchester Union*. You know how a big corporation spends a million dollars for an advertising campaign? Well, this is how we buy advertising space, by spending a couple days in jail."

Billy Murphy stared at him, brow furrowed beneath his cowboy hat. "Huh," he said. "You wanted to be arrested?"

"Yes."

"Then we did exactly what you wanted?"

"That's right."

Billy slapped his thigh. "Well, I'll be damned," he said, laughing hugely at the trick Colin had played on him. "We did what you wanted, huh?" He nodded happily, then said: "Hey! Since you wanna go to jail, anyhow, you won't run off if I go out for a minute?"

"No," Colin promised.

The state trooper went out to the corridor, returning fifteen minutes later with two sandwiches wrapped in waxed paper, two cardboard containers of coffee, and a checkerboard. "You play checkers?" he asked.

"Sure."

"All right, then."

Billy Murphy played checkers as well as he drove a car. Colin lost five games in succession, then a nurse interrupted them to ask, "Is one of you gentlemen Mr. Peabody?"

"No," said Colin. "I mean, yes, I am."

"Mrs. Peabody in the delivery room." And indeed, through the door she hadn't quite closed, there came a yell that was at once inhuman and yet instantly recognizable as the voice of Prudence Peabody. Colin shuddered. The sound, ten times amplified, was the same animal cry that she had uttered that burning afternoon near Provincetown. How could so much pain and discomfort come out of a moment like that? "Would you like to go in?" the nurse was asking him. "She'll be under anesthesia in a minute; would you like to see her before she goes to sleep?"

"I don't think so," Colin said. "Thanks just the same."

When the nurse was gone, Billy chewed his underlip and looked Colin up and down. "I thought your name was Merchant," he said.

"It is."

"And her name's Peabody?"

"Yes."

"Well, I'll be damned," the state trooper said. "What a crew!" He jumped two of Colin's pieces and got a king.

Eventually the nurse returned. "Not yet!" she said brightly to Colin. "But Mr. Stevens? You have a girl, a beautiful little girl, seven pounds three ounces. . . ."

114

"A girl?" said the other man. "But we wanted a boy."

"A girl, Mr. Stevens. Would you like to see her?"

"I guess so," the man said, and followed the nurse through the door. Before he closed it there was another inhuman yell from Prudence.

"Better lie down for a minute," the state trooper said, his voice sounding hollow to Colin's ears. "You got this game lost, anyhow." Jelly-jointed, Colin left his chair and lay down on the couch where Mr. Stevens had been sitting. Perhaps he should ask the state trooper to take him back to Narwich and swap him for Marvin Peabody. But by staying, he could help make up for the pain he had brought to Prudy. And Teddy— poor Teddy! She'd gone through the same agony a month or so ago, giving birth to his son. Colin could not believe it: the baby she lugged around in her arms this morning had been born in this same barbaric fashion. No wonder women loved their children so. They had to, to justify the pain the children had caused them. Thinking of that, he drifted into sleep. He dreamed of babies, pain, and love, and almost made sense of them, but not quite.

He awoke with a jerk, sweating and stiff in the joints, unable to remember where he was. He stared at the ceiling while he recollected what had brought him here. He was hungry, so he must have slept for several hours. A song was echoing from the walls, about a teen queen and her prince. He sat up. Billy Murphy was gone, and in his place was a young deputy from Narwich, angular and red-faced in a uniform that didn't fit him. He grinned at Colin across the transistor radio in his hand. "Congratulations," he said.

A nurse—a different one this time, older and stouter—was standing near the couch. She smiled at Colin in a motherly way, and told him that Mrs. Peabody had given birth to a baby girl and both were doing fine. Colin swung his feet to the floor, and when they seemed ready to support him, he followed the nurse into the observation room next door, where babies were lined up in front of a plate-glass window like cuts of meat in a supermarket. "There," said the nurse, pointing to an infant apart from the others, in a glass box on wheels. It was a flaming pink, as if it had been bathed in hot water. It was also bowlegged and exceedingly tiny. Colin remarked on this fact to the nurse. "Well, she's a preemie, poor dear," the nurse said. "What did you expect? About eight months, I'd say."

"Just about," Colin agreed.

She took him in to see Prudence. She was in a ward with two other women, looking like contented cows beside Prudy's dark, secret face. "Hi, kid," he said. "I'm sorry you had such a tough time."

"You should be," she told him, and Colin took this as proof that the baby was his. But she added: "That's Marvin's child, and don't you ever forget it. Just because you hung around the waiting room!. . .Where is Marvie, by the way?"

"In jail," Colin said. "I was in the car with you, remember, so I had to come along for the ride." The Narwich deputy came into the ward, his head bobbing like a turkey's. "This is my escort," Colin told Prudy. "I guess I'm supposed to go back to jail now."

"Oh, yes," Prudy said. "Back to jail! That's what men do while women are having babies—off saving the world." She laughed, then bit it off; she looked kittenish at him and reached over to touch his hand. "Thanks for sticking around," she said. "I appreciated it, knowing somebody was there. Sometimes you're not such a bastard as you seem."

Colin bent and kissed the small, dark nose. "Good night," he said, and went outside, feeling oddly happy. The Narwich deputy fell into step beside him. "Where'd you come from?" Colin asked him.

"Well, Corporal Murphy, he was off duty at five o'clock, so he called over and asked for a relief. I didn't mind. I get paid by the hour." They drove back to Narwich in the deputy's car, a Pontiac almost as old as Colin's Ford. The deputy unlocked the town hall and led Colin inside. "That's funny," he said. "There's nobody here. Don't that beat all?" The jail cell was in the basement, reached by a stairwell from the town clerk's office, and it was indeed vacant. Colin looked around, remembering it from the afternoon he'd spent here two years ago. There was a wide landing at the foot of the stairs, a barred door, and a cell with two permanent bunks and two folding ones above them. "That do beat all," the deputy said. "They was here at five o'clock, in the corridor and all over the place. I guess somebody must of raised bail for them."

"Bail?" Somehow it didn't seem right that they had posted bail!

"Yep. Twenty-five dollars apiece, they was asking. The town clerk, he telephoned the judge and asked him how much he was going to fine you, when he found you guilty, and the judge said twenty-five dollars. So that's what they set the bail at. . . . Well, what am I gonna do with *you?*"

"Let me go?"

"Nah. Can't. Maybe we could call the town clerk. You got twenty-five dollars for the bail?"

"No."

"No," the deputy agreed. "Anyhow, it's past eight, and the town clerk goes to bed pretty early. Guess you'd better figure on spending the night here. I don't mind."

"You get paid by the hour."

"That's right."

Colin shrugged. He probably wouldn't be welcome at the Quonset hut tonight. He might as well sleep in here.

In a closet under the stairs, they found a pile of thin cotton mattresses, Army surplus, and olive drab blankets to match. They dragged one into the cell and flopped it onto the nearest bunk. They tried to put a mattress in the corridor for the deputy, but there wasn't enough room, so they dragged down an easy chair from the office instead. Colin then went into the cell. The deputy locked him in, and they composed themselves for sleep. "Hey," said the deputy after a while. "I forgot. You're allowed to make one telephone call. You want to call anybody?"

117

"No," Colin said.

"I didn't think so," the deputy said. "You don't look the type."

Despite his nap in the hospital, Colin was exhausted. He melted into the mattress, but he couldn't sleep. His nerves hummed like telephone wires on a lonely road, bringing him messages of pain and abandonment and love. He wished Teddy were sleeping beside him. How warm she'd feel; how white her skin! Prudy was dark all over, like an Indian princess; she belonged to nobody. But Teddy was his woman, she was entirely his. If he asked the deputy to telephone the Quonset hut, Teddy would be here in fifteen minutes with the bail money, and they could sleep together tonight, and every night of their lives. . . .

And didn't he owe her that much, after the pain he had caused her?

Colin grinned up at the jail window, high on the opposite wall, its bars reflecting reds and greens from the gas station next door. What was he thinking? He had work to do—he was going to Moscow! That was the important thing, not a soft bed with Teddy beside him; he had work to do. Oh, they would emasculate you, these women! They would cut off your balls and make a pet monkey out of you, to dance on the end of a string and bring the pennies home, if you let them. Not him! Not Colin Merchant. He was going to Moscow.

He pulled the blanket up to his chin, and after a while he managed to sleep. At one point in the night, he awoke briefly: the deputy had joined him in the cell and was making up a bed on the opposite bunk.

9 - *Live Now, Pay Later*

THE LAST ROLL OF FILM came out of the hypo bath at nine o'clock, and where was Teddy? Boris put that roll to wash with the others, weighting the ends to keep them from curling. Then he took out the Carol Phipps collection and slipped the prize negative into his enlarger. The original had disappeared from his collection. Probably O'Rourke had stolen it, to keep him company during his exile in the North Country. While he was at it, Boris made an enlargement of Carol's swelling breasts, like snow-covered mountains, so vast a man might die of loneliness between them.

He couldn't get the image of the fair-haired young man out of his mind—the way he'd smiled and saluted Teddy, the easy way he moved, as if he'd never met with failure in his life. Somehow he seemed more of a threat than Hal Pappajohn. Hal had lost a couple of fights, at least, and did not have that cocksure smile.

Boris was submerging Carol's bosom in hypo when a pounding called him out of the darkroom. He ran to the front door, wiping his hands on the seat of his trousers. Teddy was there, standing in the shadows with her small face luminous above the collar of her duffel coat. She was carrying Baby Merchant on her left shoulder and leading another child by the hand. "Hi!" she said, in her froggy voice. "Aren't you going to invite us in?"

He stepped aside and she brushed past him, cooing encouragement to the boy she was leading, and who turned out to be the young Peabody, staggering on his chubby legs. Behind them came Tom Matthews. "Slave driver!" Boris said, glad of the diversion. "I just got out of that darkroom. I suppose you want prints tonight?"

He loved Tom Matthews, a St. Bernard of a man who was forever knocking lamps off tables, and whose hands shook whenever he tried to do anything intricate, like inserting a key into a lock. "How'd you make out?" he asked, blundering toward the darkroom.

Boris headed him off. "All I've got so far is wet negatives," he said. "Sit down and have a drink. I'll dry them in a couple minutes. . . . Hey, Teddy," he said, not trusting himself to look at her. "Can I fix you a drink?"

"Oh, yes, and I'll put the kids to bed. It's awfully late for them."

With this excuse, Boris turned and looked them over: the young Peabody knuckling his eyes, and Baby Merchant asleep —and Teddy! Her eyes glowed like jade in the lamplight. Boris couldn't remember her eyes so green before. She stood in the center of the room with her son cradled on her shoulder, holding him in place with one hand, while her other hand kept the young Peabody from collapsing. Boris herded them into the bedroom, taking advantage of the crush at the doorway to put his hand on Teddy's free shoulder. She smiled at him. "Where'd you find that one?" he asked, nodding at the boy.

"Poor tyke!" Teddy said. She deposited her own son in his crib, gently, not to awaken him, then sat on the edge of the bed and drew the young Peabody to her. "His p-a-r-e-n-t-s are in j-a-i-l," she said in a conversational tone, meanwhile stripping the boy of jacket, shoes, trousers, shirt, and stockings. "So we thought we'd come over here and spend the night. Didn't we, Tommy-my-boy?"

Frowning behind his dark forelock, the young Peabody stared up at Boris. "Where's Daddy?" he demanded.

"At a very important meeting," Teddy assured him. "Now jump into bed and get under the covers and close your eyes, and before you know it Daddy will be home."

"He'd better," the boy said.

When the young Peabody was asleep, Teddy lifted her own son from the crib and removed the pink snowsuit he was wearing. Then she changed him, powdered him, and held him aloft for his evening worship. "Hel-lo," she breathed. "What a long day we've had! my big handsome son." Baby Merchant beamed down toothlessly at her, his eyes the blue of a winter sky. Teddy kissed him and returned him to the crib. Like a doll, his eyelids closed as soon as he was on his back. "Well!" said Teddy, smiling at her success in getting the children to sleep. "I'm sorry I lost you this afternoon. I looked around and you weren't in sight, and everybody was in jail, so I went up to Marvin and Prudy's place. I figured they'd soon be home. But I waited and waited, and finally Mr. Matthews came along and offered to bring us home. He's doing a story about Marvin and the peace marchers—oh, but you know all that. . . . Isn't he marvelous? Tom Matthews, I mean; such a nice, kind man."

"Yeah, yeah," Boris said. Women were always calling Tom nice, when what they really meant was that he looked like a stallion. "Why didn't you call me? I'd have picked you up."

"Marvin and Prudy don't have a telephone," she reminded him.

Tom was thumping around in the other room. Boris hurried out to guard his possessions, Teddy following him. "Just looking for that drink you promised," Tom said. "Did you get the kids to bed?. . . God, they're small. It's hard to believe that human beings can be so small and still function."

"Sometimes they don't function awfully well," Teddy said.

In the easy way he had, Tom began to talk about children with Teddy. She hadn't confided so swiftly in Boris. He tried to keep up with the conversation, but it was hard to talk to Teddy when someone else was around, so he gave up and shut himself in the darkroom. He took the negatives out of the wash, rinsed them in Photo-Flo, and hung them from the wire that stretched above his head. Then he toasted the long celluloid strips with his hair dryer. That done, he took one strip down and cut it into three sections, which he arranged on a sheet of enlarging paper, covered them with glass, and flashed with white light from the enlarger. He flipped the paper into the developing tray. The twelve square frames of film came up in varying degrees of perfection: the arrest, Prudy arguing with

121

the state cop, the young Peabody crying in the middle of the road. They were good!

By the time Boris had proofed the five rolls of film, his good humor was restored. The pictures were good, and Teddy was home. "You can look at 'em now," he said, opening the door. They crowded into the darkroom with him. Tom Matthews whistled at the nude studies that adorned the walls. "You'll notice I'm not up there," Teddy said. "I'm not busty enough for his rogue's gallery, I guess."

Tom looked at the proofs swimming beneath the yellow surface of the hypo. "Can you identify these people?" he asked.

"No, but you can post bail for Marvin and make him do it."

"There's some swell shots in here," Tom went on, stirring the proof sheets around in the tray. "I knew you'd get what I wanted. This pregnant girl and the little boy. . . ."

"Marvin's."

". . . and the photographers dancing around them—great!"

The *Independent's* rate was five dollars a published photo, and Tom was paying with praise what he wouldn't deliver in cash. But it was good that Teddy could hear this praise. She squeezed between them and peered into the tray. "Oh!" she cried. "There's Colin!"

"Where?"

"There," Teddy said, pointing to the closeup of the fair-haired young man, head and shoulders against the sky, young and beautiful and full of scorn. "That's Colin," she said. "He waved at me, remember?" His features were delicate and unmarked by time, like a hero in the *Saturday Evening Post*. The housewife's dream. His blond hair was ready to break into a wave, but it was cut too short, as if he were rebelling against the women who'd mussed his curls in childhood.

He was beautiful, all right. And he'd in Narwich this weekend! "Has he been poking around here?" Boris asked.

"I saw him for a second this morning. We—we didn't have a chance to speak."

"He leaves you in the lurch and then he turns up when I'm

out of town? I'll bet you called him as soon as I was out of sight."

"Boris!"

"Well, didn't you?" Boris said, wishing Tom would shut him up.

"No!" She escaped to the other room. "I wish I'd stayed at the Peabodys'," she wailed from this safe distance. "I wish I hadn't come back."

"Women!" Boris grumbled for Tom's benefit.

"Mmm," Tom said, bending over the proof sheets. "But maybe you shouldn't have landed on her like that. She's a sweet kid. Scared of life but awfully spunky in spite of it. Be gentle. You'll get further that way." Boris felt like Georgie, getting advice that would never do him any good. He took a pair of tongs and flipped the proofs into the washing tank. "When can I have a closer look?" Tom asked then.

"In five minutes," Boris said, "if you get out of here and leave me in peace." He winked at Tom. "Go ahead: tell Teddy what a noble gent I am underneath." When he was alone, he perched on his stool and watched the proof sheets swirl around in the water like flat blind fish. After a few minutes there was an uproar in the other room. He heard the oracular voice of Marvin Peabody, and Georgie's yip. Boris took out the proofs and rolled them onto ferrotype plates. The drier was hot, and when they popped free from the gleaming metal, Boris scooped them up and took them out to the other room.

He had about a dozen guests, maybe half of those who'd marched this afternoon. Somebody had found the vodka. The peace marchers were huddling on the couch, in the armchairs, and on the floor between, glasses in their hands and bright looks on their faces. Tom Matthews sat at the dinette table with a notebook. Whenever anybody spoke, Tom stared at the speaker without blinking, his curiosity as open as a child's. Sometimes two people talked at once, and then Tom's eyes swiveled between them. But Teddy wasn't in sight! Boris slipped along the wall and looked in at the bedroom, where

123

she was bending over Baby Merchant in his crib. He took a deep, steadying breath. "Boris!" cried Georgie, spotting him. "Pictures?" The proof sheets were snatched from his hand, and the big huddle broke up into five smaller ones.

Tom Matthews grinned. "They're like kids opening Christmas presents," he said. "I've been sitting here, trying to figure them out. They all seemed so damned *old*. I'm glad they act like kids sometimes." Marvin Peabody, of course, was above it all. He smiled at his followers: he would allow them this little vanity.

"Look at John Trask, that Nazi," said one of the pacifists, pointing to the proof sheet in Georgie's hands. "Did you see him this afternoon, with his helmet and his arm band?"

"And that state trooper," said Georgie, "shaking his billy club at the camera. What a beefy guy!"

"With intelligence to match," said Marvin, drawn to the huddle in spite of himself.

A dark-skinned boy came up to Boris and Tom. "This has been my most interesting day in the United States," he said. He began the conversation with practiced ease, as if accustomed to pay for hospitality by praising the attractions of the country. "I was surprised and a little disappointed we were released so quickly, without spending the night in prison. In Lima, in my country, we judge the success of our protests by the length of time we are incarcerated. . . . What will happen to us now, do you know?"

"You'll be deported," Boris said. He disliked the lad's smooth skin and long eyelashes. He was pretty enough to be a girl.

"*Boris!*" said Teddy.

"I don't think so," Tom Matthews said, always the diplomat. "You'll be brought to trial in a few days and fined. If you plead guilty, you might get off with a lecture."

The South American nodded wisely. "Then we must say—plead?—we are not guilty," he said. "If there is no punishment the protest is not a success."

"I'm glad you don't mind paying a fine," Boris said. "It'll keep my taxes down."

"Oh, it is not my money," the South American said, smiling prettily at Boris. He nodded to Teddy and moved away.

"I'd like to knock out a couple of those pearly white teeth," Boris said. He turned to Marvin, who had been drawn to the table by the sight of Tom's notebook. "Who bailed you out?"

"Some of the more progressive faculty put up the money," Marvin said.

Tom jotted down this information. More pacifists drifted over to the dinette table, and Tom quizzed them about their afternoon in jail. He recorded the answers in his furious, crabbed handwriting, his tongue between his teeth. He needed a human-interest feature about the Civil Defense protest, since the *Manchester Union* would have published all the facts before the *Independent* went to press. "What now?" he asked them. "I talked to Mr. Phipps at the University Development Office this afternoon. He said that every student was expected to obey all federal and state laws. That seems to suggest you might be expelled. What about that?"

"Sometimes," Marvin Peabody said, as if reciting from memory, "a man must measure the value of what he has by the price he's willing to pay for it. Expulsion is a high price, certainly. But we're willing to pay it, if we must, to retain our integrity."

Tom Matthews scribbled furiously. It was all new to him. Boris, who had heard this stuff for years, went looking for Georgie. He found him in the corner near the FM tuner, reading a textbook. "How was the movie last night?" Boris asked.

"Oh, it was all right," Georgie said, marking his place with his index finger. "It was a Swedish thing, with subtitles."

"What time did you bring Teddy home?"

"Eleven-thirty, I guess, when the movie let out. Then I took the baby sitter home."

Boris turned him loose. Apparently Colin Merchant hadn't spent the night. The pacifists were now debating their chances of expulsion. Nobody knew any more about it than anyone else, so the argument soon became heated. Boris took advantage of the confusion to reclaim his proof sheets. "Pacifists!" he said to Tom. "Wouldn't the Army love to have them! They're the most warlike people around. . . . Here," he said, surrendering the proofs. "Mark the ones you want. I only washed them five minutes, so they'll be turning yellow soon."

Tom bent over the proofs, inspecting each frame and marking with a red grease pencil those he wanted printed full size. Meanwhile Boris and Teddy mixed a tray of drinks and passed them around. "Drink up!" he urged. "This may be your last party in Narwich. . . . Hey, Marvin! Where's Prudy? Did she elope with a state trooper?"

"I assume she's home with the child," Marvin said coldly.

"I don't think so," said Teddy.

"Then where is she, my dear, and who's at home with the boy?"

"I don't know," Teddy said. "I thought Prudy went to jail with you. I have Tommy here. He's in the bedroom asleep."

Marvin stared at her. Then he raised his hand for silence. "Just a minute, people!" he shouted. "This afternoon—did anybody see what happened to Prudence?"

A fresh argument broke out. Some maintained that she had been arrested, others that she'd remained on the sidewalk. "Yes," said the South American. "I saw her. She ran out into the street and rescued a little boy from the police and ran back to the sidewalk."

"No, that was me," Teddy. "Prudy got into a police car with —some others."

"With Colin," Georgie said. "That was the car that went past us with its siren on, when we were at the Town Hall, remember?"

Marvin called the Oldfield police, who referred him to the State Police dispatcher in Concord, who referred him to the Oldfield hospital, which told him he was the father of a baby girl. Marvin preened himself beneath the jokes that fell upon

126

his head. Then he marched to the door.

Boris had another thought. "Hey," he said, cornering Georgie again. "How come you didn't take Teddy downtown this afternoon? She said Hal gave her a ride."

"Gee, I did drop by this morning, about nine o'clock? I was going over to Oldfield to look at my new buggy—the sports car I'm buying?—and I thought she might want to come along. But she wasn't here."

"Wasn't, huh?"

"Maybe she was out riding with Hal."

"Yeah, yeah."

"Or maybe Colin came up early and took her for a ride."

Boris left him in the corner, still talking, and sought out Hal Pappajohn. He found him in the bathroom, groping Carol Phipps on the edge of the tub. Boris unzipped his fly and Carol fled, giggling. "Hey, what time did you pick up Teddy this afternoon?" he asked.

"Damned if I know," Hal said, sliding into the bathtub and closing his eyes. "Just before the children started their crusade."

"You weren't here earlier in morning, huh?"

"Nnnn," Hal said.

Boris went back to the living room. So Teddy had been out with Colin Merchant before nine o'clock. No matter when the bastard had arrived!—it didn't take long for a man to screw his wife. Boris looked at her, at the small, strong body of the girl who had come to live with him, and tried to imagine her opening up in welcome to Colin Merchant. It wasn't possible. It wasn't fair!

With Marvin gone, the peaceniks returned to the debate about expulsion. One group was scared, and would have undone the day's work had that been possible; the others were defiant. Two unlikely members of the defiant faction were Georgie and Hal, who now emerged from the bathroom. "Live now, pay later," Hal said. "If we get chucked out, that only proves what a silly damned place this is."

127

"That's what I think, too," Georgie said.

"Brave men," said Carol Phipps, pouting her plum-ripe lips. "That's fine for you, but what will I do if I'm expelled? Daddy will never let me through the door again."

"No sweat," Hal said, grinning at her. "You can move in with me."

Carol inhaled deeply, lifting her breasts under the tight white sweater. "Maybe I will," she said.

"Wait a minute," said Boris. "Hal, you weren't in that parade, and I've got the photographs to prove it. Why were you arrested?"

"Yeah," Hal said. "I went downtown for the laughs, you know—wanted to see Marvie make a fool of himself. But when everybody was being arrested, I was standing in front of that women's store, to have a good look. And that son-of-a-bitch Trask came up to me and says: Ain't you gonna take cover?. . . *Screw you, buster*," Hal snarled at an invisible Civil Defense warden. "So I got arrested."

Boris laughed. "I'll bring in the photographs and get you off," he said.

"Nah. I didn't take cover when he told me, so I can stand trial as well as the next guy."

"I didn't take cover, either."

"Nobody told you to," Hal pointed out. "I figure the whole thing was stupid, and if they're going to jail people for calling it stupid, well, fuck 'em, I'll go to jail too. Thanks anyway."

Well, Hal was a hardhead, a barnacle upon the ass of progress. He would always land on his feet, and Marvin Peabody would probably turn a profit from the afternoon's events. But Georgie was holding the short end of the stick. If he was expelled, he'd probably spend the rest of his life selling vacuum cleaners, because he'd marched down Main Street this afternoon.

The party was breaking up. When the last guest was gone, Boris dropped his hand on Teddy's shoulder and as quickly removed it. "I'm sorry I yelled at you like that," he said.

Teddy turned and pressed herself against him, but with her arms raised between them. He was engulfed with sudden warmth and the tang of vodka. "I'm so glad you're back," she wailed. "The world's been upside down with you away." She pulled back before he could think to put his arms around her. "Boris, I'm going to get a divorce," she said, walking over to the kitchenette and picking up a glass that was sitting on the drainboard.

"Did you and Colin have a fight?"

"Yes."

"The bastard! Why didn't you throw him out? What right's he got to barge in here while I'm away?"

"I couldn't stop him from coming in."

"Why not?" Boris went to the bureau and took out his father's pistol. "This is how to keep him out," he said, showing the pistol's gray flank to Teddy.

"Put it away," she begged, but she continued to stare at the weapon. "Is it loaded?"

"Yeah, there should be seven rounds. My old man used one to blow his brains out. So it'll last the family a few more generations." He gloried in the fear on Teddy's face. As far as he knew, it was the first time in his life that anybody had been genuinely afraid of what he might do.

"Put it away, please," Teddy said, closing her eyes. "Let's talk about something else."

Boris returned the pistol to its hiding place. "Why don't you make up my bed on the couch," he said, "and I'll put out some seeds for the birds."

The night was warm enough for him to go out without a jacket. He stumbled in the dark: the sky was overcast, and the pine trees sighed in the dismal manner of evergreens before a storm. Spring was coming! He filled the feeding station by touch, scattered some sunflower seeds on the ground, and felt his way back to the Hut. Teddy had put down sheets and a blanket on the couch. "How shall we manage this?" she asked. "There are three of us, you know."

129

"Oh, yeah. The Peabody brat."

"He's not! He's sweet, really."

"Sure. Well, you better take the couch. I'll sleep in the easy chair."

Teddy chewed her lower lip, studying him. "That's silly," she said at last. "The bed is big enough for both of us. I'll bring Tommy out here and put him on the couch." Not waiting for a reply, she went into the bedroom and shortly reappeared with the young Peabody in her arms. Boris went to help, but she refused with a toss of her head. "I can manage. . . . There! Aren't children beautiful when they're asleep?"

They covered the boy with the blanket, then went into the bedroom. Teddy switched off the lights. They undressed on opposite sides of the bed, Boris wishing he had taken a shower; he hadn't washed since yesterday morning. Oh, well! He lifted the blankets and crawled under, collided with Teddy in the middle, and hastily rolled back to the edge of the mattress. "Hey?" she said after a while.

"Hi," Boris said.

"Do you think that Marvin and—and the others—do you think they did any good this afternoon?"

"No."

"Perhaps they started people thinking."

"Sure, started them thinking about Communists in Narwich. Wait until you see the *Manchester Union* tomorrow."

Another silence. "Do you know what Tom Matthews thinks?" Teddy said then. "He thinks that the older generation can't understand about the Bomb. Both of you grew up before Hiroshima, so you can remember a time when there wasn't any Bomb. I can't. I can't even imagine what it would be like, living in a world that didn't have the Bomb." Good old Tom! Bad enough to be thirty-nine years old without having him remind her of the fact. "I think about it sometimes," said Teddy's voice, warm and confiding behind the screen of darkness. "I think: all right, if it comes, Marvin will go to

130

Prudence, and my father will go to my mother, and Tom Matthews will go to *his* wife, but who will come to me? Nobody! I don't have anybody. I wouldn't really mind being killed—I'd be sorry for Baby more than for myself—but it would be terrible if I were alone."

"I'll be here," Boris said.

"Thank you," Teddy said. "I think of that, too, and it makes me feel better."

Boris felt his heart expand. "Is that what you think about when you go to bed?"

"All the time! Mostly about whether anybody will be with me when it comes."

"It won't come."

"Oh, it will, in my lifetime or in my son's, or in *his* children's. . . . But mostly I think it'll be in my lifetime, and I don't want to be alone when it happens. That's why it's so hard when Colin leaves me. Because the Bomb might come at any time."

"For Christ's sake," Boris said, aching to put his arm around her. "When did you start thinking all this stuff?"

"I don't know. I remember when I was little, lying awake at night and listening to the fire whistle. I knew they'd blow the whistle when the Bomb was coming, and I used to lie awake and try to remember how many blasts meant it was happening. . . . I never could remember, at night, and during the day I'd forget to ask. . . . I didn't really know what the Bomb was, except that it would be the end of everything, and they would blow the fire whistle when it came."

Her voice trailed away. Boris didn't answer, and soon he heard the deepened sound of her breathing in sleep. He put his hands beneath his head and stared open-eyed into the dark. Poor Teddy!—to have all the troubles of young motherhood and a broken marriage and, on top of that, to be obsessed by a Bomb that would never fall. Boris at twenty had been immortal. He was a combat photographer, cowering on his belly in the jungle, but he knew that no Jap bullet could

131

touch him—not him! The war was over before he realized that he could have been killed in it. But these kids, Teddy and Georgie and the others, had grown up with the impossible knowledge of their own mortality. They were born old, knowing they would die.

Yet it was so foolish. The Bomb didn't fall, couldn't fall; it would remain in its sheath, tricking college kids into wrecking their lives because they weren't one hundred per cent sure how much life remained to them. As if Hal Pappajohn hadn't put his finger on every man's fate—live now, pay later!

He heard a B-52 jet bomber, rising out of Powell Air Force Base like a distant storm. Boris listened to its low-pitched drone, an awesomely masculine sound. There was a Bomb in its silver scrotum: that plane was taut with the sperm of holocaust, ready for the orgasm that would obliterate cities, nations, civilizations. . . . And over Siberia, another plane was doubtless rising into the night, a Russian bomber with the same virile cargo. They were playing a marvelous game, those planes and the men who flew them, frightening the children of the world, brandishing Bombs that would never fall . . . that they couldn't let fall.

10 - And Endangering Reason

THE DAYS WERE LENGTHENING. The college girls changed to shorts before heading downtown for lunch; they displayed their white legs for a few hours in the afternoon, then hurried back to their dormitories to put on sweaters and skirts before twilight. Boris was too sleepy to care. He was apt to nap in the photo lab in the afternoon, and he wasn't the only one: secretaries drooped over their typewriters, and students slept upon their books in the library. "Spring's coming," Teddy said, yawning over dinner. "My blood feels thicker than molasses. Oof!" She bit off another yawn. "Last year at this time, I was so tired that one time I fell asleep while Colin was making love to me. Oh, was he insulted! He wouldn't talk to me for days."

"What about Saturday night?" Boris asked. "Did you fall asleep then?"

"Saturday?"

"Yeah, Saturday. Are you trying to tell me you didn't go to bed with him?"

"I'm not trying to tell you *anything*. I said he'd come back to me, and he did. Now it's over. He wants to tilt at windmills and I want a divorce."

"Sure, but before you decided that, what happened?"

"Nothing happened," Teddy said. Her eyes were a mosaic of green and brown flecks, as blank as the tiles on the floor of the University art gallery. "For heaven's sake, Boris. I wasn't *raped*. You don't have to *shoot* anybody."

Well, the important thing was what she did next. If she got the divorce, it didn't much matter what had happened last Saturday night.

He went to the University Development Office next morning and asked Mr. Phipps for the name of a lawyer. "For—uh—a friend?" Mr. Phipps asked, clearing his throat. He was a thin, erect man in his fifties, his gray hair cropped like a soldier's, his manner as neat as an Englishman's. "I'd be glad to help, Boris, you know that, but not if there's going to be a scandal. We can't afford a scandal, not this week." He shuddered at the memory of the Civil Defense protest in which Carol had taken part.

"That's why I need a good lawyer," Boris said. "To avoid a scandal."

"Yes. Well. I'd suggest Malcolm Carleton. He's a young fellow, graduated from the University eight or ten years ago, but he has a splendid record. I'll make an appointment, if you like."

While Mr. Phipps made the call, Boris picked up the *Manchester Union* that was lying on his desk. The Civil Defense story had slipped below the center fold, since the only new development was the trial date—Friday afternoon. But there was a front-page editorial, which noted that Judge Harold O. Kinney of the municipal court was a veteran of Verdun, a member of the American Legion, and a one- hundred-per-cent American who might stand fast against the epidemic of liberalism infecting the beautiful colonial village of Narwich, where his forebears had fought and died for American liberties.

"Malcolm can see you this afternoon at three o'clock," Mr. Phipps announced, cradling the telephone. "Here's his address." The UDO gave Boris a slip of paper upon which the lawyer's name and an address in Concord were written. "I see you've read the *Union*."

"Nothing new."

"No news is good news, as the man said, but I'm afraid the *Union* is biding its time. We received a telephone call from the Attorney General this morning. That young man—Marvin Peabody? Well, the Attorney General asked me if Marvin Peabody really was the ringleader, or if some faculty member put him up to it."

"I doubt it," Boris said. "Marvie marches to his own drum."

"You know him?"

"Sure. He's a regular at my place. Same with most of the others." Mr. Phipps nodded, then his expression changed. His head swiveled like a doorknob from the newspaper to Boris. "Jesus," Boris said. "I'm just the photographer. Who'd pay any attention to me?"

"You're a staff member! Nobody expects us to control our professors—eggheads, you know—but a member of the *staff*? That's a horse of another color, as the man said."

"Because Marvin Peabody drinks my vodka? I mean, your daughter was in that Civil Defense thing, too. Does that make you a peacenik?"

"It makes me a damned fool," Mr. Phipps said, raising his mottled hands. "But nobody expects a father to have much control over his children, either, not these days."

Boris felt like a mouse caught in the beam of a flashlight. "What can they do to me?" he said. "Bring me to trial? Send me to jail?"

"Nothing so dramatic, I'm sure. But the Attorney General could put us in a position where we'd have to ask for your resignation, Boris. That's another difference between you and a faculty member. They have tenure. You don't."

"That's all right, then," Boris said. The flashlight had been switched off! "I can always make my living as a free-lance." He stood up to leave, and the UDO walked him to the door.

"Uh, Boris," Mr. Phipps said then. "You said that these youngsters—that is, does Carol—do you know her?"

"Well, she's been to my place a couple times, I think" Boris said, wishing he had kept his mouth shut. "At parties, sometimes, as somebody's date."

"Well, perhaps you could tell me. . . ." Boris edged toward the door. Had that missing photograph of Carol fallen into the UDO's hands? Or was she pregnant, and her father knew it, and knew perhaps that Hal Pappajohn had screwed her at the Hut? "What makes them *do* it?" Mr. Phipps asked.

"Do what?" Boris was trapped by the hand on his shoulder.

"What makes them break the law, the way they did last

Sunday? Why don't they write their Congressman if they think the law is wrong?"

"They're scared," Boris said, breathing easy again. "They're afraid they won't have time for all that."

"What makes them *drink* so much?" Mr. Phipps continued. "What makes them so *different?*"

"Jesus, I don't know. Except that they're scared."

"Well, and weren't you scared, Boris, during the War?"

"Sure, but that was just me. I didn't have to worry about the rest of the world. These kids figure that another war will finish the whole damned business."

"But there won't *be* another war. It's unthinkable. Carol's in more danger crossing the street than she is from World War Three."

"Sure, but that's only her," Boris pointed out. "One person. When the Bomb goes off, *pffft!* Everybody goes."

"I don't understand them."

"They'll grow up," Boris said. "In twenty years Carol will be complaining she doesn't understand her kids."

"You're right, you're absolutely right."

"If there isn't a war before then," Boris said, and made his escape.

~ ~ ~ ~

Teddy chewed her lower lip and frowned, as if he'd made an appointment with a dentist. "All right," she said. "I'll go. When is it?"

"This afternoon."

"Boris! Today? But I don't have anything to *wear*, and. . . . . Oh, all right. I'll go." She looked at him like a child tricked into swallowing its medicine. "But after this, please, I'd like to make my own arrangements. I didn't have any control over my marriage. Everybody had more to say about it than I did, even the baby. So I'd like to make the decisions about my divorce, if you don't mind."

"I'm sorry," Boris said. Since Sunday he'd had a hard time following Teddy's moods. Sometimes she wept without reason, but otherwise she was more self-confident than before. It was as if she had reclaimed the gold of herself that had been on loan to Colin Merchant, but didn't yet know how to spend it. "I wanted to save you the trouble," he told her. "I thought it might upset you to go looking for a lawyer yourself."

"All right, thank you, but I want to see him alone."

"Alone?"

"Alone," Teddy said. "Boris, please! This is *important* to me; it's something I have to do myself. You can't do it for me, and I don't want you sitting there as if it's your responsibility. It's not. It's mine."

Boris sighed. "Just so long as you're ready by two o'clock," he said.

Teddy's self-confidence began to ebb as soon as they were on the road to Concord. It was a bright afternoon. The weather had been warm since Sunday, and great brown patches had appeared on the open fields. Only the ditches and woodlots still contained much snow. From these shady places, some fingers of white reached out into the fields, but they were shrinking almost perceptibly under the warm March sun.

"I can't believe it," Teddy said. "I'm going to walk into an office and sign a piece of paper that says my marriage was a big mistake."

"Well, wasn't it?"

For answer, Teddy hugged her infant son, who mistook the affection for a promise of food, and cried good-naturedly when it didn't materialize. "I'll have to think of a name for him, I suppose," she said. "Poor little mistake—what should we call you?. . . Boris, what shall I name him?"

He glanced at her, crouched in the passenger's seat with her face pressed against the child's. He thought there was a tear streak on her chin, but couldn't be sure. "Colin," he said.

"No."

Good! Today it hurt, but she'd grow accustomed to saying no to Colin Merchant, and eventually she might enjoy it. And finally, hopefully, she would forget about him altogether.

They reached Concord shortly before three. The address proved to be a white frame building across from the gilt-domed state capitol, once featured in *Life* magazine as the ugliest in the United States. Boris made a U turn and parked in front of the lawyer's office. Malcolm Carleton's name was the newest and lowest on the directory outside. "You sure?" he said.

"I'm sure," said Teddy, in command once more. "This guy is all the comfort I need."

"Okay. I'll visit the old lady. I'll be back by four o'clock."

She shouldered Baby Merchant and marched up the sidewalk. The baby jounced on her shoulder, toothlessly smiling at Boris and the Volkswagen, which he no doubt regarded as his own. Then they disappeared through the door, which was a deep, glossy black. The building was trimmed in black, like a funeral parlor, and the lawyers' names were lettered in gold.

Unlike the colonial towns near the seacoast, Concord was laid out in a boring grid. Boris fired up the Volkswagen and drove north on Main Street, turned left, then left again, drove down State Street for a few blocks, and turned right. This put him on the wide, institutional avenue called Pleasant Street, which led him in a few minutes to the wrought-iron gates of the State Hospital. There were not many visitors on weekday afternoons. He found the old lady sitting in a rocking chair, just inside the great metal-sheathed doors of her ward.

"Well, Maw!" Boris shouted in his loony-bin voice. "Still cheating the boneyard, huh?" He kissed the wrinkled cheek that was slanted up to him, the skin as dry and fragile as a grasshopper's wing. The old lady looked at him. Her eyes were faded—to the color of the sky over the Ukraine, as Boris liked to think—and with a shock he realized that she had understood. This was one of her lucid days, more rare with each passing year. "I brought my girlfriend to town to see a lawyer," Boris explained. "So I dropped over to say hello."

"Why, Nikolas," the old lady said, in a voice no thicker than her skin. Then she hesitated. "That's not right," she said.

"Nikolas is dead, isn't he?"

"Yeah," said Boris.

"How long have I been in this place?" she asked.

"Ten years."

"And Nikolas has been dead for ten years?"

"Yeah." He had forgotten how to *talk* to his mother. "And I've been sober for ten years," he said, studying the visitor's section of the ward. An ancient woman was drooling in the opposite corner, beyond the piano, trying to touch her index fingers together and laughing when she failed, much as Baby Merchant was learning to do.

"Boris?" she said, and it was the first time in years she had called him by his rightful name. "I want to tell you how it is. Sometimes I sit here and I see how time is put together, like your old patchwork quilt, do you remember?"

"Sure, Maw," he said, wishing he hadn't come.

"I can look at it quick, sometimes," the old lady said, "and I see it before they move everything back together again. This chair," she said, rubbing her fingertips along the arm of it; "you look at it and they've made it into a chair. But when your back is turned, it's something else."

"What?" said Boris.

"I don't *know*," the old lady said. "The names are what they put on things while you're looking. If you close your eyes the names go away. Then there's —" She closed her eyes. The lids were so transparent that for an awful moment Boris wondered if she had learned to see with them closed. Her hands moved vaguely in front of her. "Nothing," she said, opening her eyes. "It swirls around like fog. It's *deep*, too, and I'm not in the middle of it any more. Don't you ever feel like that? Everything moving, moving; nothing has a name, and the colors are mixed up together. . . ."

Boris could not breathe. "Excuse me, Maw," he said, standing up.

"I wish it would stop," the old lady said. "If I was dead, it might. Then everything would be cool and gray and quiet."

Boris went to the window and looked out through glass that was molded over a wire mesh, like delicate chicken wire. He longed to open the window, but knew that it would cause a fuss. When he turned away, he saw Rose, his favorite among the long-term patients. She was just starting her long tightrope walk to the doors, and her mild, drugged face never looked away from her goal. Past the dead television set, past the table where Maggie was playing bridge with two patients and another warder, past Boris, past the piano that nobody played. Boris couldn't remember how many years Rose had been making this journey—four or five, maybe. She was a stocky woman who in real life might have been somebody's housekeeper.

Reaching the doors, Rose extended her strong hands and shoved at the brown-painted metal, as she always did. She would rattle them for a moment, curse under her breath, and then return to the dormitory.

But this time the great doors swung open at her touch, like a wall splitting down the middle and falling away. Rose was transfixed. She stared into the dark corridor, broken only by the stairwell and an occasional electric bulb; she leaned into the hallway with her hands still outstretched. Then she turned and ran back the way she had come. Her toes pointed outward, her head was thrown back, and her hands flopped at the wrists. Maggie jumped up from the card game and intercepted her. "It's all right, dearie, it's all right," Maggie said, putting her massive arms around Rose.

"The door is open," Rose cried, staring at the dark corridor from the security of the attendant's arms. "Won't you lock the door?" Maggie led her back to the dormitory, muttering endearments, then returned to close and lock the great doors. Poor Rose! Boris had always assumed she wanted to escape, but perhaps she'd only been afraid of who might enter.

"The people here aren't happy, you know," his mother told him. "You're better off outside, even if it frightens you sometimes."

"Sure, Maw."

"Boris? Did you bring a girl to see me yesterday?"

"That was two weeks ago, Maw."

"She was a nice girl. You should marry her, Boris. It's not good for a man to be alone. . . . I'm tired," she whispered, her head lolling forward. As if possessed of a will of their own, her hands began to grope through the folds of her dress. Boris found what she was looking for: the black wooden beads. He pressed them into her hands.

"Maybe I will," Boris said, waving his arm at Maggie. "Well, take care of yourself, Maw."

Maggie arrived with her burden of keys and let him out. Boris ran down the stairs. Outside, he leaned against the white columns of Baxter Building and drank the moist spring air, while small scattered clouds ran across the sky like sheep. It was definitely better outside.

He drove back to the lawyer's office. Teddy was sitting on the front steps with the baby in her lap. Her duffel coat was open to the afternoon sunshine, and Baby Merchant was trying to creep inside, for shade or the promise of milk. Slowly, Teddy gathered herself and her son and got into the car. "Bad?" asked Boris.

"*Awful*," Teddy agreed. She put the baby on the back seat, which she rarely did, and let him sleep there while Boris drove out of Concord on the road to the seacoast. "All the words," she said. "All the papers! First there's one called a libel, the most important, and it begins: *Now comes Theodora Merchant of Narwich, in the County of Piscataqua, State of New Hampshire, and complains against Colin Merchant of said Narwich and says. . . .*" She rattled this off like a child reciting its prayers. "There's more," she said. "You'd think Shakespeare wrote it. *Now comes Theodora!* I ought to be carrying a candle and wearing a long black robe and pointing my finger into the shadows." She extended a crooked index finger at Boris, which made her giggle. "Oh, and I need a doctor's certificate saying that Colin treated me in a way *injurious to*

141

health and endangering reason. Do you know what that means?"

"He hit you?"

"No! It means I'm so worried I can't sleep! And then there's a Something for temporary support. There'll be a hearing on that next week, probably, and something else important happens on the first Tuesday of April. I don't remember what."

"Sounds more complicated than getting married."

"Yes. Malcolm says that if everything goes right I could be single in two or three months. We were married in five minutes!"

"Yeah," said Boris. They were on first-name terms already, Teddy and her lawyer. "How old is this guy?" he asked.

"There are so *many* things to do," Teddy said. "I have to name the baby; it's necessary for the petition. And there's something about residence, too. I have to prove that we intended to live in New Hampshire, that we were in Boston temporarily. . . . Oh, I don't know!" Like a squall, misery swept across her face. "I don't *know!*" she wailed. "All those papers! And the people—the judge, the doctor, the lawyer, the witnesses! Why can't I just say *end it?* Why does it have to be such a mess?"

"Hey, hey," Boris said. "Take it easy, kid." He wanted to stop the car and put his arm around her, but they were passing through the long village of Northwood and the traffic was heavy. "Just take it one step at a time," he said. "Tomorrow we'll get Doc Perkins to sign that certificate, and then we'll think about the next step."

"Do you think so?" she asked, sniffling.

"Sure. That's the way to do it."

"All right," she said. "One step at a time. . . . Do you have a hanky?" He didn't. "Never mind," she said, smiling through her tears. "I have a clean diaper here. That'll do."

~ ~ ~ ~

Having made the decision, she couldn't wait for tomorrow, so

142

they visited the Doc after dinner. "Marry in haste, divorce at leisure," he grumbled. "As a doctor, young lady, I can't recommend divorce. You're better off staying married and getting your nooky every Tuesday, Thursday, and Saturday. It may not be as exciting as the unmarried kind, but it's better for the system." But, grumbling, he certified that Teddy's marriage to Colin Merchant was injurious to her health and endangering her reason, with symptoms of sleeplessness and loss of weight.

"I forgot that the old duffer goes to Mass every Sunday," Boris said when they left Doc Perkins's house. "He's a very moral bird underneath."

"Like you," Teddy said, slipping her arm through his. In the deep March evening, they passed other couples as they walked to the car, and they were a couple like any of the others.

11 - *Mama Piga Simba*

HAL WAS SORRY he had ever heard of Civil Defense. Wherever he went in Narwich now, somebody would crawl out of the woodwork and call him friend— peaceniks, vegetarians, Negroes, beards, you name it. One evening he came home drunk from La Cantina in Oldfield and found a little old lady waiting in the hallway of his apartment; she said she was a Peace Apostle and had been told he'd give her a place to sleep. The next night it was somebody trying to interest him in organic farming. Then it was Marvin Peabody, and he was the bitterest pill of all.

"I knew it," Marvin said, wringing his hand. "I knew you'd come over to our side. The movement needs people like you, Harold." Marvin's eyes stared mournfully into Hal's, while his fingers perspired in that endless handshake.

"Have a beer," Hal said, jerking his hand away.

"Men like you," Marvin insisted. "*Average* men. Men not previously identified with the movement, men of no great intellectual attainments but willing to throw the force of their character into the Committee's work."

"What?"

"That's right, Harold. I want to talk to you about joining the Committee."

"Listen, will you? Just *listen* for a minute: I'm not a peacenik. Do your recruiting somewhere else, okay?"

"But we were going to have a glass of beer."

"I don't have any glasses."

"I'll drink out of the bottle," Marvin said. He punched one fist into an open palm. "I *like* to drink beer out of the bottle."

"I don't have any bottles, either," Hal said. "I'm not a peacenik, and I'm not a vegetarian, and I'm not running a crash pad for the Peace Apostles, okay?"

"Well, certainly. But –"

"Now get out."

Marvin wasn't offended. "We'll talk another time," he said.

~ ~ ~ ~

And on Friday it was the trial. Narwich municipal court was a church-like room in the town hall, with high-backed pews. It was packed with friends and enemies and reporters. The Narwich chief of police was the prosecutor, or pretended to be, but there was a pale young man from Concord who sat beside him and passed him notes telling him what to say next. Marvin Peabody refused to have a lawyer, and Hal and the others followed his example.

Some pleaded guilty, some not guilty, and Georgie came up with a plea of Nolo, but each was fined the same twenty-five dollars and sentenced to the same thirty days in jail. Hal's stomach slid into his boots. Thirty days without a drink—thirty days without Carol Phipps! But then the judge suspended the jail sentence and turned them loose.

Hal grabbed her on the way out, while the peaceniks congratulated themselves and the reporters popped off flashbulbs. "Let's bug out," he said to her. "Let's go to Boston for the weekend."

"Crazy," she said.

"We'll have a ball. Colin will give us a bed, and we won't get out of it all weekend." Colin hadn't turned up for the trial, but the judge had entered a guilty plea for him and fined him with the rest.

"Okay," she said. "I'll have to pack a few things."

He liked Carol. She made love with less fuss than any other girl he knew, and when he was drinking or arguing with somebody else she would sit beside him all night and never say a word. She was the perfect woman. The blood was running hot as he waited for her at the dormitory, but he set his lust aside, knowing he would enjoy it all the more with a couple of drinks inside him and a long noisy party behind him. The sun was shining, the sky was blue, and the turnpike pointed straight as an arrow of love to Boston. It would be a good weekend.

He got lost in the alleys of Beacon Hill, so he parked the

car on Joy Street and they threaded through the hilly maze on foot, in a dusk that was languorous with spring. Here it was, Sherman Street, and there was Colin's doorway. Hal led Carol up the four dark, echoing flights of stairs to the topmost landing. There was no answer when he knocked. "Maybe he's working," Carol said, standing beside him with her suitcase in one hand and his gym bag in the other.

But the landlady wheezed up the stairs, attracted by the pounding. "He's gone to Paris," she said, looking suspiciously at Carol and Hal. "In France? He won't be back till June." She sniffed. "If ever! I hope you're not planning to take his things away. They stay here till he pays me the rent he owes."

"Europe," said Hal, envious.

"You his family, or what?" the landlady asked.

Ah, that was a way to salvage the weekend! "Yes," he said. "I'm his brother and this is my wife. We live in Milwaukee. We've been driving since yesterday morning to pay Colin a surprise visit."

"Oh!" she cried. "And him in Paris, France."

"We'll just have to turn around and drive back to Milwaukee," Hal said, faking a yawn. "We can't afford a hotel. I'm working my way through college."

"You aren't going to take his luggage away?"

"No, no," Hal said. "There's no room for it in our car."

She produced a ring of keys from her apron pocket and gave him one. "Here," she said. "Leave it in the mailbox when you go. And tell your brother he owes me two months' rent."

"Crazy," said Carol when the landlady was gone. She followed Hal inside and dropped the bags on the floor. "Goodness, what a lot of books," she said, wandering around the aparment and opening volumes at random. "Alan Watts. Thoreau. Fried Rich Something. D'you suppose he's read them all?"

While she took a shower, Hal walked down to the foot of Beacon Hill and bought groceries and gin. Then he made some calls on the liquor store's private phone. He lined up seven

146

people before the owner threw him out, including Gene Breck, who was in town for the weekend.

Hal was half in the chute before the party began, and he passed out before the last guest showed up. He awoke in the dark, silent middle of the night, dry as sandpaper, uncertain where he was. He thumped around the room. Gradually he put together the light switch, the sink, and a fair recollection of what he was doing here. He woke up Carol in the process. "What a party pooper *you* turned out to be," she said, sitting up in bed and peering at him through the thicket of her blond hair. "Can I get you something?"

"Aspirin." She bounced out of bed and padded barefoot around the room, opening things and running water at the sink. She was wearing rumpled pink pajamas. He was fully dressed except for his shoes. "Thanks," he said, accepting three white pills and a glass of water. "Say, did we screw?"

"No. Don't be so vulgar."

Vulgar! Hal swallowed the aspirin and the chaser, then looked her up and down. She was such a beautiful broad, lusty and warm; it would be hell if she started to put on airs. He peeled off his clothes while Carol watched admiringly. It was a fine thing, his body, scarred here and there by football injuries, fights, and one or two automobile wrecks, white badges of honor like the dueling scars that German students were said to collect. Hal slapped the hard flesh of his belly. "Let's go to bed," he said.

"Do you love me?" Carol asked, pouting.

"Sure. Let's go to bed."

"Tell me you love me." Well, he did, as a matter of fact, and normally he didn't mind telling her so. But he didn't like to have her *expecting* it. "All you want is my body," Carol said, twisting the cord of her pajamas around her wrist. "I want you to *love* me. I want you to respect my personality. Is that so much to ask?"

"Some other time," Hal said. "When I don't have a headache."

"Just tell me you love me," she insisted.

Hal knew when he was up against it. If he dragged her into bed, she would make him pay for it all day tomorrow; if he told her what she wanted to hear, she'd be the boss from now on. He pointed to the door. "Beat it," he said.

Her eyes flew up from their sullen inspection of the floor. "Are you *kidding?*"

"No. Screw or get out, that's your choice."

"You bastard!"

"Screw or get out," Hal said, moving naked toward the bed.

"Where can I go, this time of night?"

"That's up to you." He paused at the side of the bed, stretched hugely, and jumped between the sheets, which were still warm from Carol's body. "Turn off the lights when you go," he told her.

Carol was silent for a moment. "Okay," she said then. "I'll screw." That was a woman talking! He opened his arm along the pillows to receive her when she came.

They stayed close to the bed until Sunday evening, drinking gin, making love, and eating the elaborate sandwiches that Hal put together. Carol was an impossibly bad cook, and he couldn't bear to see things done badly. Life was too short! So he made the sandwiches and mixed the drinks while she stayed in bed. She was in a strange mood all weekend, and they had several fights, about the sandwiches and other things.

When the gin ran out, Sunday evening, Hal showered and dressed himself for the first time since Friday. He was clean to the bone, scoured out, renewed; he whistled and sang until Carol burst into tears. "I don't want to go back," she sobbed, her white breasts trembling.

"Okay," Hal said, rocking her in his arms. "Okay, we'll stay right here." What a bloody mood she was in! But she washed and dressed at his urging, and just in time, because she was putting on her lipstick when the door flew open and Gene Breck walked in. He stood there, poised on the balls of his feet,

148

regarding them expectantly. Then he snapped his fingers.

"Damn!" he said. "I'd hoped to catch you *in flagrante delicto*."

"How?" Carol asked.

"Flagrantly fucking," Breck said, smiling at her. He was about thirty, a frail man, shabbily dressed and quivering with energy. Tonight he was wearing broken-down sneakers, faded jeans, a red plaid shirt, and a suitcoat frayed at the elbows.

Carol wrinkled her nose. "There's a nicer word you could use," she said.

Breck threw himself into the armchair. "Yes, yes," he said. "All sorts of words. You, for instance, you're a biologist. You must know—oh, words! All sorts of words. Epidermis, things like that."

Hal had a vague recollection that Breck and Carol did not like each other, but he could not remember why. "I'd offer you a drink," he said, to short-circuit the argument. "But we're fresh out of gin."

Breck reached into one sagging pocket and withdrew a pint of corn liquor. He removed the cap, took a swig, and wiped the lip with his hand. Then he offered the bottle to Carol. She shuddered. Breck grinned and gave the bottle to Hal, who swallowed a mouthful of the clear, harsh liquor.

"I'm not majoring in biology, anyhow," Carol said. She sat down on the bed, crossed her legs, and swung the free one nervously. Breck stared at the white calf. Carol uncrossed her legs and pulled the skirt down over her knees. "It's Orni-thology," she said.

"Another word!" Breck said. "What else do you know? Tell me about birds; tell me about the sex life of the birds."

"Well, name a bird," she hedged.

"Ah—penguins!"

"Well," Carol said, looking to Hal for guidance. He shrugged, squatted on his heels against the wall, and nursed the bottle of corn liquor. "As a matter of fact, penguins have a very interesting sex life," Carol said, as if defending them from

Breck's scorn. Hal quit listening, although he knew when they changed the subject to bats. The corn liquor burned pleasantly in his guts; he watched the two of them like characters in a silent movie. They didn't like each other. That was a shame; Breck was a wild man, one of the greats, and Hal wished that Carol could love him as he did. But she was all on edge, talking about penguins and bats. It was stupid that people should tear each other to pieces over birds that weren't even birds, not really.

Hal rose to his feet. "*Yeah!*" he said, from the diaphragm. "Too much talk." He shook the bottle, found it empty, and pitched it into the corner.

"We should all move to Boston," Breck said, puffing at a corncob pipe. "We should. Yes. Live in the city, man! The excitement of it, the sheer excitement!"

Hal sat down on the bed beside Carol. "Show me some excitement," he said.

"Yes!" Breck's eyes glittered like artificial diamonds. He hunched forward in his lumpy black suit jacket. "Let's steal some lions," he said.

"Lions?"

"Oh, not any old lions, of course not. Stone lions. Two of them. Shit! They're just begging to be stolen, so we'll find four or five healthy chaps like you, and we'll steal them."

"Why?"

"Why not?"

Hal was impressed by Breck's logic. "Yeah," he said. "Why not?"

Carol wasn't convinced. "That's silly," she said. "Why don't you—oh!—jump out the window, then? Why not kill yourself if that's the only reason you need?"

"I will, I will! In time. It's all a matter of—what? Oh, yes, priority. There's a word for you! If I jumped out the window I couldn't steal the lions, could I?, so I have to steal the lions first. Hah?"

"You're a nut," Carol said.

"The important thing is to do it," Breck said. "Don't resist! When you have the old itch, give it a scratch! Life will kill you if you try to hold back. That's my philosophy. If life puts a pair of lions in my path, why, I steal the bastards, that's all there is to that! Don't ask me *why* unless you're ready to tell me *why not.*"

"You're a nut," Carol insisted. "I'll tell you why not: it's a sin."

"What sin? Horsecock! There's no sin, no God, no soul, no Virgin Mary and the seven dwarfs. You don't believe that stuff any more than I do."

"It's against the law, then. You'll go to jail."

"We won't get caught—and if we do? I can live just as hard in jail as I'm living right now. Maybe harder."

"It sets a bad example," Carol said. "We should make the world a good place for our children to grow up in."

"There won't *be* any world when our children grow up," Breck said. "No children, either. Flippers and things. D'you see? There's no point to it any more. There never was, only now it's out in the open. We can lie and steal and screw like bunnies, and it doesn't matter, because life is a candle's flame, and death is the next puff of wind. Whoosh! That's all we need. One puff, one little puff."

Hal lay back on the bed and took a nap. It ended with somebody shaking him—Carol—and when he sat up the situation had changed. Breck was standing by the door, grinning apologetically. "Somebody boxed me in," he said.

Hal followed him down to the street, stumbling, still half asleep. Breck owned a tired little Volkswagen. Two fat sedans were imprisoning the car front and rear. "We'll pick it up," Hal suggested. They tried, but the Beetle was too heavy, and Breck wasn't built for that kind of work. Then two drunks came along. They leaned against a lamppost and criticized the operation in loud voices.

"Roll it over," said one.

The four of them, Hal and Breck and the drunks, squatted

on the sidewalk and heaved the little car onto its side. There was a squeaking sound from the fenders. Another shove, and the Volkswagen settled on its roof in the middle of Sherman Street, its front wheels slowly revolving. Hal and Breck went around to the other side and pulled while the drunks pushed, and over it came. The fenders were ruined, a side window was cracked, and the roof was somewhat caved in, but otherwise the car was all right. Breck shook hands all around, then drove off. Hal went back upstairs, laughing happily to himself.

"You're as nutty as he is," Carol said when he told her what they had done. "Hal? You're not going to help him steal those stupid lions, are you?"

"Why not?"

"I have a term paper due on Wednesday."

"Okay. You take the car and I'll hitchhike back in a couple days."

"No! I want to stay with you."

"That's good." He yawned. "Let's go to bed."

They had a good time in bed, with the lights on for kicks, but afterward Hal was sleepy and Carol wasn't. She propped her elbow on his chest and stared into the corner of the room, her full lips thrust out unhappily. "I hate him," she said. "The words he uses, you know? Boris says the same things because he likes to shock people, but this one—what's his name?"

"Breck," Hal said, not believing that she had forgotten. "Gene Breck."

"Yes. He says those things to make me feel dirty inside, so I won't want to be a woman. So I'll feel no better than a damned female bat." She was silent for a while, then: "Hal?"

Why didn't she go to sleep, for crying out loud? "What?" he said softly, not to sound angry.

"Guess what?"

"No, what?"

"I'm pregnant." Ah! No wonder she was so moody, no wonder she was upset by the four-letter words. That damned party at the Hut. "Isn't it silly?" she said. "Me—pregnant. Me.

152

It's supposed to happen to somebody else, underprivileged girls or something. . . . Hal?"

"It's all right," he said. "Do you want to get married, or what?"

"I don't know. Do you?"

"Well, you don't want to marry *me*," Hal told her. "I'm twenty-five years old and I'm a bum. I go from party to party. I'd make a rotten husband."

She stirred beside him. "I guess I'd better have that nasty little operation, huh?" she said.

"That's probably the best thing. The only trouble is, I don't have any money."

"How much would it cost?"

"I've heard four hundred dollars."

"Ugh. Who's got four hundred dollars?"

"Not me, that's for damned sure."

"Oh!" she said. "I know." She slapped his chest and looked triumphantly down at him. "Boris! He must have oodles and oodles of money stashed away, an old bachelor like him."

Hal didn't like it. "I'd rather borrow the money," he said.

"Borrow it from Boris, then."

"He wouldn't lend it to me. To you, sure, but I'd rather you didn't. It's not fair."

"Men!" said Carol, diving down under the covers. "You're all crazy." Her voice came up muffled through the blankets. Hal got out of bed and padded across the room to the light switch. When he came back to the bed, Carol was stretched out full-length again. He crawled in beside her. "I don't know," she said. "Wouldn't it be nice to get married and have a little baby?"

"No," he said.

Carol sighed in the dark. "I guess you're right," she said.

~ ~ ~ ~

The raid on the stone lions was set for Tuesday midnight. Breck had lined up a truck and two recruits, a dark little monkey named Sam who talked mostly in literary quotations, and a Negro named Douglas. The Negro was an oily giant. Carol was thrilled by him, and kept bringing him coffee and asking him to help her open a window or light the gas stove— anything to get those broad, smooth muscles into operation. Douglas wore GI khakis that many washings had shrunk skintight.

When it was time to go, Hal drew her off into a corner. "You don't have to come with us, you know," he said. "You can wait here until we get back."

"Oh, I want to come! I want to see you being adventurous," she said, squeezing his bicep. Then she added: "I'm sorry I've been such a bitch about it all. Being pregnant, I mean."

"That's okay."

"I didn't know how to tell you, and sometimes—"

"Sure."

"—sometimes I get so sick of being tough. Don't you? I mean, people get pregnant all the time and that's the chance you take, but gee! Sometimes I want you to fuss over me. I want you to be—oh, I don't know—*excited*, I guess. I want you to be excited that I've got your baby inside me."

Hal thought about it. He wouldn't mind having a son to take into the woods, hunting and fishing, who'd ask him about automobiles and women, who'd depend on him. . . . "You'd make a good mother," he said.

"Do you think so? Really?. . . Oh, but that's stupid. Who'd want to have babies in a world like this?" He hurried her back to the party before she could change her mind. The others were ready to go. He and Breck would take the truck, and Douglas would follow in the beat-up Beetle with the others. Carol would be their lookout. "What if I see a policeman?" she asked, wide-eyed and scared now that the engines were running and the raid was about to start. "What should I *do?*"

"Just pass the word," Hal said, kissing the soft lips that were turned up to him. "Be a good girl, now." He jumped into the truck beside Breck, who was driving. It was a prewar

Chevrolet, a one-ton flatbed that shuddered to the very heart of its being when Breck let out the clutch. The passenger-side door flew open before they were halfway down the hill, and Hal had to hold it closed with his elbow. "Where'd you find this monster?" he yelled above the engine noise.

"Borrowed it off a guy in Brookline. And say! He's got an Austin-Healey he wants to race. Sports-car rally? In Narwich. That back road between the greenhouses and the reservoir. I know some guys at Harvard who'll come up, and we could put together a car worth racing, you and me. What d'you think?"

"Why not?" yelled Hal. He'd go along with any project in the world tonight. It was a wild, gusty March evening, and a sandstorm of grit was blowing down Charles Street against the windshield.

The street of the lions was deserted when they reached it. Breck drove into an alley between two dark apartment houses, and there he killed the engine. The Volkswagen followed them in. The entire block was dark. It had been condemned as part of an urban renewal project, Breck said; the tenants were moved out last week and the utilities cut off. "It's a marvelous plan," Breck said, leading his raiders around to the sidewalk. "Winston Churchill thought it up. He paid a thousand Negroes to move here from Harlem and run down the property values. . . ."

"He *didn't*," Carol protested.

"Ask Douglas! He was one of them. After the Negroes blight the neighborhood, you see, Urban Renewal moves them out and builds a highway. The Negroes settle somewhere else, blight that neighborhood, and pretty soon—no houses left in Boston! Just highways. It was Churchill's idea, revenge for the Boston Tea Party. . . . Ah, look at them! Aren't they beauties?"

The lions were pale and immense in the stray street lighting. There were two of them, staring proudly across the street with their blind stone eyes, one on either side of the apartment house entry. Their manes had been worn slick by small boys, and one had a broken ear and the other a broken tail.

Douglas got ropes and tools from the back of the truck, arranged them on the steps, and went to work with a cold chisel and mallet. The blows echoed like gunfire along the deserted street. They sent Carol down to the corner to watch for police cruisers, and Breck tried a hacksaw on the lion's rear feet, but it was no good. They rested, sweating. "Steel rods," Hal guessed. Breck grabbed the cold chisel and went to work again, crouching at the lion's feet. Douglas watched him with passive African scorn. Little Sam went poking into the alley, returning with a four-by-six timber with rusty spikes sticking out of it.

Carol came running up to them, shivering. "I'm scared," she said, tugging at Hal's sleeve. "You're making too much noise." He took her over to the other lion, the broken-tailed one, and swung her up to sit upon its back. "Keep a lookout from there," he said, pinching her thigh. "We'll be done in a minute."

Sam clapped his hands. "*Mama piga simba*," he said.

"What's that supposed to mean?"

"Mama kill lion! Swahili, I think. From the *Green Hills of Africa*. Mama was Hemingway's wife."

Hal slipped the timber under the belly of their lion. He stood on the steps with Douglas behind him. The two smaller men stood on the pedestal behind the lion and hugged him at the neck and hindquarters. "Okay?" asked Hal when they were in position. He bent his knees and got his shoulder under the timber, and behind him Douglas did likewise; he closed his eyes and forced his legs to straighten. The wood dug into his shoulder. He heaved to the limit of his strength, sparks flying up behind his eyelids. Behind him Douglas was grunting. Then the great weight flew off his shoulder, and he fell forward on his hands and knees.

"Excelsior!" yelled Sam above him. He and Breck were holding the lion in their arms, as if the great stone cat were rubbing its fur against them.

It must have weighed five hundred pounds. They carried it

with the plank under its belly, Hal and Douglas on opposite sides, while Sam lifted the front end and Breck lifted the rump. They slid the beast along the bed of the truck and roped it to the cab. Then they did the same with the second lion.

This time, Carol rode in the truck on Hal's lap. Their destination was a garage out in Brookline that belonged to Breck's friend who owned the truck and the Austin-Healey. They reached the garage at three o'clock, unloaded the lions and covered them with a tarp, then drove back to Boston, three of them crammed into the Volkswagen's back seat. Carol fell asleep in front. Breck wanted to celebrate at the Sevens, but Hal needed to get his girl to bed, so he had Douglas leave them at the foot of Sherman Street.

Hal carried her upstairs. He was too wired up to sleep, so after undressing her and coaxing her into pajamas—she wobbled like a drunk—he sat in the armchair until dawn, smoking cigarettes and chuckling. Then he crawled into bed beside Carol's soft warmth.

He slept until late in the afternoon, then jerked awake with a snore caught in his throat. Carol was puttering around in her pink pajamas. A toothbrush handle projected from her mouth, and foam had trickled down her chin. She was humming. Hal watched her while he chased the cobwebs of sleep from his brain. "Hey," he called then, in that special voice. She turned and smiled past the toothbrush handle. Hal wriggled between the sheets, waiting for her to come to him. She rinsed her mouth at the sink, spat, and dropped the toothbrush into a glass. Then she walked toward him with her lips wet and gleaming, already half in a trance. Hal made room for her beside him. Then he played with her, twining and intertwining in the elaborate games they had worked out. "*Now*," whispered Carol, her eyes glazed behind half-closed lids. In that best of all possible moments, a thunder filled the room. Hal tried to shut out the noise but couldn't. Somebody pounding on the door. "Oh, damn him to hell," Carol said, tossing her head on the pillow. "If that's your friend Breck, I'll kill him!"

Hal rose up on his hands. "Who is it?" he yelled at the door.

"County sheriff's office!" the door yelled back.

Carol's hand flew to her mouth. "Oh!" she gasped. "Hal, sweetie, don't answer!"

"Get dressed," he said. He rolled her out of bed and followed after her. "Now listen," he said, pulling on his trousers. "If it's about those damned lions, remember: you weren't with us last night. You came down to Boston this morning. By the train. Got it?"

"Ye—yes."

"Say it!"

"I came down . . . by the morning train. . . . But Hal!" she wailed, clinging so tight he couldn't buckle his belt. "What about *you?*"

"Never mind that. Get dressed."

She ran around the room in search of her clothes, dropping as many as she picked up. Hal cornered her, gathered the clothes, and fed them to her a piece at a time. Then he put on his sweater and shoes while Carol ran a comb through her hair, cursing the tangles.

Then he opened the door. A short, square man was standing there, wearing a topcoat and a hat with the brim parallel to his eyebrows. His brown eyes inspected Hal without enthusiasm. One cheek bulged from the probing of his tongue, then flattened, and he said, "Mister Merchant?"

Hal wanted to say No, to see if the chopping-block would change its expression, but he remembered that he was Colin's brother. "That's right," he said.

The deputy, if that's what he was, brushed past Hal and walked into the room. The tongue was in his cheek again. He looked at the rumpled bed, at the suitcase open on the floor, and at Carol, flushed and frightened by the sink with a comb in her hand. Hal slammed the door and walked over to the intruder. He didn't turn, obliging Hal to walk a half-circle to face him down. "This is for you," he said, extracting a long

158

envelope from his topcoat pocket and holding it up.

When Hal didn't take it, the deputy tried to stuff the envelope into his shirt. That was too much. Hal balled his fist and threw it in a looping blow at the other man's face. The punch landed with a heart-warming noise. The deputy's face snapped two inches to the left, and the hat flew off, revealing that he was bald.

"Hal!" Carol screamed.

"*Yeah!*" he said.

Then the deputy's left arm swept up and caught him under the jaw, setting him on his heels. The envelope sailed away. Hal stepped back, recovered, and landed a left on the other man's forehead, where the weather-beaten face changed into a milk-white brow. Hal tried an uppercut, missed, and pitched onto the floor, propelled by a hand on his elbow. Judo!

Well, all right. He rolled over and jumped up before he could be nailed. He landed one pretty good punch, but the deputy swayed and took it on his shoulder, and the next one missed completely. Shit! He was short, he was fast—what else? Hal tried to grab him, to hold him steady for a minute, but a chopping hand slammed into his neck and drove him down to the floor again, onto his knees. His head weighed a ton. Before he could bounce out of the way, the frock of the deputy's topcoat flew up and cracked him on the mouth. The room tilted and blurred. Hal went over on his side, blinking his eyes, trying to get a grip on the floor boards with his fingers. His vision cleared in time to show him a black shoe rising from the floor. It exploded in his face with a brilliant flash.

~ ~ ~ ~

When he struggled back to consciousness, his head was in Carol's lap and she was wiping his face with a wet cloth. His head felt enormous, a ballooning mass of hurt, and when he tried to speak his upper lip got in the way. "Yes, he's gone, the beast," Carol said. "And, oh Hal!—it didn't have anything to do with those silly lions. He wasn't going to arrest us."

"Colin?" he guessed, talking out of the corner of his mouth.

159

"Yes, something about a divorce. Teddy's *divorcing* him." Carol gave him the washcloth to hold against his mouth—the cloth was pink with blood—and helped him sit up. Hal explored the inside of his mouth, and was relieved to find that all his teeth were still there. That was one thing about fighting that always scared him: he might lose his teeth. "He thought you were Colin," Carol said, "and he wanted to serve this thing on you about the divorce. Do you want to stand up, sweetie?"

"Mirror," Hal said. Carol brought the mirror from the sink. She knelt in front of him, holding the glass for his inspection. He removed the washcloth. Blood was oozing from a cut that ran along his upper lip and almost to his nose. That was from the kick that had put him out. His left eye was swollen and squinting, and there was a bruise beginning on his cheekbone, with a few drops of blood standing out on the skin. He wiped them away and they immediately reappeared. "Chair," he said. Carol helped him to stand, and like a four-legged drunk they hobbled to the chair and sat down together. "Good," Hal said. "How come . . . he didn't run me in? The bastard."

Carol giggled. "He wanted to," she said, "but I told him you were Colin's brother, all the way from Milwaukee. I told him we'd been driving all night and you didn't know what you were doing."

"That's for damned sure," Hal said. He could talk all right, once he got over his fear of splitting his lip. "What about a divorce?" Carol jumped up and got the document. It was a legal-sized form, filled in by a typewriter with a bad ribbon, and it declared that Colin Merchant should appear in Piscataqua County Superior Court on the second Tuesday of April, to show cause why Theodora Merchant should not divorce him. "Well, that settles one question," Hal said. "They really did get married!"

"Oh, Hal! Of *course* they did!" Carol was furious, for some reason, but her anger was brief. "Why would Teddy do a thing like that?" she said. "If I were married, I'd expect it to be for life, wouldn't you? Especially if I had a nice little baby like

Teddy's. A baby needs a father, don't you think?"

"Yeah," said Hal, not sure which question he was answering.

"A marriage—oh! It should last, don't you think? It should be a safe place? I mean: somewhere you can always go and know you'll be welcome?" Carol grabbed his knees and pressed her face against them. She was crying. "Otherwise," she sobbed, "otherwise there's nothing."

12 - *Send Marvin Peabody to Russia*

WHEN BORIS SOBERED OFF and went to work for the University, in 1953, there was a lot of excitement about subversives. He'd been drunk since the end of the War. At one moment, the Japanese were surrendering to General MacArthur on the *USS Missouri*, then Joe McCarthy was rumbling and growling and tugging at his shirt collar, finding Communists in the State Department and even the US Army. Something very serious must have happened in the meantime, to put the nation in such an uproar.

Then Senator McCarthy died and was forgotten by everybody except the *Manchester Union*, which each year, on the anniversary of the great man's death, printed a black-bordered tribute to his memory. In the end, Boris dismissed the whole thing as he had earlier dismissed the Lindberg kidnapping and the disappearance of Amelia Earhart, vague tragedies he could never fully understand.

So it was like remembering a childhood disaster when the New Hampshire Attorney General began to investigate Narwich. Boris bought the *Manchester Union* every morning. "I don't get it," he complained to the University Development Officer. "Do they think Marvin Peabody is a *spy?* For Christ's sake! The Russians have better things to do with their money. They're not going to pay a grad student to march up and down Main Street."

"It's more subtle than that," Mr. Phipps said, making a cat's cradle of his long, bony fingers. "It's, uh, a matter of loyalty. Are we teaching our young men and women to be good Americans? That's what the Attorney General wants to know."

Said that way, it almost made sense, only to wobble into chaos again, like the world his mother saw from her rocking chair in the State Hospital. What were they after? Boris couldn't decide, nobody could tell him, yet he had become involved in this game of loyalty. Was he loyal? Could he prove it? What did *loyal* mean? It was madness, and it went on from nine o'clock in the morning until four-thirty in the afternoon.

He got into the habit of watching it begin. He drove to work through the bright spring morning, often with wraiths of ground mist creeping out of College Woods, and parked his Volkswagen outside the administration building. There he waited for the Attorney General's man—he who had scribbled notes to the chief of police during the pacifists' trial. He arrived as the nine o'clock bells were ringing from the clock tower. Neatly turned out in a dark brown suit, he emerged from his state car with a briefcase tucked under his left elbow. He brought his own secretary, a mousy girl who carried a portable stenographic machine. With the emblems of their professions, they marched into the administration building and vanished upstairs just as the last stroke of nine sounded across the campus.

According to the *Manchester Union*, the Attorney General's man had been provided with an office and a letter urging all members of the University community to give him full cooperation, whatever that meant. So far, he had used it to catch five professors. The word in Narwich was that they had all talked rings around him, since he was fresh out of law school, while they had been answering hostile questions for years, from students brought up in homes where the *Manchester Union* was honored. Four professors said they knew Marvin Peabody. One of them admitted that he had discussed the Civil Defense protest with Marvin but had advised him to take cover with everybody else. All five had contributed to the fund that bailed the pacifists out of jail.

The *Union* made a front-page story out of this last bit of information. It was accompanied by a statement from the Governor, who wanted the Attorney General's man to extend the investigation to the University administration. Clearly something was being hidden, the Governor said. Mr. Phipps brought the newspaper down to the photo lab and showed it to Boris. "They already knew that, about the bail money," he

163

said. "The town clerk gave a list of the contributors to the Attorney General."

"You mean that story is a lie?" Boris asked.

"Not exactly," Mr. Phipps said. "More of an embellishment, I'd say."

"Jesus," Boris said. "I'm going to stop reading newspapers again."

"I just hope they don't connect you with those crazy kids." As the week wore on and Mr. Phipps saw a year's worth of public relations going to waste, his sympathy with the pacifists had evaporated. "We can justify having a few pet liberals on the faculty. It shows that we're concerned with freedom of speech, you know. But you're different, Boris, and I don't know if we can protect you if the *Union* starts yelling for your scalp."

"I don't even *like* Marvin Peabody," Boris said.

"Neither do I," Mr. Phipps said. "He's a bad influence on the younger students, like Carol. And that reminds me, Boris. I talked to the president this morning, and it seems that the Governor will attend the trustees' meeting on Saturday. He'll probably try to have the Peabody fellow expelled. Anyhow, the president wants to write an op-ed for the *New York Times*— how he stood up for free speech, you know?—and he needs a few pictures to illustrate it. I've asked the Student Senate to organize a little demonstration on his behalf. If you'd be there?"

When Mr. Phipps had gone, Boris called Tom Matthews in Oldfield and told him about this development. Tom agreed to buy a set of prints. Boris hung up, feeling better already.

~ ~ ~ ~

Saturday dawned in a light gray drizzle. After breakfast, Boris drove into Narwich for a second cup of coffee and a copy of the *Union*. Sure enough, the Governor would attend the March meeting of the University's board of trustees, armed with a resolution to expel Marvin Peabody and the other students found guilty by Judge Kinney. There was a list of the names.

Among them, Boris saw Colin Merchant's, and his heart leapt in outrage. Why did they keep throwing that name at him?

He drove to the administration building and went to work. He photographed the University's bespectacled president and the cheering students who lined the sidewalk. He photographed the trustees, elderly gentlemen and two fierce ladies. Lastly he photographed the Governor, who tossed a left-handed salute to the students, probably thinking they had gathered in his honor. He received hostile stares in return, except from the Young Americans for Liberty, who were stationed under the clock tower with a sign: SEND MARVIN PEABODY TO RUSSIA! Boris photographed the Young Americans, too, then ducked into the building out of the rain.

The meeting lasted three hours. Half a dozen reporters, including Tom Matthews, had gathered beneath the Victorian spire by the time the trustees emerged, led by the Governor. The University president was the last to appear. He blew upon his spectacles, replaced them on his nose, and read aloud from a slip of paper. The trustees had voted, seven to four with one abstention, to suspend any student who had taken part in the Civil Defense protest. That said, he walked with his quick, birdlike step down the path to the street. The Governor passed him in a Lincoln Continental with a gumball machine on the dashboard, driven by a state trooper in forest green. He did not offer the president a ride. "Well," said Boris to Tom Matthews. "It looks like you have an exclusive. The *New York Times* won't be needing these photos, after all."

He developed the negatives that afternoon, figuring that the troops would descend on him that evening. He was right. They began to drift into the Hut before seven o'clock, and most were drunk before eight. "I don't know why you put up with them," Teddy whispered to Boris while they were mixing drinks. She dreaded the notion that he would be questioned by the Attorney General's man. "They'll get you fired!"

"What the hell," he said. "The harm's been done. Let them have their party."

It was more of a funeral than a party. The only cheerful ones were Marvin Peabody and Carol Phipps. Marvin was a hero and free to go to Russia, as the Young Americans for Liberty had suggested. But Carol was a mystery. She became tipsy early and kept bumping into Boris, calling him sweetie and running her fingers along his neck. Hal Pappajohn got drunk, told a rambling story about how he had stolen a lion, hit a student who didn't believe him, and finally disappeared. Carol came up to where Boris was lounging in the armchair, sat down heavily in his lap, and wriggled there in time to the music, drenching him with warmth and the scent of perfume. Teddy punished Boris by going to bed at ten o'clock.

Toward midnight, Hal Pappajohn returned with blood oozing from a cut over his eyebrow, and dragged Carol away.

The party lasted until three o'clock, so Boris relaxed his rule against all-night guests. Six or seven of the pacifists slept in various postures on the living room floor. Boris fed them bacon and eggs next morning, then threw them out, and he and Teddy spent most of Sunday cleaning up.

On Monday, Mr. Phipps's secretary waiting for Boris when he arrived at the photo lab. She was a motherly woman in her forties, a widow whom Boris suspected of wanting to make a match. But today she was being aloof. "*That man* wants to see you," she said. "I made an appointment for ten o'clock."

"Ugh," Boris said.

"I do hope you won't swear at him, Boris," she said, melting somewhat. He gave her a pat on the fanny as she went out the door. He tried to print up the orders that were left over from Friday, but his heart wasn't in it, and finally he flopped in the waiting-room armchair and smoked a cigarette. It was a bad omen that Mr. Phipps had dispatched his secretary. If he meant to do battle for his photographer, he'd have come in person.

Shortly before ten, Boris walked over to the administration building. The interview would take place on the third floor, unused except to store records and let students into the bell

166

tower after a football game; he climbed the stairs with acid spreading through his guts. There was one door open in the corridor. Boris went in. The Attorney General's man and his secretary looked up but did not speak, and when Boris did, the lawyer shook his head and pointed to a chair. They looked at each other. Then a great creaking and groaning began over their heads, followed by a *whoosh!* of air and a thunderous peal upon the clock tower bell. The entire office vibrated to the sound. As soon as everything had steadied, there was another mighty peal from the bell.

"Hey," said Boris into the ringing silence that followed the tenth stroke. "Anybody got the time?"

The Attorney General's man let out a sigh. Perhaps he'd heard the line before. "Boris . . . Ivashko," he said. It was a statement, not a question, but Boris knew there was a question tucked in there.

"My father came from the Ukraine," he said. "In 1912," he added.

The questions seemed routine: age, address, occupation, past employment, military service, arrests other than minor traffic violations, ever a member of . . . and there followed one of the most impressive lists Boris had ever heard. Most of the organizations had patriotic names. Boris wished that he could claim membership in one or two—the Abraham Lincoln Brigade, perhaps—just to erase the boredom on the lawyer's face. He seemed no older than Marvin Peabody. He had a dark face, handsome in a French Canadian sort of way, and he kept clearing his throat as he read from the list. "No," Boris said when the lawyer finished, slightly out of breath.

"Did you ever hear any of those names mentioned in conversation?"

"Sure."

"Which ones?" the Attorney General's man asked.

"Well, the Nazi party. And the Communist party."

"Have you ever heard of the Committee for Militant Pacifism?"

"No," Boris said, crossing his fingers below the level of the desk.

"Do you know Marvin Peabody?" the lawyer asked then. So first round was over. The secretary's fingers floated across the keyboard of her stenographic machine, encrypting the questions and answers upon a white ribbon of paper. Did you ever join any group organized by Marvin Peabody? Did you know that Marvin Peabody was coordinator of the William Penn chapter of the Committee for Militant Pacifism? Is it true that Marvin Peabody frequently called meetings in a building known as the Hut and owned by you? Was Civil Defense discussed at any of these meetings? Did you take part in any such discussion? Were you present during the Civil Defense test on Sunday, March the tenth, 1963? Did you take cover when the alarm was sounded? Why not? Is it true that Marvin Peabody and his followers had met at the Hut following their release from incarceration?

"From what?" Boris said, suffocated by all these questions.

"Jail."

"Oh, Christ, I guess so."

"They did?"

"Yes."

"Is it true that the wife of one of the arrested pacifists—Colin Merchant by name—has been living with you since late January or early February?"

"Fuck you," Boris said.

"I beg your pardon?" said the Attorney General's man, and the click-clack of the secretary's machine faltered and stopped.

"I said *fuck you*." Boris glared into the soft brown eyes of the Attorney General's man—they reminded him of butter—and forced him to look away. Boris had nothing to lose, it seemed. "Do you want me to spell it?" he asked. "*Eff*. . . .

"That won't be necessary," the Attorney General's man said. "Perhaps you'd like to plead self-incrimination?"

"If that's what *fuck you* means to a lawyer," Boris said, "it's okay with me."

"Let the record show," the Attorney General's man said to his secretary, "that the witness availed himself of the fifteenth amendment to the New Hampshire constitution relating to self-incrimination."

With a pause at eleven while the bells tolled the hour, the interrogation lasted out the morning. Boris was sweat-soaked by the end of it. He had fared badly, and in some obscure fashion his answers had proved him guilty of something, though he wasn't sure what. "I don't even *like* Marvin Peabody," he complained at the end.

"I don't see that it makes any difference," the Attorney General's man said, "but we'll insert it into the record if you like. This is not a trial, you know. We're gathering factual and unbiased information to assist the legislature in its lawmaking functions."

"Yeah," said Boris, "and scaring hell out of people."

"That will be all," the Attorney General's man said.

Boris went out. He ached for a drink, for the first time in years. Better drunk than . . . what was it? Disloyal.

What nonsense! The noontime bells were ringing, melodious now that he was outdoors; the students swept five abreast down the sidewalk on their way to lunch, and that mad interview had never taken place. How could he be disloyal, when he didn't even know what he had subverted?

CONGRATULATIONS!" said Hal Pappajohn, who had a strip of surgical tape over his right eye. "I hear you've joined the peaceniks, too! I tell you, Boris, the only way to keep clear of these birds is carry a flag in one hand and keep saluting it with the other." The word was out that, Hal said, that Boris had told the Attorney General's man to go to hell.

"That makes me a pacifist?"

"Just like me!" Hal said. "I told Johnny Trask to kiss my ass, and next thing I knew, Marvin Peabody signed me up. He'll be after you before sundown."

He was right. Marvin caught up with Boris in front of the Coffee Corner and surrounded him with cold, damp fingers. "I knew you were with us. I knew it," he said.

Boris backed off, but Marvin followed with his arm still pumping, until Boris felt that his own hand would dissolve in that earnest grip. They were now in front of Sigma Phi, and the sweat-shirted brothers stared at them. "Don't drag me into your plots," Boris said. "I'm not a part of them. I'm not a part of anything."

"You know better than that, Boris. You can't be a spectator in this day and age. You have to come down on one side or the other, and it seems you have chosen ours. I'm glad to have you aboard!"

The most frustrating part of Marvin's claim was that there was some truth to it: Boris had lost his spectator status. He'd involved himself with the peace marchers, he'd involved himself with Teddy Merchant's baby, and he'd involved himself with her divorce. And when he went home that evening, she involved him in Baby Merchant's future. "Malcolm was by this afternoon," she told him breathlessly, taking the bag of groceries from his arm and spilling a can of evaporated milk on the floor. "The hearing—for temporary support?—has been set for next week, and he says that I should name Baby before then. I've thought and thought, and I can't for the life of me think of a name. Malcolm must think I'm an awful nut." They both stooped to pick up the fallen can, and Teddy's nearness was like a kiss. How alive she was! "Boris," she said then, "what shall I name him?"

The way she appealed to him, full of trust, made him dizzy with joy. "I don't know," he said, but while he was saying it his father's image came to him: the ugly old optimist with the walrus mustache. "If I had a son," he said, tingling at the thought, "I'd call him Nikolas. That was my old man's name."

"Nikolas?"

"Yeah. With a K."

"Nikolas Merchant," she said, in a tone of wonder. "With a K!"

"Sounds good to me."

Teddy clapped her hands and raced into the bedroom. Boris followed her. "Nik!" she cried, bending over the crib. "Hello, Nik, my son! Hello, *Nikolas*." The way she said the word turned Boris inside out. He wondered if his own mother had ever pronounced his name in that manner, as if all of life and beauty and wisdom were contained in it. "Do you think he likes it?" Teddy asked, looking up at him.

"Hey, Nick!" Boris said. He leaned over and tickled the soft skin between the diaper and the sailor shirt. The baby chuckled with pleasure. "He likes it," Boris said.

"Then it's settled." Teddy scooped her son out of the crib and held him high. "Nikolas Merchant," she breathed, and again Boris felt himself turning slow somersaults.

"He's my favorite person," he said. "No, second favorite."

"Who's the first?"

"You are."

She laughed, hiding her face against her son's fat belly. "You're so nice to me," she said. "Why are you so nice to me?"

"I'll never tell," Boris said.

And next day he telephoned the town clerk, the Oldfield hospital, and Malcolm Carleton's office, formally enrolling

Nikolas Merchant as a member of society. "Now you have to take him home and introduce him to your folks," Boris told Teddy then.

"No," she said. "Not until I'm divorced."

"They've never seen their grandson. Is that fair? I'll drive you home Saturday; it won't cost you a dime. For Christ's sake!"

"So they can say I-told-you-so? Oh, Boris, you should have heard my father, one day when I was lonely and telephoned him. It was awful. *I told you he was a bastard*," she growled; "I told you it wouldn't last; *I told you so.* . . ."

"He wanted you to come home."

"Great!" Teddy said, and laughed in the cynical manner she was cultivating. Her divorcee's laugh. "A great way to bring me home."

"One lousy weekend, can't you spare your folks that much?"

"After I'm divorced," she said, but less stoutly than before.

"This weekend," Boris said. "I'll drive you home Saturday."

"Well. . . ."

"This weekend," Boris said.

"All right, but I'll take the bus. I can handle them better if nobody else is around."

Boris agreed. But Saturday morning after breakfast, when Teddy began to wonder aloud about bus schedules, he said, "It's a nice day; I'll drive you over. I have nothing better to do."

"But. . . ."

"And your old man can bring you back tomorrow. You've probably missed the bus by now, anyhow."

"All right," she said. Her face wore that softly glowing look that women assumed after a surrender, and Boris pulsed with yearning. She was the first woman to wear that expression for him since the Siamese girl, half a lifetime ago, when he was nineteen and would never die.

Teddy's home was in Leah, a mill town on the river

separating New Hampshire from Vermont; a sleepy place with a park and a bandstand and an American flag drooping in the sun. No subversives in Leah! They arrived just before noon. The house was on a residential street across the railroad tracks, surrounded by lilac bushes and willow trees in bud; it had a warm and clumsy look. Teddy's mother was stoutly handsome, a square-faced woman maybe ten years older than Boris, but no wrinkles or gray hair. They made polite conversation for half an hour, then Boris excused himself. "I have a three o'clock appointment," he said, to impress the mother. "Nice meeting you, Mrs.—" He ended on a mumble. He'd almost called her Mrs. Merchant.

The women chorused good-by—how alike their voices were!—and he escaped into the spring afternoon. His shirt was damp. It had been tough, watching his tongue every second, but altogether it had been a success. Teddy was happy to be home, and she would thank him for bringing her that happiness; and at the very least he must have impressed the mother as a better man than Colin Merchant.

~ ~ ~ ~

Turning into his driveway, he saw a small white roadster with the hood yawning open and Georgie bending over it, explaining the workings to Carol Phipps. She listened with a look of pure blonde boredom. Boris got out of his Volkswagen and ambled over. "Hey, Georgie," he said. "New car?"

"Isn't she a beauty? Runs like a watch, like a dream." Georgie lowered the hood and ran his palm along the roadster's flank, his eyes glowing with the pride of possession. "I just took Carol here for a spin."

"Good idea," Boris said, moving between them and nudging her with his hip. "How about spinning with me for a while, gorgeous?" Carol tossed her hair, heavy and yellow like corn silk.

"Gee," said Georgie, squinting at his watch. "I'm late!. . . I'm working at the Italian sandwich shop downtown, until I straighten things out?" He waited for Boris to nod approval. "I

173

better be going," he said then. "You want a ride downtown, Carol?"

"Never mind, sweetie," she said. "Boris will give me a lift." Georgie lowered himself into the roadster and gave them a wave. After the little car had vanished down the road to Narwich, snarling and spitting like a castrated cat, Boris said, "How about a drink?"

Carol looked at him with her blue eyes flat as poker chips. The pink tip of her tongue came out and ran along her lips. "I thought you'd never ask," she told him.

She was teeetering on a question. She jiggled her feet while he opened the door, and once inside she paced around the room. "What's up?" Boris asked, sprawling in his favorite armchair. He was stiff from the drive to Leah and back. "What's biting you, sweetheart?"

"Oh —" Carol walked toward him, then away. "God! it's stuffy in here," she complained, smoothing her palms along a rump like the curve of a pear. In the same gesture she thrust out her breasts. "Why don't you open a window or something?"

Boris got up and unlatched one of the casements. He mixed Carol a vodka and orange while he was up. She accepted the glass, looked into it, and drank half in one swallow. Then, shuddering faintly, she perched on the arm of his chair and drank the rest. "You haven't asked me to pose for you lately," she said with a pout. "Have you found somebody prettier? Or did you get Teddy to take off her pants?"

"Go to hell," Boris said.

Carol sighed. "What about another drink," she said, "just a little one?"

"Fix it yourself."

Carol shrugged and went over to the kitchen alcove. Boris studied her back, tightly sheathed in sweater and skirt, remembering the time she'd posed for him in Georgie's trailer. That body! Perhaps he could finish the job this afternoon, get her naked before his Rolleiflex. "You're a funny duck," Carol

174

said. She laughed in her throat and came over to perch again on the arm of his chair arm. He grabbed the thigh that was offered to him, warm and full beneath his hand. Carol worked steadily at her drink, frowning at it, swirling the contents around, and finally taking a sip; she repeated this process until the glass was empty. Then she sighed and leaned perilously over to deposit the glass on the floor. When she straightened, she slid into the chair beside Boris, like a big blond cat.

"Boris, d'you like me?" she asked. "I mean, if I was in trouble, would you help me?"

"Help you?"

"If I was in trouble. You *said* you would."

"Hah," Boris said, going very still inside. Carol was pregnant and Hal had walked out on her, as they all did, sooner or later. "Have another drink," he said. He disengaged himself and stood up. He mixed the drink, a strong one, and handed it to Carol. Then he sat down on the couch facing her. "Okay, baby," he said, leaning across the space that separated them and tapping her knee. "Did Hal Pappajohn knock you up?"

"You know it," she said, being tough.

"So you decided to be nice to old Boris?"

"It's not like that!"

"Hal won't help you, or you wouldn't be here. Am I right?"

"Yes," she admitted. "No. I mean, he *can't* help, because he doesn't have any money. Boris, what can I do?"

"You know what you can do," he said, grinning at her. "You can't get any more pregnant, so you ought to go out and sleep with every guy you know. Haven't you always wanted to do that?"

"Starting with you, I suppose?"

"Sure. Charge us each ten dollars, and in a month's time you'll have all the money you need."

She winced. "You son of a bitch," she said. "You should try being a *woman* for a couple of days. Try having cramps and

175

headaches and tampons every time the moon is full, and just *try* waiting for your period when you know it's not going to come. Then tell me how funny it is."

Boris sat down on the arm of the chair. "Baby," he said, "I think everything is funny. When you look like I do, you gotta have a sense of humor."

"Boris?"

"Yeah."

"Will you lend me the money?"

"You couldn't pay it back."

"All right, will you *give* it to me?"

"How much?"

"Four hundred dollars."

Boris snaked his tongue across his lips, which were so dry they seemed ready to crack. Four hundred was a lot for a photograph. But he'd never have another chance like this—who knew what poses he might coax from her? And she needed his help, she genuinely did. "Okay," he said, and Carol's breath went out in a rush, like a balloon when the end is released. Boris stood up and went over to the bureau. There was a pigeonhole drawer on top, and in this niche Boris kept his Bronze Star medal, a packet of contraceptives, and his checkbook. He didn't have four hundred dollars in his checking account, but he could borrow it from the University credit union and cover the check before she cashed it. "Carol Phipps," he said, tearing off a blank check and taking out his fountain pen.

"Make it out to cash."

He did as she asked, then waved the check slowly in the air. "Come and get it," he said to her. She stood up, as if she too were in a dream, and padded silently across the floor. At some point in the game she had kicked off her shoes. Barefoot, she seemed broader and closer to the ground—a panther of a woman! She held out her hand for the check, but Boris whisked it away. "Let's talk about it in the studio," he said, standing the check on edge against the pigeonhole drawer.

Carol shrugged, as if she had known all along what the transaction would entail. There was a half-smile around her mouth and eyes. She padded barefoot into the bedroom. Boris grabbed the Rollei off the dinette table and followed her. That walk! That body! And he had the whole afternoon to capture her on film, in all the poses he could devise—poses enough for a lifetime of private lusts.

Scarcely pausing inside the bedroom door, Carol hit the light switch to turn it off and continued in her feral walk to the window, where she pulled the shade and drew the curtains together in one smooth motion. "Hey!" she said, spotting the camera in his hand. "You can leave that in the other room, sweetie. No dirty pictures! That's final." She sat down with a bounce on the edge of the mattress, crossed her arms, and peeled the sweater over her head. She folded it neatly and placed it on Teddy's bedside table. Then she unbuttoned the skirt at her hip, opened the zipper with a little chirp, and stood up briefly to kick it off, catching the garment with her toe; she folded that also and put it on top of the sweater.

"Well, come *on*," she said, patting the bedspread beside her. "What are you waiting for?" When he didn't answer, she pulled down the covers and dove beneath them—into Teddy's bed. There was a great amount of wriggling, then her hand emerged long enough to drop a bundle of underclothes on the floor. Boris felt dizzy: she was naked and waiting for him, expecting him to make love to her. Hal Pappajohn's girl! That rugged Greek bastard—how would Boris compare? But he couldn't back away. He'd never have another chance like this. He went to the bed, stripped, and slid under the covers beside Carol. Just in time! Her head emerged, ripe as a plum in the artificial dusk. Boris shrank before the directness of her gaze: it seemed there was nothing but the clear blue cellophane of her irises between him and her naked soul. "*Boo!*" she said. "What are you waiting for, silly?"

Boris flipped the blanket down. He put his hand on the plump curve of her belly. The hand looked like a spider,

177

resting there, but what the hell! He'd paid for the privilege. Anyhow, this much was familiar. Every year or so Boris would find a model who allowed him to explore her body with lips and fingertips. This was no different, no different at all. It was merely the *wholeness* of Carol Phipps that had unnerved him for a moment. He began with her breasts and worked his way down to the honeypot. Carol sighed agreeably beneath him. "There!" she said. "Oh, that's nice. . . ." She began to roll gently from side to side. "Now," she urged. "Stick it in!" Boris aligned his belly with hers, striving to remember across the chasm of twenty years the combination that unlocked the mystery of her sex. The warmth of Carol Phipps seemed to melt his bones. "Hey," she said. "What's the matter?" Her exploring hand had found, not the triumphant phallus she expected, but a daisy wilting in the sun. "My goodness," she said.

Boris imagined that he'd drift upward like tumbleweed, weightless and dry. She stirred beneath him, then pushed him away. He rolled face down in the knotted sheets. The bed creaked and joggled; he heard her bare feet padding across the floor, then silence, then the sound of rushing water from the bathroom. He opened his eyes. The emptiness of the room was like a blessing. Quickly, he scrambled out of bed and got dressed. Thank God, she was gone.

He decided to shoot himself. It was a quick way out, and the weapon was handy, so he went over to the bureau and got his father's pistol. He was astonished by its weight; it had never seemed so heavy before. Cradling it in both hands, he carried it to the couch and sat down. He looked at it: the glossy gray flank, the checkered hand-grip, the pungent odor of gun oil, the gritty *weight* of it! But he could raise it no higher than his chin. Two impossible weights were dragging at his elbows, and finally they pulled the pistol down into his lap. Well, he'd smoke a cigarette first.

While he was inhaling the sweet gray smoke, he saw how it would be: Teddy would come home from Leah and find him sprawled on the couch, and she would scream. Baby Nikolas

178

would be frightened. He'd add his thin cries to hers, scream upon scream.

Poor Teddy! He couldn't frighten her that way. And what would be the result? He'd never see her again, never again hear Baby Nikolas crow with happiness—the child that he had named! Boris wept a little, then butted the cigarette and took the pistol back to the bureau. He would get drunk instead, the first time in ten years. He got the vodka bottle, sat down on the couch again, and poured himself a drink. Ah, there was the cure! But he couldn't bring himself to taste it, remembering, like glass bells tinkling in the breeze, the drinks he and the Siamese girl had shared as a prelude to making love, twenty years ago, half a lifetime ago.

He could remember them all—all the wonderful erections, beginning with pretty Miss Ogburn in the sixth grade. How he'd lusted after Miss Ogburn! And later, the nudes in the photography books at the Oldfield library, until he was in high school and could buy girlie magazines over the counter. There'd been no shortage of erections in high school. There were hundreds of them, thousands, now gone forever, wasted beyond recall. If he could only bring one of them back again, only one!

Then it happened. Sluggishly at first, like sap beginning to run in the springtime, the blood began to stir. Boris howled. What a trick his body had played on him!—an hour late, and he'd never again have a chance like that.

He poured the drink into the sink, then washed the two glasses, his and Carol's.

~ ~ ~ ~

Toward evening, the telephone rang. It was Mr. Phipps, and Boris panicked that Carol had told her father about this afternoon. But it was only the matter of that interview with the Attorney General's man. "I've seen the transcript," Mr. Phipps said, "and it's worse than I expected. Boris, why did you *say* those things?"

"Somebody had to," Boris said.

"But not you! Boris, they'll release that transcript, and the *Manchester Union* will crucify you."

"I'm just a two-bit photographer."

"Oh, Boris, what an innocent you are!" There was a squeaky noise as Mr. Phipps lighted his pipe. "These people aren't looking for the truth. They already know the truth—that the University is full of liberal ideas—and they want to nail somebody, to make the rest of us watch our step. You happen to be what they've pushed up against. I'm afraid you're in for some nasty publicity."

"I don't care," Boris said. After the beating he had taken this afternoon, what would a little more embarrassment matter? "Do you want me to resign?"

"I didn't say that. But Boris, please understand my situation. My *daughter* was part of that demonstration. If I go to bat for you, they'll suspect my motives. No, what we've got to do is to put our house in order, as the man said. Ah. . . ."

"What?" Boris said, sniffing trouble.

"This woman who's living with you, Boris. And a former student! Do you realize how that will sound when the *Union* gets through with it?"

Boris felt sick. Would they actually drag Teddy and Nikolas into their nasty little plot? Sure they would. The bastards. "Don't sweat it, boss," he said. "I'll resign."

"You don't have to go that far, Boris. If you just get the girl out of town. . . ."

"No, I'll resign."

"Perhaps that *would* be the best thing, Boris. Mind you, I'd never ask it of you. . . ."

"But it would get everybody off the hook, right?"

"Well—yes. Yes, it would."

"Okay. Tell the business office to cash me in." Boris felt a sudden thrill of freedom, perilous but grand. "I'll clean my stuff out of the photo lab tomorrow."

"No, no," Mr. Phipps said. "A replacement won't be easy to find. If we have your resignation in hand, we can meet any

180

criticism as it arises. And perhaps it won't be necessary."

"How does the first of May strike you?"

"Could you make it a bit later? After graduation?"

"Okay. June 15."

"Good enough. . . . See you Monday," Mr. Phipps said, as if to be on the safe side.

Boris cradled the receiver, wondering if the afternoon had really happened. The walls of his world were falling away, one by one. First his manhood had forsaken him, then his job, two things that had always seemed so certain that he had never questioned them. And now they were gone.

Nor was that the end of it. When he went to the New Hampshire State Hospital on Sunday, they told him that his mother had died in her sleep on Friday night. "I thought she was getting better," Boris said. "Last time I was here, she was talking just as sane as we are."

"It often happens that way," the receptionist told him. She was a kindly woman with sharp, watchful eyes. "They're often most lucid just before they die. It's as if they don't need the old defenses anymore."

"But in *April*," Boris protested.

"That often happens, too," the receptionist said, smiling sympathetically while her watchful eyes scurried over his face, as if worried he'd make a scene. "We lose our old folks in the autumn because they can't face the thought of another winter, and in the spring, because they're worn out from getting through it."

They gave him a cardboard carton of her clothing and such, and the name of the funeral parlor that had taken the body. Boris removed the old wooden rosary beads and told the receptionist to give the rest to Rose, the gentle catatonic. Then he went to see the undertaker. He arranged to have his mother brought to Oldfield on Tuesday, by which time he could find a plot near his father's grave.

14 - A Man Must Do What He Must

AT TEN O'CLOCK, the sun climbed above the chimney pots and struck Colin in the face. Normally this was his alarm clock. But this morning he lay deliciously in bed with his eyes closed, a red glare in place of vision, and waited for the concierge's daughter to bring his breakfast. He would tumble her today—he swore it! At last he heard the elevator, a gaseous rumbling in the bowels of the hotel. It stopped, gasping, at his floor. Yes! He heard the sliding doors clang, then footsteps coming down the corridor toward his room. He rolled onto his side. Now his eyes were shielded from the sun, and Colin opened them.

Balls!

Rickover came into the room, tall and handsome and perfectly dressed, bearing the breakfast tray. "This is the big day, you sloth!" he cried, sliding the tray onto the bedside table. "Up, man, up!"

Colin subsided. He searched the floor with his left hand, located his shirt, and took a Marlboro from the breast pocket. Rickover lit it for him, and lit a stubby Gauloise for himself. The room soon smelled like a wet horse blanket. "After breakfast," Colin said. "I'll get up after breakfast."

Rick took a cane-bottomed chair from the corner and sat down on the other side of the breakfast tray. He poured coffee and hot milk from two silver jugs, one in each hand. Then he took a flaky crescent roll from the tray and bit into it. Colin did the same, and closed his eyes. His entire head seemed full of the warm pastry, crisp on the outside and angel-soft within, smelling like a bakery out of childhood. Then a sip of café au lait. Then a deep drag on his cigarette. "Late night, I suppose?" Rick said. "Try to bear in mind, Colin, that we are here on business."

Indeed, the Committee for Militant Pacifism had flown Colin from New York to Paris—fourteen hours in a Douglas

DC-7—with instructions to find Clayton Rickover, in charge of the march through the Continent. Rick's earlier helper had deserted, hitchhiking to Italy with a beautiful Polish refugee, and Colin had turned up in New York just as the Committee was looking for a replacement.

"The people from London are landing at Calais this afternoon," Rick said, reaching for the last pastry. He divided it, offered half to Colin, and popped both halves into his own mouth when Colin shook his head. "We'll keep this room for a few days," he went on. "How's your money holding out? All right? Good. . . . We may need the room because Pierre—you'll meet Pierre this morning—says that the authorities may not allow our group to enter the country."

"How can they stop us?"

"The French police have a lot of power, and they're terrified of Communists."

"We're not Communists!"

"Well, some of us are—Pierre's a Party member—but that's beside the point. We're pacifists, and that's bad enough. It's quite possible that our people won't be allowed to land." At the promise of action, Colin bounced out of bed. He dressed, put a change of socks and his toilet kit into the net bag he'd bought the other day, and followed Rickover down to the lobby. They took the stairs, since the elevator held only one passenger.

Pierre was a small, unkempt Frenchman with a perspiring face. He didn't speak English, so Rick chatted to them in turns. They crossed the city by taxi. Colin pressed his face to the window, loving the sidewalk cafes, the outdoor urinals like green pillboxes, the chestnut vendors at their carts, the tiny automobiles with canvas roofs, the policemen in their squat caps—and the girls! Especially he loved the girls. They walked with more grace than any women he'd ever seen, and their bodies were softer, more finely proportioned; every one of them looked she was the mistress of a duke.

"Pierre says: you should find yourself a nice French girl." Rickover translated this sentence in a dry, ironical voice. "He says that she will put her tongue into your mouth and teach you to speak French."

Well, what could you expect from a Communist?

The boat train was electrified. It hurled itself out of the Gare du Nord like a stone from a catapult, stopped at wayside stations with a violence that tumbled suitcases from the overhead racks, and was off again before anybody could complain. They sat in a second-class compartment with three French soldiers and a doe-eyed girl who read a book without once lifting her long lashes at Colin. He nudged her foot, as a test, but she ignored him, so he turned to the food Pierre had brought along. There was a loaf of uncut bread, a hunk of cheese in white paper, and a bottle of cheap red wine. By the time they finished eating, the train was hurtling to a stop at Calais Maritime. Beyond the station and the hurrying flocks of people, Colin saw the fat flank of a channel steamer.

This turned out to be the departing ferry, bound for Dover, so Rickover led them to the snack bar for coffee and a last-minute briefing. Pierre kept slapping his oily forehead and jumping up to telephone yet another friend in the press corps. By two o'clock, when next steamer was due, they'd been joined by three French reporters. The newspapermen wore black business suits with wide, sloping shoulders, and each carried a small twin-lens camera like the one Boris had used, that day in Narwich.

At two-fifteen, a boat's whistle called them out of the cafeteria. The incoming steamer was passing the breakwater, entering the harbor's calm embrace. Tiny figures on the foredeck waved handkerchiefs to other figures, equally tiny, standing on the breakwater. The ferry was as long as a football field, with a dark hull, white topsides, and a red and black funnel. Colin finished his cigarette before it heaved up against the dock and he could read the name on the bow: *Invicta*. The gangways were run out and the first-class passengers came ashore. They filed directly into the customs shed.

"We'll stay out here," Rick said. "We can go inside if our

people are permitted to land. If they're not!—we're better off on the dock." He repeated this logic in French for Pierre and the reporters. By comparing Rickover's translations, Colin was beginning to pick up a basic French vocabulary—*ici* for *here*, and so on. Another week and he'd speak the language well enough for most purposes, like seducing the concierge's daughter.

The second-class passengers were coming down the gangway now, and he could make out a knot of angry young men near the bow. They were arguing with three uniformed French officials. "They're not to land!" Rick said. He spoke rapidly in French, and Pierre turned and went toward the customs shed at a plump-hipped run, his shoes squeaking on the dock. "They're not to land," Rick repeated. "Oh, the silly French!"

At the ferryboat's stern, Colin saw another group, three young men and two laughing British sailors. While the crewmen watched from the rails, one of the young men swung out and straddled the cable that stretched from the boat to a capstan on the dock. He was blond and crew-cut, barefoot, dressed in shorts and a checkered flannel shirt. Gawkers materialized on the boat and ashore. One of the French immigration people rushed to the stern, shoved the onlookers aside, and began to shout and wave his fist at the young man on the cable. A crowd had gathered at the capstan that was his goal. Rickover and Colin ran along the dock to join them, ducking under the gangway, as did two or three policemen from the customs shed. "Jump!" Rick yelled. "Swim for it!"

The young man hesitated. Seeing the policemen, he nodded, then clumsily lowered himself until he was hanging by his hands from the cable, twenty feet above the water. Ah!—he dropped. He hit the water with a tremendous splash, but immediately bobbed to the surface and began to swim on a line parallel with the dock. The newspapermen kept pace with him, snapping photographs.

Now his friends jumped ship, one diving cleanly into the water, the other hanging for a moment from the rail before getting up the courage to drop. He fell close to the steamer's side, hit a projecting porthole cover, and tumbled outward to hit the water on his back. A murmur rose from the crowd. But the young man came to the surface, spitting, and began to swim toward shore. "Marvelous," said Rickover. "Come on!" he yelled at the pacifists remaining on the boat. Then he was gone, running toward the bow, to encourage those still arguing with the immigration officials.

Colin would help the swimmers. He ran along the dock, which stood too high above the water for them to climb. The dock was now crowded with running people. Over his shoulder Colin saw other pacifists diving from the boat and hitting the water with varying degrees of skill. A hot joy burned in his face. What a day, what a ball! After a hundred yards or so, Colin came to the end of the dock. Here was a concrete ramp where two or three fishing boats were drawn out of the water, as if for repairs: this was where the swimmers would come ashore. He skirted the edge of the dock and walked down to the ramp. A crowd soon built up behind him, smelling of seaweed and sweat and French cigarettes; he stood in the sun with his heart pounding.

Two swimmers came in sight. "Over here!" Colin shouted, making a megaphone of his hands. They were the pair who'd jumped from the stern. They came out of the sea like two Vikings, streaming water and grinning. One was lean and Yankee-seeming; the other, the injured one, was huskier and sported a short brown beard. Colin went to shake hands but wound up hugging them instead.

"How did you get ashore?" the bearded one asked, looking at Colin's dry shoes.

"I was here already," Colin said. He propelled them up the ramp. "Three of us came down from Paris to meet you."

The crowd of Frenchmen, mostly workers in berets and coarse blue jackets, parted to let them through. Then the breech suddenly widened and a policeman marched through from the other side. "*Allo!*" the policeman shouted.

"Howdy," said the Yankee type.

The policeman was small, no taller than Colin, but swarthy and hard-eyed. He carried a long riot stick that he pointed at Colin's belly. "I guess we're under arrest," the bearded pacifist said. He was holding his left arm; the shirt was torn and a trickle of diluted blood was running down. "Hey," he said to the policeman. "You got a first aid kit?"

"*Marchons!*" the policeman replied.

They walked three abreast, with the policeman behind them, up the ramp and along the dock. The crowd followed, and it was growing in size. Finally the policeman shifted his position so that Colin and the two swimmers were between him and the crowd, a precaution that obliged him to walk close to the edge of the dock.

"Hey," said the bearded swimmer. "Let's push him off."

"Just cut out and run!" said the Yankee. "He can't catch us all." He sprinted forward. His comrade hesitated, then turned and ran toward town, on a path that would take him past the customs shed. The crowd cheered him. Some of the workers, tough young men, began to taunt the policeman. He grabbed Colin's right arm and turned him to face the crowd. Son of a bitch! Colin put his right foot behind the policeman's and jerked his own arm back. He was free! And the policeman was off balance, reeling at the edge of the dock, and a young tough pushed him over. The splash was spectacular. The policeman came to the surface still clutching his riot stick, and struck out to capture his uniform cap, which was floating beside some orange peels a few yards away.

What a ball!

Colin ran back toward the ship. Just as he burst from under the gangway, he came up against more blue uniforms and red-trimmed caps: they were holding the bearded swimmer. The police were careful not to wet their uniforms, holding the pacifist's arms behind his back and twisting them upward, ignoring the blood that was dripping from his elbow. Then one of them grabbed Colin. "I was here already," Colin protested, "*Ici!* I was *ici.*" He showed his passport with the entry stamp at Orly airport. After a conference, they released him. Colin winked at the bearded pacifist and dodged into the crowd.

People were surging across the dock. Some taunted the police and others insulted the pacifists, and a third group, which seemed to consist of students, was singing an anthem beneath a sign in English: NO A-BOMB! A few fights were in progress. Through it all, however, the police were winning. Colin counted six pacifists, dripping wet, being dragged up the gangway, back to the boat.

~ ~ ~ ~

In town, things were quieter, although a great many people were talking excitedly and moving toward the docks. Then a chubby Frenchman emerged from a cafe and grabbed Colin's arm. Pierre! He was glistening with sweat and excitement, and he poured long French sentences into Colin's ear, urging him into the cafe. Three dock workers were crouched over drinks at a table by the window, and another man was sitting alone near the bar. He was wrapped in a blanket that he held together at his throat; a pool of water was collecting beneath the table. There was something familiar about the face, despite the gloom and the straggling wet hair that shielded it. Colin went over and found himself looking into the mournful eyes of Marvin Peabody.

Ah, Narwich! The trees would be lemon-green with new buds, and Teddy would be there, and his own fat blue-eyed son. Suddenly, desperately, Colin wanted to go home. "How's everybody in Narwich?" he asked.

"Well, Colin, what luck!" Marvin said. A pudgy white hand emerged from the blanket. "Just the man I wanted to see."

"How's Teddy?"

"She's fine, they're all fine," Marvin said. "Teddy has filed suit for a divorce, as you probably know. But tell me —"

"No! Did she really?" As if in a dream, Colin saw her small figure slipping away from him. "I suppose I had it coming,

188

walking out on her like that," he said.

"A man must do what he must do."

Colin winced. He'd said the same thing to Teddy, last month in Narwich. He was glad he'd missed with the concierge's daughter. He wouldn't want Teddy's divorce to be justified by anything he did on the road to Moscow. But of course he had already betrayed her, with Prudence, and he'd betrayed Marvin also, who had been his friend at the time.

Colin sat down beside his former friend and ordered a hot chocolate from the waiter, an evil pirate with hairy arms and a dirty apron. Pierre sat down also. He seemed puzzled that the Americans knew each other. "How's Prudence?" Colin asked. "How's—the baby?"

"Both doing fine," Marvin said. "She and Teddy are planning to move in together, find jobs, you know, and divide the housekeeping chores."

Colin was relieved that Teddy was moving out of the Hut, but wasn't sure if he wanted the women living together. They might share confidences as well as the housekeeping.

Shivering occasionally, Marvin told him how the University had disgraced itself, and how he'd decided to join the march to Moscow. He'd flown to London, taken part in a Ban-the-Bomb demonstration, and walked to Dover with the main body. He'd seen Bertrand Russell! "Marvelous," he said. "The British are years ahead of us, Colin. Pacifism is quite acceptable there, like being a Democrat in New Hampshire, not popular but acceptable, especially among the educated classes. I'm delighted to have this chance to investigate the peace movement in Europe. Odd how things work out, isn't it? A month ago nothing seemed more important to me than finishing my thesis. But now. . . ." He flicked his fingers at the insignificance of scholarly research.

"Marvin," said Colin, "anything you do will always seem the best thing to do."

~ ~ ~ ~

Toward four o'clock, a young Frenchman in tight pants and

turtle-neck sweater—a student, Colin supposed—rushed into the cafe. After a joyful reunion with Pierre, he led them through the rear door and along a succession of streets and alleys. Eventually they arrived at a cheap hotel. The young man led them up to the top floor and into a room that was already full: people sitting on the bed, the floor, and the windowsill, with a bottle of wine going from hand to hand. The window was open from the top. Over it was draped an assortment of wet garments, including a brassiere. Colin skimmed the room and found two girls in the crowd, both pretty. One was wrapped in a blanket. Big brown eyes.

"Here's another!" shouted Rickover from the bed. "And you, Colin!—I thought you'd been deported with the rest."

Colin introduced Rick to Marvin, and in turn was introduced to a bewildering number of Americans, British, and French. Only four of them had jumped ship; the others were local pacifists, sympathizers down from Paris, or passengers caught up in the excitement. The girl in the blanket was Ursula. She was a bit on the heavy side, but she had a pretty, gamine face, out of which two spaniel-brown eyes gazed intensely at Colin. "This is my apprentice," Rick said to the group. He was standing now, with his hand on Colin's shoulder. "I'm afraid he has a lot to learn. In the middle of our demonstration this afternoon, while the eyes of the world were upon us to learn the principles of nonviolent resistance, *this one*," he roared, putting an arm around Colin, "threw a gendarme into the harbor!"

Colin didn't point out that it was actually one of the locals who'd pushed the policeman off the dock.

Rickover would set up a new headquarters at this hotel, with most of the new arrivals staying with him. They'd wait for the main group to attempt a second landing tomorrow. Meanwhile Colin would return to Paris and finish the work they had begun, with Pierre to help. Colin did not especially like the idea of working with Pierre, but it seemed that the Frenchman had a friend on the government-owned television network who could arrange an interview with one of the newcomers. "My French isn't *fluent*," Marvin Peabody said, "but I daresay it would serve."

Colin sat down beside Ursula. "How's yours?" he asked.

"I beg your pardon?" she said, the brown eyes huge.

"Do you speak French?"

"Oh, yes," she said. The voice was nice, with a husky quality that perhaps came from too many cigarettes. "I majored in French at Berkeley."

"Here's your TV star," Colin shouted to Rick, avoiding Marvin's eyes. "Here's a lovely young student to melt their Gallic hearts."

Rick smiled with his fine white teeth. "All things considered," he said; "*all* things considered, I think it would be to everybody's advantage if Ursula went to Paris with my young apprentice. Yes." He nodded over his private joke.

Ursula smiled at Colin: from strangers, they'd become accomplices. He wondered what she looked like beneath the blanket—plump, no doubt, with broad hips and big breasts. And a fulsome vagina, probably. No matter! He grabbed the wine bottle on its rounds and toasted her brown eyes with it. "To Paris!" he said.

They would take the six o'clock train, which was a local, not the electrified *Fléche d'Or*. Rickover went with them to the station, giving Colin last-minute instructions, while Pierre and Ursula walked ahead. She had borrowed a white shirt and a pair of jeans from one of the French students. The shirttails were knotted in front, exposing the small of her back, smooth and tanned and unbearably sexy. "I'll send you a telegram confirming my address here," Rickover said, guiding Colin by the elbow. "It will reach Paris before you do. Keep yourself available, recruit as many marchers as you can, and help Pierre with any scheme that seems worthwhile. With luck, the main group will be on the road to Paris in a day or two."

"What if they're turned back tomorrow?"

"No problem. They'll just land at Ostend the day after. In

191

any event, you can figure on having seven or eight days before we reach Paris. Please devote *some* of them to business."

Pierre and the girl had reached the downtown railroad station. Colin had loaned Ursula his net bag. She carried it loose in her right hand, sodden and heavy with the garments that had been draped across the window. With any luck, he'd be there to help, when she dressed herself in them again.

15 - A Jolly Good Fellow

THE LETTER FROM PARIS arrived on Saturday, which mean that Boris was there for the excitement. It was the twenty-second of April—his birthday! The woods were speckled green and yellow; the sun was brassy-hot in a deep blue sky and glittered off the corrugated steel shell of the Hut. He had been enjoying the lusty morning, sitting on the front step while his harem did the housework, and wondering if it were true that he was forty years old. Then the mailman came, bringing Boris his bank statement, a bill from the Douglass Funeral Parlor, and an airmail flimsy addressed to Prudy. Some birthday presents! Boris flipped through the sheaf of canceled checks but didn't see the one he'd made out to Carol Phipps.

He called Prudy. She was ecstatic, fumbling at the blue aerogram until Boris wanted to snatch it from her. Teddy came out, wiping her hands on her apron, equally excited. Boris lit a cigarette and paced the yard, though staying within earshot.

"*Reached London,*" Prudy recited, reading the highlights. "*I shook hands with Bertrand Russell. . . . Rumor that de Gaulle wouldn't let us land in the Fifth Republic. . . . Oh!*" Prudy's dark face burned with pride. "You'll never guess what Marvie did—he jumped ship and swam ashore!" She dashed into the Hut, dragged out the young Peabody, and sat him on the step to hear his father's adventures. She read this part in full. "Oh, and Teddy!" she cried then. "He's seen Colin." Boris looked up to see how Teddy had taken it. Her eyes were wide open and her lips were parted, but half hidden by the fingers of her right hand. "Listen to this," Prudy said. "*I was sitting in a cafe tabac, whilst the gendarmes were combing the waterfront for me, when who should walk in but Colin Merchant. He had flown to Paris to work with Clayton Rickover, that annoying young man from Harvard. Looked fine, but I fear*"

193

that our Colin has absorbed some of Rickover's pretensions. Well, the rest is about the hotel where he's staying."

Prudence and Teddy looked at each other. For a moment Boris thought Teddy would snatch the flimsy from the other girl's hand. "Hey," he said, to break it up. "Are we going to eat?"

Teddy bit her lip and went into the Hut: lunch was her responsibility. Prudy sat down on the step beside the young Peabody and read Marvin's letter over again in silence. Boris leaned against the Volkswagen and admired her round, tanned knees. Far down the road, the day was annoyed by the sound of a sports car going through gears, whining like an angry insect. That would be Georgie. "Daddy is way, way across the sea," Prudy said to her son, in a voice as clear and sweet as the child's. "He's gone to a country called France, where the men wear little cloth caps called berets and people drink wine instead of milk."

"Will he come home soon?" the young Peabody asked.

"Oh, yes—soon." Prudy looked at Boris and dared him to call her a liar. "Meanwhile," she said, "we have Uncle Boris to look after us."

"Can I have some wine?" the boy said to Boris. "Can I?"

They had moved to the Hut two weeks ago. The original plan was for Teddy to move into the Peabody apartment with Prudence, but Boris convinced them that they could all save money by living at the Hut. And they did, of course. They arranged a split shift at the Coffee Corner, with Teddy working from one o'clock to six, and Prudy from six to eleven. While one worked the other took care of the children. They did the household chores in the morning; Teddy prepared lunch and Prudy cooked the evening meal. The system ran with appalling efficiency. Fortunately the season was turning around to summer and Boris could spend Saturday outdoors, safe from all that efficiency. The other days weren't so bad. During the week he ran the photo lab, Prudy was away all evening, and the children mostly slept; and on Sunday everybody rested for a fresh bout of efficiency on Monday.

The buzzing of Georgie's roadster came steadily closer. Finally the little car rocketed around the corner and turned into the yard, spitting gravel like the spray from a turning speedboat. Georgie killed the engine. He seemed sorry to be at rest; he sagged, as if some previous gloom had caught up with him and settled again on his shoulders. "Hi, Boris," he said listlessly. "Hi, Prudy. Is Teddy home?" He walked into the Hut without waiting for an invitation, and the young Peabody, who for some reason had become devoted to Georgie, trotted after him upon fat legs.

Boris went over and sat down beside Prudence. The concrete was too hard for comfort, so he moved to the other side of her, where he could hunker with his back against the sun-warmed metal of the Hut. He patted the firm contour of her thigh. "Nice leg you got there," he said. "You'll have to pose for me sometime."

Prudy sniffed, but she was pleased. And it was true: now that Mary Margaret Peabody was sleeping in the bedroom instead of inside her belly, Prudence looked as trim as a college girl. Boris had forgotten what an attractive bitch she was. He told her so. "Hah!" she said. "You should see my bruises. My tummy is all over black-and-blue."

"Bruises go away," Boris said. "Why don't we take a few pictures this afternoon, to give us an idea of what we're working with? I won't print them. They'll just be guidelines, you know."

Prudy sighted across the top of her precious letter. "In the first place, you old billygoat, I haven't said that I would pose for you, bruises or no bruises, and in the second place I don't have time to talk to you all morning. Now clear out and let me finish my letter." Boris patted her knee, warm from the sun, and went inside to see how the others were making out.

There was a crisis after lunch. Baby Nikolas came up soiled just as Teddy was leaving for work, and she panicked, torn between mother love and her job. After a lot of fuss Georgie drove her to the Coffee Corner, Prudence changed the diaper, and Boris went off to walk in College Woods. Some birthday!

~ ~ ~ ~

When he returned to the Hut, he found that Prudy had company. O'Rourke was sprawled in the armchair, drinking a bottle of beer and dribbling cigarette ashes upon the rug, which Teddy had vacuumed that morning. His briefcase sat on the floor beside him like a pet dog. "Does the P.T.A. know you're in town?" Boris asked. "Have the Girl Scouts been warned?"

O'Rourke shook his head. It wasn't as gaunt as before, that bony face, thanks to two months on home-cooked food. "You laugh!" he cried, striking his chest with his free hand, meanwhile peering at Boris. "You mock this tortured soul, so pure it must find ease in the rosebud skin of puberty—ah, Boris, you have no heart! As a matter of fact," he added, "I have a job."

O'Rourke had been hired to direct a summer theater on the seacoast. It was a new venture, and he would spend the month of May in Narwich to recruit actors and stagehands. "Oh!" Prudy cried. "I used to do costume design for the University theater. Do you have a job for me?"

"Design?" O'Rourke said. "*Costume* design? My dear girl, you are not a designer—you are an *actress*!"

"Do you think so?"

"Is this outfit going to pay you a salary?" Boris asked.

"We divide the profits," O'Rourke said. "Never fear, my friend, under my direction the Yankee Players cannot fail. I have here. . . ." He drew a sheaf of papers from his briefcase, the outer sheets stained from the salami sandwich his mother had packed for him. It seemed that O'Rourke also planned to write the plays he would direct. He read some dialogue to Prudy, who was enchanted.

"Which role would I have?" she asked.

Boris meanwhile called Georgie at the Italian sandwich shop and told him to expect an overnight guest. There was no room for O'Rourke at the Hut.

196

Prudence had the evening off, for some reason, and Georgie came by to inspect his lodger. Then Hal Pappajohn dropped in, looking belligerent. There was a secret in the air, and Teddy was at the center of it: her eyes were bright and her cheeks were flushed. Georgie's eyes followed her wherever she went. Boris felt a surge of panic. What if he had missed something? Were they about to announce their engagement? When the party seemed ready to burst from tension, Teddy went into the bedroom and closed the door. Boris wanted to hit somebody. What were they hiding from him?

She reappeared with a birthday cake in her hands. It had green and white frosting, and four candles that gleamed in her eyes. The sweetheart! Boris wanted to cry; and Teddy, the cake, and the heart-shaped flames all blurred and mingled together. How long had she been planning this?

They made him blow out the candles and listen to the Happy Birthday song and cut the cake, while they sang "For He's a Jolly Good Fellow." Even Hal Pappajohn joined the singing; he kept glaring left and right, as if threatening anybody who might remember that he had sung birthday greetings to Boris. Only O'Rourke was above it all. He was slouched in the armchair with his eyes fastened on Prudence Peabody. She sat on the couch with Hal. Each drink brought them closer together while O'Rourke watched with his black, glittering eyes. He looks like a hawk, Boris thought. No: he looks like me. Didn't Marvin Peabody mistake us for brothers? "Speech!" cried Georgie at the end of the song.

"Yes," said Teddy, clapping her hands. "Make us a speech, Boris."

How good his name sounded on her lips! "Well," he said, and paused to clear his throat. "Well, I just hope I meet such fine people during the next forty years." He looked at Teddy when he said it, and her eyes were gray and marvelous: they almost loved him. Boris felt that he had taken a big step. He wanted to add something even more revealing, to lay out his heart in front of them all, who had given him a birthday party. But his mind was dry.

Luckily the young Peabody tottered into the room at that moment, rubbing his eyes. Prudence jumped up from the couch and fussed over him, her dark cheeks flaming with love, or guilt. She gave the child a piece of cake, kissed him, and sent him back to bed. Then she sat down on the couch again, but at a safe distance from Hal Pappajohn. "It doesn't seem the same without Carol," Teddy suddenly said.

They all looked at Hal. "Yeah," he said. He hunched slightly, like a boxer protecting his stomach.

"Have you heard from her?" Teddy insisted.

"She's in Boston," Hal said, crouching deeper into himself. He glared at Teddy, but she was determined to needle him.

"Do you know her address?" she asked.

"I guess I could find out if I wanted to."

"Oh, Hal! Of course you *want* to."

"If I ran after Carol now," he said, "it would be the same as a proposal. Can you feature me as a husband?"

"You'd make a fine husband!"

Boris stood up. Each time they said Carol's name, the syllables rang sourly on his memory, like notes on a broken bell. If only he could hate Hal Pappajohn! Carol was pregnant by him, Prudy wanted to sleep with him, and Teddy probably envied them both. But Hal was a big, friendly police dog of a man, falling all over himself with strength—who could hate him? So Boris went out for a walk. The evening was warm and bright, with half a moon that enabled him to find his way easily between the trees. How many loving couples were lying in College Woods tonight?

When he returned to the Hut, they were deciding Georgie's future. "I don't know," he said. "What's the use? I've lost a semester of school and today I got a letter from Nova Scotia, and if I don't get my degree in June, they'll break my contract. . . . I don't know. I'm twenty-two years old, and I'm

198

going nowhere."

"You're just feeling blue," Teddy said. "Things will look better in a few days, you'll see."

"Maybe, but that won't change the fact that I'm twenty-two years old and not qualified to teach math at a country school in Canada. I can't sell Italian sandwiches all my life! I couldn't support a wife that way, let alone any children." They all looked at Teddy, as earlier they had looked at Hal. She tried to smile.

O'Rourke plunged into the silence. Gazing at the ceiling, he said in a hollow, prophetic tone: "All this searching, searching—it's a waste of time, my young friend. You desire a meaning for life? You require a goal? Well, you can stop searching, because it's right there in front of you."

"Where?" said Georgie.

O'Rourke abandoned his study of the ceiling and once more stared at Prudence. Hal Pappajohn, meanwhile, slipped off the couch and sat on the floor at her feet, with his shaggy head resting against her thigh.

"The meaning of life," O'Rourke said in a gloomy voice, "is . . . life."

Prudy jumped to her feet. "Then you haven't *said* anything," she protested.

O'Rourke nodded, pleased that he had hooked Prudence. "All great ideas are simple," he conceded. "Usually they are just new ways of looking at old problems. Copernicus, for example. . . ."

"You're saying a thing is the same thing as itself," Prudy said, sitting down. She missed the couch and slid to the floor beside Hal, who put his arm around her. "It's a, it's a. . . ."

"Tautology?"

"Yes."

"The basic problem remains, that's true," O'Rourke said. "There are many different ways to fill out the moments of life, and no doubt some are better than others. That's where your confusion arises, my friend—George? Yes: George. You have

199

simply asked the wrong question. Life doesn't go anywhere, so it can't have a goal, can it?"

"But," said Georgie.

"Life is not a vehicle," O'Rourke said grandly. "It is an *instrument*."

"But. . . ."

"Astonishing how many problems vanish when you stop searching for the answer and look at the question instead."

Hal Pappajohn clapped his hands. His left arm was around Prudy, and the applause jostled her breasts. She melted against him, her eyes glowing and out of focus. "Jesus, you're smart," he said to O'Rourke. "It must hurt to be so smart. Tell me—are you happy?"

O'Rourke twitched. "Me?" he said. "I am a wise man, a prophet. Wise men are never happy. Isn't that right, Boris?"

"How would I know?" Boris asked. "I'm no wise man."

"Oh, but you are!" O'Rourke cried.

This too made Hal angry. "Then who the hell wants to be a wise man?" he demanded.

"Nobody! We just can't help it."

"Balls," said Hal, still angry. "I know what Georgie should do. This guy I'm working with, Gene Breck? He runs a foreign car shop in Maine." He was talking to Georgie now, and he shifted his body so that Prudence was sitting between his legs. She was feverish at the arms and legs that were clasping her. "We've talked some hotshots at the University into sponsoring time trials in a couple weeks, and we've got a car that we're going to enter. And Breck knows some guys at Harvard and Boston University and so on. You've got a car, Georgie. Enter it! Jesus, man, that's the cure for the blues—action! *Do* something, keep moving, make a big yell! Don't listen to this bird," he said, jerking his head at O'Rourke.

"Gee, I never thought of racing my car."

"Why not?" Hal said.

"Don't you *dare!*" cried Teddy, who was sitting on the arm of the couch, out of the brightest circle of light. "You'll be

200

killed, racing against people like that."

Georgie lifted his head proudly. "I can manage," he said.

"Stout fella!" said Hal. "Let's drink to it."

Boris mixed another round of drinks, but when he returned to the couch he found that only Georgie and Teddy were still active.

"Prudy felt woozy," Georgie explained. "So Hal took her out to get some fresh air." O'Rourke, now that the conversation had moved elsewhere, was asleep in the armchair. Teddy also was not drinking: she was angry at Georgie, who looked sadly at the tray of drinks. "No, thanks," he said, shaking his head. "It's getting late. I'd better mosey on home."

"Well, take that carcass with you," Boris said. Together they shook O'Rourke half awake, then walked him out to the roadster and wedged him into the passenger seat. Georgie got behind the wheel. Boris released O'Rourke, whose head lolled about and finally came to rest on Georgie's shoulder. In this fashion they drove off into the night. Boris listened for a while after the snarling motor had faded in the distance, but he heard no sound of Prudence and Hal, so he went back to the Hut.

Teddy was tidying up from the party. "All that *talk*," she sighed. "I have a headache coming on." She was restless, prowling around the room in search of more dishes. "It's very strange," she said. "I never felt better in my life, yet I get headaches so easily."

"We'll make an appointment with the Doc."

Teddy went to the kitchen alcove, to heat milk in a saucepan. Baby Nikolas was on the bottle now. "Poor Tommy," she said then. "What if he wakes up and wants to know where his mother is? He's four years old; he's old enough to remember. . . . And his mother is out in the woods with a man who isn't his father." Was she jealous? "Sometimes I lie awake at night, wondering what's going to happen to me," Teddy said. "Will it be Hal Pappajohn? Or somebody like him? Someday it's going to happen, Boris, I know it; someday a man is going to ask me out and I'll say Yes and we'll end up in bed; I know it. Why else would a man date a divorcee?"

"Because you're pretty, you're young!"

"Thank you," she said. The milk was steaming in the saucepan. She went to the stove and turned off the burner, scorching her fingers in the process. "Damn!" she said. Shaking her fingers to cool them, she used the other hand to pour milk into a baby bottle from the row that stood on the counter. Then she capped the bottle and shook a drop of milk upon her wrist; the gesture, so easy and motherly, made Boris tremble with love. She was indeed young—and pretty! Her cheeks flushed with warmth, Teddy filled another bottle. There were two infants now. Mary Margaret Peabody had come home from the hospital last week; she weighed six pounds and slept in the crib with Nicholas. Teddy poured the remaining milk into a glass and colored it with chocolate syrup in case the young Peabody woke up. "Oh, I don't know," she said when she was done. "I'm no bargain, God knows, but I suppose I'm pretty enough that a lot of men would be willing to take me to bed. Especially since I'd be so easy—a divorcee and all. . . . Here, take the glass."

Boris did so, aching for words to comfort her and finding none. They went into the darkened bedroom. The young Peabody was asleep in the big bed, which once had belonged to Boris, more recently to Teddy; now Prudence shared it with the boy. There was a new cot against the wall where Teddy slept, and the crib beneath the window. The room had an overpowering sweetness to it—talcum powder and cosmetics and diapers and windows closed against the night air.

They sat on the edge of the bed. The young Peabody was restless, and Teddy stroked his rumpled hair—black like his father's—while Boris fed the baby. Nikolas sucked happily at the bottle. Boris felt a rush of pity for him, that little bundle of warmth, who was so pleased with his artificial nipple. How easily he was fooled! What chance would he have against the more subtle trickeries of life?

"Someday," Teddy whispered, "I'll go to bed with one of them. It's bound to happen. I'll have an affair with one of them, and eventually he'll find some prissy little virgin to fall in love with, then it's goodbye, Mrs. Merchant, and thanks for the lay. . . ."

"Shut up!" Boris said, also whispering.

"Why shouldn't I say it, since it's true? I'll howl and moan and in six months I'll be in bed with a different man, and each time it will be easier; each time there'll be less pretense of love. . . . Oh, Boris! I don't want to be a tramp. I don't want my little boy to wake up at night and not find me because I'm out in the woods with Hal Pappajohn."

"You'll get married."

"Who'd marry me, no education and a ready-made family? What kind of a dowry is that?"

"Plenty of men would be proud to marry you."

"Do you really think so?" Baby Nikolas hiccuped, and Teddy took him from Boris. "I feel like a cheat," she said, "putting him on the bottle so early." She cradled the baby against her shoulder and burped him. "But I'm not doing it because I'm lazy. I did love to nurse him, my little man, but my milk dried up. . . . And there's something to be said for it," she added, gazing through the night-blackened window. "At least I'll be having my periods again. I'll be a woman again."

16 - *Georgie, You're a Winner!*

TOM MATTHEWS WANTED photos of the sports-car race, so Boris phoned the *Sunday Advertiser* in Boston. He needed more outlets, if he was to support his harem as a free lance photographer. The city editor told him to send down a crash picture by the Saturday evening bus. "An injury is okay, if it's messy enough, but a fatality is best," the man told him. "Get some Massachusetts people in the picture if you can."

"I'll see what I can do," Boris promised.

Teddy was having no success in keeping Georgie out of the race. Every day, he was out on the back roads around Narwich, withering the lilacs with his exhaust. Evenings he spent with Hal Pappajohn, tinkering with the engine. Teddy refused to talk to him, but on Saturday morning she was in a fever of excitement to see him win. "We'll all go!" she cried. "I'll tell them at the Coffee Corner that I'm sick; we'll make a picnic lunch and spend the day."

"I'll be working," Boris pointed out.

"We won't be in your way, you'll see!"

It was the second week of May, and Saturday was hot with the breath of summer. Boris waited outside the Hut and smelled the sun upon the pines, the lilacs, and the asphalt road that ran to Georgie's trailer. He looked at his watch: ten o'clock! The first trial heat had been scheduled for nine, and still the women weren't ready. Boris went inside. There was a crisis in progress, because Prudence had dressed her son in short pants; he was shrieking and pulling off his shirt, shoes, and underwear. Prudy followed him around the living room, dressing him again, while Teddy calmed the babies. "All *right!*" cried Prudy at last. "Go get your damned jeans. . . . Oh, Jesus," she said when the boy had trotted into the bedroom. "I love him, but! He's too much for me to understand."

The boy returned with his trousers of blue denim. Boris

recognized Marvin Peabody in the little face: stubborn, persuasive, and absolutely right. "Put them on!" he demanded, and Prudence knelt to obey.

They were ready at half-past ten. Boris carried the picnic basket and a satchel full of baby gear, the women shouldered their infants, and the young Peabody lugged a favorite stuffed lion. He wanted to ride in front. Boris said no, but the boy howled and Prudence begged for peace, so the women and the babies squeezed into the rear seat, and the young Peabody had his way.

"Boris!" Teddy wailed just before they reached the main road. "Please stop for a minute." She scrambled out of the car and was sick in the bushes. "I don't know what's the matter with me," she said when they were underway again. "I was sick the other morning, too."

"We'll get you to Doc Perkins," Boris said.

"I know what he'll say," Prudy said.

"Prudy!"

"Well, it looks mighty peculiar to me. Morning sickness, bright cheeks, all the food you've been eating. . . ."

"I'm not!" Teddy cried. "I can't be!"

Surely she would know. Boris tried to turn around, but now he was on the main road and the traffic was heavy. But he knew by her voice that she was telling the truth. She wasn't pregnant. She couldn't be. Women knew these things, didn't they?

The trials were at the experimental farm, a vast tract of field and forest and dirt roads, west of the village. The sponsors had strung a banner across the highway between two telephone poles:

FIRST ANNUAL NARWICH GRAND PRIX

Automobiles were parked two deep along the road. Low-slung sports cars flashed up and down the highway, and others turned into the side road that led to the horticultural farm. Boris followed a fat Corvette down this road, displaying a

Press sticker on his sunshade. The Detroit convertible was turned back by a campus cop; Boris was waved through. He drove as far as he could go, until he was stopped by a glittering wall of parked cars, including a Jeep with a sheet-metal body and a red gum-ball machine on top. "Ambulance," he said, pointing to the Jeep.

"Oh, dear," said Teddy.

They climbed out of the Volkswagen, and Prudy and Teddy debated what to do with the children. "Let's take them with us for now," Teddy said. "When we're tired of carrying them around, we'll bring them back to the car and take turns baby-sitting."

Boris checked his cameras. He had the Leica with the telephoto lens for action shots, and the Rolleiflex for close work. He saw Teddy wrapping Baby Nikolas in a blanket. How beautiful she was!—flushed with motherhood, eyes sparkling and her imperfect mouth opening in a smile. He framed her face in the reflex viewer and took the picture. Then he slung the Rollei on his left side, the Leica on his right, and stuffed his pockets with film, filters, and his exposure meter. "All set," he said.

They tacked between parked automobiles and joined the line of spectators. A chubby red car was on the starting line, the driver's head framed by a roll-over bar; beyond him the starter was snapping a checkered flag back and forth. The driver raced his engine with each snap of the flag, until the little car was throbbing from the torque, faster and faster. Then the flag whipped all the way down. The roadster leaped forward, its front tires lifting off the pavement for a moment. It roared straight for the grassy triangle where the road turned left, and where a policeman was standing with a cluster of spectators. Like a red bomb, the car hurtled toward them until the last possible moment, then *downshift—hard left*—and it vanished over a rise and down the slope beyond. Boris heard the car shift again, then squealing tires and a rising whine from the motor, then finally the last shift into top gear. The motor faded in the direction of the reservoir.

Another car was ready at the starting line. A hard-faced young man spoke into a field telephone, then nodded at the starter. Again the business with the checkered flag, the squealing start, and the rush toward the island where the spectators watched. This driver made a bad business of the corner. He went into the turn too fast, and his tail lights flashed red. The telephone operator and the starter grinned at one another. "I don't understand," Teddy said. "How can it be a race if the cars go one at a time?"

"Time trials," a young man told her. "Guy on the telephone gives the word when the flag goes down, and they start a clock at the other end. They're racing against the clock, not against each other."

"Aren't we all?" Boris said. "C'mon," he said to Teddy and Prudence. "Let's find Georgie." He led them through the crowd, over a fence, and into the western pasture where sports cars grazed like mechanical sheep. Most were foreign-built, sparsely elegant, but there were a few Corvettes and Thunderbirds, and a homemade job that looked like an overgrown soapbox racer. He saw Georgie's little white car near the fence with its hood gaping open, like a crocodile that was in the process of swallowing Hal Pappajohn.

"There he is!" Teddy cried, pointing to a huddle nearby. Most were wearing loose gray coveralls splotched with grease. They were listening to a pep talk by a man who seemed older and dirtier than the rest. He wore sandals, dungarees, a blue work shirt, and a scorched corncob pipe; his chin was covered by a stubble of beard. "You're holding back," the dirty young man was saying. "Yes. Brake lights and things. No more of that!"

Georgie stood a bit apart. He was dressed in olive-green Army fatigues. "Hi, Boris," he said when they joined him. "Hi Teddy, hi Prudy . . . *hello* there!" The young Peabody, flustered by the attention from his hero, ducked behind the sweet reverse curve of his mother's leg. "That's Gene Breck," Georgie said of the dirty young man with the corncob pipe. "He and Hal are living on an old centerboard sloop in Portsmouth harbor. Hal wants to sail it to England."

They walked to where Georgie's car was parked. Hal withdrew his head and shoulders from the engine compartment, straightened up, and grinned at them through a mask of grease. His gaze lingered upon Prudy, who looked away. She turned to Georgie. "Are you having fun?" she asked.

"I'm not in the same league as these guys. Look at them!" He gestured at the lilac-colored car just beyond them, a sweet instrument of speed that was being tended by two men and a girl. "The guys are from Harvard," Georgie said, "and she's from Radcliffe. The money they've got! That's just their racing car—they have a green one for touring. Gene Breck will be driving for them."

"I'm sure you're every bit as good as he is," Teddy said.

"No," he said. "They've got it all—money, skill, everything."

"Aw," Hal said amiably. "You're not racing against that car. You're racing against ten, fifteen cars with the same displacement as yours, and if you'll pay attention to what I'm saying, you'll be all right. You gotta *hit* that first turn." Hal twisted his body like a small boy playing airplanes. "Run her up as far as she'll go, then *shift!* before you're into the turn, then *pull her around*. You can shave five seconds if you do that at every turn. . . . Listen, next heat I'll go up to the finish line and watch how you manage that. It's tricky, I know. I drove over it yesterday. All washboard."

"Aren't you racing?" Teddy asked.

Hal grinned at her. "Breck and I had a car we were gonna enter, but I totaled it the other day. Went off the road into a stone wall."

"Drunk, I suppose," Prudy said.

"Me? No, I was scared by an airplane. One of the jets out of Powell. It came zooming over the crest of a hill, fifty feet off the road. Scared the bejesus out of me."

Gene Breck was shouting from his vantage point near the

gate, yelling names from a clipboard in his hand. "Well, I gotta go," Georgie said, hearing his. He climbed into the cockpit of his car, donned a crash helmet, and started the engine. Hal fastened the hood. "Wish me luck," Georgie said.

Teddy moved Baby Nikolas to the side and kissed Georgie's cheek. "Be careful," she said.

"Women!" Hal said. "He wants luck and she gives him *careful*."

Georgie eased the roadster into the field, where five or six others were already lining up. Boris photographed them. Then he turned to the men and the girl who were tending the lilac-colored racer. Gene Breck came over to join them. "Saw your lady in Cambridge this morning," Breck said, looking at Hal with burning, bloodshot eyes.

"Who?"

"The blonde with—yes!—mammaries. *Mama piga simba!* From the lion hunt."

"Carol?" Hal said.

"The same. She was decorating Harvard Square when we picked up the cars. Yes." The dirty young man climbed into the lilac car and refused the crash helmet with a shake of his head.

Hal bit his lip, glanced at Prudy, then ran after him. "Hey!" he called. "Did you get her address?"

In silence, not to hurt Prudy's feelings, they walked over to watch the start. The cars from the previous heat were coming down the road. They went through the gate and fanned out into the field. Meanwhile the telephone operator hunched over his instrument, the starter raised his checkered flag, and the first car rolled up to the starting line. It was a nice moment. Boris raised his Leica and caught the scene over Teddy's shoulder. Then he ducked through the fence and took some pictures of the crowd. Somebody with an armband chased him off the track, so he climbed through the fence again and slouched around the pasture with his Rolleiflex. It was a good place to work. There were so many cameras around that nobody paid attention to his.

209

After a while Teddy caught up with him. She was childless. "Oh!" she cried, "did you see Georgie go? Everybody said what a wonderful start he made." Her eyes were glowing, green in the sunlight, gray when they walked into the shadow of an oak tree.

"Where are the kids?" Boris asked.

"Prudy took them back to the car," Teddy said. "I think she's afraid she'll run after Hal if she has the chance." She pointed to the roll-over bar behind the cockpit of a nearby roadster. "Is that to protect the driver?" she asked. "Why doesn't Georgie have one?"

"Because he's a damned fool," Boris said. "Because Hal talked him into racing and neither of them knows anything about it."

Teddy decided to watch from the starting line, and Boris walked along the fence to the second turn, savoring the compact black weight of the Leica and the Rolleiflex. He needed them. Otherwise he wouldn't have the courage to walk in front of the cold, scornful eyes of the fraternity boys who were watching the race.

A car had gone off the road at the second turn, plowing through the barrier of baled hay. It was bogged down in the field beyond. Half a dozen students were trying to manhandle it back to the asphalt, sweating and straining under the noon-time sun. Boris photographed them and walked on toward the reservoir.

Another car flashed past. This was a straight downhill run, over a causeway that crossed the reservoir. Beyond the reservoir, the road climbed again into the woods, and at the top of the hill he came upon the finish line. The asphalt was broken by frost-heaves, and it was indeed corrugated like an old-fashioned washboard. "Hey, Boris!" He went toward the voice and found Georgie among a knot of drivers and officials. "Boy, is that rough!" he said, flushed with pleasure and excitement. "I thought I was going to take off. Boris, I was doing eighty-five when I came up that hill!"

"Yeah, man," said Hal Pappajohn. "Two minutes, thirty seconds. Second-best time of the heat."

"Here comes Breck!" shouted one of the drivers. "Hit the dirt!"

The car exploded out of the trees below them, like a lilac-colored rocket; it shot up the hill and danced madly upon the washboard surface at the end of the course. "Jesus," said Hal. The dirty young man grinned behind his corncob pipe. Then the car went into a skid and plowed sideways through the stakes that marked the finish line. Officials and drivers ran in whatever direction they had been facing. The car came to a halt a hundred yards off the road, its left flank dented along most of its length. "What was my time?" Breck asked, stepping out of the car and rolling the stem of the corncob around in his mouth.

"Your time? Jesus, manyou smashed the clock. How would I know your time?"

Breck's was the last car in this heat. It was still running, so he led the convoy back to the starting line. Boris and Hal squeezed into Georgie's car and rode back with him. "You've got it now," Hal was saying. "Don't worry about the finish. This is heavier than Breck's car; it won't break loose."

"I'd hate to put any dents in this baby," Georgie said.

"You won't, you won't! And if you do, Breck and I will fix it cheap."

It was past one o'clock, so when Georgie reached the starting line, Boris dropped off and made his way to the Volkswagen. The family had already eaten. The babies were asleep in the back seat, and Teddy was playing tag with the young Peabody between the parked automobiles. Boris gulped a sandwich and went back to work. Prudence went with him. She carried a bag of sandwiches for Georgie and Hal, who were tinkering again beneath the roadster's hood. "Pop one into my mouth," said Hal, whose hands were slippery with grease. Prudy broke a sandwich in half and fed it to him. Hal chewed it, his cheeks distended and his eyes fastened upon

211

her. "Wow," he said, swallowing the last of it, "that hit the spot. . . . You know what we should do? We'll have a victory party tonight for old Georgie. Over at the boat—you ever seen our boat, Prudy?"

"No."

"We'll get some gin and have a party."

"I don't think so," Prudy said. "We'd have to take the children, and it'd be awfully late for them." Boris walked away, wondering if she would follow or stay with Hal. After a moment he was aware that she was just behind him. He turned around. "It's not what you think," she said. "I had too much to drink that night."

"Sure."

"I did!"

"Baby, you don't get drunk and then run wild. You get drunk because you *want* to run wild."

Prudence seemed startled by this piece of wisdom. "All right, maybe I did," she said. "I'm twenty-three and I have a son that's four. How many years do you think I have, that I should be a nun while my husband chases around Europe?"

"I just don't care very much for Hal Pappajohn."

"Or for Colin Merchant?"

"No, he's another bastard."

"Boris, dear, I think you don't like *men*. Because whatever you say about them Hal and Colin—they're both men."

Boris went back to work. Teddy caught up with him at three o'clock. "I'm getting a headache from all the noise," she said. "And Tommy is restless. It's nap time; we'd better go home."

Boris tossed her the car keys. "Pick me up at five," he said. He would work for a while at the second turn, which seemed the most likely place for a car to go off the road. And the bursting hay bales would make a fine picture. He took up a position near an oak tree that would give him shelter if necessary. The ambulance driver had also picked this as a good spot for an accident. He'd parked his Jeep in the pasture beyond

212

the turn, its flat nose pointing toward the race course as if to sniff out trouble.

Boris guessed the little cars were hitting fifty-five or sixty miles an hour by the time they rounded this curve. The noise was shattering. Most of them shifted down to third or second gear, for more traction through the turn, and back to top gear as soon as they were out of it and shooting down the straight-away toward the reservoir. All of them made it, unfortunately. After a while Boris went over to talk to the ambulance driver. This proved to be Johnny Trask, the Civil Defense warden who had arrested Hal Pappajohn. "Hey," Boris said. "How's business?"

"So-so. You a photographer?"

"I own a couple cameras, anyhow." Boris peered into the Jeep. It was not like the ambulances he had seen during the War, with two stretchers rigged up high; Trask had simply removed the front passenger seat and welded brackets to the dashboard and tailgate to hold a single stretcher. "You do this yourself?" Boris asked.

"Yeah. You wanna take a picture of it?"

"I guess not," Boris said.

Trask turned his back and talked to the observer in charge of this corner, manning a field telephone like those at the start and finish lines. Boris was about to return to his oak tree when the telephone jangled. "Observer here!" the official said. "Hey! Is that right?" He listened wide-eyed to the voice on the other end of the line, then slammed down the receiver. "Accident at the finish line," he said to Trask. "Guy flipped ass over tea-kettle." They sprinted for the Jeep.

Boris was closer to it than they were, and he went in over the tailgate, taking the rear seat. The observer gave him a dirty look and squeezed in the front. Johnny Trask hunched over the steering wheel and sent the Jeep blasting through hay bales onto the paved road. When they passed over the cause-way between the twin ponds of the Narwich water supply, Boris saw a covey of sports cars at the top of the hill he'd just

213

left. Then the Jeep climbed to the horticultural farm where Boris had once photographed those prize cantaloupes. There was a swerve, a belly-knotting jolt, and at last the ambulance came to a halt. Boris jumped out. He checked the Rolleiflex, saw five exposures remaining on the roll, and ran after the others.

The car was on its back like an upended turtle, one wheel still revolving slowly. There was a smashed headlamp on the grass nearby. The car was white, like Georgie's little roadster. Boris brought the camera up to his eyes, framed the picture through the sports-finder, and pressed the shutter release. Four or five men were straining at the overturned car. Beautiful!—the flowing lines of their bodies, the cords standing out on their necks.

Three more cars mounted the hill and skidded to a stop. Hal Pappajohn jumped out of the lead car. "Is he okay?" Hal shouted. "Jesus H. Christ! What was his time, what was his time?"

"Two minutes five seconds," one of the men panted, looking up from his labors. "Give us a hand, you guys."

"Best of his class!" Hal shouted, capering across to the wreck. "Good for Georgie!" They positioned themselves on one side of the car, heaved, heaved again, and on the third try flipped it over. The windscreen was flattened, and there was a small puncture in the hood. Other than that, and the missing headlamp, the car didn't seem badly damaged.

Georgie remained on the ground. Like his car, he seemed to be in one piece, lying on his back with his wide-open eyes staring up at the sky. Boris ran around to the other side of him. It was another beautiful shot, with the rescuers surrounding Georgie and the little car in the background, its windscreen smashed.

"You okay, kid?" Hal was shouting. "Georgie, you're a winner!"

Georgie didn't answer, and Boris went over for a closer look. Sweat stood out in little drops on Georgie's forehead and cheeks. "I think he'd hurt," somebody said. "I think we should get him to the hospital."

Johnny Trask flung himself upon the Jeep's tailgate, tore it open, and hauled out the stretcher, which he dragged back to where Georgie was lying. Four of them snuggled the stretcher against his side and rolled him onto it. Georgie gasped but didn't speak. Hal shouldered his way through the knot of men and took one handle of the stretcher, on the same end as Johnny Trask. The finish-line official and the beautiful young man from Harvard took the other end. Together they carried Georgie to the Jeep and slid him through the tailgate, like a log into a furnace.

"Hey, get out of there!" Hal yelled at the official, who was boosting himself into the rear passenger's seat. "Me and this guy are riding with him. We're his buddies."

"Yeah," shouted a driver. "Get out of there, Smitty. Let his buddies ride with him."

Smitty climbed down, Boris got in, and Hal squeezed in at the front. Georgie was still sweating. Boris took a handkerchief from his hip pocket and wiped the young man's forehead, but he was soon sweating again. When the Jeep started down the hill, Georgie winced and closed his eyes. "Boris?" he said.

"Yeah, what?"

"Did they cut off my legs? I can't feel anything in my legs."

"Hell, no! They haven't touched you."

"Oh," said Georgie. "That's all right, then." He was silent for a moment, and then, as the Jeep was passing the reservoir, he said: "Boris, if anything should happen to me —"

"Nothing's going to happen, for Christ's sake."

"No, but if it does, would you look after Teddy for me? I was hoping to marry her when the divorce came through and I had a steady job," Georgie said. His lips peeled away from his teeth in the expression that Boris had come to accept as a smile. "But maybe I won't be able to do that. So would you look after her for me?"

"Yeah, kid. Sure." And who did Georgie think had been

looking after Teddy all these months?

"Maybe you should marry her, Boris. She needs somebody steady."

"Maybe I will, kid."

"Yes, that's what you should do," Georgie said, and did not speak again.

17 - It's Not as if She Were a Virgin

A LANE WAS CLEAR FOR THEM to the main road, and Johnny Trask took it at fifty miles an hour, the heel of his hand sounding a continual warning from the horn. Georgie's lips were slightly parted, and his eyes squinted against the sun or some interior warning, but he was alive. Then the corner. Boris was thrown against the Jeep's sheet-metal canopy, which flexed and boomed under his head, and when he righted himself Georgie was dead. An eraser had passed across his face, wiping away the wrinkles that had formed, along with the intelligence and the warmth, transforming him into a corpse. The Jeep continued to hum along the road to Narwich. The horn continued to blat. But Georgie was gone—plans cut off, mistakes absolved, dreams reduced to ash.

~ ~ ~ ~

That evening, Boris developed his photographs. They were even better than he hoped, and he made up a package and put it on the eight o'clock bus to Boston, when it stopped outside the Coffee Corner. Teddy met him at the door when he returned from the village, her eyes brimming. "The police just called," she said. "About Georgie?" She chewed her knuckles between each sentence. "They called to say he was dead."

"Why us?"

The tears spilled over and ran in two glistening streams down her cheeks. "Georgie had you listed in his wallet—in case of accident?—and your telephone number." Boris put his arm around Teddy and led her to the couch, then tried to detach himself so he could fix her a drink. But she clung to him, sobbing like Baby Nikolas when he dropped his bottle. Boris patted her shoulder, felt foolish, and began to massage the shoulder instead. Teddy's sobbing burst out on a higher pitch.

"It's all right," he said, putting his other arm around her. "I love you."

That stopped her. She raised her face to him, her eyes still closed, her cheeks streaked and gleaming in the lamplight, her lips puffy. She wanted to be kissed! Boris bent and pressed his lips to her. They were softer than he had imagined possible. Then the telephone rang. It was the *Manchester Union*, wanting to know Georgie's life story for the Sunday paper. Boris was astonished at how little he was able to tell the reporter.

In the morning, he went over to the trailer and put Georgie's things in order, while O'Rourke perched on the edge of the sink like an unhappy vulture. "There it is!" he cried. "A few weeks ago I was advising the lad about life, and now he's dead."

"Hell," Boris said, "nobody gets out of this world alive."

"No, but some of us have *lived* in the interim," O'Rourke said.

Boris found a rent receipt, and told O'Rourke that he might as well use the trailer until the end of May, since it was paid up. There were other receipted bills, an unpaid one for overdue books at the University library, a passport application, and a number of letters from a school superintendent in Nova Scotia. Boris wasn't sure what he was looking for; whatever it was, he didn't find it. O'Rourke was right: Georgie had departed life without having done much living.

Next day Boris talked to the University registrar and learned that Georgie was a state ward. A couple in Manchester had reared him in return for a weekly check from the Department of Welfare, and their interest seemed to have ceased with the checks. "We can't afford the burial, anyways," the woman said when Boris phoned. "Won't the state pay for it? Or maybe you can find his old man. He's still around Manchester somewheres. You want me to ask?"

"Never mind," Boris said. "I'll take care of the funeral."

"That would be the Christian thing to do," the woman agreed. "He was a well-behaved youngun, Georgie was."

But she didn't come to the funeral, which was held in the University chapel, a small Gothic structure on the western fringe of College Woods. The Protestant chaplain got permission for Boris to use it for the funeral. That was a Wednesday, the day after the coroner's inquest, and a grounds crew went out on Tuesday afternoon to clear the beer bottles and contraceptives from the grounds.

Boris and Teddy walked to the service through the woods. The sky was overcast, and the wind was raw enough for him to wear a raincoat over his Sunday suit. Above the clouds the jet bombers were droning.

The chapel contained a few rows of backless pews. About half were occupied. Boris saw Mr. Phipps, his hair gleaming silver in the light of the altar candles, and Doc Perkins, Hal Pappajohn, and two or three University students. There was also the dirty young man with the corncob pipe—Hal's friend —and some other young toughs from the First Annual Narwich Grand Prix. The casket was covered with flowers and evergreen wreathes. Boris was surprised by the bouquets. He checked the cards and found that the largest were from the Narwich Sports Car Club, the Cambridge Mass. Rally-ers, and Breck's Auto-Body and Foreign Cars in Kittery, across the river in Maine. Teddy wept.

After the service, a little caravan followed the hearse to the main road, turned west, and drove to the cemetery, off Route 4 on the way to Concord. The funeral director had disguised the surroundings with a carpet of artificial grass. The gravediggers were hidden by a little hill, beyond which they played cards in the back of a green pickup truck. The Protestant chaplain said a few words. He was obliged to raise his voice at the end, while a B-52 droned unseen behind the clouds. Then the casket was lowered from the funeral director's winch, the canvas straps were removed, and a handful of dirt was thrown into the grave, where it rattled on the lid of the casket. Teddy began to weep again. Boris put his arm around her, remembering that precious moment when he had kissed her, but she moved away, to the edge of the grave. "I'm all right," she said when he followed her. "I just want to say a little prayer for

219

Georgie." Looking at the tight little curls on the back of her neck, Boris remembered Georgie's last words, about marrying Teddy. Should he tell her?

Hal Pappajohn and some of the others had wandered over to admire the headstone, and Boris followed them. Breck's Auto-Body had provided the stone. It was pink marble, tall and slender. Nobody had anything to say, so Boris walked back to the grave in search of Teddy. She was standing with Doc Perkins, who was wearing his old winter topcoat. A cigar, as frayed as the coat, projected from his mouth. "Boris!" he growled. "Why haven't you been around to see me?"

"What would I want with a sawbones?" Boris said. "I'm the picture of health."

"Yeah, they have your pictures in the textbooks—emphysema, underweight, dehydration—hell yes! But you wrecked yourself years ago, Boris. There's nothing to be done for old crocks like us, but this young lady is a different matter." He squeezed Teddy's arm. "How long since you've had a checkup, hah?"

"I'm fine," Teddy protested. "A little tired, that's all."

"Anemic, too, I'll wager." The Doc spat out the pulpy remnants of his cigar. "Come along with me now," he said, "and we'll have a look at you. I have two babies to deliver this week, so there's no sense making an appointment. I'd probably have to break it."

"I . . ." But Doc Perkins was already walking across the field with his slow, bearpaw tread. Teddy looked to Boris for help.

"Why not?" he said. In the end, she agreed to follow Doc Perkins in the Volkswagen, and Boris hitched a ride back to the Hut with Hal Pappajohn. "Come in for a drink," Boris suggested.

"I guess not," Hal said. "I got some thinking to do." They nodded goodbye, and Boris walked to the front door, aching as if somebody had beaten him. The old lady's funeral had been a lot easier. That was a short, tearless affair in Oldfield, with

220

only Teddy for company, and a few women friends who were afraid of Boris, and who dabbed continually at eyes from which no tears came. Georgie's death was a different matter. It required some justification, which was probably what Hal wanted to think about. If he'd had kept his mouth shut, a few weeks ago, Georgie would be alive today.

Boris went into the Hut, where he was almost knocked down by a naked woman, her arms and shoulders flashing golden in the artificial light. She was chased by a dark, angular shadow that could only have been O'Rourke. Boris shook his head, but the figures did not vanish. They circled the room and rushed past him again. This time he recognized the woman as Prudence Peabody, and saw that she wasn't entirely naked. She wore a bath towel, held in place by her left hand. Thus handicapped, Prudy should have been an easy catch, but O'Rourke remained the same distance behind her, his breath rasping in his throat.

Boris closed the door. When they rushed past him for the third time, he tripped O'Rourke, who tumbled to the floor, his bones clattering. Prudy was stopped by the noise. She whirled on her bare feet and stared wide-eyed at Boris. "*Shsssh!*" she hissed. "*Don't wake the children!*" O'Rourke tried to stand but couldn't get off the floor; he remained on his knees, massaging his elbow. He continued to stare at Prudy. She circled the couch and came around to stand beside Boris. "I was taking a shower," she whispered, "and *that one* came in and tried to rape me." Her skin was still damp and glowing from the hot water, and Boris could smell the perfume of the soap she had used.

"Why didn't you let him?" he said. "What difference would it have made?"

"Yes!" cried O'Rourke from the floor, still staring at the golden flesh above and below the towel. "My words exactly!" he said. "Just to nuzzle her a few times—that would have been an unspeakable happiness. It's not as if she were a virgin, is it? I would never rape a virgin, Boris, you know that. But Mrs.

Peabody is a multipara, and indifferent to me besides; she would scarcely have noticed my assault."

"Be quiet," Prudy told him, then turned back to Boris. "He's your friend," she said. "If you ever let him through that door again, I'll *castrate* him." Boris let his eyes wander down the indignant body. Her hair was wet, and beads of water ran down to vanish between her breasts. He reached out and took a corner of the towel. "Hey!" she said.

Well, why not? He swung his weight against the towel, peeling it away like the string from a top. Prudy spun, recovered, and tried to hide herself with her hands. Then she stopped and looked scornfully at them. "All right," she said. "Go ahead—take a good look."

O'Rourke moaned and covered his face with his hands. He rocked on his knees very slowly. To Boris, the astonishing thing was the *color* of Prudy's skin—yellow, it seemed, the yellow of buttercups, and with the same fire burning beneath the surface. Then she turned and walked to the bedroom. Boris collapsed on the couch, laughing until his belly ached. O'Rourke! Of all the people in the world, O'Rourke, cowering in front of that glorious nude—it was impossibly funny. Boris saw the Rolleiflex, sitting on the coffee table a few feet away. The laughter surged up in him again: he could have photographed them, Prudence and O'Rourke; he could have captured that scene forever, the woman victorious and the man on his knees.

"You know," O'Rourke was saying, "she didn't seem too offended, did she? I wonder if next time, perhaps. . . ." Boris went off again, laughing until he could only gasp and dab at his eyes. "I could have caught her," O'Rourke said, standing up. "But I was afraid she would scream and perhaps disturb the children."

"Yeah," Boris said, swallowing a chuckle that threatened to overcome him. He looked around for something to divert his attention, and found two envelopes addressed to him on the coffee table, weighted down by the Rolleiflex. "Well, you can always put her into your book," he said to O'Rourke. "Along with Lucia from that school in Connecticut."

The first envelope was from National News-Pix and contained a check for fifty dollars. Wow. For fifty dollars, the Boston *Advertiser* must have pushed Georgie's photo all over the country. Boris admired the slip of paper for a moment, put it down, and opened the second envelope. It also contained a check—the one he'd made out to Carol Phipps! On the back, where her signature should have been, there was the scarlet imprint of two plum-ripe lips. Boris turned the envelope inside out, but Carol hadn't enclosed any news of herself, nor supplied a return address. "Well, well," Boris said, and burned the check to a gray husk in the ashtray.

O'Rourke was entranced by the flame. "Was that money?" he asked, as the blue tongue of flame flickered and went out. "Because if you have money to burn, Boris, my oldest friend, may I trouble you for a twenty?"

"I don't think she's for sale," Boris said.

"It has nothing to do with Mrs. Peabody, I assure you. It's that young lad, Georgie. My erstwhile roommate. . . . Why did he moon so much? Why did he fret and fuss so much? Why didn't he join the Peace Corps and be done with it?"

"Why don't you?" Boris asked, and a grin spread across O'Rourke's face, like a hatchet smiling. "The *Peace Corps?*" Boris said.

"Not exactly. The regimen would be too severe. But do you remember the time I was stranded in Magnolia, Georgia, when the inhabitants were lynching Freedom Riders? Well, Magnolia is in the news again." He showed Boris a photo clipped from the *New York Times*. It showed a Negro whose trousers were being shredded by a German shepherd dog while two policemen stood over him with riot sticks, as if to protect the dog. "The civil rights marchers are falling faster than autumn leaves," O'Rourke said. "If I had a modest sum to cover expenses, I thought I'd go down and offer my services to the cause of integration."

Boris tried to imagine O'Rourke fighting for civil rights. "You always said that demonstrations did more harm than good."

"But what if I was wrong?" O'Rouke slapped his forehead with his open palm. "I keep thinking, what if I'd been a young man in the 1930s and didn't go to fight in Spain? What if I'd lived in the time of *Coeur de Lion* and didn't join the Crusades? What if I had been a Legionnaire and didn't crucify Christ? What a fool I would have been! How I'd hate myself today! Think of it, Boris—to know that life had called, and that you were out in the back shed, jerking off. . . . Besides," he added, "how could a demonstration do more harm than good if I were part of it?

Boris turned over the National News-Pix check and endorsed it to O'Rourke. The money was Georgie's. What better use for it than to send O'Rourke off to strive for civil rights in Magnolia?

18 - Kein Atomwaffen

COLIN SUFFERED, that first week on the road. His feet blistered. His skin burned and peeled and burned again. His thighs cramped. He called himself a fool for joining this adventure, but he kept going, and by the time they reached the frontier he felt strong again; and once in Germany, he was hiking with the best of them. He took his turn under the placards, and when they marched into Frankfurt he shared the strong man's duty, carrying an extra pack at the end of the day, for one of the girls or one of the lame. His boots rang on the cobblestones, and his chest was full of the ancient air of Germany, which had washed over vineyards and ruined castles before finding its proper home in Colin Merchant's breast. If only Teddy could see him now!

"Look!" cried Marvin Peabody, sweating under his pack, but cheerful all the same. "They're way ahead of us," he panted. "Oh, we could take some lessons from them!" He pointed to the posters on a tall wooden fence across the street. Each depicted a grinning skull against a towering mushroom cloud, and carried this legend: KEIN ATOMWAFFEN! No atomic weapons for Germany.

They were walking down a long hill in a district their guide said was the ancient part of Frankfurt, called Sachsenhausen. Colin was impressed by the number of beer halls—one on every corner, almost—and by the delivery wagon rolling up the street, pulled by a beautiful pair of gray draft horses and laden with wooden casks of beer.

The youth hostel was a modern structure, near the river separating Sachsenhausen from Frankfurt. Clayton Rickover had taken the train from Paris, set up an advance headquarters here, and then moved on again. He was now in Berlin, arranging for their passage through East Germany. "What did I tell you?" Marvin groaned, dropping his pack in the common room. "Our Mr. Rickover simply doesn't care for walking. I thought he looked a bit unhappy on the march to Paris."

Rick had left instructions for a demonstration tomorrow, along with a sack of mail. There were no letters for Colin, so he ducked out for one of those draft beers. The marchers weren't supposed to drink, but he'd built up a mighty thirst, that first week out of Paris. In the *gasthaus*, he soon had an audience of stout men and their wives and teenage daughters, who no doubt were in need of American husbands. They giggled at his jokes and tried to teach him how to say them in German. Well, beer was *bier*, anyhow!

He went back to the youth at nine o'clock, rescued his pack from the common room, and searched the men's dormitories until he found one occupied by the pacifists. A bit tipsy, he rolled out his sleeping bag on an empty bunk. "That you, Colin?" asked Marvin Peabody from the neighboring bunk. He came over to help. "Terrible news," he said, taking a swipe at the sleeping bag. "Poor Georgie!"

"What about him?" Colin straightened, banging his head against the upper bunk. Tears sprang to his eyes. He wanted to sneeze; he held it back, and when the sneeze was gone so was his buzz from the beer. "What happened to Georgie?"

"Killed in an automobile accident. A race of some sort. Died on the way to the hospital, Prudence says. . . . She sent you a message, by the way." Colin had a swift, tearing sense of Prudy's nearness, screaming behind the green double doors of Oldfield hospital. He accepted the note from Marvin. It was folded twice and sealed with Scotch tape. "I told him to come with us," Marvin said. He abandoned his attempt to straighten the sleeping bag, and instead sat down on it. "Too bad, too bad!" he said, shaking his head. "He might have done yeoman work over here, but he always lagged behind when he should have forged ahead. Remember how he wouldn't go to Washington with us? I shouldn't be surprised if that wasn't what undid him in the end, his hesitations."

"Go to bed, Marv," said Colin. A headache was building up

at the base of his skull.

"Yes, that's the ticket," Marvin agreed. "It's a long day tomorrow, and a busy one." He clumped away to his own bunk.

Colin went to the hallway, wondering about Marvin Peabody, who so calmly delivered a sealed message from his wife to another man. Or had he read it and sealed it again? Colin freed the tape with his fingernail: it came off easily enough. The note read: *Teddy is pregnant. You bastard. What are you going to do about it?* Colin returned to his bunk. Another baby! Was there no end to his ability to beget children?

There was a fire escape outside his window, and he went through it and down the skeleton steps. After scouting through the back streets, heading downhill, he came to the river. It flowed dark and oily between well-tamed banks. Colin found a gravel path leading along it. The night air was damp. After walking a few hundred yards he came to a narrow, old-fashioned footbridge, and mounted a flight of concrete steps to reach it. It must have been standing here when American soldiers reached Frankfurt in 1945. There would have been German machine gunners in those buildings on the other side of the river, not the jolly types he had met in the *gasthaus* tonight, with fat wives and buxom daughters, but young men, hard-eyed and lean and shooting to kill. Yet the GIs had crossed. What in the world could have made them cross?

He leaned against the rail and looked down at the black, oily surface of the Main, broken only by an occasional silver ripple. Really, a man's life was no more substantial than one of those gleams that disturbed the water but left it unchanged.

A streetcar rattled across the vehicular bridge, half a mile downstream; and in the silence that followed Colin could hear distant laughter. That was better!

He considered his own personal history. What monument had he erected to his existence? Well, there were the babies, carelessly begotten and then abandoned: Teddy's young son, Prudy's baby girl, and now the clump of protoplasm in Teddy's womb. There was the pain he had inflicted upon the women, screaming behind the double doors of Oldfield hospital. And the shame he'd given to Marvin, delivering messages from his wife to the man who had cuckolded him.

What terrible things he had done!

~ ~ ~ ~

The road smoothed things out. It seemed to bring him closer to the people he had injured. True, he was walking in the wrong direction, but it was a penance of sorts to carry Ursula's pack through the hot, dusty afternoon, especially since her virtue had proved as immoveable as her politics. The extra weight was his offering to Teddy, who was carrying his child alone.

Anyhow, he'd actually come to *like* the pacifists. They believed in something larger than themselves, and they had suffered for it. They'd sit around a campfire at night, or in a hostel common room, and talk about the Actions they had joined. One balding man had trespassed on a nuclear testing site near Las Vegas in 1957, and was sentenced to six months, suspended; a year later he took part in Omaha Action, lying in front of trucks carrying materials to build an Atlas missile base, which yielded him a broken nose and three months in jail. He was beaten up a few times by the other prisoners, until they found he wouldn't fight back; after that, they left him alone.

They were like the Korean war veterans who'd been his cadre in basic training. The Actions were their campaigns, and jail sentences their medals. Even Ursula had spent thirty days in prison. Hiram Thornton, the Vermont Yankee who was Colin's best friend on the march, had been jailed as a conscientious objector, and his brother was serving a six-year sentence for boarding a Polaris submarine in New London, Connecticut. "Six years," said Colin, awed by this kind of courage. "I thought I was being noble when I spent one night in jail."

"Civil Defense protest?" asked one.

"Yes."

"Where?"

"Narwich, New Hampshire."

"Oh, yes—heard about that. You posted bond and paid your fines."

"Not me," Colin said, with a side glance at Marvin Peabody. Marvin was scowling. "I didn't have the money, so they kept me in jail overnight. Next day they let me go. I never heard any more about it."

"Often happens that way," said the other, mollified. "Authorities back down when they find a man determined to follow his principles to the end."

Six years! Six years without a woman! He ached to be home with Teddy. But next morning he arose womanless with the others, shook out his sleeping bag, and continued to walk in the wrong direction.

~ ~ ~ ~

Five days after Frankfurt, they reached the Iron Curtain, though they were told not to call it that. And in fact it was only a small swing gate across the highway. On this side, American GIs in starched fatigues stared curiously at the marchers. Beyond the gate, Colin saw East German troops in uniforms that reminded him of photographs he had seen of the Nazi time, except for their helmets, which resembled steel toadstools. An officer in a cloth cap greeted the marchers on behalf of the German Democratic Republic. He told them, in heavily accented English, that a bus would soon arrive from the village to pick them up. It had been donated by the free workers of the Republic. "There must be some mistake," Marvin Peabody said in a loud voice, and slowly, as if speaking to a deaf man. "We are walking. On foot, yes? *Aus fuss?* From San Francisco to Moscow?"

"I think—you did not—go by foot—across the ocean," said the officer, smiling with his mouth only.

Colin decided that the officer was Russian, and that the

other brown-uniformed, cloth-capped soldiers he saw in the background were also Soviet troops. He whispered his guess to Hiram, who shrugged. "Why not?" he said. "Shouldn't be any more surprised to see Russians on that side than Americans on this." But Hiram too spoke in a whisper, and even Marvin seemed impressed by the East Bloc soldiers.

In his patient English, the Russian officer explained that entry had been arranged for them, yes, but his instructions specified bus transportation. He had no authority to allow them to enter otherwise. "It is not I who makes this rule," he said, his mouth smiling, his eyes cold. Besides, he said, the free democratic workers had arranged a rally in the village, and they mustn't be late. While he was talking, the bus arrived. It wasn't the drab military vehicle Colin had expected, but a streamlined tourist bus with windows tinted orange against the sun. "He does not wait," the officer warned. "He returns now to the village."

The pacifists went into a huddle. "Let's wait here," Colin urged. "You won your point in France, remember? You tried to swim ashore when they wouldn't let you down the gangway, and then you tried again next day. And they let you in! Let's camp here until they allow us to walk through that gate."

"Makes sense," Hiram said.

Marvin shook his head. "Our goal is to reach Moscow," he said, "not to embarrass the various governments along the route of march."

"You were happy enough to embarrass the French," Colin said.

"That was different," Ursula snapped. "Honestly, Colin! Everybody knows how *reactionary* the French can be. They didn't want us to enter at *all*."

"Ursula is right," Marvin said. "There's a subtle difference here. The French wanted to keep us out, while these people are offering us transportation to help us along. They just don't understand that we prefer to walk. I'm sure we can straighten it out when we reach Berlin."

"For God's sake!" Colin said. "That Russian officer just doesn't want us walking through the countryside. And isn't that what we're supposed to be doing? It doesn't matter if we reach Moscow; what matters is the people we meet along the way."

He would lose. The bus waited beyond the gate, its motor running; the cloth-capped Russian officer lounged against the guardhouse with his hard eyes fixed upon Hiram's placard; the soldiers of East and West stared at the marchers in similar bafflement. Somehow what was proper in France was not proper here.

"Quickly please!" the officer cried. "The bus is now returning." Marvin Peabody picked up his pack and went to the guardhouse, where a uniformed official glanced at the American passport, nodded, and returned it with a slip of paper inserted between the leaves. Three or four others also went to get their visas. The rest huddled in small, leaderless groups, faced with the choice of following Marvin or splitting the march.

"I'm tempted to stay," Hiram said. "But I don't want to bust up the whole affair. Maybe we should go to Berlin and see what your friend Rickover thinks."

"Not me," said Colin, wanting to run through the gate and drag Marvin Peabody off the bus. "I'll walk to Moscow or stop right here."

"Huh!" Ursula said. 'You didn't walk from San Francisco to New York. You didn't walk from Liverpool to London. You didn't even walk to *Paris*!"

Neither had she walked to Paris, but he was smart enough not to say that. "True," he said. "But all the more reason not to hop a bus now, just because a Russian officer wants me to."

"Honestly!" she cried. "Colin, you. . . ."

"The bus is leaving," the officer interrupted, and indeed the bus was turning around on the far side of the barrier. Ursula picked up her knapsack. Colin went to help her, but she pulled away.

"If you don't come," she said, "we won't see each other again." She battled with the straps, got one of them twisted, and it took both Hiram and Colin to straighten her out.

"Staying?" Hiram asked.

"Yes," Colin said.

They shook hands, and the tall Vermonter escorted Ursula to the guardhouse. By now almost all of the peace marchers had passed through the pedestrian gate. Colin waved to Hiram as he helped Ursula aboard the bus; she didn't turn, so Colin couldn't wave goodbye to her. The door closed upon them, the motor revved up, and the bus pulled out into the highway, swaying slightly, and vanished on the road to the East. Colin felt very lonely there at the barricade. What should he do now? He didn't have enough money to pay for passage back to the United States.

Suddenly, he wanted to run after the bus. He could catch up with his comrades in the village mentioned by the Russian officer; he could be back with them tonight. Why was it so important to walk? Why be more proud than those who were jailed in Omaha and Phoenix and San Francisco?. . . But the moment passed. He wasn't going to ride a chartered bus through East Germany, like a tourist from Indiana. That wasn't his style. Anyhow, the Russian officer probably wouldn't let him through.

Colin shouldered his knapsack and walked back to the US Army checkpoint, a small white building athwart the Autobahn. He'd hitch a ride back to Frankfurt and ask the American consul for advice.

~ ~ ~ ~

The first vehicle to stop at the checkpoint was heading east: a little French car that contained two GIs in civilian clothes. They handed furlough papers to the military policeman at the checkpoint; he recorded some information on his clipboard, returned the papers, and waved them on. Colin stooped to the level of the driver-side window. "Hey," he said. "You guys going to Berlin?"

"Yeah," the driver drawled out of a chunky, ugly face, like the gargoyles on the cathedral of Notre Dame. "What about it?"

"How about a lift?"

"You English, or what?"

"I'm from Boston," Colin said.

"Well, that's all right, then. Hop in." Colin squeezed into the back seat with the AWOL bags and clothes on hangers. He had to rest the pack on his lap. The little car jolted forward to the East German barrier, where the GIs surrendered their furlough papers and Colin his passport. "You a student or what?" said the driver.

"Just bumming around."

"Well, hi-ho for the gallant island of democracy," the driver said when their travel documents were returned. "Did you know we can't stop along the Autobahn or take any pictures? It's a fact. I don't know whether that's the Army talking, or the Commies. They're both crazy, if you ask me. Rules is all they're good for, making rules!"

They reached Berlin at ten o'clock that evening. The city did resemble an island: they burst into its circle of light like sailors off the darkened sea. When the sun went down, apparently, life stopped in East Germany. They hadn't seen a lighted window anywhere along their route, just the occasional naked lightbulb at railroad station. In contrast, West Berlin seemed the finest place Colin had ever entered, with soft neon lights casting a halo into the sky, and a four-engine plane roaring down for a landing in the heart of the city.

The soldiers, Larry and Sam, had the address of a cheap hotel a few blocks from the Kurfiirstendam, West Berlin's main street, and Colin volunteered to split the cost with them. They agreed. The three of them dumped their luggage—in a spacious bed-sitter with a bay window—and went out to get drunk.

Berlin was full of surprises. There were broad modern streets that ended in a mountain of rubble, or a gutted

233

building, untouched since 1945; there was a strange orange beer that sparkled like champagne; there was the Wall dividing East and West. The city reminded Colin of a story he'd read about the Red Death, in which the best and the most beautiful of the kingdom barricaded themselves inside a castle and partied while plague raged outside. West Berlin was like that castle. The plague was the German Democratic Republic, where the Second World War had never quite ended.

Larry and Sam planned to stay three days in the city, and offered to take Colin back to Frankfurt at the end of their stay. But first Berlin threw another surprise at him: Rickover! Colin ran into him on the Kurfürstendam, his last evening in the city. Because they were in a foreign land, the meeting seemed especially marvelous. They hugged each other, pounded shoulders, and went to a sidewalk cafe to drink *Weisse mit Schuss Himbeere*, the orange brew that sparkled like champagne. It was dusk. The sky was shading into violet, and the soft neon lights of the Kurfürstendam were rich and brave. Down at the end of the broad avenue, the skeleton of a church stood black against the sky, a reminder of the war that had ended so strangely, with the victors dividing the city against each other.

"I should have known!" Rick said, smiling handsomely. "You're a hard-head; I should have met you at the frontier. . . . But you're back with us now, aren't you? We're leaving East Berlin in the morning. I just slipped over here for a last look at beauty, and one last civilized drink. Whatever one says about them, the Communists haven't yet mastered the art of the cocktail hour."

Colin was tempted. "Are you traveling by bus?" he asked.

"Damn it, yes! I talked myself blue, but they still think we're a passel of spies. The Poles are easier. We can walk from the Polish frontier to Warsaw, but then it's by bus again to Moscow. We'll be hammering on the Kremlin gates this time next month. Come with us, Colin!"

"I guess not," he said. "It's not just the bus. I learned in

Frankfurt that my wife is going to have another baby." The word moved him strangely, and he realized that he'd never before called Teddy his *wife*. "She was pretty upset when I decided to come on this march, and I don't want to wait two more months before straightening things out. Who can tell what will happen in two months? Hell, a friend of mine was killed a couple weeks ago in an automobile accident. I want to see Teddy—my wife—before something like that happens to me."

"Ah," said Rick.

"And to tell you the truth I've been sort of disappointed in the marchers, some of them. Not you, or Hiram Thornton. . . ."

"Or Ursula?"

"Well, even that didn't work out the way I had hoped."

"Ah," said Rick again.

"They're so irresponsible! They leave their families in the lurch, they make excuses for the Communists that they wouldn't make for the French. . . ."

Rick sighed. "Perhaps we are a bit irresponsible," he said. "But how can you blame a condemned man for lacking enthusiasm for the thrifty details of life? Here we have an entire world under sentence of death."

Colin trembled, as if the last, final fire were already sweeping around the world. "All the more reason to stay home and settle my own affairs," he said. "How can I go marching to Moscow when there's somebody back in New Hampshire who needs me?"

"Every man has his own answer to the news that he will die," Rick said. "Some drink, some pray, some ignore it, and a few stand up and yell. I want to be one of those who die yelling."

"You're not married."

"No."

"Well, I am, and I want to work at it for a while. Then maybe I'll start thinking about how to save the world."

"You never will," Rick said. "There are world-savers and

235

home-builders, and never the twain shall meet."

Colin had a vision of crying babies, soiled diapers, and money worries. Sure enough, he was condemning himself to a dull life. Never to see the Kremlin spires, never to save the world! "Maybe I can't do both," he said, "but I have to take care of my family."

"Do you have passage money?"

"I'm going to ask the American consul in Frankfurt."

"No good." Rick reached for his wallet. "Those days are gone forever." He extracted a ten-mark note, which he placed on the tablecloth, and a little blue envelope. "I bought a round-trip ticket," he said, smiling. "You see, I'm not as irresponsible as you think. . . . Take it. You can pay me back sometime."

They sat in silence for a while. The sky had turned to a deep purple, almost black. To their right they could see the red glow of a propaganda sign, flashing defiance at East Berlin.

19 - Why the Hell Not?

EDDY WAS PREGNANT and, worse, she had lied to him. She'd let that fair-faced young man make love to her, and now she was carrying his child—his second child! "He was my husband," she said. "I had to do it—I *wanted* to. I like sex. It's *fun*."

"You said. . . ."

"Well, I didn't want you to *shoot* him. Or yourself."

At least she'd worried about that! "Well," he said. "Do you want to call off the divorce?"

"No! I told Colin I'd divorce him if he went on his stupid peace march, and I will." She began to cry. "Oh, *why* was I put on this earth?" she wailed.

"To have children, I guess."

Indeed, it seemed so. For the past few weeks, she'd been gaining in weight and beauty. Her cheeks were pink, her breasts filled out, and her walk became steady. A woman fulfilled! Boris was proud to have her in charge of his household, even if the beauty was another man's work.

But what about his hope of marrying her?

He spent the night smoking on the couch while the women and children slept in the other room. How much noise they made!—turning, sighing, coughing, uttering scraps of sentences. Did Teddy sleep so restlessly when she was with Colin Merchant? By morning, Boris was ready to admit that he had known it all along. Of course she'd slept with her husband! And he should have known she was pregnant, too. Hadn't Prudy been hinting at it?

And Teddy had to marry him now! She couldn't work beyond September, say; Colin Merchant wasn't here to support her; and she was less likely than ever to go home to her parents. What choice did she have except to marry Boris? Viewed in this light, her betrayal was a piece of great good luck.

He yawned, butted his final cigarette, and made a pot of coffee at the kitchen alcove. It was the end of May; classes were over, and the movie hall was staging its annual Cartoon Marathon to help the students prepare for finals. The new photographer would be taking over soon, and Boris had to figure out how to support a wife and child—two children!—without a steady job.

But his luck continued to run. At eight-thirty, with the hot breath of summer detectable through the morning freshness, he went to the photo lab and found Mr. Phipps waiting for him. The development officer was the image of good news, his skull-like head creased and shining with happiness. "We're in the clear, Boris!" he cried, his lips peeling back in a grin. "Here, read this." He pushed a copy of the *Manchester Union* at Boris. The headline declared:

RED PROBE SHOWS

'SECURITY RISK'

IN OLDFIELD SCHOOL

Boris skimmed the story. A high school civics teacher had once joined the Communist Party. "What's this got to do with us?" he asked

"That's the Attorney General's report," Mr. Phipps said, as if the civics teacher's martyrdom were a personal victory. "That's it! The entire report is about this one Red he found, the only one in New Hampshire, apparently, and not a single word about the University."

"I don't have to resign?"

"No!" cried Mr. Phipps, slapping him on the back. "I couldn't believe it, either. As soon as I read the story, I called a friend in the Governor's office and asked: what's going on? Are you saving the big blast for the Sunday paper? Well, it seems the Attorney General had a falling-out with his assistant —the lad who questioned you? He resigned a month ago. The Attorney General refused to use any of the testimony he collected, so you're in the clear."

"And Marvin Peabody and the troops? You didn't have to boot them out of school?"

"Well, that was a bit different," Mr. Phipps said. "They *did* break the law. However!" he said, clearing his throat, "I wouldn't be surprised if the trustees took some corrective action at their next meeting. Young Peabody and his friends may be readmitted in September."

Boris read the story again, more closely. "So this poor bastard joined the Communist Party in 1936," he said. "And he fought in Spain. So what the hell? I remember the Spanish Civil War: all the good guys were fighting over there when I was a kid."

"I know," Mr. Phipps said. "I contributed a few dollars to the Abraham Lincoln Brigade, myself."

"Was the investigation in Narwich as stupid as this one? Did it mean as little?"

"I suppose so, Boris." Mr. Phipps looked out the window at the campus, sleepy in the late spring morning. "I argued against the expulsions," he said, "though I couldn't say much because Carol was one of them. . . . We haven't heard from her since she left home, you know. But!" He turned back to Boris, rubbing his hands. "That's in the past. The important thing now is to repair the injustice to you. We want you to stay on."

"But there's a new man coming in."

"He'll be your assistant," Mr. Phipps said. "I never did like the idea of turning the photo service over to him. Too young."

"I promised to do some free-lance work. . . ."

"You'll have an assistant! You haven't taken a vacation in ten years; nobody'll complain if you miss a day's work now and then. Outside work reflects credit upon the University, just as when a professor writes a book. Yes. And speaking of vacations, why don't you take one, now you have somebody to look after things? My brother-in-law owns a camp on Cape Cod. Why don't I borrow the key for a few days?"

"All right," Boris said, and they shook hands on it.

~ ~ ~ ~

"Life begins at forty," Boris told his reflection in the mirror that night. "Well, I'll be damned." He'd burst the cocoon of his life! He was an executive, with an assistant to handle the dull jobs. A magazine called *Gusto* had ordered a set of prints from the rally, and the Halcyon Fire and Casualty Company wanted to use Georgie's death picture in an advertisement. Even Tom Matthews was paying $10 a published photo now, to keep up with the competition. What with one thing and another, Boris figured, he could support as many children as Teddy was likely to produce.

The next evening, after a haircut at the Greek barbershop, he couldn't find an opening to propose. Then it was Saturday. Boris skulked around the Hut all afternoon, rehearsing his speech, and almost fainted from excitement when she came home from the Coffee Corner at six. He decided to wait until after dinner. Then the kids were restless; the young Peabody demanded attention and wouldn't leave Teddy's side until they packed him off to bed at nine. Then they had to wash the dinner dishes.

After they put the dishes away, he went outside to calm his nerves. The moon was rising like a bloody egg yolk above College Woods. The trees sighed in the dark. Boris shivered, although the night was almost summer-warm; it seemed a time for dreadful happenings. He went back to the Hut and called Teddy out to look at the huge, red-orange moon. "It's an omen," she whispered. "There's going to be a war." She was scaring herself, like the young Peabody conjuring dragons beneath the bed. Boris put his hand upon her shoulder in what he hoped was a reassuring manner. Perhaps, when the rising moon had turned to silver, he could put his question into words. Women were supposed to wax sentimental with the moon.

An automobile killed that hope. Headlights swept into the yard, turning the pines gray-green and reducing the moon to a reflection in the sky: a long Chevrolet convertible with the top down. "Oh!" cried Teddy. "It's Malcolm—my wonderful Malcolm." She danced away to greet him. Boris jammed his hands into his pockets and followed her. He wished he could dislike the lawyer, who ate wheat germ and drove with the top down in all weather. But it was hard to dislike him. He was, after all, the man hired to cut Colin Merchant out of their lives. "I was visiting a client," he said, getting out of the car without turning off the headlamps. In their glare he had the look of a dissipated elf. "So I thought I'd come over and see how you were getting along."

"Oh, you're sweet," Teddy said. "Boris, isn't he sweet?"

"Yeah," Boris said. "Any news about the divorce?"

"Yes, as a matter of fact. The judge schedules one day each term for uncontested divorces, and it will be July fifteen. Six weeks from now. How does that suit?"

"Oh!" Teddy's hand flew to her eyes, as if to shield them from the glare.

"Something wrong?" Malcolm Carleton asked.

"Oh, no. Nothing wrong. It's just so sudden. I thought it would take a bit longer, somehow."

"We can wait until the fall term," the lawyer said.

"No, that's worse. July is fine. . . . July fifteen."

"Let's drink to it," Boris said, afraid she'd burst into tears. They went into the Hut, the lawyer detouring to shut off his headlights and collect his briefcase. Boris mixed the drinks, with a double for Teddy and orange juice for himself. They sat down in a formal row on the couch.

"I have the libel," Malcolm said. He took a sheet of paper from his briefcase and scanned it with his small, bright eyes. His head glowed brick-red in the lamplight. "Shall I read it?" he asked.

"Wait," said Teddy. She placed her drink on the floor and went into the bedroom. With the door open, Boris could hear Baby Nikolas fretting. Teddy returned with her son in her arms. "Go ahead," she said. "He should hear it, too."

241

Malcolm Carleton cleared his throat. "Now comes Theodora Merchant of Narwich," he read without expression, "in the County of Piscataqua, State of New Hampshire, and complains against Colin Merchant of said Narwich and says. . . ."

Teddy sniffled and dug through her pockets in search of a handkerchief. Boris reached over and took Baby Nikolas on his own knee. The infant was awed by the ritual: he swayed from the hips and goggled at Malcolm Carleton, who was continuing in the same dull voice: "Yet the same Colin Merchant, wholly regardless of his marriage covenant and duty, has been guilty of extreme cruelty toward the libelant, in that he has frequently struck the libelant with his hands and fists and threatened to kill her; that he has twice abandoned the libelant for extended periods of time without provision for her support, and is presently outside the continental United States, address unknown. . . ."

Teddy wept into her handkerchief, and Baby Nikolas began to gurgle. Boris joggled the child. The tiny fingers opened like the petals of a flower and closed again upon his thumb. Poor little guy! He was willing to accept any thumb that was handy, whether it belonged to his father or not, the libelee whose address was unknown.

"*Wherefore*," said Malcolm Carleton, taking a deep breath, "your libelant, Theodora Merchant, prays that a divorce from the bonds of matrimony between herself and the libelee, Colin Merchant, be decreed in her favor; that she be granted the temporary and permanent custody of said minor child; that temporarily and permanently the libelee be enjoined and restrained from molesting and interfering with the person or liberty of the libelant and from entering any premises wherein she may reside; and for such other and further relief as justice may require."

"Is that necessary?" Teddy asked. "About threatening to kill me? He didn't really mean it, you know."

"It's customary," the lawyer said.

"All right," Teddy said. "If it's customary." She reclaimed

Baby Nikolas and carried him back to the bedroom.

"Divorce bothers the wife more than the husband," Malcolm Carleton said. After a second drink, he stood up to leave.

Boris went with him to the car. "Tell me something," he said.

"That's what you're paying for," the lawyer agreed.

"How long—how much time...."

"Before she can marry again?"

"Yeah."

"No time at all," Malcolm Carleton said, getting into his car and starting the engine. "She can remarry the next day if she wants. Happens all the time."

"What if she has a baby?"

"After she remarries? The law presumes that it belongs to her second husband. If she stays single the credit goes to husband number one."

"Happens all the time?"

"Yes."

Boris went back to the Hut. He found her sprawled on the couch. "Now comes Theodora!" she said. "Oh, Boris, maybe I should wait until he comes home—wouldn't that be the fair thing?"

"For Christ's sake. Was he ever fair to you?"

"What about the baby?" Teddy asked in the same helpless voice. "Shouldn't I wait until after the baby is born?"

Now. Ask her now! "Hey," he said.

"What?"

"Will you . . ." He choked on the verb.

"Boris," she said, sitting up. "What's the matter?"

". . . marry me," he said, the words coming out in a cracked whisper. "Teddy—will you marry me?" That was better! "You don't want that baby born without a father," he said before she could say No. "Marry me, and he'll be mine; I talked to Malcolm Carleton and he said the baby would be mine. So he'll have a father forever. Okay?"

"But I don't love you, Boris."

243

"Maybe you will, some day. Hell, it's fifty per cent habit, isn't it?"

"Do you think so?"

"Sure!"

Teddy bit her lip in the way that had become so familiar to him, and his heart turned over with love. "Yes," she said. "No. Oh, I don't know."

"Never mind. I'll ask again in a couple of days. Okay?"

"Oh, you're so good to me, Boris—why are you so good to me?"

"Because I love you," he said. And then he did it: brought his arms up to encircle her waist, and bent his neck to kiss her on the lips. He thought his heart would burst. Teddy returned the kiss with a little motion of her lips. Then she moved closer and butted her forehead against the hollow of his shoulder. They sat like that for a long time, until Prudence came home like a small whirlwind from her evening at the Coffee Corner.

"Three offers tonight," she said, sweeping off her kerchief and brushing an imaginary strand of hair into place. "I don't know whether it's the full moon or final exams, but the boys are really randy. . . . Oh, and speaking of randy young men, take a look at this!" She pulled a newspaper from her jacket pocket. There was a wire-service photograph on the front page. It showed a white man and three Negroes kneeling on the sidewalk in front of a restaurant while a group of toughs crowded around them. One had his foot up to kick a black man in the back. The caption explained that the "biracial group of demonstrators" had been evicted from the restaurant and doused with eggs, ketchup, and flour. "Isn't that your friend O'Rourke?"

"Well, I'll be damned," Boris said.

~ ~ ~ ~

Hal Pappajohn telephoned on Sunday afternoon. Like O'Rourke, he hadn't been seen in town since Georgie's funeral. "Hey, Boris," he said. "You having a gig tonight?"

Oh, God! It was the first Sunday of June, when Boris was accustomed to visit his mother in Concord and relax with his young rebels at the Hut. But the old lady was dead and the rebels were scattered. "I guess not," he said. "But come over for a drink if you want."

"Why don't you guys come here? Bring Teddy, bring that Peabody dame, bring the kids. . . . Oh, and bring a bottle. I've got a surprise for you."

Boris covered the mouthpiece with his hand and told the women that Hal was back. Teddy was enthusiastic. Prudence was not. "I'll stay with the children," she said.

"We'll hire a baby sitter," Boris said, and uncovered the mouthpiece. "Okay," he told Hal. "Eight o'clock."

It was past eight before Prudy and Teddy got the kids to sleep, and nine before Boris crossed the bridge that separated Portsmouth from Kittery in Maine. Hal's boat was moored at the Simpson Cove Yacht Club. This consisted of a general store, a hut containing a lounge and a shower room, a fuel pump, and a float to which *Nomad* was attached by umbilical cords of water hose and electric cable. It was on the north bank of Portsmouth Harbor. To reach it, Boris had to drive past the US Navy shipyard, blazing with light, building nuclear submarines to lurk beneath the ocean and give fits to Marvin Peabody.

A mist was rising from Simpson Cove when Boris parked the Volkswagen behind the general store. The tide was low, so he was obliged to lead the women down a gangway that was slippery with dew and pitched at an angle. Prudy giggled. "A girl doesn't have a chance with Hal Pappajohn, does she?" she said. "Imagine trying to escape from this place in spike heels!"

Nomad was not a large boat, but there was headroom for Boris if he didn't straighten his shoulders. A centerboard trunk ran through the middle of the cabin, with the leaves of a table hinged to it; there were bunks on either side that doubled as couches for daytime use. Toward the stern, a sink and cookstove were tucked beside the cockpit steps, while the forward end of the cabin was curtained off. Prudy was ecstatic. She danced around the cabin, touching the kerosene lamps and the brass hand pump and the alcohol stove on pivots that remained from the days when *Nomad* actually went to sea. "Some night I'll fill Breck full of gin," Hal said. "I'll cut the lines with an axe and sail this old tub to England. *Yeah!*" He was already drunk, his eyes bright and cold as diamonds, his shirt open to the third button to expose the curly black hair on his chest.

Prudy wouldn't look at him, but chattered to Gene Breck, slouched on one of the bunks with his bare feet propped against the centerboard trunk, and smoking his awful corncob pipe. "What do you keep behind the curtain?" she asked.

"That's the bridal suite," Breck said in a drawl, staring her up and down.

Hal bounced to his feet. "Come out of there, bitch!" he roared at the curtain. As if she'd been waiting for this call, Carol Phipps emerged from the forward compartment. Her full lips gleamed in the lamplight, quivering over a private joke; her blue eyes sparkled.

"Hello, everybody," she said, letting the curtains drift together behind her. "Boris, dear!" She brushed his cheekbone with her plum-ripe lips, then squeezed by to greet the women, leaving him flushed with the heat of her passage. "Hal, sweetie, have you offered our guests a drink?" She was holding her left hand askew. At first Boris thought she'd sprained it, but then he saw a plain gold band around the third finger. He looked at Hal's left hand. Sure enough, he was wearing the twin of Carol's ring.

"Well, why the hell not?" Hal said. "I always wanted to be a family man, and here I had the chance, so I decided to grab it." He seized Carol's plump thigh and gave it a squeeze. She smiled tolerantly.

"The drinks, sweetie, the drinks," she said.

Hal took the bottle of gin from Boris and went to the galley. "So I went down to Boston," he yelled over his

246

shoulder, "and do you know where I found her? In Colin's apartment. Yeah! So we looked up a justice of the peace and got married. Why the hell not?"

"Not too strong for me, sweetie," Carol said.

The *Nomad* crew sat on one couch, with Carol between the two men. Boris sat across from them with Teddy on his right and Prudence on his left. "Why not?" Hal roared. "That's what I said to myself. If you sit on your ass, life'll drag you along anyhow; you just get the skin worn off. Don't fight it, that's my motto. Don't argue with life. You want to get married? Get married. Why the hell not?"

"Is everybody's drink all right?" Carol asked, and Breck raised his eyebrows.

"What will you do now?" Prudy asked.

"I'm going to find a summer job," Carol said, "and we'll get an apartment, because Hal will be going back to school in September. The baby will be coming in November. . . ."

Teddy sat quietly on the couch, smiling at Hal and Carol in turn. Then she turned to Boris. "Please," she whispered, "let's go outside for a minute—all this smoke, this talk!" They went on deck. When *Nomad* became a houseboat, the cabin was extended toward the stern, so it crowded out most of the cockpit. Boris and Teddy went up on the cabin roof and sat there hugging the mast. They found themselves staring at the wall of checkered light that was Portsmouth Navy Prison, the glow diffused and unearthly through the fog. Water lapped against *Nomad*'s hull, and the planks creaked where they rubbed against the float. "Hal is a changed man," Teddy said. "Isn't it amazing?"

Boris took a breath. "Have you—thought about what I asked you? About marrying again?"

"Oh, yes!"

"What did. . . ."

"I don't know, Boris," she whispered. Their voices seemed very loud on the water. "I'm very fond of you, but I don't love you, not that way."

"I don't care. I want to marry you anyhow."

She was silent for a while. They heard the mournful call of a whistling buoy, and the fog was brightened at intervals by the lighthouse on Whaleback reef, as if some cosmic photographer were flashing their portrait, over and over again. "All right," Teddy said then. "But I want to be your mistress first. And if it works out we'll be married."

"You want. . . ."

"Well, the physical thing is pretty important. Wouldn't it be awful if we were married and then discovered we didn't like each other in bed? We'll have an affair, Boris, a really-and-truly affair. Won't that be fun?"

Boris wasn't sure. Once he was married to Teddy, the sex bit would be no problem: he would have all the time in the world to learn how to please her. But a test case. . . . He was not certain that he wanted to risk his marriage on a test case, as if happiness were a wager and sex a roulette wheel. There was that business with Carol Phipps—but Teddy was different! He was in love with Teddy. "All right," he said. "There's a place on Cape Cod I can borrow. We could go down there for—a honeymoon. What do you think?"

"I've always wanted to visit the Cape," Teddy said in her husky voice, creeping closer to the mast, and to him. Boris put his arm around her. In silence they watched the mist rising on Simpson Cove. A sailboat was chugging slowly through the anchorage under engine power, with one man at the tiller and another up front with a searchlight, arguing about the location of their mooring. As if disturbed by the argument, a gull materialized out of the mist and settled upon *Nomad*'s bowsprit. It ruffled its feathers and peered brightly at Teddy and Boris. "Oh, look at him!" Teddy cried.

Boris looked at her instead, her heart-shaped face just visible in the light from Whaleback reef. "I love you," he said. "You're the first person I've loved in twenty years."

20 - *That Was a Bit of a Bust*

BORIS HAD NEVER SEEN the world so beautiful. The days were bright with sun; the nights were full of stars. Each afternoon stretched a bit longer than the one before, until it was summer, and the roads around Narwich were heavy with the scent of lilacs. On the fourteenth of June, he signed his contract as Director of Photographic Services, turned the lab over to his new assistant, took an advance against his month's salary, and borrowed the key to the Phipps cottage at the Cape. He was off to make his peace with life!

Teddy had never been so beautiful, either. Her eyes sparkled like tiny mosaics of lavender and green; she kept dropping small objects and bumping into large ones, and her cheeks flamed whenever he declared his love, which he did at regular intervals. They were shy with one another now. Luckily the Coffee Corner was closed for two weeks between spring semester and summer school, so Prudence was usually at home to fill the silences. She seemed amused by it all.

On the road map, Cape Cod extended into the Atlantic Ocean like a beckoning arm, with Provincetown clasped in its hand. It didn't seem far, but they were late in starting and the roads were crowded with weekend drivers. They reached the cottage at six, after driving through a landscape that might have been seared by a celestial blowtorch. It was on the outskirts of Provincetown: gray with bright red trim, a tiny honeymoon house among the dunes, with windows that looked down a bone-white beach to the sea. Teddy clapped her hands and began moving things, not resting until she had rearranged the furniture, unpacked the suitcases, and swept the floors. The cottage would have fitted entire into the living room of the Hut, so they had it arranged to Teddy's satisfaction in less than an hour. Then they had dinner. Afterward they fashioned a crib from suitcases and blankets, and put Baby Nikolas to bed. "There!" Teddy said. "Now we can relax."

But she continued to stand.

Boris sat on the couch and lit a cigarette. The ocean surged outside the window, hurling itself upon the beach in a slow, pulsating rhythm. The ocean air was damp upon his face. He couldn't think of anything to say.

"I—" Teddy's voice was unexpectedly loud in the room, and she broke off and began again. "I should wash the dishes," she said in a quieter tone.

"Tomorrow," Boris said. "Why don't we wait until tomorrow?"

"All right. I am tired, aren't you? Well, not *too* tired. . . ."

"It was a long drive," he agreed, to give her a way out if she wanted one.

Teddy sat down, but at the far end of the couch. He'd have to stand up, walk a few steps, and sit down again if he wanted to be close. He decided to wait a few minutes. It would seem more natural that way: he'd stand up, yawn and stretch, walk around a bit. "I know!" Teddy cried, jumping to her feet. "Let's have a drink. You too, Boris—let's!"

"You go ahead."

"Not unless you drink with me," she said in her throaty voice. "Aren't we starting a new life? Drink to it with me!"

Her eyes were joyful, almost purple in the lamplight. "Okay," he said. She mixed the drinks. Boris sipped at his, the first in ten years. Well! It was good. He could just make out the astringent taste of gin, under the sweet cloak of orange juice. He drank it off and held out his glass for another.

"Not so fast," Teddy giggled. "I don't want you to pass out." But her glass too was empty.

Boris felt the second drink. The light in the room seemed brighter, the ocean less noisy, and all things possible: he slid along the couch and put his arm around Teddy's waist. "I love you," he said, the words fuzzy at the edges.

"Kiss me, then," she said.

He bent his head, but only managed to kiss the corner of her mouth. Then Teddy bounced up to fill their glasses again.

The third drink seemed stronger. His throat tried to lock it out, and he discovered a desperate need for air. "Excuse me," he said, lurching toward the window, but changed direction and ran to the bathroom, where he was so sick he wanted to die. "I'm sorry," Teddy wailed, fussing around with sponges and towels. "I forgot you weren't used to drinking. . . . Oh, I *am* sorry, Boris."

Together they got him cleaned up and into the bedroom. Boris stretched out on the double bed. Humming softly, Teddy removed his shoes and spread a blanket across him; the light went out, and a soft hand brushed his face. He fell asleep.

~ ~ ~ ~

At dawn he snapped awake. The ocean still hurled itself against the distant beach, and the sea air was clammy around his face. He was *freezing*. Nearby, however, there was a promise of warmth, and he turned toward it. Teddy was sleeping fully dressed on the bedspread, crouched into herself with her shoulders bent and her hands tucked between her knees. She was facing him, but all he could see was the top of her head and the curve of her cheek, ivory-white in the dawn.

God, it was cold! He searched on the floor and came up with the blanket, which had slipped to the floor during the night, and which he now wrapped around himself and then spread across Teddy. "Mmmm," she said, and her eyelids fluttered open. She regarded him with eyes that were gray as anthracite in the uncertain light of dawn. "Uhh," she said, closing them again. One arm speared upward until she rapped her knuckles against the wall; then she turned away, and back, and stretched. Finally she rolled against him with her arms drawn up and her hands covering her face, and went back to sleep. His heart swelled with love. So did his body, turning strong and lustful, as if he were a flower and Teddy was the sun. It would be all right. Everything would be all right.

"Teddy," he whispered, putting his hand on her shoulder. She moved closer to him. "Sweetheart," he said. "Wake up."

Teddy yawned with a quick intake of breath. Her teeth clicked. "My!" she said. "It's morning."

"I love you," Boris said.

"Mmmm," she said. She was a married woman, with one child in the crib and another on the way—couldn't she give him a bit of help?

"Do you have an Alka-Seltzer?" Those fine fat discs had once been his standard breakfast.

"Aspirin," she said. "In the bathroom? In a little bottle."

He walked to the bathroom in his stocking feet and found the aspirin on top of the toilet tank, with other of her supplies. More bottles were ranged along the glass shelf above the washbowl. What a lot of stuff! He popped three tablets into his mouth and chewed them. Then he brushed his teeth, shaved, and took a shower. The shower stall was metal, which boomed whenever his elbows hit it. But the water was hot, and he was warm when he finished. He was also naked, so he wrapped a towel around his middle. That did nothing to hide his bony knees and chest. He peered into the bedroom. Her eyes were still closed, and he was padded across the floor and slid under the covers before she opened them.

But she was on *top* of the covers. And she was wearing a cardigan, and a blouse under that, and wool slacks that came down past her knees. How was he supposed to get through so much clothing? Carol Phipps had undressed herself, and of course the same was true of the girl in Bangkok. "Teddy?" he said.

"Mmm?"

"Maybe if you got under the bedspread?"

"Oh! I'm so stupid—I'm sorry!" Off came the cardigan and the blouse and the slacks, and she got under the covers. "That's better," she said, her voice husky, that welcoming sound. Boris put his arms around her. His hands glowed with the warmth of her body, smooth and mostly naked; the glow ran like quicksilver through his veins, until he was throbbing with heat. She was still wearing the bra and panties, of course.

252

He began to rehearse in his mind the trick of unclasping a bra from the front.

Then Baby Nikolas cried. The noise began on the floor beyond Teddy, then bounced from the walls, so that it attacked Boris from every side. It was shrill, mechanical, and somehow jolly, as if Baby Nikolas knew what the grownups were planning and thought it a fine joke to stop them.

"Oh, dear," Teddy said. She got out of bed, went to the makeshift crib, and plucked the baby out of his nest. Cooing softly, she took him to the kitchen. Boris heard the rattle of a saucepan and the hiss of the gas jet, then the *fhlup!* when it ignited. He took the opportunity to dig a shirt and clean underwear out of his suitcase, and to retrieve his pants from the bathroom. Teddy emerged from the kitchen and put Baby Nikolas back in his nest, with the bottle propped at an angle to his mouth. "Well," she said, looking at Boris in his clean clothes, "you've had a shower, so I suppose I ought to."

When he heard the water storming against the shower stall, he found his shoes and put them on. He'd wait until tonight. That would be better. He went to the window and looked out on an eroded hillside of sand, and beyond that the beach and the slate-gray eternity of the Atlantic Ocean. The horizon burned with color. Boris waited for the sun to come up, but the mood was broken by an automobile exhaust, un-muffled, that seemed to explode out of the sand dunes on either side.

Behind him, Baby Nikolas was fussing. Boris went over and adjusted the bottle so the last of the milk would flow into the pursed, sucking lips. The blue eyes grinned at him. Boris made a fist and shook it, and Baby Nikolas chuckled, causing the bottle to roll away from him with milk leaking from the nipple. Boris replaced it, then sat down on the edge of the bed. His eyes burned.

After a few minutes Teddy came in. She was now wearing a plain cotton dress, belted, very matronly. Her hair was wet from the shower. Not looking at him, she went to the bureau and took a cigarette from the pack that was lying there. With the cigarette drooping from her lips, woman fashion, she struck a match and lit it. Then she sat down on the bed. She propped her elbows on her knees and smoked by leaning forward to the cigarette, instead of bringing it to her lips. She looked at little Nick in his barricade of suitcases. The bottle had fallen aside again, empty, and he was amusing himself by kicking his fat pink feet into the air. "Well, that was a bit of a bust, wasn't it?" she said.

"It would have been fine if he hadn't yelled. That broke the mood, you know?"

"I'm sorry, Boris. But what was I supposed to do, tell him wait while Mommy gets *laid*?"

"It'll work out, you'll see," he said. "When we're married."

"Hah!" Teddy leaned forward to take a puff from her cigarette. The ash was long, and when she inhaled it spilled on her lap. "Damn," she, brushing them off. "You were sorry for me, so you thought you'd marry me. Well, thank you very much, but I don't want a loveless marriage."

"It wouldn't be loveless—I love you!"

"You don't. You don't even want to *screw* me, that's pretty obvious. Oh, God!" she cried, bringing her hand to her mouth and biting the knuckle. "Doesn't anybody want me? Am I so homely? I know my figure isn't much, but doesn't anybody want me?"

"Teddy, for Christ's sake!"

"I'm sorry." She sniffled and stood up, beating stray cigarette ashes out of her dess. "It's better this way," she said. "It wouldn't be fair to marry you."

"Who's talking about fair? I love you!"

"Oh, Boris, it's no good." She walked away from him toward the window. "You couldn't be my husband, any more than you could be the father of my baby," she said over her shoulder. "Colin is the one. He's the only one there'll ever be." She leaned against the window, her face to the rising sun. "Colin. . . . *My God!*" she cried.

254

"What? What's the matter?" Boris followed her to the window. Across the damp crown of her head, he saw what had startled her: a naked swimmer. A young man. He was emerging from the ocean, which glittered off to the horizon in an iron blue. Water streamed from the swimmer's body and surged around his ankles as he walked clear of the waves. The rising sun touched his skin with gold. He was the prototype of man, born from the sea, slender, fair, and unmarked by time.

Then he ran up the beach toward them, leaping like a colt in the joy of his youth, and vanished behind a dune.

21 - Let the Whole World See!

COLIN DANCED ONE-LEGGED on the sand, dressing as fast as he could, not bothering to dry himself or brush the sand from his feet. Wow! He had never been so cold. Nor so awake, though he hadn't slept for twenty-four hours—more than that! —not since leaving the Paris youth hostel yesterday morning. How many miles was that? How many time zones? Paris to Boston in the Pan Am Clipper, four big jet engines whooshing him across the sea. (No DC-7s for Rickover!) Then to Narwich in his loyal old Ford, recovered from the alley off Sherman Street. An awkward reunion with a sleepy Prudy Peabody, then south again to Provincetown. Wow!

When he was dressed in the plaid shirt, khaki trousers, and hiking boots that had been his uniform for three months now, Colin walked back to the road. From time to time a tremor ran through him, caused by the swim he'd just finished or the excitement he was about to cause. From time to time, he caught a glimpse across the sand dune of that little red-and-gray cottage where his wife had spent the night with another man.

He reached the black Ford, sagging on its springs. He'd intended to smoke a cigarette and wait for his watch to creep along to eight o'clock, but it was only six-thirty. He'd never last until eight! So, trailing cigarette smoke behind him, he turned and walked to the cottage. His heart thumped in his chest. What should he do with them? Slap Teddy until she cried! Beat the photographer until he begged for mercy! But he was no Hal Pappajohn. Oh, he may have hit Teddy once or twice, when he'd been drinking, but he hadn't hit another guy since fifth grade.

And really, what did one night matter? Sex didn't leave a mark—none, anyhow, that wasn't gone before the next encounter. If it were otherwise, Colin would be as scarred as anyone. Teddy deserved a fling! It evened the score somewhat, so he could start the new life with an easy conscience.

He mounted the flagstone path and knocked twice on the door. "Come in!" cried a husky voice—Teddy's voice. He hesitated, remembering Prudy's warning about the pistol. What if the photographer was on the other side of the door with the gun? No—Teddy wouldn't allow it. Colin turned the doorknob and stepped inside.

They were waiting for him, all right, standing in the middle of the room like two people in a Swedish film—motionless, angular, and apart. "Get out," the photographer said. "We don't want you here." He was a tall, hawklike man, blackened by time and burning with an energy that made Colin tremble. Hatred! Colin had never seen such a power of hatred. "Bastard," the photographer added for good measure.

"Never mind, Boris," Teddy said. "He won't stay long. He never does."

It was true, then. They were leagued against him. But he had to try! "Teddy," he said, coaxing her, looking into her eyes —what sweet eyes she had! Cool and thoughtful. What color were they? He was never quite sure. "Come for a walk with me," he urged. "I want to talk to you."

"No," the photographer said.

"You can talk right here, Colin Merchant," Teddy said, but not so bitterly as before.

"No, he can't," the photographer said.

"I love you," Colin told her, torn between the need to look at her and keep an eye on the other man. "Come outside for a minute."

"Anyhow," Teddy said, "what do you mean, barging in here this time of the morning? Why didn't you come last night if you were going to come at all?"

The photographer turned away and walked to the couch, where he flopped down. There was no gun in sight, so Colin pressed his advantage. He told Teddy about the thousands of miles he'd traveled since yesterday morning. "I haven't slept in two days," he said, which was almost true, if you added the time zones he'd crossed. "Trying to find you again."

"Really?"

She was softening! "I love you, Teddy," he said. "Don't you understand?"

"Oh, I understand. You're in love *this minute*. But what about tomorrow? I want something that will *last*." Colin's heart swelled with the desire to protect her—this fierce, frightened girl who was his wife. She needed somebody to look after her, that was all. But Colin Merchant could be just as reliable as the photographer, if that's what it took. Why not? It was a better life than marching across Europe under a sign that nobody heeded.

"That's what I came here to say," he told her. Again, it wasn't much of an exaggeration. "I'm going to settle down, if you'll come back to me."

"This minute," she said again.

"That's all there is!" he cried. "This minute is all we've got!"

"Not for me. I have a son."

"Yes, and that's something else. Where is he? I want to see my son."

"You do?" Teddy softened, glowing with the love he remembered so well. Well, there was something to be said for children, after all. They were a drag in fair weather, but useful in a storm, when without their pull astern the old ship might broach and go under. "All right," Teddy whispered.

The photographer bounded to his feet with a fresh reserve of hatred. He picked up the telephone. "If that bastard doesn't get out of here in one minute," he said, "I'm calling the police."

"Oh, God!" she cried. "You pull me this way, he pulls me that way. . . . Why do you *tear me apart?*"

"Thirty seconds," the photographer said.

Then the baby cried—a husky, piping cry, not at all unpleasant. Colin had expected something more fretful. "That's my son!" he said. "I want to see him."

258

"Yes," Teddy said. "It's a father's right." She went into the bedroom and returned with a blanket-wrapped bundle in her arms. "We'll go for a walk on the beach," she said, her voice now firm. "We'll be back in ten minutes," she told the photographer, who was still holding the telephone. "He has a right to see his son." Colin opened the door before she could change her mind.

Outside, he walked so fast she couldn't keep up with him. There was a winding driveway between the cottage and the road, and a ridge of sand loosely held in place by grass and weeds, and when he reached the car she wasn't in sight. So he prepared a surprise: he stood on his head. "Oh, *Colin!*" she cried when she came over the rise—just in time, too. He was about to fall over. "You *idiot!*" He flipped onto his knees and swiveled around to grin at her. He cheeped out of the side of his mouth and scooted toward her, monkey-fashion, dragging his knuckles along the sand. Teddy shrieked. He grabbed the hem of her dress, then her hand, and pulled her down on top of him, cheeping all the while. Then they kissed. It was a hot, vibrant kiss that Teddy was the first to break. "Don't hurt Baby Nikolas," she said, uncovering the good blue eyes of his son. They stared unblinkingly at him.

"Nick-o-louse!" he jeered. "What a name!"

"Well, *you* weren't here to name him. . . . What would you have chosen?"

"I would call him—Everyman!" Colin cried. He did a backward somersault. "Wow!" he said, coming to rest in a sitting position. "Nice friends you have. What was he going to tell the police? *Help, officer! My girlfriend is being bothered by her husband!*"

Teddy giggled. "Oh, Colin," she said. "The telephone isn't connected." They shared a laugh, looking into each other's eyes, and then she came over to kneel close beside him on the sand. "I'm glad you've come back," she whispered. "Even if it's just for a little while."

She was so *real*, her eyes open to him and welcoming any

hurt he might give—trusting him. Brown, weren't they? Or that other thing—hazel. The eyes of his wife! And that other defenseless creature was his son. Colin felt a thrill of possession, and he stood up and gestured toward the car. "Let's have breakfast," he said. "I haven't eaten since I got off the plane. Yesterday morning I was having café au lait in Paris—can you believe it?"

He told her about Paris and Calais and Frankfurt and Berlin as they drove into Provincetown. He couldn't find a parking place on the narrow main street, so he left the car on the municipal pier, where fishermen were cutting bait and gulls were hovering. He took Teddy's hand, warm and trusting like her eyes, and led her across the square where a giant anchor had come to rest, for the benefit of tourist photographs during the day and folk singers at night. Colin had often perched on that anchor, last summer in Provincetown.

He ordered ham and eggs at a snack bar on the square. Over coffee, Teddy said: "All right, now I have something to tell *you*." Her eyes were determined and rather scared. "Did you know that I've filed suit for divorce? Well, I have, and that's not all. I—I'm—oh, Colin!"

"I know," he said, trying to sound reassuring. "You're pregnant. It's all right."

"But how did you *know?*"

"Prudy wrote and told me. That's why I gave up the peace march." It wasn't the entire truth, but it was close enough. "That's why I came home."

"Really? Oh, why didn't you come sooner, then?"

"So you wouldn't have shacked up with that creep?" Colin took a deep, steadying breath. "Well, that's all right, too."

Teddy stared at him, a little pucker-frown between her eyebrows. "Well, I like that!" she said. "He doesn't care if his wife sleeps with another man! Well, for your information, Colin Merchant, nothing happened last night. Nothing at all."

"Oh, Teddy, don't be afraid of me."

"It's true! You're still the only man I've ever had, the only one I've ever wanted." He felt relief and disappointment, both, and a shivering gratitude that he hadn't mentioned his romp with Prudence Peabody, on Cape Cod last summer. Let it be, let it be. Teddy wouldn't be so ready to forgive if she needed no forgiveness herself.

"I believe you," he said. "Let's get out of here." All this talk about last night was making him itch with desire. And the counterman was getting interested in the conversation. "We'll go for a ride."

"I told Boris. . . ."

"Five minutes!"

"All right."

He drove out of Provincetown on the brave ribbon of highway that seemed about to sink at any moment beneath the sand. The sun was well up now, and the air had a purity that dazzled their eyes and made Berlin and Paris seem drab in comparison. Colin followed the highway to Race Point, on the outer knuckle of the Cape. He parked near the Coast Guard station, beside the automobiles of other early-morning tourists, and led Teddy down the sandy cliff to the beach. The wind was off the ocean. Colin turned up the collar of his shirt for the illusion of warmth it gave, and Teddy snuggled the baby under her leeward arm. "Here!" he said, suddenly aflame with love. "Let me carry him."

"Really?" She placed the child in his arms like an offering. Then she put her left arm around his waist and her right hand on his elbow, and the three of them progressed as one person across the sand.

"This is a good place," Colin said at last, nudging Teddy into a cleft between two dunes. "It's out of the wind." They sat down on the sand, still twined together, and waited for the sun to warm them. Colin continued his tale of Europe, telling her how he had decided to come home and find a job and support his family.

"And then what?" she asked, still not quite believing him.

"I don't know. Maybe I can get back to my sculpture,

261

maybe I can create something worthwhile. But it doesn't matter. The important thing is to live a good life, a full life. When I heard about Georgie...."

"Oh, yes! Poor Georgie."

"Prepare! That's all I've done. First I had to graduate from high school, and then I had to do three years in the Army, to get the GI Bill, and then I had to finish college. . . ."

"And then you had to marry me."

"Yes, and then I left you, because I still wasn't ready to start living— I had to reform the world! Well, I'm done with that. I'm going to live in it while I can." He pressed against her. "Will you come with me?" he asked.

"Yes! Oh, Colin, I love you so!" Then her hand flew to her mouth. "Oh, dear," she said.

"What?"

"Boris."

"What about him?"

"He'll be terribly upset."

"So what?"

"He's been so good to me, Colin—you've no idea."

He laughed. "I did have an idea," he reminded her, "but you said I was wrong."

"*Colin!*"

"Are you sure you didn't sleep with him last night?"

"I—we slept in the same bed, but we didn't . . . make love." Her hands fluttered, and she buried them in her lap. "He didn't even kiss me."

"What is he—a monk?"

"It's not that." She smiled, a shy little twist of the mouth. "I think maybe he's a little bit afraid of women, you know?"

"You didn't sleep with him?"

"Not that way, no."

"Not last night? Not ever?"

"I told you: no."

"Then it's been a long time, hasn't it?" he said, letting his voice go low and vibrant. Teddy shivered. "*Hasn't* it?"

262

"Yes."

They kissed. Then Teddy pulled away. "Give me your shirt," she said.

"What?"

"So I can put Baby Nikolas down—you see? He's asleep." Colin took off the shirt, and with one hand Teddy spread it on the sand. She put the baby in the center, very white against the red plaid, and covered him with the little blanket she had brought. "There!" she said. She took his hand. Her arm—as tanned as his, but golden instead of bronze—was covered with tiny goose-bumps. "I saw you on the beach this morning," she said. "You thought you were all alone, didn't you? But I was right there with you. Are you all salty from the ocean?" She touched his neck with her tongue. "Ooooh!" she said, laughing in her throat. The sun flamed on Colin's neck. He ran his fingers along Teddy's calf, under her dress, along her thigh. She wasn't wearing panties! "Not here!" she said. "Somebody will see us." But she lifted herself away from him, and helped him by moving her hips.

"Let the whole world see! We're married."

"We're not! I have a paper from the state of New Hampshire that says we're getting divorced, that you can't come near me."

"To hell with New Hampshire," Colin said. "You're my wife, and no piece of paper can change that."

Her eyes went misty. "Do you love me?" she asked.

"Of course I do."

"Well, say it."

"I love you."

"And I love *you*." Colin was half-sitting, half-lying against the sandy ledge. He put his hands on Teddy's waist and pulled her onto him. Gently at first, he made love to her while the surf roared upon Race Point and the sun flamed into their cleft between the dunes. Then the surf merged with the blood that was surging in his ears, and the sun with the blood flaming in his eyes, and all the world pounded with him in the

263

need of making love. Until the sun pinwheeled, the surf exploded, and Teddy shuddered in his arms. They lay together for a long, sunny time. Then she stirred. Her face swam into his range of vision, a great golden orb that came down and kissed him on the eyes, again and again. "I love you," she whispered. "Only you. No one but you."

~ ~ ~ ~

Boris crouched in the easy chair with his father's pistol dangling from his right hand, a comfortable weight, and listened to the ceaseless drive of the ocean, a dark and powerful sound. He turned the pistol, supporting the muzzle with the palm of his left hand. It was a .32 caliber hammerless Colt such as his colonel had carried during the War; it was also said to be popular with detectives and gangsters—and women, because it was small enough to carry in a purse. It was a pocket-sized version of the Bomb—dark gray, metallic, and foolproof.

He was still admiring its handsome flank when he heard the car returning—a popple of exhaust, a creaking of springs, tires crunching on the gravel, a slamming door. Teddy's quick footsteps mounted to the cottage. "Hi!" she said. "Goodness, this place is gloomy. D'you mind if I leave the door open? Boris?" She saw the pistol. "What are you doing with that thing?"

"Cleaning it," he said. "The salt air is tough on steel." He put the weapon on the side table. "Where's Nikolas?"

"In—the car." She twisted her fingers together. "Boris. . . ."

"You're going away."

"Well—yes." She flashed an uncertain smile.

"He ran out on you twice, you filed for a divorce, you said you'd marry me, and now you're going back to him—just like that?"

"You don't *understand!*"

"Oh, I understand. He didn't make a fool of himself in bed."

"Boris! It wasn't your fault, what happened; it was me, it was both of us. We just don't love each other that way."

264

It was nice of her to share the blame. If only. . . . He swallowed the question, but it bobbed into his throat again, so he asked it: "If things had happened differently—you know—would you be going go away with him now?"

"I think so." Her face glowed with happiness, as if he had reminded her of something particularly wonderful. "It would have been more difficult, of course, but I think I would have gone back to him, and I think he would have forgiven me. I belong to him. . . . You say: 'Please be mine.' But Colin says: 'You *are* mine.' And that makes all the difference." She bent and kissed him. She moved away before he could return the kiss, but not before he caught the tangy scent of sex, like ammonia, and saw grains of sand on her neck. Of course! Colin had made hot, successful love to her, on the beach, untroubled by the long night or the bright day, untroubled by anything in the world except his young, hot need. Colin was successful: she would go with him. Boris had failed: he would stay behind.

Teddy went into the bedroom and began to pack. He couldn't bear the sound, the drawers opening and closing, and he put the pistol on the side-table and covered his ears with his hands. After what seemed a very long time, she emerged from the bedroom with a suitcase in each hand and the overnight case under her left arm. She carried them to the door and put them down. She looked around the room, found a pale blue kerchief on the couch, and tied it inexpertly around her head. The kerchief was a present from Boris, as was the overnight case. "Let's see," she said. "What else have I forgotten?"

"Try the bathroom."

She nodded, went into the bathroom, and emerged with a plastic bag of soiled diapers, which she folded and placed in one of the suitcases. "Boris," she said then. "*Thank* you. You've done so much for us, for Nikolas and me."

"I—enjoyed it."

"Goodbye, Boris."

"So long," he said.

She gathered the cases, one in each hand and one under her arm. She went outside. Boris sat in the chair as if nailed to it, scarcely breathing, waiting for her to be gone. Luckily he didn't have to *do* anything. He didn't know how he would have managed, if the parting had required him to *do* something. He heard a car door slam, another door, low voices, then Teddy saying high and clear: "I don't know. . . ." But Boris never learned what it was she didn't know, because her words crumbled the wall holding back his grief, and misery rushed over him in long, black, soundless waves.

When the torrent had swept past, leaving him gasping but still safely nailed in place, there was nothing in the yard but silence. She was gone.

Boris took his father's pistol and went to the door, which she had left open. (And didn't she always leave doors open, jar caps untightened, milk unrefrigerated?) It was getting on toward noon. Except for the sun, everything was where it had been at dawn. Boris was astonished that this should be so. He'd expected uprooted trees, shattered buildings, bodies of animals and people—wreckage to match the desolation in his heart. But everything was as it had been.

He went outside and walked along the ridge of sand and scrub, until he came to the beach. There were two beaches, really—a strip of loose white sand beginning where the dunes left off, and beyond it a smooth ramp of wet sand leading down to the sea. The tide was low. Boris walked out on the exposed sea-bottom, like a polished slab, until he was standing in the froth of the strongest waves, at the line where the land gave way to the sea. The water tossed endlessly, restlessly, driving an occasional long wave against the beach, as if to test its strength and wet his shoes.

He heaved the pistol up to the level of his eyes and looked at it, dark gray and cold like the sea, but not alive like the sea. A dead thing. A lump of metal, designed by a lunatic for the use of fools. Throw it away!

But he'd keep the bullet as a souvenir. Tingling with excitement—he'd never seen the bullet that would smash his skull—Boris examined the back of the barrel, where the hammer would have been if the pistol had had a hammer. It must work like the carbine he'd carried during the War. So he grabbed the slide with the thumb and forefinger of his left hand and tried to pull it back. God, it was stiff! It kept springing forward again, but he could see the beginning of the slot on the right side, where the empty cartridge would be ejected. But there was no bullet inside.

So he attacked the underside of the hand-grip, where a latch kept the magazine in place. That too was stiff, but he was able to force it open and let the magazine drop into his palm. It was empty.

It couldn't be! But it was. Perhaps his mother had emptied it—poor mad, dead mother—or the Oldfield police who'd investigated the shooting. Or maybe there'd only ever been the one bullet, the one that had smashed his father's skull.

The excitement snapped in him, like a window shade flying up, and a burst of air rasped through his throat. Empty! Always empty, all the times he'd used it to scare his guests, all the times it had comforted him, a key to let him out of life if life became too much to bear. Escape had never been possible. The gun was empty.

He danced a little jig upon the sand, then realized that he was dancing in ankle-deep water. The tide was returning. He drew back his arm and hurled the pistol seaward. It made a solid, stone-like splash. *Bloop!* He danced back to the strip of loose, dry sand beyond the high-water line. Here he sat on his heels and watched the tide come in, gaining upon the land with the patience of eternity. The water was gray-green when it washed over the sand. Each wave came a bit nearer than the one before, then fell back, boiling, into the gray cauldron from which it had emerged, as if to assure the land that its intentions were honorable. But the next wave came nearer still.

He bounced to his feet and began striding up and down, a

267

few yards along the sand and back again. Well, was he any worse off than before? And what had he lost, after all? Teddy had never really been his. He was no worse off than before, and he had gained the ability to suffer. Perhaps the accounts were settled now. Perhaps life would smile on him now; perhaps life would reward him with a love that was truly his.

"Yes!" he cried to the sun, high and scorching overhead. "Send me another! I want to live!"

Postscript

LIFE DID SEND Boris another, or rather the same one. Teddy left Colin again in 1969, after two more babies—both girls—because he wanted to reenlist and see combat, the better to understand life at its extreme. They'd settled in Oldfield, in a nice white house on Lincoln Street, the down payment paid by her parents. Colin had finished his senior year and gotten a job teaching art at Oldfield High. There was no need for a second divorce, since Colin refused to recognize the first; so when he was killed in a traffic accident on the road from Tan Son Nhut airfield to downtown Saigon, all Boris had to do was to get a marriage license, take over the mortgage, and move into the master bedroom. They were, I think, reasonably happy, though I know nothing about their sex life. (It probably worked out. These things usually do.)

Teddy lives there still, though the children have long since graduated from the University and moved to distant places and started families of their own. Boris died of a heart attack in 1993. He was sixty years old.

Like Colin, O'Rourke died young. He was a passenger in a car driven too fast by Hal Pappajohn, who had his left ear torn off in the crash. Carol forgave him—she always forgave Hal—and they too bought a house in Oldfield. Hal developed a business installing granite countertops for doctors, dentists, University vice-presidents, and other prosperous people, while Carol managed rental apartments in Oldfield and Narwich for absentee landlords. Both are retired now and, like Teddy, are still in the house where they've lived for more than half a century.

Marvin Peabody was the great surprise of our generation of Narwich students. Rather than finish his MA at the University, he and Prudy moved to Iowa City and he got an MFA at the Iowa Writers Workshop, his thesis a novel about student protestors that, published by Doubleday in 1967, received kind notices in *The New Yorker* and the *New York Times*. He was, by then, teaching creative writing at Cornell, in upstate New York, and his novel about faculty politics and infidelities was short-listed for the National Book Award. (His students were sure that Prudence had written the steamy parts.) Thereafter, until he died, Marvin turned out a novel every two years, all respectfully reviewed by his colleagues, whose books in turn were respectfully reviewed by him.

Prudy survived him and still lives in Ithaca. I met her not long ago, at our fiftieth class reunion, and after a few drinks she told me that Marvin never learned that their daughter—whom they named after Freya, goddess of married love—wasn't his child. Nor did she ever tell Freya that her name was something of a private joke.

I was impressed by Prudy at that reunion, and I don't think it was just the drinks. In her seventies, she is a very handsome woman. Freya, she told me, is a public defender in Sitka, Alaska. Tommy settled even farther away: he's a long-line fisherman in the western Aleutians, catching tuna for the politically correct market. I know this because Prudy wore a Dutch Harbor cap to the reunion—*It Ain't Your Father's Fishing Hole*—and of course I asked about it.

You wouldn't recognize Narwich now, or the University. Indeed, I scarcely recognize them myself, though I live on the outskirts of town. The population doubled during the 1960s and has doubled again since then, with 15,000 students arriving last month, fighting for parking space with 15,000 residents. I go to town as seldom as I can, and thanks to the internet and Amazon that is seldom indeed. I even vote by absentee ballot. Boris's Quonset and Georgie's house trailer have long since been replaced by a cavernous student housing complex with its own bus stop.

I'm afraid I've lost track of the others who passed through this story, though I married one of the girls who used to party at the Hut, just as I did. I couldn't figure out how to write myself into the book. Unlike Marvin Peabody—and perhaps unlike O'Rourke, though his novel was never published and probably never completed—I just don't seem to have the knack for it.

— *Daniel Ford, Narwich, New Hampshire, October 2018*